Sacred Ground

Also by Barbara Wood

Perfect Harmony
The Prophetess
Virgins of Paradise
Green City in the Sun
Soul Flame
Domina
Childsong
Yesterday's Child
The Magdalene Scrolls
Hounds and Jackals
Night-Trains
(with Gareth Wootton)
The Watchgods
Curse This House
Vital Signs
The Dreaming

Barbara Wood

SACRED GROUND

St. Martin's Press

New York

www.stmartins.com

LIBRARY OF CONGRESS CATALOGING-IN-PUBLICATION DATA
Wood, Barbara.
    Sacred ground / Barbara Wood.—1st ed.
        p.   cm.
    ISBN 0-312-27537-4
    1. Women healers—Fiction.   2. Mothers and daughters—Fiction.   3. Prehistoric peoples—
Fiction.   4. California—Fiction.   I. Title.
PS3573. O5877 S23 2001
813'.54—dc21

                                                                            2001031818

Design by Kathryn Parise

First Edition: September 2001

10   9   8   7   6   5   4   3   2   1

*This book is dedicated with love
to my husband, George.*

Acknowledgments

Research in museums and books is all well and good, but never so enlightening or enriching as dealing with actual human beings. These special people need to be thanked:

Elmer De La Riva of the Agua Caliente Band of Cahuilla Indians for a private tour of the haunted Taquitz Canyon and for sharing the legendary shaman's terrifying story; Dr. Michelle Anderson, professor of Native American Studies, who generously shared her experiences in reservation field work; Dr. Raymond Wong, forensic pathologist, for explaining the legalities of dealing with bones; Mike Smith for allowing me access to his impressive collection of very old and rare Southern California Native American art; Richard Martinez for walking me through the legal quagmire of Indian land claims; Shana Dominguez, who took me to my first powwow and gave me lessons in the Buckskin Dance; and the members of the Pala, Pechanga, Morongo, and Santa Ynez (Chumash) bands of

Mission Indians who freely shared their family histories and lore, and their hopes for the future of Native Americans.

Finally, eternal gratitude goes to Jennifer Enderlin, my wise and prescient editor, and to Harvey Klinger, the world's greatest literary agent.

Peace to you all!

Sacred Ground

Chapter One

Erica gripped the steering wheel as the four-wheel-drive vehicle flew up the dirt road, caroming around boulders and slamming into potholes. Sitting next to her, white-faced and anxious, was her assistant Luke, a UCSB graduate student working on his doctoral dissertation. In his twenties, his long blond hair tied in a ponytail, Luke wore a T-shirt that said *Archaeologists Dig Older Women*.

"I heard it's a mess, Dr. Tyler," he said, as Erica steered the car up the winding fire road. "Apparently the swimming pool disappeared into the ground just like *that*." He snapped his fingers. "It said on the news that the sinkhole stretches the whole length of the mesa, and it's underneath movie stars' homes, and that rock singer who's been in the news, and the baseball player who hit all those runs last year, and some famous plastic surgeon. Under *their* homes. So you know what *that* means."

Erica wasn't sure what *that* meant. Her mind was focused on only one thing: the astonishing discovery that had been made.

At the time of the disaster she had been up north working on a project for the state. The earthquake, striking two days ago and measuring 7.4, had been felt as far north as San Luis Obispo, as far south as San Diego, and as far east as Phoenix, jolting Southern California's millions of inhabitants awake. It was the biggest temblor in memory and was believed to have been what had triggered, a day later, the sudden and astonishing disappearance of a hundred-foot swimming pool, diving board, water slide and all.

A second astonishing event had followed almost immediately: when the pool sank, earth had avalanched into it, exposing human bones and the opening to a previously unknown cave.

"This could be the find of the century!" Luke declared, taking his eyes off the road for a moment to glance at his boss. It was still dark out and there were no lights along the mountain road, so Erica had turned on the vehicle's interior light. It illuminated glossy chestnut hair brushing her shoulders with a hint of curl, and a tan complexion from years of toiling in the sun. Dr. Erica Tyler, whom Luke had worked with for the past six months, was in her thirties and, while he wouldn't call her beautiful, Luke thought she was attractive in a way that registered in a man's gut rather than in his eye. "Quite a feather in some lucky archaeologist's cap," he added.

She glanced at him. "Why do you think we just broke every traffic law on the books getting here?" she said with a smile, and then returned her attention to the road in time to avoid hitting a startled jackrabbit.

They reached the top of the mesa from where the lights of Malibu could be seen in the distance. The rest of the view—Los Angeles to the east and the Pacific Ocean to the south—was blocked by trees, higher peaks, and the mansions of millionaires. Erica maneuvered her car through the congestion of fire engines, police cars, county trucks, news vans, and the armada of automobiles parked along the yellow police tape cordoning off the site. Curiosity-seekers sat on hoods and car roofs to watch, drink beer, and ponder disasters and their meanings, or perhaps just to be entertained for a while, despite warnings shouted through bullhorns that this was a dangerous area.

"I heard that this whole mesa used to be some sort of retreat run by a nutty spiritualist back in the twenties," Luke said as the car rolled to a halt. "People came up here to talk to ghosts."

Erica recalled seeing silent newsreels of Sister Sarah, one of LA's more colorful characters, who used to hold séances for Hollywood royalty such as Rudolph Valentino and Charlie Chaplin. Sarah had held mass séances in theaters and auditoriums, and when her followers numbered in the hundreds of thousands, she had come to these mountains and built a retreat called The Church of the Spirits.

"Know what this place was originally called?" Luke went on as they unbuckled their safety belts. "I mean before the spiritualist owned it? Back *when*," he said, the word 'when' conjuring up parchments with wax seals and men dueling at dawn. "Cañon de Fantasmas," he intoned, tasting the dusty words on his tongue. "Haunted Canyon. Sounds spooky!" He shuddered.

Erica laughed. "Luke, if you want to be an archaeologist when you grow up, you're just going to have to not let ghosts scare you." She herself lived daily with phantasms and ghosts, spirits and sprites. They peopled her dreams and her archaeological digs, and while ghosts might elude, confound, tease, and frustrate her, they had never frightened her.

As Erica got out of the car and felt the night wind on her face, she gazed spellbound at the horrific scene. She had already seen news photos and had heard eyewitness accounts of the event—how the earthquake had somehow destabilized the ground beneath the gated community of Emerald Hills Estates, an exclusive enclave in the Santa Monica Mountains, causing one swimming pool to suddenly sink into the ground and threatening the rest of the homes with the same. But nothing had prepared her for what her eyes now beheld.

Although the eastern sky was starting to pale, night was still a dark, stubborn bowl over Los Angeles so that emergency lights had to be brought in, man-made suns placed at intervals around the perimeter of the site, illuminating one square block of a super-ritzy neighborhood where houses stood like marble temples in the milky moon. In the center of this surreal scene was a black crater—the devil's mouth that had swallowed the swimming pool of movie producer Harmon Zimmerman. Helicopters buzzed overhead, sweeping blinding circles of light over surveyors setting up equipment, geologists moving in with drills and maps, men in hard hats warming their hands on cups of coffee as they waited for daybreak, and police trying to evacuate residents who were refusing to leave.

Flashing the ID that identified her as an anthropologist working for the State Archaeologist's Office, Erica and her assistant were permitted to climb over the yellow police tape keeping the crowd out. They ran to the crater, where Los Angeles County firefighters were inspecting the rim of the cave-in. Erica quickly searched for the entrance to the cavern.

"Is that it?" Luke said, pointing with a lanky arm to the other side of the crater. Erica could just make out, about eighty feet below ground level, an opening in the side of the cliff. "Looks dangerous, Dr. Tyler. You plan on going in?"

"I've been in caves before."

"What in blazes are *you* doing here!"

Erica spun around to see a large man with leonine gray hair come striding toward her, a scowl on his face. Sam Carter, senior state archaeologist from the California Office of Historical Preservation, a man who wore colorful suspenders and spoke in a stentorian voice. And who was clearly not happy to see her.

"You know why I'm here, Sam," Erica said as she pushed her hair back from her face and looked around at the chaos. Residents of the threatened homes were arguing with the police and refusing to leave their property. "Tell me about the cave. Have you been inside?"

Sam noticed two things: that Erica's eyes were bright with an inner fever, and that her sweater was buttoned wrong. Clearly she had dropped everything and driven down from Santa Barbara as if she were on fire. "I haven't been inside yet," he said. "There's a geologist and a couple of cavers exploring it right now for structural soundness. As soon as they give the go-ahead, I'm going to take a look." He rubbed his jaw. Getting rid of Erica, now that she was here, was not going to be easy. The woman stuck like glue once she put her mind to something. "What about the Gaviota Project? I assume you left it in capable hands?"

Erica didn't hear him. She was watching the gaping hole in the hillside and thinking of heavy boots tramping over the cave's delicate ecology. She prayed they hadn't inadvertently destroyed precious historical evidence. The archaeology in these hills was paltry enough, despite the fact that people had lived here for ten thousand years. The few caves that had been found yielded very little because in the early part of the twentieth century bulldozers and dynamite had brutalized these wild mountains to make way for roads, bridges, and human progress. Burial sites had been plowed under, village mounds scraped away, all traces of previous human habitation obliterated.

"Erica?" Sam prompted.

"I have to go in," she said.

He knew she meant the cave. "Erica, you shouldn't even be here."

"Assign me to the job, Sam. You're going to be excavating. And bones were found, it said on the news."

"Erica—"

"Please."

In frustration, Sam turned on his heel and headed back through the Zimmerman's trampled garden to an area at the end of the street where a makeshift command center had been created. People holding clipboards and talking on cell phones milled around folding metal tables and chairs, where two-way radios had been set up, surveillance monitors, a bulletin board for messages. A catering truck parked nearby was being patronized by people wearing various official uniforms and badges: Southern California Gas, Department of Water and Power, LAPD, County Office of Emergency Management. There was even someone from the Humane Society trying to round up loose animals from the evacuated area.

Erica caught up with her boss. "So what happened, Sam? What caused a swimming pool to suddenly sink into the ground?"

"County engineers and state geologists have been working around the clock to determine the cause. Those boys over there"—he pointed down the street, where men were setting up drilling equipment beneath bright spotlights—"are going to run soils tests to find out exactly what this housing development is sitting on." Sam swept a beefy hand over the topographical maps and geological surveys spread out on the tables, their corners anchored by rocks. "These were brought up from City Hall a few hours ago. This here is a geological survey from 1908. And here's one from 1956, when this area was being proposed for a residential development that never got built."

Erica's eyes went back and forth over the two maps. "They aren't the same."

"Apparently the current builder didn't run soils tests on every building pad—which he wasn't required to do. The tests he did run showed stable ground and bedrock. But that's at the north and south boundaries of the mesa, which it turns out are the two ridges embracing the canyon. Remember Sister Sarah back in the twenties? This was her religious retreat or something and it seems she had the canyon filled in and never got permission or informed City Hall. The work was apparently done without standard compaction procedures and a lot of the fill was organic—wood, vegetation, garbage—that eventually rotted away." Sam's sleep-deprived eyes scanned the street, where fountains and imported trees graced expensively tended lawns. "These folks have been sitting on a time bomb. I wouldn't be surprised if this whole area was on the verge of collapsing."

While Sam spoke, he watched Erica as she stood with her hands on her hips, shifting from foot to foot like a runner eager for the race to begin. He had seen her like this before, when she was "onto" something. Erica Tyler was one of the most passionate scientists he had ever met, but sometimes her enthusiasm could be her undoing. "I know why you're here, Erica," he said wearily, "and I can't give you the job."

She whirled on him, her cheeks two spots of red. "Sam, you've got me counting abalone shells, for God's sake!"

He was the first to admit that putting Erica in charge of a mollusk midden was a waste of her brains and talent. But after the shipwreck debacle last year, he thought it best that she cool her heels in a low-profile job for a while. So she had spent the past six months excavating a newly discovered mound that turned out to be the refuse heap of Indians that had lived north of Santa Barbara four thousand years ago. Erica's job was to sort, classify, and carbon-date the thousands of abalone shells found there.

"Sam," she said, putting her hand on his arm, urgency in her voice. "I need this. I have to salvage my career. I need to make people forget Chadwick—"

"Erica, the Chadwick incident is precisely the reason *why* I can't put you on this job. You're just not disciplined. You're impulsive, and you don't possess the necessary scientific detachment and objectivity."

"I've learned my lesson, Sam," she said. She felt like screaming. The Wreck of the Erica Tyler, people in inner circles had called the Chadwick fiasco. Was she going to be made to pay for it the rest of her life? "I'll be extra careful."

He scowled. "Erica, you made my office a laughingstock."

"And I've apologized a thousand times! Sam, be logical about this. You know that I've studied every example of rock art this side of the Rio Grande. There is no one better qualified. When I saw that cave painting on the news I *knew* this job was for me."

Sam drove his thick fingers through his mane of hair. It was so like Erica to just drop everything. Had she even bothered to turn the Gaviota Project over to someone else?

"Come on, Sam. Put me to work doing what I was born to do."

He looked into her amber eyes and saw the desperation there. He didn't know what it was like to be discredited in one's own profession, to be laughed at by colleagues. He could only guess what these past twelve months had been like for Erica. "I tell you what," he said. "A member of the Search and Rescue team volunteered to go back in and take pictures. We should have them any minute. You can have a look at them, see what you make of the pictographs."

"Search and Rescue?"

"After the pool sank, it was learned that Zimmerman's daughter was missing. So the County Sheriff launched a search for her in all that mess. That was how the cave painting was discovered."

"And the girl?"

"She turned up later. Seems she was in Vegas with her boyfriend at the time of the earthquake. Listen, Erica, there's no point in you hanging around here. I'm not putting you on the case. Go back to Gaviota." Even as he said it, Sam knew she wouldn't obey orders. Once Erica Tyler got something in her head, it was impossible to shake it loose. That was what had happened last year, when Irving Chadwick discovered the underwater shipwreck of what he claimed was an ancient Chinese boat on the California coast, proving his theory that people from Asia didn't just come across the Bering Strait, but had arrived in ships as well. Erica had already been enamored of Chadwick's hypothesis so that when he invited her to authenticate pottery found in the shipwreck, she had already made up her mind that this was indeed proof.

Sam had tried even then to dissuade her from jumping to conclusions, to convince her to move slowly and cautiously. But Erica's middle name was exuberance. She had gone ahead with her public announcement that the pottery was genuine and for a while she and Irving Chadwick basked in the spotlight. When the shipwreck was later proven to be a hoax, and Chadwick confessed to having engineered it, it was too late for Erica Tyler. Her reputation was in ruins.

"They said on the news that bones have been found," she said now. "What have you found out so far about them?"

Sam picked up a clipboard, knowing she was stalling for time. "All we have are small fragments but they were found with arrowheads, which was enough reason to call my office. Here's the Coroner's report."

While Erica scanned the findings, Sam said, "As you can see, according to the Kjeldahl test, the quantity of nitrogenous components in the bone is less than four grams. And the benzidine-acetic test shows no evidence of albuminous material."

"Which means the bones are older than a hundred years. Was the Coroner able to determine how much older?"

"Unfortunately, no. And we can't do it through soil analysis since we have no way of determining exactly which soil the bones had been resting in. This canyon was filled in seventy years ago, and then last year the soil was disturbed during trenching for the swimming pool. When the earth beneath liquefied and gave way because of the earthquake, causing the pool to sink, the earth on the sides spilled in. It's all mixed up, Erica. We did find the arrowheads, though, and crude flint tools."

"Which point to an Indian burial ground." She handed him the clipboard. "I take it NAHC has been notified?" she asked, looking around for someone who looked like they might be from the State of California Native American Heritage Commission.

"They've been notified all right," Sam said in a wry tone. "In fact they're already here. Rather, *he's* here."

She read Sam's look. "Jared Black?"

"Your old adversary."

Erica and Black had tangled on Native American legal issues before, and the outcome had been decidedly unpleasant.

A young man came running up then, his face smudged with dirt, caver's helmet askew on his head. He held out the Polaroid snapshots he had taken inside the cave and apologized for their amateur quality. Thanking the young man, Sam divided up the pictures, handing half to Erica.

"My God," Erica whispered as she stared at them one by one. "These are . . . *beautiful*. And these symbols—" Her voice caught.

"So what do you think?" Sam muttered as he squinted at the pictures. "Can you identify the tribe?"

When she didn't respond, he looked at her. Erica was staring at the pictures in her hands, her lips slightly parted. For a minute Sam thought she had gone shockingly pale, but then he realized it must be due to the fluorescent lighting hastily strung around the disaster site. "Erica?"

She blinked like someone brought out of a trance. When she looked at him, Sam had the odd notion that, for just an instant, she didn't know who he was. Then, with color returning to her face, she said, "We have the find of the century in our hands, Sam. This painting is vast, and I've never seen such an excellent state of preservation. Think of the native history we could fill in once these pictographs have been deciphered. Sam, don't send me back to those abalone shells."

He released a sigh. "All right, you can hang around for a day or two and give us a preliminary analysis, but"—he held up his hand—"you are to go back to Gaviota after that. I can't put you on this project, Erica. I'm sorry. It's interdepartmental politics."

"But you're the boss—" She suddenly stopped and stared.

He followed her line of vision and saw what had caught her attention. In this chilly hour just before dawn, with everyone unshaven, bleary-eyed, craving coffee and sleep and a fresh change of clothes, Commissioner Jared Black, with not a hair out of place, wore a tailored three-piece suit with French cuffs, silk tie, and polished loafers as if he had just stepped out of a courtroom. As he approached, dark irises glittered beneath frowning brows.

"Dr. Tyler. Dr. Carter."

"Commissioner."

Although an outspoken advocate on Indian issues, Jared Black was himself pure Anglo, having once claimed that it was his Irish heritage that made him empathetic to the plight of oppressed peoples. He addressed Sam Carter. "When do you expect to make a tribal identification of the cave painting?" His tone implied that he wanted an answer soon.

"That will be up to the people I assign to the job."

Jared didn't look at Erica. "I will be bringing in my own experts, of course."

"*After* we have conducted our preliminary analysis," Carter said. "I'm sure I don't need to remind you that that is standard protocol."

Jared Black's eyes flickered. There was no love lost between him and the senior state archaeologist. Carter had vocally opposed Black's appointment to the Commission, citing Jared's extreme prejudice against the academic and scientific communities.

Erica's own clash with Jared Black happened four years ago, when a wealthy recluse named Reddman had died and left an astonishing collection of Indian artifacts to be housed in his mansion, which was to be turned into a public museum named for himself. Erica had been brought in to identify and catalogue the priceless collection, and when she traced them to a small, local tribe, the tribe hired attorney Jared Black, who specialized in land rights and property law, to sue for possession of the objects. Erica asked the state to challenge the suit on the grounds that the tribe planned to rebury the objects without prior historical analysis. "The heritage in these bones and artifacts," she had argued, "belong not just to the Indians but to all Americans." It had been a passionate issue, with crowds picketing in front of the courthouse—Native Americans demanding the return of all their lands and cultural objects; teachers, historians, and archaeologists insisting upon the creation of the Reddman Museum. Jared Black's wife, a member of the Maidu tribe and a passionate Indian rights activist—a woman who had once thrown herself in front of bulldozers to stop a new freeway from being pushed through Indian land—had been among the most vocal in favor of "keeping the collection out of white man's hands."

The case dragged on for months until Jared finally uncovered a fact that had not been previously known: that unbeknownst to state and local authorities, Reddman had dug up the objects from his own property, an estate covering five hundred acres, and had kept them without permission. Arguing that because the objects indicated a living mound—and Erica, although working for the other side, was forced to admit that the estate had most likely been built on the site of an ancient village—Jared Black declared that the property had not therefore legally belonged to Mr. Reddman but to the descendents of those who had lived in the village. The five hundred acres, as well as over a thousand Indian relics—including rare pottery, basketry, bows, and arrows—were handed over to the tribe, which consisted of exactly sixteen members. Reddman's museum was never built, the artifacts never seen again.

Erica recalled now how the media had played up her and Jared's battle in and out of court. One now-famous photograph of the two arguing, snapped on the courthouse steps, had been sold to the tabloids and run under the headline "Secret Lovers?" because a trick of the lighting and the unlucky timing of the cameraman's shutter had captured Erica and Jared in one of those quirky, split-second freeze frames that give the very opposite impression of what is really happening: Erica's eyes wide as she looks up at him, her tongue touching her lips, her body inclined in a suggestive way, with Black, towering over her on the upper step, arms outstretched as if about to sweep her into a torrid embrace. Both had been outraged by the photograph and its false message, but both had decided to let the matter drop and not add grist to the gossip mill.

"And I'm sure I don't need to remind *you*, Dr. Carter," he said to Sam, "that I'm here to see you keep your desecration to a minimum, and that the instant the MLD is found I am going to personally and with great satisfaction escort you and your fellow grave robbers off this site."

As they watched him go, Sam thrust his hands into his pockets and muttered, "I definitely do not like that man."

"Well then," Erica said. "I guess it's a good thing you aren't assigning me to this case, because that would really annoy Jared Black."

Sam looked at her and caught the hint of a smile. "You really want this job, don't you?"

"Have I been too subtle?"

"All right," he said at last, rubbing the back of his neck. "It goes against my better judgment, but I suppose I can send someone else to Gaviota."

"Sam!" She impulsively threw her arms around his neck. "You won't regret this, I promise! Luke," she said, grabbing her assistant's arm, causing a half-eaten bear claw to fly out of his hand. "Let's gear up!"

✻

"I'm surprised Sam Carter assigned you to this project, Dr. Tyler," Jared Black said coolly as they gathered at the top of the cliff.

"I know a few things about rock art."

"As I recall you also know a few things about Chinese shipwrecks."

Before Erica could respond, he continued, "I trust you have familiarized yourself with the latest update of the Native American Graves Protection and Repatriation Act, which states that whereas the scientific removal and analysis of historical artifacts might be recommended, said analysis is to be *nondestructive* and—"

She pointedly ignored him, recognizing the challenge in his tone, knowing he was trying to goad her into an argument. She resented his implication. Jared Black knew very well that Erica had a reputation for being one of the most cautious anthropologists when it came to the handling of artifacts and that *all* of her tests were nondestructive.

Erica kept her irritation in check. She had no choice but to allow Jared Black to oversee every step of her operation. While Erica's job was to determine which tribe the bones and the cave painting belonged to, it was Jared's to locate the MLD—most likely descendent—and turn whatever Erica found over to them.

She felt Jared's eyes on her, and she wondered if, like her, he was remembering the time they first met. It was in the County Court building and Erica was there for the first deposition hearing in the Reddman case.

She and Black hadn't known each other then, they were simply two strangers sharing an elevator. At the first stop, the doors opened and a woman in maternity clothes stepped in. At the next stop, a woman with a boy of about five got on and as the elevator began to rise, the little boy stared wide-eyed at the pregnant woman. Seeing his curiosity, she said in a tolerant tone: "I'm expecting a baby. I'm going to have a little girl or a little boy just like you." The boy frowned as he pondered this, then he said, "Will they let you exchange it for a donkey?" The woman smiled patiently while the boy's mother reddened. At the next stop all three got off, the doors closing shut. Erica and the stranger were silent for a moment, then they both started to laugh. Erica remembered noticing his deep dimples and how attractive he was. He in turn had given her an appraising look that said he liked what he saw. Then the doors had opened and people were there to meet them. Erica had stood stock-still when she heard him addressed as "Mr. Black." And when the attorney for the Reddman estate called her Erica, Jared also came to an abrupt halt. They had looked at each other, both realizing in the same instant their horrible gaff. They were enemies, generals in opposing war camps. Yet they had unwittingly shared a private joke, had laughed together, and had even flirted a little.

It appalled and embarrassed Erica to think that, even though it was only for three minutes, she had been attracted to this man.

The cave opening was eighty feet below the ridge behind the Zimmerman property, and as dawn broke over the eastern mountains, bathing the Los Angeles basin in fresh, smogless light, Erica adjusted the chin strap of her helmet. Beside her, also gearing up, was Luke, looking excited and wild-eyed. This was going to be his first experience with a new dig and he adjusted his caver's sling and locking carabiner with the vigor of an ancient warrior girding his loins for battle.

Jared Black was also strapping himself into a harness, and Erica noticed that he had changed into more rugged attire—a borrowed set of coveralls that said Southern California Edison on the back. But there was no excitement showing on his face. Instead he presented a grim expression, causing her to think: He's angry. Why? Didn't he want this assignment? Had he been forced to take it? Erica would have thought Jared Black would welcome such a choice opportunity to spotlight the work of the NAHC and his own personal crusade for Native American rights.

Or was his anger personal? Had he still not forgiven her for what she had said the day she and her group had lost the Reddman case: "Mr. Black's words smack of hypocrisy when he claims on the one hand to be a proponent of safeguarding historical culture while at the same time consigning historical material evidence to the ground and therefore to oblivion."

"Are you ready, Dr. Tyler?" the climber asked as he made sure Erica was clipped into the rope, double-checking her harness and all attachment points.

"As ready as I'll ever be," she said with a nervous laugh. Erica had never rappelled down a cliff before.

"Okay, just follow my lead and you'll be fine."

Standing at the edge of the cliff, the climber turned and faced away from the edge, showing the others how to lean back and then start a controlled descent, demonstrating how to allow rope to feed through the figure eight by releasing pressure on the strands running through the right hand, his other arm held outstretched behind him as he dropped slowly and cautiously. When they reached the lip of the cave, the climber helped Erica inside, then assisted Luke and Jared, who followed.

The four released their ropes and faced the dark, cavernous interior. The cave might have been small but the darkness looked huge. The only relief in the intimidating blackness were the frail spots of light from their helmet lamps. When they shuffled their feet, the noise echoed thinly off sandstone walls and died away in the lightless distance.

Despite her impulse to rush inside and see the painting, Erica remained at the entrance and methodically swept her flashlight over the floor, walls, ceiling. When she had satisfied herself that there was no surface archaeological material, nothing they might inadvertently destroy, she said, "All right, gentlemen, we can go in. Be careful where you walk." Her flashlight beam swept up the stone walls and across the vaulted ceiling. "As we proceed, what we must do is send ourselves back in time and try to imagine the things that people are likely to have done here and the traces that these activities might have left behind."

They moved slowly forward, booted feet careful of where they trod while eight circles of light danced like white moths over sandstone formations. Erica observed quietly: "We're lucky this cave is in the north slope of the mountains, which is drier than the south slope, which gets the brunt of Pacific storms. Shelter from the rain is what helped to preserve the painting. And possibly other artifacts."

They explored in silence, beams slithering over the smooth contours of rock, illuminating blackened surfaces and patches of lichen, all four intruders alert, senses sharpened, watchful, until finally they arrived at the far end.

"There," said the climber, meaning the painting.

Erica approached with apprehension, one foot placed meticulously in front of the other. When the carbide lamp on her helmet shone on the pictographs, her breath caught. The vibrant colors of the circles, the reds and yellows, like blazing sunsets! They were beautiful, fantastic, lifelike. They were also—

"Do you know what these symbols mean, Dr. Tyler?" the climber asked, tilting his head this way and that as he tried to make sense of what appeared to be a nonsensical collage of lines, circles, shapes, and colors.

Erica didn't respond. She stood transfixed before the painting, eyes unblinking, as if the luminous suns and moons on the wall had hypnotized her.

"Dr. Tyler?" he repeated. Jared and Luke exchanged a glance. "Dr. Tyler," Luke said, "are you okay?" He tapped her on the shoulder and she jumped.

"What?" she gave him a perplexed look. Then, recovering, said, "I was just . . . I hadn't expected to find such an intact painting. No graffiti . . ." She was a little breathless. "To answer your question about these symbols," her voice a little stronger, a little forced, as if she had to remind herself where she was, "the heart of religious belief in this area was shamanism, a form of worship based on personal interaction between a shaman and the supernatural. The shaman would eat jimsonweed, or in other ways enter a trance, and walk in the spirit world. This was called a vision quest. And when he came out of the trance he would record his visions on rocks. This is called trance-derived art. At least that is one of the theories explaining Southwest rock art."

The climber leaned close. "How do you figure this is the work of a shaman?" he asked. "I mean, couldn't it just be graffiti and not really mean anything at all?"

Erica stared at the largest circle, which was blood-red with curious points emanating from it. *This means something all right.* "There have been laboratory studies of this phenomenon, it's called the neuropsychology of altered states. And what the studies have discovered is that there are universal images described by people in different cultures, whether they be Native Americans, Australian Aborigines, or natives of African cultures. They are believed to be luminous geometric forms somehow spontaneously generated in the optical system. You can try it yourself. Stare briefly at a bright light and then quickly close your eyes. You will generate these same patterns—dots, parallel lines, zigzags, and spirals. What we call metaphors of trance."

He frowned. "But they don't *look* like anything."

"They're not supposed to. These symbols are images of a feeling or of a spiritual plane, something that in reality has no corporeal structure and therefore no image. However . . ." She frowned when her flashlight illuminated an unidentifiable figure, elongated with what appeared to be arms or antlers stretching out. "There are other elements that are puzzling."

Luke turned to her, momentarily blinding her with his helmet lamp. "Puzzling? Like what?"

"Notice that some of these features don't conform to the known record of trance imagery. This symbol here. I've never seen it before, not in all the rock art I've studied. Most of these symbols you will find in other pictographs and petroglyphs scattered around the Southwest. These handprints, for example. In fact, the handprint in rock art is universal and found all over the world. It reflects the belief that the rock face was a permeable boundary between the natural and the supernatural worlds.

It's the door through which the shaman entered to visit the spirits. But these other symbols"—she pointed, being careful not to touch the surface—"are completely new to me." She paused, her soft respirations sounding in the cave like a breeze. "There is something else puzzling about this painting."

Her companions waited.

"While it contains pictographs that are characteristic of the ethnographic cultures of this area, this mural also contains motifs that are typical of Puebloan rock art. In fact, this art reflects a mix of cultures. Southern Paiute, Shoshonean. Somewhere in southern Nevada."

"Can you date the painting, Dr. Tyler?" asked Luke in an awed tone.

"We can place an immediate date of before 500 C.E. because of the atlatls depicted—these objects here, spear throwers—instead of bows and arrows, which came into use in the New World around the year five hundred. For more definitive dating, we would need to use electron microprobe analysis and radiocarbon dating. But for now I would say this painting is around two thousand years old."

Jared Black spoke for the first time. "If the artist came from southern Nevada, that's quite a trek, considering he would have had to walk across Death Valley."

"The bigger question is *why* did he do it? The Shoshone and Paiute never ventured beyond their tribal lands. Although they moved around according to food availability, they were very territorial and stayed within the limits of their ancestral grounds. What was it that made this person break away from the clan and come all this way, making what can only have been a very treacherous journey?"

Jared's eyes were shadowed beneath his helmet, but Erica sensed his piercing gaze. "So this is possibly Shoshone?" he said.

"It's only a guess. According to studies of drought cycles, about fifteen hundred years ago environmental changes in the eastern California deserts brought the ancestors of the Gabrielino Indians to Los Angles, a Shoshonean-speaking language group. However, if these people had a tribal name for themselves, it has been lost over time."

Jared pressed: "But this *was* done by one of those ancestors?"

She tried to keep her impatience in check. Jared Black was a man who demanded instant answers. "I'm not sure because I believe this is older than fifteen hundred years. And keep in mind that 'Gabrielino' was a general catch-all name given by the Franciscans to the diverse tribes in this area." She gave him a pointed look. "So we have to be very careful with our terms here."

"Are you sure you don't know?"

She felt her irritation with him start to shift to anger. She knew what he was implying, he had made the same accusation during the Reddman case when she had said she needed more time to identify the tribal affiliation of the bones and artifacts. In that instance, Jared had been right: Erica *had* been stalling for time. But in this case, she was telling the truth. She had no idea which tribe was responsible for the painting.

Stepping back from the wall, Erica noticed that directly beneath the painting the floor was different from the rest of the cave floor. It rose up in a contour that didn't strike her as a natural formation. She looked up at the ceiling. There was no evidence of breakdown. Then she squatted in several places and rubbed the soil between her fingertips. It was the same all over, uniformly deposited by winds blowing into the cave. "Since the painting doesn't pinpoint a specific tribe," she said, "then I suggest we look elsewhere for our evidence. This curious mound, for instance."

Luke's blond eyebrows arched, his eyes bright with hope. "You think there's something buried here, Dr. Tyler?"

"Possibly. The smoke residue on the walls indicates that campfires or torches were burned in here, which might mean this mound is levels of habitation over centuries. I want to explore this raised area."

"So now the locusts descend," Jared murmured.

"No locusts, Mr. Black. Just me. I'll be the only one working here to ensure the least possible destruction to the mound."

"Excavation *is* destruction, Dr. Tyler."

"Believe it or not, Mr. Black, there *are* archaeologists who don't believe in excavating a site simply because it's there. It must be a threatened site. Or, as in this case, there is a need to determine the tribal identity of our cave artist. We might have stumbled upon a fabulous repository of history."

"Or graves that shouldn't be disturbed."

She looked at Jared, his face cast in sharp planes by the chiaroscuro lighting, then she turned to Luke. "First we'll run a geochemical analysis of the soil and measure the phosphate content. This at least will tell us if this was once an inhabited site. In the meantime, I think it would be a good idea if you cleared some of this wall. Under all that soot might be more pictographs."

As she turned to say something further to Jared Black, she saw to her surprise that he had gone to stand at the cave's entrance, a tall, broad-shouldered figure silhouetted against the morning sunshine, one hand resting on the wall, the other holding his helmet, which he had removed. Jared Black seemed poised at the edge of the cliff as if ready to fly away.

There was a surreal aspect to the moment, the darkness of the cave with the feeling of the weight of the mountain pressing down, the closeness of the sandstone walls, the silence that was a kind of peace, and yet there was the opening to bright Pacific sunlight and beyond it the sounds of work crews, police, news choppers whirring overhead. Why was he standing there? What was he looking at?

And then Erica wondered: why had he arrived here with such a large chip on his shoulder? Jared Black seemed to have come with all the open-mindedness of a grizzly bear protecting its cub. If only there were some way she could make him see that it was possible for them to work together, that they did not have to be adversaries. But for some unfathomable reason he seemed determined to make her the enemy. The Reddman case was four years ago, yet it was almost as if, she couldn't help thinking, the adrenaline from that battle and the high from the subsequent victory were still fueling his passion. Jared Black was a man preparing himself for a fight and Erica had no idea why.

She continued to scan the cave with her flashlight, until her beam caught on something on the floor. "Luke, what do you make of this?"

He looked down and saw that earth had been dislodged, exposing something grayish white on the cave floor. "It's fresh. Looks like the earthquake disturbed the soil here."

Erica dropped to her knees and, using a whisk brush, gently cleared away the loose soil.

"My God," Luke said, his eyes widening.

Jared came back in and stood in silence as Erica uncovered something with her brush, an object that looked like a rock with a hole in it. And then another hole. And then . . . teeth.

It was a human skull.

"This is a grave!" Luke whispered in awe.

"Whose?" said the climber nervously.

Erica, feeling a sudden rush of adrenaline and excitement, didn't respond. But she knew. Somehow, before excavating, before finding proof, she knew that they had found the remains of the artist of the sun painting.

Chapter Two

MARIMI
Two Thousand Years Ago

As Marimi watched the dancers performing in the center of the circle, she knew that tonight was going to be a night of magic.

She could already feel the magic in her fingers as she skillfully wove the oval cradle board, laying the tender willow branches crosswise in preparation to support her newborn child; the surface would later be covered with buckskin and a basket sunshade added above the baby's head. She could feel the magic in her womb as the new life stirred there, her first child, due to be born in the spring. She saw the magic in the supple limbs of her young husband as he danced in celebration of the annual pine nut harvest, a handsome, virile hunter who had introduced her to the ecstasy of physical love between a man and a woman. Marimi heard magic in the laughter of the men as they danced, or gambled, or told stories while smoking their clay pipes; she heard it in the music of the musicians as they blew whistles made of hollowed bird bones and flutes made of elderberry wood; there was magic in the merry gossip of the women as they wove their brilliant baskets by the light of many campfires; in the children's squeals as they played hoop and pole games or wrestled on the damp forest floor; and there was magic, too, in the faces of the young people falling in love, smiling behind their hands as they chose future mates. A "spirit" night, her mother called it, when the ghosts of ancestors were called forth by the souls of the trees and the rocks and the rivers to celebrate the Oneness of All Things. A time of great joy, a good night, a special night, Marimi thought.

Except that Marimi's joy on this night of celebration was laced with unexpected fear.

Across the great circle around which the families watched the dancers, a pair of hard black eyes were fixed on her—Old Opaka, clan shaman-woman, magnificent in her buckskins and beads and precious eagle feathers. Marimi shivered beneath the piercing gaze and felt bumps of fear sprout on her skin. Opaka terrified everyone, including the chiefs and the hunters, with her vast and mysterious knowledge of magic and because she spoke to the gods, because she alone out of all the clan knew the secret of communing with the sun and the moon and all the earth's spirits and how to invoke their powers.

Ordinary persons were unable to speak to the gods. If a clan member wished a favor of the gods, the intercession of a shaman was required: a barren wife wishing for a child, a homely virgin desperate for a husband, an aging hunter whose skills were fading, a grandmother whose fingers could no longer weave baskets, a pregnant woman seeking protection from the evil eye, a father wondering if the dried-up creek beside his family's shelter would ever run with water again—they shyly and with great reverence approached the shaman of the clan and humbly presented their case. Each petition was accompanied by payment, which was why the shamans were so wealthy, their huts the most richly adorned, their buckskins the softest, their beads the most elegant. The poorest families could offer only seeds while the richest brought sheep's horn and elk hides. But all were allowed to approach the shaman, and all received an answer from the gods through the shaman's mouth. In this case she was Opaka, the most powerful figure in Marimi's clan. Marimi had once seen the old woman make a man sicken and die, simply by pointing at him; Opaka was that powerful.

But why was she now watching Marimi especially, out of all the people, her eyes like pinpoints of black fire?

Trying not to let her fear show, the young wife returned her attention to her basketry, reminding herself again that tonight was a special night.

This was the time of the annual gathering, when once a year all the families of the People—who called themselves Topaa—came from the four points of the world, from as far away as where the earth supports the sky, leaving their summer homes to meet in the mountains for the pine nut harvest—a gathering of some five hundred families, each with its own round grass shelter and campfire. Using long poles to remove the cones from the trees, they roasted the nuts and ate them, or ground them into a meal which they mixed with deer meat and gravy, and then they stored what was left over for the coming winter months. While the women gathered the nuts, the men conducted a communal hunt for rabbits, driving them into nets and clubbing what they needed for winter food supply.

Marriages were arranged at this time, no simple matter since the rules governing who could marry whom were complex—the lineages had to be examined and considered, the gods must be invoked, the omens read. Although the Topaa were all of the same tribe, they were members of different clans, which in turn were divided into families, second and first. The clans had an animal totem: Cougar, Hawk, Tortoise. The second family, comprised of grandparents, aunts and uncles and cousins, called themselves after their lineage: People From Cold River, People In Salt Desert. The first family consisted of mother and father and siblings, and the family's name was based on their local food source, occupation, or geographic feature—"eaters of buffalo berry," "creek dwellers," or "white knives" because they made cutting tools from a local white rock quarry. Marimi was of the Red-Tailed Hawk Clan, her second family were People From the Black Mesa, her first family was "hunt jackrabbit." The young man who had chosen her for his mate was of the Tortoise Clan, the Dust Valley People, "pipe makers." He had delighted Marimi with his antics at the last harvest, prancing and preening in front of her shelter, playing his flute, miming his skill at spear throwing, but not speaking to her for that was taboo. And when she had set out a basket of sweet roots, to indicate her interest, he had arranged for his father to meet with hers, and the two men had conferred with the headmen of their clans to work out the complex negotiations, to determine gifts, and whether the bride should go to the groom's family, or the other way around. If the husband came from a family of few women, then his wife went with him. If the wife came from a family of widows and unmarried sisters, then the husband went with her. In Marimi's case, her father was the only male among eight women. He gladly welcomed Marimi's new husband as a son.

Also at the harvest, the people were reminded of the boundaries of the tribal land, and the children were taught to memorize the rivers, the forests, the mountain ranges that separated Topaa land from that of neighboring tribes—Shoshone to the north, Paiute to the south, and with whom the Topaa neither traded, nor intermarried, nor waged war—and the children were made to remember that it was strictly taboo to hunt, collect seeds, or to take water from the land of another tribe.

At each pine nut harvest the families erected shelters on their ancestral plots, where their family had been meeting and harvesting since the beginning of time. The very spot where Marimi had spread her mat and where she now wove her baby basket was the same place her mother and grandmother and grandmothers all the way back to the beginning had also spread their mats and woven baby baskets. And someday, her first born daughter would sit in this same place and weave her baskets as she watched the same dances, the same games. In this way did the yearly pine nut harvest serve as more than merely to collect winter food. Here was where the people learned the stories of their ancestors, because the way of the Topaa was bound to the past, thus ensuring that what went before was so today, and would be tomorrow until the end of time. The annual gathering taught a person where he or she stood in Creation. It showed a man or woman that he or she was part of a Great Design, that the Topaa and the land, the animals and the plants, the wind and the water were all connected and intertwined like the complex baskets the women wove.

After the pine nut harvest, the clans would stay and winter in the mountains, and when the first green shoots came up from the ground, the enormous settlement would break up, with the families dispersing to their ancestral homes until the next harvest. Marimi and her husband, her mother and father, and six sisters would return to their land, where they hunted jackrabbits, and where Marimi's family had lived since the time of Creation. There she would bear her first child, becoming a mother, thus raising her status in the clan so that next year when they returned to the pine forest, the people would address her with new respect and deference.

It was upon this happy future that Marimi tried to focus her thoughts while the chill from Opaka's enigmatic gaze crept into her flesh like a dread. Why was the shaman-woman staring at her?

The ways of the clan shamans were mysterious and deep, and taboo for anyone to even contemplate let alone talk about, for the shamans alone possessed the power to move between the real world and that of the supernatural. Always, before the harvest began, before the first family erected its first shelter, the shamans' god-huts were built. Everyone participated, even children and the elderly, cutting the best branches and twigs, offering the best skins and kindling so that the god-hut would welcome the gods and bring blessings to the harvest and to the people through their shamans' vision quests. The world being the uncertain and terrifying place that it was, bountiful harvests could never be predicted nor counted upon, and so it was imperative that before the first cone was dislodged from the first tree, the shamans went into the god-huts and journeyed in their trance states to communicate with the supernatural powers, to receive instructions and prophecies and sometimes new laws.

This was why Marimi was suddenly afraid on this night of celebration. Opaka had the power of the gods, and Marimi was certain there was malevolence in her gaze. Why? Marimi could not recall what she might have done to incur the elder's wrath. If the source of the rancor were another tribe member, Marimi would go to her clan shaman and beseech her to ask the gods for protection from that person. But in this case it was the shaman herself who was casting an evil eye upon Marimi!

And then suddenly she was remembering Tika, and Marimi was filled with a blinding panic.

Tika had been Marimi's mother's sister's first daughter, and ever since they were little she and Marimi had been like sisters. They had undergone the sacred puberty rites together, and when Tika and twelve other girls had run in the initiates' race, and Marimi had won, reaching the shaman's hut before the others, Tika had been the only one to cheer. It was Tika, at the last harvest, who had carried secret messages back and forth between Marimi and the young hunter, since it was taboo for them to speak while marriage negotiations were in progress. And it was Tika who had given Marimi and her new husband the gift of a basket so magnificent in design that it was the talk of the whole clan.

And then misfortune befell Tika. She had fallen in love with a boy Opaka intended for her sister's granddaughter. If it had been any other boy she had lain with, Tika would not have been made outcast, Marimi was certain. But when the two were found together in an uncle's grass shelter, the medicine men and women sat in counsel and smoked their wisdom pipes and decreed that the girl should be outcast, although not the boy, since they decided it was the girl who had seduced him into breaking tribal law. As the tribe didn't execute any of its members for even the severest crime, because they feared retribution from the ghost, the guilty were condemned to a living death. Their name, possessions and food were taken from them and they were cast out of the protective circle. Once declared outcast, a person could never be brought back in. No one was to speak to or look at the outcast, nor to give food or water or shelter. The family members cut off their hair and mourned as if their loved one had truly died. When Tika became one of the Nameless Ones Marimi's heart wept for her. She recalled seeing her friend at the edge of the pine trees, hovering like a lost soul. Marimi wanted to go out to Tika, to cross the protective circle and take food and warm blankets. But that would have made Marimi an outcast, too.

Because they were already "dead," outcasts did not live long. It was not just the difficulty in obtaining food, or exposure to the elements, it was because the spirit inside them died when they were pronounced outcast. With the will to live gone, death was not far behind. After a few days, Tika was no longer glimpsed at the edge of the camp.

"Mother," Marimi said quietly now to the woman who sat cross-legged at her side, singing as she wove an intricate basket. The singing gave life, and therefore a spirit, to the basket. The song also enabled the fingers to spin a myth or a magical tale into the pattern. Marimi's mother, using a pattern of diamond shapes, was imbuing her basket with the story of how the stars were created long ago. "Mother," Marimi said a little louder. "Opaka is watching me."

"I know, daughter! Take care. Avert your eyes."

Marimi's gaze flickered nervously about the noisy settlement, where the smoke of five hundred campfires rose to the sky. Her summer home was in the high desert, where the common vegetation was sagebrush, but these mountains were forested with pine and juniper, and this leafy haunt of ghosts would otherwise have terrified Marimi if she and her people were not within the protection of the circle. At night, as families lay on their fur blankets listening in fear to the sounds of ghosts moaning in the trees, they hoped that the shamans' talismans that had been set out around the perimeter of the settlement were strong enough to keep the spirits out. This was why no one begrudged payment to the shaman, because a powerful shaman meant that the clan was safe and that the gods watched over them. Everyone remembered the terrible fate of the Owl Clan, whose shaman had accidentally fallen to his death from a steep precipice, leaving thirty-six families without someone to represent them in the spirit world and to speak to the gods on their behalf. Before one cycle of the moon, every man, woman, and child had sickened and died so that Owl Clan no longer was.

With her feeling of dread growing, Marimi forced herself to concentrate on her baby basket. But now her fingers worked stiffly and without grace as she realized in dismay that the magic she had sensed this night was not necessarily *good* magic . . .

✷

As Opaka kept her eyes on Marimi across the circle of dancers, she recalled a time when she herself had been that pleasing to look upon. Sitting on her rich buffalo hide, surrounded by gifts of food, beads, and feathers brought by people seeking favors and blessings from the gods, Opaka thought bitterly that Marimi's round face, laughing eyes, sensuous mouth, and hair like a shining black waterfall—which had caught the attention of more than just the young hunter who had married her—had once been Opaka's features, before age and too many soul-journeys out of her body had worn her down. Now Opaka was bent, white-haired, and nearly toothless.

But this was not why she hated the girl.

The poison that flowed in Opaka's aged veins had sprung up six winters ago, during the Season of No Pine Nuts, when the families had arrived at the forest to find the pinecones already fallen and rotting on the ground. When they realized the gods had made the season come too soon so now the people would starve, a great wailing arose, and the shamans had retreated into the god-huts to burn fires of sacred mesquite and to fast and swallow jimsonweed and chant and sing and pray for visions from the gods that would show the people where pine nuts were. But the gods had not answered the shamans' prayers and so it appeared that a dreadful famine was upon the Topaa.

And then Marimi's mother had come to Opaka with the most extraordinary tale.

Her daughter, then nine summers old, had fallen victim to a terrible affliction that filled her head with pain and blinded her eyes and deafened her ears. The mother had bathed the child's head in cool water and kept her in the shade of the trees, and when the sickness passed Marimi told her mother about a pine forest on the other side of the river. It was only a dream, her mother said, brought on by hunger and the strange head sickness. And she cautioned her daughter to keep silent about her vision, for it was up to Opaka to tell the clan where to find food. But Marimi persisted in her vision of a woodland of pine trees, in a land beyond the Topaa boundaries where no other people dwelled and no ancestors had lived, so it would not be taboo to journey there and to harvest the abundant pine nuts.

And so when the shamans emerged from their hut and said that there would be no pine nuts this season and that there would be no rabbit hunt since no one had seen rabbits in the forest, that the woodland was barren because the gods had turned their backs on the people, Marimi's mother had thought she should seek Opaka's counsel regarding her daughter's vision. The woodland, the child had said, lay in the direction of the rising sun, across a river and atop a fertile ridge.

But Opaka said that the land she spoke of lay beyond their tribal boundaries. It was taboo for the people to go there. Yet the child insisted it wasn't taboo. The spirit in the dream had told her so. Instructing the woman to speak of this to no one else, Opaka had quietly gone on a journey of her own and sure enough had found the forest with plentiful pine nuts. Returning to the camp, she had gone into the shaman's god-hut to undergo a spiritual journey and had emerged to announce that the gods had led her in a vision to a place of bountiful pine nuts, a place where no other ancestors had lived.

Four brave young men were chosen and given spears. They were instructed to run toward the sun, but if they entered taboo ground, they were not to return.

While they were gone, the people danced and sustained themselves on bee larvae and honey and on such pine nuts as could be scavenged from the terrible waste. And when the hunters returned, they told of a bountiful woodland on the other side of the river where no people and no ancestors had lived.

It had turned out to be a good season, the Season of No Pine Nuts, and was talked about at every gathering and around every campfire. The tribe had feasted well and had returned to their summer homes with baskets filled with nuts. The girl was not mentioned. The vision was credited to the shamans, who could speak to the gods, thus proving the power of the shamans, proving the power of Opaka.

Opaka had kept her eye on the girl since, noting the occasions when Marimi was stricken with head pains and spoke of visions. When the girl entered womanhood and won the race at her puberty ritual two summers ago, a victory which awarded her a place of honor in the eyes of the tribe and which Opaka had hoped would go to her sister's granddaughter, Opaka having no granddaughter of her own, Opaka had intensified her vigil. When the girls emerged from the final puberty rite, spent in a ceremonial hut where they had undergone vision quests, and each had declared that the rattlesnake was her spirit guide—the snake being a strong masculine symbol and good luck for virgins hoping to become fertile mothers—Marimi had announced that the *raven* was her spirit guide, defying tradition.

But what alarmed Opaka most was that the girl was able to have visions without the benefit of jimsonweed, which the shamans required. What would happen to the social structure of the tribe if just anyone could commune with the gods? Chaos, savagery, lawlessness would result. Only those specially chosen and initiated into the secret shamanic rites might communicate with the Other World. In this way did the universe remain in balance, in this way was order kept. Opaka saw the girl as a threat to the future stability of the tribe. Especially now that she was pregnant and soon to have her status elevated to that of a mother.

A privilege Opaka had never known.

Chosen when she was only a baby, taken from her mother and sent to live in seclusion with the clan shaman, Opaka had been raised and instructed by the old woman in the ways of mysteries and secrets, medicine and healing, and how to talk to the gods. It had been an initiation of endurance and trial, with grueling months of loneliness and sacrifice as she was trained in hardship and without love, to think not of herself but of the tribe, to live a husbandless life, childless, a virgin even in her old age. Opaka was unable to recognize the emotion of envy, having been raised to become the richest and most powerful person in the clan, so what had she to be envious of? Jealousy was also a foreign concept to her and so she couldn't recognize it when she felt it. Opaka would also not have believed, had anyone told her, that she could be afraid of a simple girl. People who spoke directly to the gods didn't suffer from petty human frailties. And so, blind to her inner rancor and bitterness and her deep terror that one day Marimi might compete with her for god-power, Opaka told herself now that the secret she plotted against the girl was for the good of the tribe.

✳

A group of young women came by, Marimi's unmarried friends, to tease her about not getting cold tonight when the winter chill invaded their shelters. *They* only had their furs and hides to keep them warm, whereas lucky Marimi had the heat of a man. "If we hear your cries," said one girl who was soon to be married to a hunter from the Falcon Clan, "shall we come and rescue you?"

"But what if the cries are *his*?" teased another. "Shall we come and take your husband away?"

Marimi blushed and laughed and chided her friends for being silly virgins, but she loved the attention and was indeed looking forward to her husband's lusty embrace that coming night.

As she was about to offer her friends a basket of berries, which she had picked that afternoon, a woman suddenly broke into the circle, pushing aside the dancers, screaming as she carried an unconscious child. She flung herself before Opaka, beseeching the medicine woman to save her son.

The encampment fell silent, leaving only the sounds of flames crackling in campfires and babies wailing in distant huts.

Marimi recognized the boy. He was Payat, of the Mountain Lion Clan, his second family were the People From The Red Canyon, his first family were "lives by the salt flat." A dreadful hush descended upon the encampment as Opaka struggled to her feet and went to bend over the boy, who was moaning in pain. She touched various points of his body, laid a hand on his forehead, closed her eyes, and held her hands out, palms downward, over his writhing form. And all the while she murmured a mystical chant which no one understood.

Finally, she opened her eyes, straightened as best she could, and declared that the boy had broken a taboo and now there was an evil spirit in him.

A collective gasp rose from the crowd. People shifted nervously and some even backed away. Women who were menstruating or breast-feeding rushed inside the protection of their shelters, while men handled their spears nervously. A person possessed by an evil spirit was a frightening thing, for the spirit could fly from the possessed one at any moment and enter the body of anyone nearby.

Opaka declared the boy Untouchable, that he was as good as dead and beyond the help of the gods, and then she conferred with the chief and subchiefs over what to do with him—he certainly could not be allowed to remain among the people. In the meantime, Marimi edged closer to the scene.

Payat's mother was bent over him, sobbing and begging for the evil spirit to leave his body. Two hunters were ordered to lift her away from the boy, for Opaka had declared it taboo to touch him. While everyone's attention was on the hysterical woman, Marimi moved yet closer, curious to know what had happened. She knew she should keep away, because she was pregnant and should not be in the presence of a taboo person, but she had never seen a possessed person before. But as she drew near, she saw only a little boy who was grimacing in pain and of shocking pallor. What terrible crime could so young a child have committed, she wondered, to deserve the infliction of an evil spirit?

Then Marimi saw something that the others seemed not to—in the boy's hands, crushed yellow blossoms. And suddenly she knew: the child had eaten buttercup leaves. That was how the evil spirit had entered Payat! Everyone knew that the buttercup plant housed an evil spirit and that to ingest it caused sickness and death. If the leaves were still in his stomach, Marimi wondered with sudden insight, mightn't it be possible to expel the spirit?

Without thinking, she rushed forward and before anyone could react, lifted the boy, turned him over, and stuck a finger down his throat. He started at once to vomit.

The onlookers cried out when they saw an arc of green liquid spew from Payat's belly, and when it pooled on the ground they all exclaimed that it was in the shape of a beast. The evil spirit had left the boy's body!

Immediately men rushed forward to throw ashes upon the green devil, thereby smothering it before it could find another host.

When Marimi gently laid the boy on the ground, he groaned and asked for his mother. The woman quickly gathered Payat in her arms, sobbing and laughing at the same time, and held him tight to her bosom as the onlookers murmured and remarked about the miracle. In all their memory, they couldn't recall such an event. They looked at Marimi with new eyes, some in admiration, others in wonder, a few in wariness.

When Payat coughed and opened his eyes, and everyone saw that the color was already returning to his face, they began talking at once, lifting Marimi's name up to the night sky.

"Silence!" Opaka cried suddenly, raising her medicine stick, which was decorated with feathers and beads.

The crowd fell back. All eyes were fixed upon the white-haired medicine woman who, though small and frail-looking, was a powerful vision. And every tribe member knew, in the terrible moment of silence that followed, that the most serous crime a Topaa could commit had taken place before their eyes: a girl had defied the edict of a shaman.

*

The shamans of all the clans gathered in the god-hut, where their mystical smoke was seen spiraling up through the opening in the roof. A somber mood befell the settlement. Marimi cried fearfully in her mother's lap while her young husband paced angrily in front of the shelter as everyone awaited the verdict.

When the shamans emerged, Opaka solemnly declared Marimi and the boy outcast. They were dead.

"No!" Marimi cried. "We did no wrong!"

Marimi's husband spat at her and turned his back.

She flung herself at her mother's feet, begging for help. But her mother turned her back and commenced the keening that would not let up for five days and five nights.

With great ceremony, while the tribe stood in a circle, their backs to Marimi and the boy, Opaka divested them of their names, their clothes, and their possessions. They would have no spear to catch food, no basket to carry seeds, no fur to keep out the cold. They were to live beyond the encampment, beyond the circle, on their own, ghosts in bodies, with no one looking at them or speaking to them, their fleshly fates in the hands of the gods.

*

They were dying.

As Marimi and the boy sat huddled at the edge of the settlement, not crossing the boundary marked by Opaka's talismans and the mystical symbols she had carved into tree trunks, they listlessly watched the dancing in the clearing, the women at their basket weaving, the men at their games of chance. The first and second families of Marimi and Payat were in mourning. They had cut off their hair and smeared mud on their chests and faces and would refrain from eating meat for one full cycle of the moon. All the aunts and female cousins were forbidden to weave, the uncles and male cousins were barred from the dance, and Payat's brothers and Marimi's widowed husband would not be allowed to hunt for one moon. Nor were any in the families to engage in sexual intercourse, to eat with nonfamily members, to walk across the shadow of Opaka or any of the shamans.

For seven nights, the outcast pair had struggled to survive. With pangs of hunger constricting their bellies, Marimi and the boy had managed to find a place to sleep for the night, a hollow in the ground which Marimi lined with leaves. She had drawn Payat against her to share warmth, but both had shivered all through the night, and the little boy had cried in his sleep. During that first long night, Marimi had gazed up at the stars, feeling a strange numbness creep up her limbs. It was not the loss of her own life that filled her with despair, but that of her unborn child. She had placed her hands on her abdomen and felt the fitful life within. How was she going to nourish herself enough to feed the child? If Marimi shivered from cold, then did not her baby also? And when its time came, in the spring, would it be born dead from Opaka's curse?

Without her buckskin skirt and rabbit fur cape, without the comfort of the campfire and the fur blankets inside the shelter, Marimi had been gripped with the fiercest cold she could ever have imagined. Her fingers and toes were numb, her blood felt like frost. She had never shivered so violently as she had when clinging to little Payat, whose tears froze on his face as he cried and cried for his mother.

Marimi hadn't known which was worse, the cold or the terror.

Every morning, when the sun rose, the shamans of the clans would say the proper prayers and send sacred smoke to the sky, scattering seeds to the four points in order to placate the gods, to show respect and gratitude. Powerful talismans, blessed by shamans, hung in the doorways of family shelters to keep evil and sickness out. The huts were built in the shapes of circles, the most sacred of symbols, and then arranged in a circle around the great circular dancing ground. The whole encampment of hundreds of families formed a circle for as far as the eye could see, and there was safety inside the circle.

But Marimi and the boy were expelled from the circle, forced to fend for themselves in the hostile and dangerous land beyond the protection of the shamans.

There were ghosts everywhere in this strange and terrifying wilderness—they lived in the loamy soil and in the menacing shadows, they lurked in the brambles and briars, they hovered overhead in the branches, watching the unprotected humans, ready to descend and possess their bodies. Marimi had never been in the woods alone, she had always been in the company of her family, with the shamans going ahead with their sacred smoke and rattles to make the way safe. But now she was naked and alone, beyond the circle, in a dark place where she heard the whispers and rustlings of ghosts and spirits as they skittered and flitted past her, teasing, taunting, threatening.

Worse even than this, she and the boy were cut off from the stories. It was the tales told at the campfires that connected the Topaa to one another; it was the myths and histories recited at night that joined one generation to another, all the way back to the beginning of time. Marimi's father, like all Topaa fathers, passed along the stories that he had learned at his father's campfire, where they had been learned from earlier fathers, all the way back starting with the first story and the first father to tell that story. But Marimi and Payat had been severed from the stories and therefore from their clans and their families, never to be brought back into the embrace of the tribe. They haunted the edge of the encampment, living on juniper berries and such pine nuts as had been overlooked by the harvesters. But these were not enough, so that Marimi and the boy soon grew weak from hunger. Days and nights came and went, until they had no strength even to find berries. Marimi knew that she and Payat were now facing death, and there was no shaman they could ask to intercede with the gods on their behalf.

✳

She watched the moon through the branches. It was taboo to stare at the moon, for that was the privilege of the shamans. The clan still talked about the cousin who had stared at the moon for so long that he had been punished by fits in which he foamed at the mouth and thrashed his limbs on the ground. But the moon could be generous also. When Tika's older sister could not get pregnant, she presented a gift of rare kestrel feathers to Opaka, who went into her god-hut and beseeched the moon for the favor of a child. The sister was blessed with a boy the next spring.

Knowing that she should avert her gaze from the celestial orb, Marimi could not. Weak and faint from hunger, her soul like a last dying ember among cold ashes, she was beyond fear and caring. As she lay in their little hollow, Payat's bony body curled against hers as he slept too deeply, Marimi kept her eyes on the glowing circle in the sky. Her breathing slowed, her heart fluttered behind her ribs. Her thoughts came on their own as, without realizing it, she silently spoke to the moon: "The crime was mine. This boy is innocent, as is the child in my womb. Punish only me and allow them to live. If you grant this, I will do whatever you ask of me."

The light from the moon seemed to intensify. Marimi didn't blink. She stared up through the branches as the lunar luminescence grew whiter, fiercer, until it covered the entire sky. Suddenly a sharp pain sliced through her head and Marimi realized in dismay that even in her ghost state she must still suffer the affliction that had plagued her since childhood. It was the moon punishing her. Marimi had had the arrogance to speak to the gods and now she would know only pain until she died. Then let it be so, Marimi thought as she delivered herself to its power and slipped into a deeper sleep than she had ever known. As her last conscious thought drifted away on waves of pain, she thought: I am dying.

But Marimi didn't die, and while she slept her spirit guide, the raven, appeared to her in a dream. He beckoned, and as he flew ahead, Marimi followed until she came upon a small glade in the woods where a clump of milkweed grew.

When she awoke at dawn, barely alive but filled with a strange new compulsion, Marimi crept weakly from her bed of leaves and followed the vision in her dream. When she found the small glade where the milkweed grew, she ate ravenously of the starchy root which, though bitter, was nutritious. Then she took some back to Payat and coaxed him to eat.

They survived on milkweed after that, and as they grew in strength, Marimi and the boy were able to fashion small traps and supplement their gruel with squirrel and rabbit meat. Marimi found sticks to make fire and soon fashioned a round shelter out of branches and leaves. She and Payat scratched out a living far from the harvest settlement, alone with the ghosts and spirits of the unfriendly forest, but Marimi was less afraid than before, because at the moment of her deepest despair, when she had felt abandoned by her people, when she knew she and the boy were one step from death, she had had a revelation: she had prayed directly to the moon without the help of a shaman, and the moon had answered.

✳

One night the affliction came upon Marimi again as she slept, sending pains through her skull as if ghosts with spears attacked her. And in her agony she heard her guide, the raven, instruct her to follow Opaka. Marimi was frightened at first, but as she was compelled to do what her spirit guide told her to do, she suddenly realized she had nothing to fear. She was a ghost and ghosts could go anywhere they wanted to. Therefore, she was free to spy on Opaka as she went about her daily work.

Marimi stood in the dappled sunlight, in full view of Opaka, as the old woman harvested raspberries. The whole tribe knew that medicine men and women used the berries and leaves of the raspberry in the manufacture of astringents, stimulants, and tonics, and in teas and syrups for curing diarrhea and dysentery, canker sores and sore throat. While anyone could gather raspberries, what the people did not know was the proper way to harvest the plant, the propitious times, the correct prayers to recite during harvesting, for without these the plant was powerless.

Marimi brazenly observed how Opaka approached a plant before harvesting it, the words of respect she spoke, the sacred signs she drew in the air with her beads and feathers. And when Opaka discarded a plant after drawing it from the ground, Marimi saw that its root was broken, which meant it had lost its spiritual power. As Opaka did most of her harvesting at night, Marimi made note of the moon's phase, the position of the stars, the thickness of the dew upon the leaves.

Marimi also listened as Opaka instructed her sister's granddaughter in the ways of herbs and medicines, showing the girl how to age alder bark first before boiling, as the green bark will cause vomiting and stomach pain, and how to allow the decoction to stand for three days until the yellow color had turned black. When administered during the full moon, Opaka told her sister's granddaughter, alder tea strengthened the stomach and stimulated appetite. The berries also made an excellent vermifuge for children.

Sometimes when Opaka left her shelter, which stood apart and secluded from the rest of the camp, Marimi would go inside to see what the medicine woman was doing with the plants she gathered. In this way did Marimi learn the secret of the inner bark of slippery elm, which Marimi had seen Opaka harvest and set out to dry. Next to the bark, on a buckskin, were a mortar and stone with some of the bark already ground to a fine powder. Drying on a string were slippery elm suppositories which Marimi knew were used vaginally for female troubles, and rectally for bowel difficulties.

Through the long winter, as her baby grew beneath her heart, everything Marimi observed and heard she committed to memory. The terrors of the forest were forever around her, threatening, lurking, keeping her alert to malicious ghosts as she sought to protect herself and Payat from being possessed by an evil spirit. But Marimi felt an inner strength growing within her, and a sureness of purpose and knowledge. The moon had saved her for a reason, and so she kept her bargain with the moon. Whenever Marimi came upon a pond that was littered with leaves so that the moon's reflection could not be seen, Marimi scooped the leaves from the surface, allowing the moon to shine proud and beautiful on the water. And when she came across night-blooming flowers in the woods, such as evening primrose, she would clear branches overhead so that the moon would have an unobstructed view of the beautiful blossoms opening up to her.

Thus did they survive, the sturdy girl and the trusting boy as they haunted the edge of the encampment but never daring to cross into the circle. Marimi didn't wonder about the future because the Topaa never did. There was today and times past, but tomorrow was a vague and puzzling concept, since tomorrows always turned into todays. She wished she could consult a shaman about what to do when spring came—were she and Payat to remain in the woods, or were they to seek summer homes near their families? What did the living dead do? And how did they learn to be ghosts? When Marimi and Payat had been cast out, there was no one on the other side to teach them. Marimi and the boy should have died, but Marimi had prayed to the moon and the moon had shown them the way to survive. Had they broken yet more tribal taboos by not dying?

Marimi was too young to ponder for long the complex questions that plagued her. And so she set them aside, instead facing each new dawn with the basic task of survival for another day, and leaving the mysteries of life and death to the shamans.

And then came the day when she learned of her true power. After weeks of being haunted by Marimi, Opaka had grown increasingly wary and nervous, emerging cautiously from her shelter, or entering the forest with trepidation, looking this way and that for the girl. Her old hands began to shake, her temper grew short, her distress increased daily. She must not acknowledge the creature and yet the creature was forever shadowing her, straining her aged nerves. At last, unable to take it any longer, Opaka startled Marimi one day at the creek by suddenly whirling around and crying out, rattling her sacred sticks and chanting in a language unknown to Marimi.

Marimi stood her ground, tall and proud, her swollen belly evidence of her vital life force and the strong will that had kept her from dying. The old woman fell silent and their eyes met. Even the forest grew quiet, as if the spirits and ghosts, the birds and small animals were aware that a monumental turning point had been reached. Finally, Opaka averted her eyes, turned away from the ghost-girl who had refused to die, and disappeared through the trees.

✳

Finally came a dawn when the blinding sunlight pierced Marimi's eyes like a knife, sharp and swift. She lay immobilized, enveloped in agony, but through the pain came a vision—her spirit guide, the raven, sitting on a branch, blinking his cunning black eye at her. And this time she heard him whisper, "Follow me."

Marimi gathered up the herbs and plants she had collected during her sojourn in the land of the dead, and the rabbit skin pouches she had made and filled with seeds and leaves and roots. She took Payat's hand, and said, "We are leaving this place." Filled with a strange new resolve and no longer afraid of the tribe's laws and taboos, she went to her family shelter, where everyone was still asleep, and helped herself to her possessions, which her mother had not yet buried. Marimi squatted next to her sleeping mother and, alarmed at how old and wasted she had become from her long period of mourning, bent close and whispered, "Mourn for me no longer. I am going to follow my raven. My destiny lies no more with this family. I can never come back, Mother, but I will carry you in my heart. And whenever you see a raven, stop and listen to what he says, for he might be the one carrying a message from me. The message will be this: I am safe. I am content. I have found my destiny."

She left, wearing her best clothes: a long buckskin skirt and a rabbit skin cape around her shoulders, grass sandals on her feet. Rolled on her back was her sleeping mat which she had woven herself from cattails, a rabbit skin blanket, and the cradle board she had woven for the child to be born in the spring. She carried a basket for gathering seeds, a spear and a spear thrower, fire-starting tools, and pouches containing medicinal herbs. In this way did she come to understand why the raven had instructed her to follow Opaka and learn the medicine woman's teachings. It had been to prepare Marimi for her great journey.

The Topaa might wander far and wide in their eternal search for food, but there were limits and all were taught at an early age that "the land over there" belonged to the ancestors of another tribe and so it was forbidden for Topaa to walk there. But Marimi sensed, as she and Payat followed the raven who flew before them, that they were going to be led, for the first time in the history of her people, into forbidden territory.

They walked all day, and when they reached the westernmost boundary of Topaa territory, Marimi approached the escarpment with fear and caution because this was a new land, where no Topaa had ever walked, with unfamiliar rocks and plants and, therefore, unfamiliar spirits. She looked out at the desert valley stretching away to the horizon. She didn't know the rules here, the taboos. She knew that she must be cautious with every step for she might accidentally offend one of the spirits. As she was about to take the first step on the incline down the escarpment, she said, "Spirits of this place, we mean you no harm, we mean you no disrespect. We come with peace in our hearts." Firmly grasping the boy's hand, Marimi lifted her right foot and set it resolutely upon the forbidden soil.

Payat began to cry. He tugged Marimi's hand and pointed back to where they had come from, crying for his mother.

But Marimi took him by the shoulders and, looking deeply into his young eyes, said, "We cannot go back, little one. We can never go back. I am your mother now. I am your mother."

Sniffing back his tears, Payat delivered his small hand into Marimi's, and said, "Where are we going?"

And she pointed toward the sun, a giant red ball in the western sky, her guide, the raven, outlined sharply against it.

❋

Payat noticed the vultures first, circling overhead.

"Why doesn't Raven lead us to water?" he asked, his lips parched and cracked.

"I don't know," Marimi said, puffing with the exertion of having to carry the boy on her back. He was too weak to walk. "Maybe he's looking."

"Those birds want to eat us," Payat said, meaning the vultures.

"They are just curious. We are strangers in their land. They mean us no harm." It was only a small lie, enough to comfort the boy.

Marimi and Payat had traveled far, for many days and nights, along stark jagged cliffs and through deep canyons, across fields of boulders and vast areas of flat sand where they saw cacti taller than a man, always following the raven, who flew westward, ever westward.

At each nightfall the raven would come to a rest—on a rock or a cactus or a tree—and Marimi and the boy would make camp, to awaken the next morning to follow the raven again in his flight toward the west. Where was Raven leading them? Were they to join another people? Marimi was worried because her child was going to be born soon and it was unthinkable that it should be born without a shaman in attendance to ask the gods for blessings. How would her baby receive protection and beneficence from the gods with no shaman there to speak on its behalf?

During their long trek Marimi and Payat had survived on beans from the mesquite, wild plum, dates, and cactus buds. When hunting was good, they had feasted on a stew of rabbit, wild onions, and pistachio nuts. For water, when they could not find a stream or a spring, they sucked on the thick stems of prickly pear, which were full of water.

Wherever they walked, they showed etiquette toward the land. All things were treated with respect and ritual. Taking any part of a tree, killing an animal, using a spring, or entering a cave was prefaced by ceremony, however simple, in the form of a request or an acknowledgment. "Spirit in this spring," Marimi would say. "I ask pardon for taking your water. May we together complete the circle of life that was given to us by the Creator of All." She also fashioned snares with bait, and as she and the boy hid behind rocks, she kissed the back of her hand to make a sucking sound, which attracted birds. And when they caught small game thusly, she apologized to the animal and asked that his ghost not take revenge on them.

Once, when the ground roared and trembled so mightily that she and Payat were thrown off their feet, Marimi shook with terror until she re-traced their steps and discovered the cause of the earthquake. She had inadvertently crushed a tortoise burrow. She begged forgiveness of Grandfather Tortoise and cleared the opening to the reptile's home.

She never forgot her debt to the moon. When she and Payat had a meal, they never ate the whole of it but always left some behind, an offering to the goddess who had saved them.

Occasionally they had come upon evidence of people having recently occupied a site—blackened stones, animal bones, shells from nuts. But sometimes the evidence was from long ago, when they would come upon petroglyphs that looked as if they had been carved in the rock back at the beginning of time. Marimi sensed the ghosts of those ancient people all about them as she and Payat crossed the foreign landscape, over the hot sand, in and out of the shade of massive date palms. She wondered what the ghosts thought of these strange intruders trekking over their ancestral land, and she always asked their pardon and assured them she and Payat meant no disrespect.

The moon had died and renewed herself five times since the night Marimi prayed to her, and in that time Marimi had watched the moon and marveled at her power. Only the moon could die and be reborn in an endless cycle of death and birth, and only the moon cast light during the night when it was needed, whereas the sun shone his light during the day when it wasn't needed. And when she walked in the moonlight, despite the burdens she carried on her back and inside her body, Marimi found her stride widening, she felt moon power flowing in her veins. With each step, her strength grew.

And while she journeyed ever westward across the endless expanse, she let her thoughts fly to the stars, to linger there and then to return with new knowledge. Marimi knew something her people had never known: that an individual could pray directly to the gods without the intervention of a shaman. She had also learned that the world was not necessarily a malevolent place, as the Topaa believed. There were spirits everywhere to be sure, but they were not all evil. There were those who could be friendly and could be called upon for help and guidance, such as birds that circled the sky at sunset, indicating a water hole below. Whereas the shamans of the Topaa taught their people that only fear ensured survival, Marimi learned during her long sojourn among the silent boulders and cacti, the slinking coyotes and tiptoeing tortoises, that mutual respect and trust also ensured survival.

When she saw how beautifully the moon lit up the desert landscape at night to light their way, Marimi marveled at how the Topaa could believe her to be an angry and fearful goddess. Not only was it taboo to look upon the moon, but the people were afraid of her because of her tremendous power over menstrual blood, birth cycles, and the dark mysteries of women. Likewise did the Topaa fear the sun because it burned the skin and caused fires and droughts and was angry all the time, being placated only through the intercession of a shaman's prayers. But Marimi and Payat learned to love the feel of the warm sun on their limbs in the mornings, and they observed how flowers turned their faces to follow the sun's path across the sky. Marimi came to understand that what her people had feared could also be loved, and she began to regard the sun as like a father, stern but benevolent, and the moon as like a mother, gentle and loving.

But now they were in a land where there was no water, no berries or seeds, and the only shrubs were bitter and waterless. Even small animals didn't come out of their burrows. Marimi was carrying the boy on her back, and because her sandals had disintegrated long ago, her bare feet were cut and bleeding. They sucked on pebbles to stave off thirst. They stopped at dry streambeds, which often have water just below the surface, sinking at the lowest point on the outside of a bend in the channel as the stream dried up, and it was along these bends she dug for water. But none could be found.

Finally, they had to stop, Marimi easing Payat to the sand and then stretching her lower back. Her baby moved restlessly, as if it, too, were thirsty, and when she looked for her raven, she could not find him.

Had her spirit guide abandoned them in this harsh wilderness? Had she and Payat inadvertently offended a spirit somewhere along their trek, perhaps disturbing a snake's nest or not showing enough gratitude when she sliced open the last prickly pear they came upon?

Shading her eyes, she scanned the barren landscape, where only stunted, withered plants grew, and a dry wind whispered mournfully across the sand. In the distance she saw silver waves shimmering up from the hard-baked clay, but she had learned by now that this was not water but a trick played by desert spirits. Finally, she looked up at fierce Father Sun. It was to him she must pray, she realized, for the moon was in her sleeping house.

But as Marimi raised her arms and sought the proper words, she was suddenly stricken with her head sickness, causing her to drop to her knees and press her hands to her eyes. As the pain swept her away, she saw a vision of a lost child, trapped among rocks. She saw it from the sky, as if through the eyes of a bird. And then Marimi saw people searching for the child, but in the wrong place, and moving farther away from him in their search.

When the pain subsided, she said urgently to Payat, "Raven led me to a lost boy. We must find him before the vultures make a feast of his body."

Within the embrace of a barren, rocky watercourse, they found the boy, unconscious and dehydrated, but still alive. "Oh, you poor little boy, poor thing," Marimi crooned as she knelt at his side. "Look, Payat, see how his foot is caught." The child's ankle was raw and bloody, and the rocks were scarred where he had clawed to free himself.

Marimi sat back on her heels and listened. She lifted her nose to the air and sniffed. She closed her eyes and summoned up the vision the raven had shown her from the air. "There is a stream," she said to Payat. And she pointed through the boulders.

Marimi first slaked Payat's thirst and then her own, then she brought water to the child, dripping it between his lips. She collected ground ivy from along the bank and wrapped the fresh leaves around the child's ankle. There were fish in the stream, which Payat caught with a basket, and the three ate well that night at a campfire that burned as brightly as the full moon.

The next day the boy, already recovering from his ordeal, said his name was Wanchem, but he didn't know his clan or his family name, and he didn't know in which direction he lived. As Marimi wondered how she could get him back to his people, she saw that the raven was calling again, impatiently circling in the sky. Marimi had no choice but to follow. And so, shouldering her basket and blanket, clasping her spear, and hefting Wanchem onto her hip, with Payat at her side, she set forth once again toward the setting sun.

✳

Finally, they reached the western edge of the desert, where fierce mountains rose straight up, sharp and jagged. Marimi found a pass through the mountains, and after days of hardship the trio emerged on the other side to find a great lush rolling plain before them. It was green such as they had never seen, and dotted with trees as far as the eye could see, with streams and ponds, and gentle hills. When they descended into the valley, they found an ancient animal track and, knowing it would lead them to food and water, followed it. And indeed along the way they came upon trees laden with fruits and nuts, and streams running with fish and clear water. Marimi wanted to stop and say: Here is our home. But the raven kept flying ever westward, and Marimi followed, unquestioning.

They continued along the track through glades and open fields, past marshes and great ponds of a black substance that bubbled on the surface and stung the nose with its stench. Westward the trio continued, encountering a few people along the way who were friendly but who spoke a language unknown to Marimi. These people lived in small round shelters and shared their food with the travelers. Marimi stopped occasionally to look at a sick child or a sick elder, and to share the healing herbs she carried.

And then the air began to change and it was unlike any she and Payat had inhaled. It was fresh and cold and smelled of salt. And when Marimi saw the green mountains in the distance, she was filled with a sense of coming to an ending. Soon, she assured Payat and Wanchem, Raven would stop for his final rest.

*

As they drew near to the foothills of the green mountains, dark clouds gathered in the sky. A wind arose, buffeting Raven and impeding his progress. Around and around he circled in the sky, while Marimi hugged the two boys to her, drawing her rabbit fur blanket around them. When the storm broke, they huddled beneath the shelter of a great oak tree and watched in fear as streams overflowed and gushed down gullies and ravines, threatening to sweep the three frightened humans away. They watched in horror as cliffs broke apart and gave way, sliding down in great muddy avalanches. The wind roared and the storm thrashed the sturdy oak. Marimi lost sight of her raven and she wondered in terror if she and the boys had broken a taboo and were now being punished.

And then her birth pains struck.

Leaving the boys beneath the tree, she plunged into the downpour to search for shelter. Blinded by rain, she groped and stumbled over rocks and brush, searching the rocky base of the mountains for somewhere dry and out of the storm.

Finally, through the torrent, she glimpsed the black bird-shape, gliding sleekly into the wind and rain, drawing her toward a towering jumble of rocks. Here Raven perched, shaking his feathers and blinking at her in silent communication. Marimi explored around the rocks, slipping and sliding on the sodden ground, and found that the boulders hid the entrance to a ravine. Going farther into the small canyon, she blinked and saw the entrance to a cave, where she and the boys could be warm and dry and protected from the storm. Later, after her baby was born and her strength returned, Marimi would go back to the boulders and carve two petroglyphs into the rock: the symbol of her raven, in gratitude for having guided them here, and the symbol of the moon, for having answered her prayers.

∗

Marimi was not surprised when she gave birth to twin girls. She came from a long line of women who gave birth only to daughters. When Marimi's strength returned, the raven flew to the top of the ridge, with Marimi and her babies, Wanchem and Payat following. There they climbed to the crest and stood transfixed for a long time.

They had arrived at the edge of the world, for before them stretched the largest expanse of water Marimi had ever seen. There was the land of the dead, she thought, the place to where the Topaa went after they died. It was breathtaking in its majesty.

The raven had come to rest in an oak tree. He had something in his beak. He dropped it, before flying off forever. Marimi picked it up, a strange, beautiful stone, perfectly round and smooth, blue-black like a raven's feather. When she curled her fingers around it she felt the power of the raven-spirit in it.

She looked again out at the body of pale blue water and saw, closer in on the distant shore, tall thin columns of smoke from cookfires. She said to the two boys and to the babies in her arms, "We will not meet those people, for they will have customs and taboos and laws that are different from ours. We were outcast and now we will be our own people. This is our home now. We will call this the Place of the People," she said, putting together the words in her language: *Topaa*, meaning "the people," and *ngna*, meaning "the place of."

*

They stopped living in the cave at Topaa-ngna and moved to the marshy plain just inland from the ocean, not far from the foothills. They built round shelters and hunted small game and went once a year into the mountains to harvest acorns. Marimi visited the cave whenever she sought counsel from her raven and from the moon. She would feel the spirit gift come upon her and she would blindly make her way up the little canyon, her head filled with pain, and she would sit in the darkness of the cave while the visions came upon her. In this way were the laws of her new family given to her.

Marimi understood the vital importance of a person knowing his clan and his second family and first family. Because if a person didn't know these, he might commit taboo without knowing it. So she tried to construct Wanchem's lineage. Because the raven led her to him, she decided he was of the Raven Clan. His second family were People Who Live With The Cactus. And his first family was Marimi's new one: "people who eat acorns."

The little family flourished and grew. In their fourth winter in the mountains snow fell, covering every branch and creek. A bear hunter, having lost his way, sought shelter in Marimi's cave, where she found him. He stayed with the family until spring and then continued on his way. In the summer, Marimi brought forth the hunter's babies, another pair of twin girls.

As the children grew and soon faced adulthood, Marimi started to worry about taboos and family ties. The rules weren't hers but had been decreed by the gods at the beginning of time: that brother should not marry sister, nor first cousin on mother's side marry first cousin on mother's side. If these rules were broken, a tribe could sicken and die. But Marimi knew that first cousin on mother's side could marry first cousin on father's side, so what the family needed was new blood. She went into the cave for counsel and the raven told her to find a husband in a neighboring tribe and bring him back.

Taking her spear and a basket of acorns, Marimi traveled eastward to a village she had passed through seasons ago. There she offered shell-beads, which were highly valued, and promised the new husband plentiful acorns and fishing. But he must accept Topaa ways, she said, and become one of them. His family agreed that this was a good thing, to have ties with a coastal tribe, who were rich in otter skins and whale meat. The chosen husband was Deer Clan, People Who Live On Trembling Ground, "dwellers in the marsh." Now he joined "people who eat acorns."

When Marimi's first daughters entered womanhood, they married Payat and Wanchem. One of the hunter's daughters also married Payat, because Marimi had made him chief of their small tribe, and the chief could have more than one wife. The second hunter's daughter found a husband in a traveler from the east, who had come in search of otter skins and had decided to stay. Marimi's husband from the Deer Clan gave her three sons and four daughters, who in time married and increased the tribe.

As the seasons came and went, Marimi taught her daughters and granddaughters how to weave baskets, how to chant and sing so that the basket was given life and therefore a spirit. She taught the young ones the rules and taboos of the Topaa: that when grasshoppers and crickets were scarce, they were not to be eaten; at the acorn harvest, the acorns were not to be harvested to depletion but some were to be left to ensure a bountiful harvest next time; a husband did not sleep with his wife during the five days of her moon; the hunter bringing back meat did not eat of it, but ate of another hunter's meat. Because without rules and without knowing the taboos, she said, a person didn't know how to conduct his or her life. The Topaa knew from nature that there were rules: cat never mated with dog, deer did not eat flesh, the owl hunted only at night. Just as animals lived by rules, so must the Topaa.

One autumn a blight struck the oak trees and the acorns dropped to the ground like ash and small game vanished from the land, so that not even a squirrel could be roasted on the fire. The family began to starve and Marimi remembered how she had once prayed to the moon for help. She prayed again now, respectfully, promising gratitude in return. And a miracle occurred: the next night fish washed up on shore living and flopping, and Marimi had everyone run with baskets up and down the beach, collecting the living fish, which when dried provided enough food until the spring, when berries and seeds appeared in plenty. In gratitude, the next time the fish ran ashore, Marimi had her children throw a certain number back, telling them that what we take from the gods, we give back to the gods.

Marimi taught her family the importance of telling stories, how the stories must be handed down so that the clan would know its history and the ancestors would be remembered. And so every night at the campfire, she told them how the world was created, how the Topaa were created, she told them stories of the gods, and the fables that taught lessons. She told them how they must pray respectfully to Father Sun and Mother Moon, that the Topaa were the children of the gods and that they needed no shaman to speak on their behalf. Like all parents, the sun and the moon liked to hear their children's voices, but only if they were respectful and obedient and promised to be reverent. Under such terms did the gods protect their children and provide well for them.

Every now and then, as the years passed, Marimi would pause in her labors and look to the east, where a small yellow sun was breaking over the summits, and she would think of her mother and the clan, and she felt a special pain in her heart.

*

When Marimi's hair was as white as the snow that had brought the bear hunter long ago and she knew she must soon make the journey west over the ocean to join her ancestors, she spent all her days in the cave, mixing paints: red, from alder bark; black, from elderberries; yellow, from buttercups; purple, from sunflowers. With these she painstakingly recorded her journey across the Great Desert in pictographs on the cave wall so that future Topaa would know the story of their tribe.

Finally, she lay dying, surrounded by her family. Although they were now nine families from five tribes and four clans, and brothers of one group had married sisters from another, and strangers who had wandered in to marry extra daughters, ultimately, the youngest generation were all descended from Marimi. She had taught them to hunt and to gather nuts, to weave baskets and sing the songs of their ancestors, to revere Mother

Moon, and to live harmoniously with the spirits that inhabited every animal, rock, and tree. She told them never to forget that they were Topaa.

Payat was there, himself now a grandfather, and he smiled sadly as Marimi laid her hand on his head in benediction. "Remember," she said, "there will be no outcasts in my family, there will be no living dead as you and I once were. Teach our people not to live in fear and helplessness as we once did, but in love and peace."

She said: "And remember to tell the children our story, about our journey from the east, about how we caused the earth to tremble when we stepped on Grandfather Tortoise's burrow, how we found Wanchem by the magical stream, how Mother Moon protected us and lighted our way. Teach our children to remember these stories and to tell them to their children, so that Topaa in generations to come will know their beginnings."

Marimi then summoned her great-granddaughter, who had since infancy suffered from blinding headaches and visions, which Marimi no longer saw as an affliction but as a blessing, and she placed her hand upon the girl's head, and said, "The gods have chosen you, my daughter. They have given you the spirit-gift. So now I give my name to you for I am to join our ancestors, and by taking my name you will become me, Marimi, clan medicine woman."

They buried her with great ceremony in the cave at Topaa-ngna, sending her spirit to the West with her medicine pouches, her spear thrower, her hairpins and earrings. But the sacred raven's spirit-stone they kept, draping it around the neck of the chosen girl, now named Marimi, who would be the clan medicine woman and whose duty it would be to tend the cave of the First Mother for the rest of her life.

Chapter Three

Your name is Walks With The Sun and you were out with a hunting party; you strayed too far and got lost, so you settled here and made this place your home.

No, Erica, thought as she studied the photographs she had taken of the skeleton in the cave. This woman would never get lost.

You are Seal Woman and you sailed down from the northwest in a long canoe, you and your lover running away from tribal taboos that forbade you to marry.

Or you came from islands far to the west, long sunk back into the sea, and you were named for a goddess.

Pinching the bridge of her nose between her thumb and forefinger, Erica leaned back from her worktable and stretched, rolling her head and shrugging her shoulders to get the stiffness out. She looked at the time. Where had the hours flown?

As she reached for her cold coffee she contemplated the mess piled on the workbench—artifacts waiting to be examined and labeled and catalogued. Erica was in the trailer that had been converted into a lab filled with scientific equipment, microscopes, tall stools, and a bulletin board covered with pins and notes and drawings. It was early evening and she had been sorting the last of the day's finds. She was the only one in the lab; everyone else was either still at dinner in the cafeteria tent or socializing around the camp.

When Erica had uncovered the skull in the cave floor, Sam Carter had authorized her to commence a full-scale excavation. They got the go-ahead from the Office of Environmental Preservation, and while Sam was to be the field director, he gave Erica the honor of conducting the hands-on work, despite sharp criticism from both within and outside the State Archaeologist's Office. However, he had cautioned her: "Be objective, Erica. After the embarrassment of the Chadwick shipwreck, there were those who wanted you fired. But you're a good anthropologist and I don't think your career should go into the toilet because of one impulsive mistake."

Promising to be careful, Erica had approached the job with her characteristic vigor and exuberance, wasting no time getting started marking out the cave floor with stakes and string, and then meticulously scraping off the soil with the edge of a trowel blade, curbing her eagerness to plunge through the soil layers and find the riches of history underneath. The scraped-off dirt was placed in buckets and hauled topside, where volunteers sieved through it to see if it contained archaeological material.

Outside the cave, the noisy business of geologists, engineers, and soils specialists got under way in earnest along Emerald Hills Drive.

And Jared Black, of course, had *his* job.

They were in a race. Jared's task was to locate the most likely descendant as quickly as possible and then to turn the cave and its contents over to that person or tribe. As soon as that happened, Erica suspected she would be out of a job. She was Anglo, and once the cave was owned by Native Americans they would want their own people on the excavation, possibly even halting the excavation altogether and sealing the cave. And so Erica was working long, hard hours, desperate to decipher the mysteries of the cave before Jared Black accomplished his goal.

The first visitor he had brought to the cave was Chief Antonio Rivera of the Gabrielino tribe. He was there to possibly identify the painting and therefore allow Jared to start the legal wheels in motion. As the visitor was of advanced age, he had been lowered to the cave in a chair, and while Chief Rivera had sat and gazed at the pictographs, Erica had paused in her work to watch him. The face mapped with a million lines and creases, coppery and weathered, remained a mask as the small, alert eyes flitted from one symbol to another, stopping, fixing, staring, absorbing, and then moving on. He had sat motionless for nearly an hour, his eyes drinking in the magnificent mural, body rigid, rough cracked hands flat on his knees, until finally he had heaved a ragged sigh and risen from the chair to say, "It is not of my tribe."

One after another Jared brought tribal members into the cave— Tongva, Diegueño, Chumash, Luiseño, Kemaaya—some young, some old, men and women, in suits or jeans, short hair or braids, to stand or sit and ponder the perplexing mysteries of the ancient mural. And each, upon leaving, shook his or her head to say, "It is not my tribe." Some of the visitors looked at Erica with clear displeasure, recalling ancient taboos about women trespassing in holy places. Some were even uncomfortable about themselves being there. A woman from the Purisima tribe north of Santa Barbara became highly agitated and left, saying that she had broken the taboo which forbade women to look upon the sacred symbols of a shaman's vision quest and that now her entire tribe would be cursed because of her being here. Some visitors, however, looked favorably upon Erica and her work. One young man, a member of the Navajo tribe and a professor of Native American history at the University of Arizona, shook Erica's hand and said he looked forward to hearing of her progress.

Jared also produced Anglo experts, men and women trained in universities to know Indian ways. These, too, with their degrees and book knowledge, shook their heads and departed.

The painting wasn't the only mystery in the cave.

The 1814 one-cent piece she had found the day before, for example. In 1814 it was illegal for Californios to trade with Americans. American ships were not allowed to dock at San Pedro or San Francisco, and anyone who jumped ship was caught and deported. So how did an American coin get into the cave? Erica knew it couldn't have been dropped there years later, when California was part of the United States, because the relief was so sharp. One could clearly see the wreath embracing the words *One Cent*, and around that, *United States of America*. On the other side, the Liberty head with a wreath on her curly hair surrounded by twelve crisply defined stars and the numbers 1814, all sharply defined. A coin that had been in circulation for years would be worn smooth from so much handling. This one had been recently minted when it was lost. And so there was a mystery here.

There were more.

Erica looked at the black-and-white photos tacked to the bulletin board showing the remarkable discovery Luke had made while cleaning the cave walls: words etched into the sandstone wall of the cave: La Primera Madre—*The First Mother*.

Who was the First Mother? Was this possibly a clue as to the identity of the Lady?

That's what they were calling her: the Lady. The woman whose intact skeleton had been gradually exposed by Erica over the past weeks, complete with burial objects, remnants of clothing, and even wisps of long white hair.

Determining gender had been easy: the pelvis was clearly that of a female. Age at time of death, which Erica placed between eighty and ninety, was determined by looking at the teeth, which were worn down nearly to the jaw, indicating a lifetime of eating food contaminated with coarse sand and dirt. Determining the historical age of the skeleton was another matter and required carbon-14 analysis. The bone tissue dated between nineteen hundred and twenty-two hundred years old, and the fact that a spear and a spear thrower had been buried with the woman instead of bow and arrow also placed her prior to fifteen hundred years ago.

Erica had also been able to deduce that the Lady had been a medicine woman. Buried with the skeleton were pouches of seeds and small woven baskets containing herbs. Most of it had disintegrated but microscopic analysis had so far identified several of them as healing herbs.

What Erica couldn't resolve, however, was tribal affiliation. The woman had been tall, which meant possibly Mojave, who were among the tallest tribes on the North American continent. The burial objects were not

Chumash, nor had the Chumash buried their dead this side of Malibu Creek. The woman couldn't have been Gabrielino since they cremated their dead. Her funerary objects were intact, and the Indians of the Los Angeles basin ritualistically broke the deceased's possessions—snapping an arrow in two, breaking a spear—so that the objects would die and their spirits could join their owner in the afterlife.

But whoever she was, whatever her tribe, those who buried her had done so lovingly and with great care and reverence. The Lady had been found on her side, arms folded at her chest, knees drawn comfortably up in what looked like a fetal or sleeping position. She had been wrapped in a blanket of rabbit skins, most of which had disintegrated but which could still be seen in small patches on the skeleton. Several shell-bead necklaces were strung around her neck, and strands of shell-beads on both wrists. Pollen analysis indicated she had been laid in a bed of flowers and sage, and small offerings of food—seeds, nuts, berries—had been placed near her hands. Around the body the woman's personal possessions had been carefully laid: feathered hairpins, engraved bone earrings, a flute made of bird bone, and various objects which Erica could not identify but suspected held ritualistic significance. Traces of ochre suggested the corpse had been painted red before interment.

While sounds from the camp drifted through the open window—someone playing a guitar, teams tossing a volleyball—Erica sent herself back through time. She gazed at the photos taped above the workbench, taking in the white hair and fragile bones that had once been part of a living, breathing woman, and suddenly felt an overwhelming need to know the Lady's story.

Stories were what made people real, what gave them souls. Erica would never forget the day she had first started wanting to know people's stories, the day her life's course was set forever. She had been twelve years old and visiting a museum with a school group. They were in the anthropology wing looking at the dioramas while the teacher lectured about the lives of the Indians depicted in the reconstructed village behind the glass. Erica had been suddenly filled with an inexplicable awe to think that these people had died long ago and yet here they were, showing people in the present how they lived! What a wonderful thing to do, to not let people die and be forgotten, but to keep them alive and remembered.

Who are you? Erica silently asked the eggshell skull with its delicate cheekbones and touchingly vulnerable jaw. What was your name? Who loved you? Whom did you love in return? Alone in the cave, amid the shadows and silence, handling the Lady's brittle skeleton so sweetly curled on its side, Erica had been rocked with unexpected emotion. It had been like tending to a child or nurturing a baby. She had felt fiercely protective of the forgotten, lonely bones, wanting to gather them to her breast and keep them safe.

That was when her resolve had been born: to learn the woman's identity before Jared Black found the cave's legal owners.

Perhaps the latest find, unearthed from the cave that afternoon, would provide a clue. The strange object was roughly the size and shape of a small football and consisted of a rabbit fur bundle tied with animal sinews decorated with shell-beads. Erica had found it at a level lower than the 1814 coin but above the soil layer from which she had extracted pottery shards. Since the Indians of the Los Angeles basin didn't fire clay but instead traded with visiting Pueblo peoples for pottery, Erica scoured reference catalogues of Southwest pottery that had been dated and identified. She had been able to determine, by the lead ore content in the glaze and the sandstone temper, that the pots had been made in Pecos, a large Indian pueblo on the Rio Grande, around the year 1400. That still left a range of four hundred years. Further analysis was required to determine more precisely the year that the rabbit fur bundle had been left in the cave.

Erica was certain there was something inside. *An offering left by a descendant who had come to the cave to pray for a miracle—a woman hoping for a child, a warrior desiring a maiden.*

Erica wanted to open it, but her eyes ached. Deciding to go for a walk and get some air, she picked up a book from amid the clutter on her workbench and tucked it under her arm.

✳

The land behind the Zimmerman property was actually the north crest of the canyon, with the producer's mansion sitting on the south crest, across the sinking backyards. Here, among oak, dwarf pine, and chaparral, trailers and tents had been erected to accommodate the archaeologists and volunteers who had come to sieve, clean, sort, catalogue, photograph, analyze, and run tests on everything that was being brought out of the cave and out of the Zimmerman pool crater—mostly, it was human bones.

During the day, the area buzzed with activity. While police, disaster teams and myriad city workers dealt with homeowners, curiosity-seekers, and news crews, licensed land surveyors were mapping the ground conditions of the mesa and comparing them to historical mapping. They worked all over the neighborhood with levels, theodolites, drills, backhoes, electronic distance-measuring equipment, seismic analysis units, and various types of small sampling tools to collect soil for laboratory analysis. Another backyard had partially sunk, creating a dramatic scene of an elaborate Renaissance-style fountain cracked in two and tilting.

Archaeologists weren't the only ones living at the site. There were people from the Seismographic Institute, monitoring delicate instruments which they had placed all over the mesa and Emerald Hills Estates; uniformed rent-a-cops hired by the homeowners to protect the mansions from looters; and construction workers brought in to shore up the cliff, the swimming pool crater, and the inside of the cave—guys in hard hats flirting with the leggy anthropology majors who had been recruited from UCLA. Many of the hard hats were Indians hired under new legislation initiated in part by Jared Black, who had argued that construction-site monitoring of Indian burial mounds not only provided jobs for Indians, it also raised cultural awareness for tribal members, helped pay for tribal training programs, and provided experts that developers and government agencies needed in order to comply with state and federal environmental impact laws.

There were other Indians here as well, protestors on the other side of the police barriers who demanded that the excavation be stopped even though no one knew which tribe the cave and the skeleton belonged to. There were also Indians who wanted the dig to continue in hopes of getting an identification. Jared Black was often seen talking to the protestors, trying to mediate between clashing Native American groups. Already one fight had broken out, the protestors taken away in handcuffs. Emotions were running high. Since the NAGPR Act of 1990, skeletons were being removed from museum collections around the country for reburial. The Smithsonian had already returned two thousand skeletons, with the remaining fourteen thousand to follow. But the problem with the Emerald Hills Woman was that her tribal affiliation was as yet unidentified and so some tribes were worried that a member of a rival tribe might handle the bones and possibly put a curse on them and her descendants.

As Erica crossed the noisy camp, she looked over at Jared Black's ostentatious forty-foot Winnebago, parked a distance away from the humbler tents and trailers. There were no lights on inside. She had seen him leave early that morning, tearing out of the parking area as if the backseat of his Porsche were on fire. Apparently he hadn't yet returned.

Jared was not an idle man. Even though he was on the State Native American Heritage Commission, he still had his private law practice with a prestigious firm in San Francisco. He was currently having his staff run searches on local deeds and historical references to the cave, poring over the records of the Franciscan Missions, digging through city, county and state archives, trying to find if Indians had ever been owners of record or if there were references to any particular tribe in that area.

Erica had been inside the RV once, when Jared had called a meeting between her and Sam and members of a local tribe. The Winnebago was equipped with state-of-the-art electronics, an entertainment center, king-size bed, Sub-Zero refrigerator, dishwasher, microwave oven, automatic ice maker, plush carpeting, and glass cabinets displaying crystal stemware. It was ritzier and loaded with more conveniences than any apartment Erica had ever lived in. Jared Black, the lawyer and Indian rights activist, was a flashy show-off, in her opinion, reveling in the spotlight. Jared had a secretary, on loan as a courtesy from a local law firm, who came every morning and then left with a full briefcase. People were in and out of Jared's RV all day long—attorneys, politicians, tribal representatives. His professional life was an open book.

Jared Black the *man*, on the other hand, was something of an enigma.

At the end of the day, when work shut down and city crews went home, and Erica and her team put away their tools and dispersed to the cafeteria tent or to private living quarters, Jared Black also closed down for the day, the visitors stopped coming, the lights went on in his RV, his door remained closed. He never joined the others for dinner but dined alone. And then around eight, he would leave, carrying a small athletic bag, and return two hours later, his hair damp. Erica imagined he went for a workout somewhere, perhaps to play handball or to swim laps, but it wasn't just two or three nights a week, it was every single night almost without fail. *He's a personal trainer to prizefighters and kung fu stars. He climbs the outside of the Bonaventure Hotel every night, with permission of course. He wrestles alligators that are going to be made into Gucci wallets.* Whatever it was, it accounted for his build. Even in a three-piece suit, it was obvious Jared Black possessed a trim, hard body.

From what Erica could see, he had no social life. She wondered about his wife, why she hadn't come to join him. He had gone away for four days a couple of weeks back, Erica presumed it was to go north to San Francisco, where he lived. *He and his wife engaged in passionate and un-bridled lovemaking. They made love everywhere—in their bedroom, in Golden Gate Park, in a cable car—an insatiable love fest to make up for lost time and to tide them over in the celibate months to come.*

Jared's pieces didn't fall together the way other people's did. Erica couldn't find his story. Although she knew the surface facts about him, she could not unearth the artifacts that were buried beneath his complex layers.

Erica did know one thing about Jared Black, however: she didn't trust him.

A booming voice pierced her thoughts. "There you are!" Sam Carter, emerging from the cafeteria tent with coffee stains on his tie. "I was just coming to see you." The news wasn't good. "I've just gotten off the phone with the OEM. We're at the mercy of nature, Erica, that's all there is to it. Those aftershocks yesterday, another swimming pool sinking, they're saying this whole canyon could go in a second. You have to be ready to move out at a moment's notice."

"But I'm not finished!"

"The Office of Emergency Management doesn't want to take responsibility for your safety should another big aftershock strike—and they *are* expecting one."

"I'll take responsibility for myself."

"Erica, your safety is *my* responsibility and if the OEM says we have to clear out, then we clear out."

He saw the book she was holding. When she caught his questioning look, she handed it to him. *Rare Medium, Well-Done: The Strange Life and Ministry of Sister Sarah.* The title was taken from the headline of a story that had run in the *Los Angeles Times* in 1926 reporting the smashing success of the medium's mass séances at the Shrine Auditorium, where over six thousand hysterical people had claimed to see and speak to spirits. "Doing a little light reading before bedtime?" Sam said.

"I'm curious to know what drew Sister Sarah to this spot. Why she chose this canyon for her Church of the Spirits."

"Probably because it was cheap. A lot of land in this area was cheap in those days. No roads, no utilities. I'd guess it was a pain to live here." He flipped through the black-and-white photos and paused at a dramatic portrait of Sarah in her white robes, marcelled hair, vampish eyes. She looked more like a silent-movie star, he thought, than a spiritualist. And then he seemed to recall that that was how she had gotten her start. Hadn't she been "discovered" or something?

Handing the book back, Sam squinted over at the Winnebago, and said, "I'm looking for our commissioner friend. Have you seen him?"

"I don't think he's home."

"Where do you suppose he goes every night?"

"He's taking guitar lessons from a retired jazz musician."

Sam gave her a surprised look, then saw the wry smile. "Someday, Erica, that imagination of yours is going to get you into trouble."

. . . *"My father is a spy and my mother is a French princess who was disowned by her family for marrying him."*

. . . *"Erica, dear, why are you telling lies to the other children?"*

"They're not lies, Miss Barnstable. They're stories."

. . . *"Class, Erica has something to say to all of you. Go on, Erica, tell the class you're sorry for telling lies."*

"Have you unwrapped the fur bundle yet?" Sam asked, knowing she already had a story for it even though she didn't know yet what it contained. That was what had gotten her into so much trouble with the Chadwick shipwreck: too much imagination and too much eagerness to know the story. If the facts didn't tell it, then Erica's mind did. In her hands a piece of pottery wasn't just a piece of pottery, it was the anger of a wife furiously working the clay and thinking about her husband making eyes at his brother's wife—a lazy husband who was no good at hunting so that his wife was forced to labor over pots to trade for fish and meat while her husband considered breaking a tribal taboo that was going to destroy them all. Erica brought passion to her work. No scientific detachment for her. "Look at this!" she would cry, holding aloft a dirty, moldy something, and saying, "Isn't it great? Can't you just *see* the story behind it?"

The stories didn't have to be true, merely possible.

Maybe that was why she was such a loner. Maybe her stories were enough. Sam marveled at the ease with which Erica had moved into the camp, using her few possessions, the way she always did, to transform a tent into a home. She didn't have a permanent residence; her address was a P.O. box in Santa Barbara. She was incredibly mobile, able to take reassignment at the drop of a hat and often laughingly referred to her "vagabond" life. There was a time when Sam had envied her rootlessness because he himself was tied to a heavily mortgaged home in Sacramento, with his adult children and small grandchildren living a few streets away, and his ex-wife, with whom he remained on good terms, still in the neighborhood, and his invalid mother residing in a nearby nursing home. To be able to just pick up and go anywhere, no explanations, no promises to call or hurry back, had been a midlife dream for him. He had stopped envying Erica, however, one Christmas when they were on a dig in the Mojave Desert and Sam had flown home to spend the holiday with his family while Erica had stayed behind to catalogue bones. He learned afterward that she had had Christmas dinner at the local desert truck stop, sharing processed turkey and canned cranberry sauce with three truck drivers, two California Highway Patrol officers, two young hikers, a local park ranger, and a grizzled old prospector named Clyde. Sam thought it was the loneliest thing he had ever heard.

He sometimes wondered about her love life. He had seen men come and go in her life, but they never stayed for long. How did the affairs end? With Erica saying, "You have to go now"? Or did her partners soon tumble to the fact that the physical was all she would allow, that her heart was off-limits? There had been a time, when they had first worked together, when he had experienced a brief infatuation with her, but Erica had gently told him that she admired and respected him and didn't want to risk spoiling their friendship with complications. Sam had thought at the time that she had rejected him because he was twenty years older, but since then he had decided that Erica wasn't going to let *anyone* inside her carefully guarded walls. He suspected it was because of her past. No one could say Erica Tyler had had an easy life.

"I wonder why Jared's wife doesn't come to visit him," Erica said now as she and Sam continued to stare at the dark RV.

He gave her a startled look. "Jared's wife? You mean you don't *know*?"

*

"Hi, son, your mother and I were just talking about you and wondering how you were doing."

Jared started for the answering machine, then stopped.

As he dropped his briefcase and car keys on a table, he listened to his father's voice come through the speaker: "We were reading about you in the newspaper . . . the work you're doing there in Topanga. We're very proud of you." Pause. "Well, I know you're busy. Give us a call. At least call your mother, she'd like to hear from you."

Jared hit the mute button and stared for a long time at the phone. I'm sorry, Dad, he wanted to say. All the words have been spoken. There aren't any left.

Turning on lights and fixing himself a drink, he picked up a fax he had just received from the Congressional Native American Caucus in Washington. But hard as he tried to focus on the words, he finally had to lay the letter aside. His father's phone call had triggered the pain again, and the anger.

He began pacing the length of his RV, from driver's seat to bedroom, pounding his fist into his palm. He needed to go to the Club. He could feel the rage building up in him like lava inside a volcano. Only an hour at the Club, thrashing himself to his physical limits, could vent the power of his fury. But they were closed tonight for maintenance, leaving tigers and tigresses to prowl the streets of Los Angeles in search of outlets for their energies and frustrations. Like most members of the Club, Jared didn't go there for physical fitness.

As he looked around at the clutter inside this temporary home/office— the computer that never slept, the bank of phone lines that never stopped ringing, the fax that never stopped spewing out messages, and the papers, stacked, spread, lying everywhere as if a snowstorm had blown through dropping three inches of documents, briefs, memos, letters, deeds, writs— he realized that the motor home, despite its size, was too small to contain both himself and his anger. He grabbed a jacket and flung himself out into the brisk night.

✳

At the edge of the mesa, on a promontory overlooking the ocean, stood a fabulous old Victorian gazebo left over from Sister Sarah's Church of the Spirits. The builder of Emerald Hills Estates had had it restored and then landscaped the area to make a small communal park for the residents. Unfortunately, the hillside had been declared unsafe and there were warning signs to stay away, so the gazebo was never used. Which was why Erica loved it.

Ever since she had first started coming here a few weeks ago, she felt a sense of peace in this spot. She wondered if it was because she was away from the camp and her work, beyond the energy and vibes of the enthusiastic volunteers and staff. Or was it simply the ambience of this delicate gazebo, a relic from a more peaceful past, symbol of a simpler age?

She looked at the book in her hand. What had drawn Sister Sarah to this place? Had she sensed an inexplicable peace on this hilltop, or—

Erica felt a chill as a new thought suddenly came to her: in those days the canyon wasn't filled in, the cave was accessible. Did Sarah go inside and see the painting and decide that it was a sign that here was where she should build her church? Sarah claimed to have built her temple of spiritualism in this area because it was conducive to reaching the Other World. But what exactly did that mean? Had she chosen to build her church of the paranormal here because it was called Haunted Canyon? Was she attracted to the notion that spirits were already supposed to be in residence? Erica had only just begun to read the biography of the enigmatic figure of the twenties, a woman whose face had been known by every person in America, who was seen everywhere in newspapers, magazines, newsreels—a flamboyant personality whose theatrics and mesmerizing voice were the butt of editorial cartoons and social comedians, and yet whose personal life and background were practically unknown. Sister Sarah had sprung out of nowhere, become an overnight sensation, and then had disappeared just as quickly under mysterious circumstances, leaving her church fragmented and in shambles.

Erica stepped into the gazebo, which shone like a wedding cake in the moonlight, and as she laid her hand on the wood she felt it hum with stories—of stolen kisses and broken promises, of moonlit trysts and séances for the dead. Music and love and disappointment and greed and spiritual contemplation had been absorbed by these old boards over the decades until the gazebo quivered with the remnants of lives that had passed through it.

Erica looked out at the water and wondered if her mother, wherever she was in the world at that moment—on the Champs Elysées in Paris, on a beach in the Caribbean—felt she wasn't complete because she had abandoned her child. *She is walking through Central Park right now, on the arm of her second husband, a dentist, and feeling that there is a piece of her missing, not knowing that three thousand miles away that missing piece is walking, breathing, dreaming.*

As she pushed her hair back, she realized with a jolt that she wasn't alone. Someone was already here, on the other side of the gazebo, at the very edge of the promontory. Jared Black! Standing with his feet apart, hands on hips, as if he were having an argument with the ocean.

He suddenly turned around and Erica was stunned by the expression on his face. It was like looking into the heart of a storm.

The moment hung suspended between them, like a freak lull in the wind and everything in the night froze for an instant. They had never been alone together. In the weeks since the project began, whenever Erica encountered Jared there were always other people around, issues to deal with and matters to settle. They had absolutely nothing to say to each other in private company. She wondered now which one of them would walk away first.

To her surprise, Jared turned from the cliff's dangerous edge and came up the creaking steps of the gazebo to stand beneath the elegant roof trimmed with gingerbread. "Sister Sarah must have preached from here. This structure was designed with acoustics in mind."

Erica looked up at the underside of the roof. "How can you tell?"

"I studied architecture once," he said, adding with a smile, "back in the Pleistocene Era."

The smile shocked Erica, as did the joke. And then she realized that the smile and joke had been forced. *He is covering up for something I was not meant to see. The look on his face, his fury at the ocean.*

"I usually have this place to myself," she said, feeling strange currents in the air and unable to identify them. "The signs frighten people away."

"Signs can sometimes accomplish the exact opposite of what they were meant to do." He fell silent, watching her.

Erica tried to think of what to say. She had the odd notion that Jared was holding himself in check, that if he let go just a little, if he was negligent in his vigilance for just a moment, he would turn into something he did not want people to see.

"I've been getting calls from Hispanic interest groups," she said for lack of anything better to say. Ever since the news broke about the *La Primera Madre* graffiti, Erica was being contacted by people who wanted to come and see it, journalists asking her to comment on what "The First Mother" might mean, Mexican-Americans making a claim of ownership of the cave.

"We're the flavor of the hour," he said with another smile.

She and Jared fell silent again and Erica thought of a hundred things to bring up that needed to be discussed—her growing concern about the lack of security around the cave, for one—but ultimately all she could do was voice what was foremost on her mind. "Sam Carter just told me about your wife. I didn't know. I was lecturing in London at the time and was out of touch with the local news. I was sorry to hear about it."

His lips formed a grim line.

"She was so young," Erica said. "Sam didn't say how . . ."

"My wife died in childbirth, Dr. Tyler."

Erica stared at him.

"We lost the baby, too," he added softly, turning his eyes toward the dark sea.

Erica was shocked. Suddenly she felt as if she were standing with a total stranger. "You must miss her." It sounded lame, but something needed to be said.

"I do. I don't know how I've made it through these past three years. It just doesn't seem fair. Netsuya had so much ahead of her, so many plans and dreams. She wanted to redress two centuries of grievances and restore her tribe's history to them." He looked at Erica. "She was Maidu. I don't have to tell *you* what an undertaking that would have been."

As an anthropologist specializing in California natives, Erica was familiar with the story of the Maidu, which was similar to that of every other West Coast tribe. Although they had been unaffected by the Spanish missions, which had spelled doom to the coastal cultures, the Maidu nonetheless met their fate during the Gold Rush, when white men, in their greed for the precious yellow metal, destroyed anything that stood in their way, be it mountains or people. Malaria and smallpox had decimated much of the tribe, and then the miners had driven away game and destroyed fish habitats by using gold-mining techniques that ravaged rivers, killing fish and their spawning beds. Life as the Maidu had known it for centuries winked out almost in an instant.

"After Netsuya graduated from law school," Jared continued, speaking to the night, his back to Erica, "she started on a plan to provide housing, senior care, health care, cultural resources, as well as tribal economic opportunities and academic scholarships for her people. But her real dream was to someday see a Native American occupying the office of Governor of California."

Erica listened to his words fade away on the wind. When silence followed, and he remained faced toward the ocean, she said, "Netsuya is a pretty name. What does it mean?"

He brought his gaze back to Erica. She tried to pinpoint the color of his eyes. Steel gray didn't quite touch it. They were the color of shadows, she thought, and mystery. "Actually, I don't know," he said. "Her real name—well, the name she was baptized with—was Janet. But when she took up the cause of her people, she adopted the name of her great-grandmother." He kept his eyes on Erica. She couldn't read his expression. There was the anger she had seen since the day he had arrived, but other emotions as well, rippling across his handsome features like the surface of a dark pool disturbed by a breeze.

She remembered his attitude the day he first arrived here, with a chip on his shoulder, making Erica wonder why he had come with such aggression. She wondered now if it had something to do with his wife. It was well-known that prior to meeting Netsuya, Jared, specializing in property law, had been the legal representative of corporations, heirs, and citizens with land disputes and that it was only after he married an Indian rights activist that he took up their cause. Now it was almost exclusively all he did. Erica imagined some sort of death wish, Jared's wife telling him to carry on the fight. A ghost was a powerful motivator.

When Jared leaned against a carved post, folding his arms, Erica was struck by the thought that he was trying to relax, to be friendly. And when he looked up at the stars, and said, "The Maidu believe that the soul of a good person travels east along the Milky Way until they reach the Creator," Erica refused to let her guard down. Reminding herself that they were still opponents and that Jared's main reason for being at the project was to take it out of Erica's hands, she looked at her watch, and said, "It's getting late and I still have work to do."

He brought his gaze away from heaven and fixed his eyes on a point somewhere out on the black, rolling ocean. Erica sensed that he was weighing something important or wrestling with something internal. When he looked at her, she braced herself. But when he said, "I understand you found something unusual in the cave today," she had the odd feeling that that was not at all what he had been about to say.

"You're welcome to come to the lab and watch while I open it."

As they started to leave the gazebo the silence was suddenly shattered by a tremendous roaring sound.

"What is *that*?" Jared said.

They looked up and saw a police helicopter hovering over Emerald Hills Drive, its high-intensity beam focused down on one spot.

As they ran back down the path and through the compound, they saw a crowd gathered in the street in front of the Zimmerman house. Homeowners—husbands, wives, kids, and pets—holding boxes and suitcases, sleeping bags and pillows. Harmon Zimmerman, wearing an Adidas jogging suit, was shouting at the security guard, who had apparently gotten spooked when he saw all those people streaming through the security gate and so had called the police. Sirens could be heard coming up the canyon.

"What the hell did you call the cops for, you idiot?"

"It's m-my job, sir. It's what I'm supposed to—"

"Yeah, it's your job all right because *we hired you*, you moron. We're paying your salary. Why did you call the cops on *us*?"

When the flustered guard couldn't reply Jared stepped in, and said, "The man just told you. He called the police because that's what he was hired to do. Why do you have a problem with that?"

Zimmerman turned on him: "And you, hotshot lawyer, between you and that woman"—he jabbed a finger toward Erica—"you've managed to drag this out so long that our houses are getting ripped off, our lawns are going to seed. This looks like a freaking ghost town."

Erica looked down the dark, deserted street. There were houses only on one side. Across the way were trees and then a gentle slope down into the next canyon. Beautiful homes, but the lawns were becoming choked with weeds, roses growing wild. The whole look was one of neglect, like Sleeping Beauty's castle, Erica thought. The maiden fell asleep and nature was reclaiming her kingdom. And it would take more than a handsome prince to rescue this situation. The entire neighborhood had been declared unsafe. The city soils engineers had drilled the length of the street and found that the whole canyon from its blind end at the north to its opening to the south was all liquefying and spilling out into lower can-

yons. It was almost as if, Erica thought, the canyon were restoring itself
to its original state, after humans had interfered with it and tried to alter
its natural formation.

Cyclone fencing had been put up around Emerald Hills Estates and
the only access in and out was through gates that were locked at night.
Despite this precaution, as well as private security guards, the homes were
prime targets for looters. Even though all furnishings had been moved
out, they still contained valuable accessories. The police had already
caught two men trying to steal the gold bathroom fixtures in one house,
and one homeowner had dropped by to check on his house only to discover all the kitchen appliances gone, imported marble stripped from the
bathroom walls, copper wiring and piping ripped out. All without a sound,
without a trace of when and how the thieves had done it.

So the homeowners had decided they were going to move back into
their residences despite the fact that the city wouldn't allow them to
because of the ground instability and that there were no utilities. Zimmerman and the others were demanding that the original developer refill
the canyon and properly compact it, and reinforce it with steel and con-
crete supports, rebuilding the development to make it stable again.

"We thought this would be resolved weeks ago," Zimmerman, spokes-
man for the irate homeowners, continued, "and that we'd be moving back
in. This is dragging on indefinitely." He poked Jared in the shoulder.
"You with your Indians"—and then poked the air in front of Erica—
"and you with your bones—"

The police, who had parked their cruisers outside the fence, were now
running in on foot.

"We're not leaving!" shouted the magazine publisher, who owned a
nine-thousand-square-foot Tudor-style mansion where the tennis court
had sunk three feet into the ground.

Zimmerman crossed his arms, and said, "We're not moving. This is
where we live and this is where we're staying."

Jared said, "This area is unstable, it isn't safe."

"You know how much that house cost me? Three million. *Before* the
pool and the expensive rose garden, which is now totally ruined I might
add because of everyone tramping through. The insurance isn't paying,

and it's sure as hell I can't sell. So you think I'm just gonna walk away from it? We've all been strung along and pushed around enough. There you are, hotshot from Sacramento, hawking Indian rights. But what about *our* rights? Some of us, our life savings went into these homes. Some of us came here to retire. Where do we go? You tell me that. No sir, here is where we take a stand and nobody's going to move us off *our* property."

Erica stepped in and said, "Mr. Zimmerman, I promise you we are moving as fast as—"

"And I'm promising *you* something, lady. I've already got my lawyers on this. We are going to have that cave sealed, this canyon filled in, and our properties restored to us. And you can take your Indians and your bones and shove 'em. You got that?"

✳

The dental tweezers and surgical blade lay ready for Erica to cut open the mysterious rabbit fur bundle. Sam was there, perched on a stool, his stomach growling because he had put himself on a diet—again. And Luke was checking his film, lighting, and shutter speed.

"Gentlemen?" Erica said. "Are we ready?"

Before either could respond, Jared came into the trailer, snapping the aluminum door shut behind him to block out the cold night wind. He had stayed behind to get further information from Zimmerman. "It's what I expected. They're going to move against the developer's completion bond, asserting that the development wasn't graded properly. If the court finds in their favor and orders completion of the project, then the builder will have no choice but to fill in the canyon."

"Can you stop them?"

"I'm sure as hell going to try." Jared looked at the tray and frowned. "Is that an animal?"

"No, it's something wrapped in an animal skin."

"Old?"

"I'd estimate about three hundred years. Dr. Fredericks, our dendro-chronologist, took core samples from nearby indigenous trees and determined that a terrible fire devastated much of this area three centuries ago. Microscopic and chemical analysis of a thin layer of soot and ash on the cave floor matched bark material in those cores. This fur bundle came from beneath that layer, which means it was left there at least three hundred years ago. It could be Chumash. These beads are similar to the ones they used as currency."

Drawing the light closer and adjusting the gooseneck lamp so that it spotlighted the object, Erica applied the very fine tweezers and dissecting blade to the sinews that tied the rabbit skin. Luke took pictures at each step of the procedure.

Beyond the thin walls of the trailer they heard sounds of people walking by, laughing, calling out to one another, while inside, Jared, Sam, and Luke stood behind Erica, softly breathing.

She snipped the sinews and painstakingly drew them aside. Then she gently clasped the edges of the brittle fur as if she were working on a living human being. Finally, the last layer of skin came away.

They stared in shock. "What the heck!" Luke blurted. "How did *those* get here?"

"Good Lord," Sam murmured, sweeping back his mane of hair.

"At what level did you say you found this?" Jared asked in disbelief.

Erica's voice was filled with wonder. "Just below the year sixteen hundred." She blinked in amazement. "I'm not an expert in this area, I would have to consult a historian, but judging by the craftsmanship and materials, I would hazard a guess that these were probably made around four hundred years ago. Of Dutch manufacture, I believe."

"But that's impossible," Luke protested, "there weren't any Europeans in California yet! Not for another two hundred years."

"So history tells us, Luke, but there is no doubt as to its age. Just as there is no doubt," she said as she lifted the surprising object to the light, "that this is a pair of eyeglasses."

Chapter Four

MARIMI
1542 C.E.

"Sea monster! A sea monster!"

Everyone ran to the shore to see where the boy was pointing. Sure enough, out on the waves, floated an animal no one had ever seen before.

The medicine woman was sent for. She arrived with her magic smoke and special sun-staff, a tall young woman wearing a fine skirt of woven grass and a small cape of sea otter skins, with tubes of pelican leg bone decorated with quail feathers piercing her earlobes, and between her bare breasts many strands of shell-bead necklaces, among them a leather thong at the end of which was a small leather pouch containing the raven's spirit-stone, handed down through the ages from the First Mother. She was Marimi, so named because she was the Guardian of the Sacred Cave in Topaangna. When she was younger she had been called something else, but when she had started to exhibit symptoms of the spirit gift—

pains in her head, visions, and trances—she had been chosen to be the successor to the old medicine woman, also called Marimi, and dedicated to the service of the Topaa and the First Mother. It was the greatest honor a clan member could receive, and Marimi was daily thankful for having been blessed with the gift, even though her service to the First Mother meant the renunciation of marriage and sexual congress with men. If at times, late at night alone in her hut, thoughts of love and children should creep into her mind, or when she counted her seasons and realized she was still very young and faced a lifetime of chastity, she reminded herself that the virginal state was necessary to keep herself and her spirit pure and that it was but a small sacrifice to make for the privilege of serving the First Mother.

She squinted out over the water. "Not a sea monster," she pronounced. "A man."

Voices buzzed like flies. "A man? One of our own? But no, no one is missing. All the boats came back today. The sea-hunters are all accounted for. What is a man doing on the water?" And then gasps and whispered speculations: "A member of the tribe to the north? The dreaded Chumash? He has come to cast spells on us! Send him back out to sea."

Marimi raised her arms and the crowd on the beach fell silent. Standing majestically on a dune, with gulls wheeling overhead against the bright blue sky, and the fresh wind blowing from the sea stirring her long black hair, Marimi watched the lifeless man out on the water and came to a decision. She called for a boat and immediately everyone ran back to the village to hoist upon their shoulders one of the big oceangoing hunting canoes made of driftwood planks sewn together and caulked with asphalt. In these impressive vessels, able to hold more than a dozen men, the Topaa hunters went out daily with their spears, nets, and hooks to hunt whale, porpoise, seal, and ray. But now they pushed their canoe through the waves to go after different prey. Everyone watched as the oars dipped into the water in unison until they reached the floating man where, using a whale hook, the hunters snared him and hauled him in.

The tide swept the canoe ashore, depositing also the mystery upon the wet sand, revealing that it was indeed a man, lying prone and unmoving on a wooden plank. The people gasped again. "Not Chumash! Look at the skins on his body! And his feet are the size of a bear's!" They drew back, afraid.

The chief came forward to confer with Marimi. While powerful in his own right, the chief's power was of a different nature from Marimi's. Together they would decide how to deal with this unexpected turn.

In the past weeks the people had sighted strange creatures far out to sea, with massive square wings and fat bloated bodies. Hunters had paddled out and come back to report that they were not creatures at all but seagoing boats unlike any the Topaa had ever seen. Members of a southern tribe passing through, who had gone north to trade with the Chumash, reported that white-skinned men had landed on the islands in the channel, and there they had traded and feasted with tribal elders and then had set out upon the water again in their marvelous canoes.

Friendly visitors, they said, whose ancestors lived far away.

Was *this* one of those visitors? Marimi wondered as she took in the salt-crusted body clad in the strangest skins she had ever seen. The man was lying facedown on a wooden plank. Why had he been put out of his canoe?

She gave a command and two men rolled the stranger over. Everyone cried out. He had two sets of eyes! "A monster!" "A devil!" "Throw him back to the sea!"

Marimi called again for silence as she studied the stranger. She could see that he was very tall with a curiously narrow face, large arched nose, and pale skin. And those eyes! She wondered if he was an ancestor since he had come from where the spirits of the dead dwell, out in the West over the ocean. Perhaps after death, the spirit was given a second pair of eyes.

Marimi knelt and placed her fingertips to his cold neck. She felt, just barely, the faint throb of life. She would have preferred to retreat to her cave and seek the counsel of the First Mother, but the stranger was at the threshold of death, there was no time.

Marimi straightened up and ordered five strong men to carry him to her shelter at the edge of the village.

✳

She recited a mental prayer. That second pair of eyes! Were they magic? Could he see her even though his eyelids were down? *Was* he some sort of monster?

But he came from the West, where the ancestors dwell. . . .

"They are friendly visitors," the southern traders had said.

First, she must undress him. She started with his peculiar hat, which was not made of grass as Topaa hats were but of a foreign skin, and when she gingerly peeled it back she cried out. His head was on fire! She frowned. But how could his hair be aflame and yet not consume his scalp? She looked closer. Then she cautiously touched the sunset-colored curls. He had sailed out too far in his ship and his head had brushed the sun. That could be the only explanation. The strange flaming hair was also very short, trimmed almost to his scalp, yet his chin and upper lip had long hair, pointy and curled! Topaa men wore their hair long and had no hair on their faces.

She contemplated the layers of skins covering his body from neck to toe, leaving only his face and hands exposed. She could not imagine what she was going to find underneath. The men of her own tribe wore nothing save for a rope around their waists from which they hung food and tools. Was this visitor the same under his skins?

Marimi didn't know that his skins had names, or that she was in fact peeling away some of the finest fabrics made in Europe, or that the fashion and design of these layers were intended to broadcast the nobility and wealth of the wearer. First there was a black padded velvet doublet with slashed sleeves to show off the fine white linen shirt underneath; over the doublet was a belted jerkin of red brocade that went to the knees in a pleated skirt, through which a red velvet codpiece protruded. The hose were white and gartered at the knee, the heavily padded breeches were of black velvet. His hat, which she had set aside, was low-crowned and wide-brimmed black velvet trimmed with fur and pearls. The shirtsleeves ended in ruffled cuffs at the wrists and the shirt was pleated at the neck. Finally, when she freed his feet from their strange bindings, she found them to be soft and without calluses, as his hands were also soft and smooth, like a child's—yet he was a grown man.

When all the skins were off and he was completely naked, she saw the sun-fire hair at his loins as well. How had the sun touched him there? His skin was soft and pale, as white as the foam that rides the morning tide. And then she saw the angry color along his legs and arms and in a scalding ring around his neck. She knew at once what afflicted him.

But first water, which she managed to drip between his chapped, cracked lips while she cradled him, her strong arm beneath his shoulders. When he was able to swallow without coughing, she laid him back down and brought her healing kit to his side: a case made of bulrushes containing a small pestle and a mortar made of a transparent crystal rock, flint knives, a fire-starter, and various healing talismans. She retrieved a stone believed to be alive because it had been treated with herbs containing tremendous life power and then smeared with hummingbird blood and oil from an eel and then wrapped in downy, white feathers. She placed this on the stranger's forehead. Then she laid across his chest a necklace strung with beads fashioned from eagle and falcon bones. She saw that he already wore a necklace made from a yellow, glittery substance she had never seen before, almost the color of his hair, and the charm at the end of this necklace looked like two sticks tied at angles, and she could see the tiniest figure of a man on it.

Going to one of her many baskets, she selected a handful of dried, flowering shoots. After steeping them in hot water, she allowed the tea to cool and then bathed his rashy skin with it. He awoke briefly, muttering in his delirium, "Pox, pox," and tried to push her away. For the bruises he had received while being buffeted about on the wooden plank and the merciless tide, Marimi boiled the leaves and branches of chaparral to make a moist poultice. She also made a tea of the leaves and gave it to him as a tonic.

She was fascinated by his hairline. It wasn't straight across his forehead, like her own, but grew back from an arrowhead-shaped point, making her think of an eagle she had once seen when she had gone up in the hills to visit the cave of the First Mother. His fiery golden eyebrows emphasized the eagle look, but when on occasion his first set of eyes fluttered open in delirium, Marimi saw no eyes that were those of a bird. Mother Moon, they were the color of the sky! Had he stared too long at the heavens and now they were caught there?

But she didn't touch his second pair of eyes, for to do so might be taboo.

He had moments when he was able to take nourishment, and Marimi fed him a healthful gruel of acorns and rabbit meat. When he looked at her his eyes didn't focus, so long had he been upon the waves and so long without water that his senses had not been restored. But she was able to feed him and give him water, and bathe his flaming limbs in the cool, herbal tea until gradually his color improved, his breathing grew tranquil, and she knew his health was returning.

✳

When he came to the first thing his eyes set upon were two plump, brown breasts. "God's bones!" he exclaimed. Then he looked down at himself and saw that he was naked. "Mother of God!" he boomed, jumping to his feet and suddenly clutching his head in dizziness.

When the spell passed and his head was clear, he looked at the bronze girl sitting in the center of the hut with a basket of leaves in her lap. She wore a grass skirt and nothing else. She was looking up at him with a startled expression.

"Where are my clothes?" he shouted, snatching up the fur blanket and wrapping it around his waist. "Where's my crew?" And then he froze. "But wait. I was dying." He examined his arms and legs, where only a trace of the rash remained. "The pox is gone. And I am not dead."

To his astonishment, the girl started to giggle. Hiding her mouth behind her hands, she laughed with glee, which only infuriated him all the more. "What's the matter with you? Are you a half-wit? And where in the name of all the saints and angels *am* I?"

He strode to the opening of the shelter and looked out at a soupy dawn, where tendrils of fog snaked along the ground and the air was filled with the salty smell of the sea. Through the mist he saw other round huts like the one he stood in, and people crouched at cookfires.

Feeling a tap on his shoulder, he spun around and found himself almost eye to eye with the girl. God's breath, she was tall! But she no longer giggled. Instead she touched his arms here and there, light little landings as if butterflies flitted along his skin. And she was babbling in her savage tongue, explaining something, or trying to. Gesturing. Pantomiming the crushing of something, and the boiling of something, and the pouring of that something over his limbs.

"What are you saying, girl? That you can cure the pox?" His red-gold eyebrows came together. "That's why they put me overboard, you know. When I came down with the sickness the captain and crew thought I had a contagion that would kill them all. I'm a chronicler, y'see, traveling with Cabrillo. I became ill after we stopped in at a bay to the south of here and we went ashore for water. As soon as the poxy rash appeared on my skin, the sailors, those syphilitic sons of whores, put me asea off one of those cursed islands where others like you live. No one took pity. Not a Christian soul among them."

He paused, rubbing his jaw. "I remember being put upon the waves," he said softly, "and saying my Our Fathers and Hail Marys. I remember seeing the ships pull anchor and sail away, and me on a piece of wood drifting on the merciless tide, away from the islands. And my skin on fire with the pox. I wondered if there was a worse end to a man than that. And then . . ." His eyes turned inward and he tried to remember. "I passed out from thirst. And that is the last I recall. Until now."

The girl listened with wide, keen eyes and the patience of a nun, he thought, as if she had understood everything he said. But of course she hadn't. "How did you do it, when not even our ship's doctor could help me?"

By gestures he got his question across. Motioning for him to wait, the girl ran out of the hut. In the meantime, he found his hose and breeches and managed to get himself halfway decent by the time the girl returned, carrying a stone with a twig upon it, prattling again in her incomprehensible tongue.

"I don't understand," he said, and reached for the twig. She cried out and drew back. Then she laughingly explained with gestures that it was this plant that had caused the sickness on his skin. He narrowed his eyes at the offending cutting of leaves in clusters of three with small, greenish flowers. He was a learned man who prided himself on his knowledge of botany. This species, he was certain, was unknown in Europe.

He was able to piece together what had happened: the plant was indigenous to this land and grew in profusion here. According to the girl's gestures, it commonly afflicted her people, which was why they had a remedy. But as a foreigner, he would not know of its poisonous properties and must have walked among it when he and the crew went ashore in the southern bay.

She handed him a basket containing long, barky, reddish purple stems with dark green leaves and numerous brownish yellow flowers. He recognized it at once as mugwort, also known as the *Mater Herbarum*—the Mother of Herbs—and it was used all over Europe to cure common ailments, also as a tea and a flavorful herb in cooking.

"It was but an ordinary rash I had then?" he said finally. "What even children and old people know how to treat? And those blackguards," he shouted, *"put me to sea for it?"*

She looked briefly startled, and then she smiled, and then she started to laugh again, recognizing indignation and the embarrassed fury of a man who had thought he was dying only to be told it was just an itch.

"You half-wit child," he groused, angrily searching the grass shelter for the rest of his clothes. "Why do you find everything so funny?"

When he started to pull his shirt on, she grabbed his arm and violently shook her head.

"Why not? It's *my* clothes and I'm not going to go about naked as you do!"

She shook her head again, sending long hair flying like raven's wings, he couldn't help thinking. She rubbed his arms and then gestured the length of his body, then to his great shock she shoved one hand in his armpit and with the other pinched her nose closed.

"God's bones," he said. "You think I *stink*? Well of course I do, woman, it's the odor of an honest man's sweat. What do you think perfumes are for? You savages wouldn't know about perfume, but go about offending with your smells."

When he followed her out of the hut he found a crowd waiting. "God's teeth! Is everyone naked here?"

A few drew back at his outburst, but after the girl had quickly explained in her rapid tongue, they smiled and a few laughed. She spoke rapidly to a man with feathers in his hair, gesturing wildly, the stranger thought, not at all like the well-bred Spanish ladies he was used to keeping company with, until the feathered man nodded in understanding and, with a grin, took the visitor by the arm and started to lead him away.

"Where are you taking me? For the stewpot? Is that it? Are you savages going to eat me?" But it was only into a long, low grass shelter that he was taken, where the heat was intense and naked men sat and sweated and inhaled smoke and then scraped their skins of inner poisons.

When he came out of the sweat lodge cleansed, feeling decidedly refreshed, and wearing his breeches and shirt that had also undergone a pleasant fumigating, he found the girl waiting for him.

He looked at her more closely, now that his head had cleared. After peering into the girl's intelligent eyes, and realizing what she had done for him, he said in a more tempered tone, "God's teeth, you *are* rational beings. The captain said you were beasts without mind or reason. But by wit and will you saved my life," he said. "And I wasn't grateful. For that I ask your forgiveness. I awoke from death to find myself alive, and all I could think of was the blackguards who threw me off their ship. I am Don Godfredo de Alvarez. At your service." He bowed. "If there is some way I can repay the favor?"

She stared blankly.

"Well, this is going to be interesting then, with no common language between us and no translator. How can I communicate to you that I wish to show my gratitude? But then what gift have I to offer, except the clothes on my back—which, I might add, you have already stripped me of once!"

Then he saw how she was looking at him, how the others in the crowd that had gathered pointed and murmured. His spectacles!

When he removed them from the bridge of his nose, the onlookers gasped. Some even turned and ran off in fear. "No, wait," he said. "They're nothing to be afraid of." When he held them out to the girl, she backed away, horrified.

He settled them back on his nose. "I purchased these from a lens maker in Amsterdam, who charged me a thief's price for 'em. But without them I cannot guide my quill on parchment, nor can I read my blessed books."

The man with feathers in his hair, whom Godfredo took to be the chief, stepped forward and pointed to Godfredo's hand, asking a question. Godfredo frowned, and then, understanding, said, "It's a ring, made of silver." But when he held it out to the chief, the man drew back. This caused Godfredo to look at the grass skirts and animal skins, the shell-beads and bird bones, the spears with arrowheads made of stone. "Do you not know of metal?" he said in perplexity. Godfredo had just come from New Spain to the south, where the conquered Aztecs had knowledge of metal and wove textiles, where they had built massive stone pyramids and temples, made paper, lived by a complicated calendar, used writing, and attended schools of science and learning. Yet their neighbors so close to the north followed none of those modern ways. Why, Godfredo wondered now in deep puzzlement, had God spared *these* people from such knowledge? And was it a blessing or curse that He had kept them in innocence?

He grew thoughtful again, studying the bare-breasted Indian girl who held him with liquid black eyes. God's teeth, he thought. A man could believe he was dreaming.

But the smell of the sea was too real, the cry of the gulls, and the bitter memory of having been put over the side for having a rash. "And they kept all my things," he swore through clenched teeth. "My books and my parchments, my gold and my fineries. That they put me adrift in clothes can only speak to the blackguards' superstitious fear that to put a naked man out to sea brings bad luck upon a ship." In that moment Godfredo made a silent oath that by the Precious Blood of Christ and Santiago, when the next ships arrived he was going to be on one, and when he returned to New Spain he was going to see to it that Cabrillo and his poxy crew regretted their mothers had ever spawned them.

✳

A crowd had gathered on the beach to watch the antics of the stranger. Men squatted on the sand and made wagers as to what the fellow was doing—some said it was a shelter he was building, others speculated it was a canoe. Children followed the visitor as he trekked up and down the beach to fetch driftwood and seaweed, and then inland to haul back dried oak branches. Women brought their basketry and sat and wove while they watched the man named Godfredo grunt and strain at his peculiar labor. Marimi also watched. She alone knew what he was doing. And she alone felt his pain. His own people had cast him out, just as the First Mother had been cast out generations ago. How his heart must be crying, how lonely his soul. To be cut off from the tribe, from the stories, from the ancestors! She prayed that his bonfire worked, that his people would see it and come back for him and take him home.

Godfredo went every day down to the beach, carefully building up the hill of wood and grass, tending it, keeping it dry with skins and palm fronds. Then he would stand for hours, watching the horizon for a sail, prepared to light the fire as soon as he saw one and send up smoke puffs as a signal, in the way shipwrecked mariners had done for centuries. And after his rescue, he would seek his revenge, for what Don Godfredo de Alvarez felt in his heart was not pain or grief or sorrow, as Marimi thought, but fury, pure and strong, and the determination to make those bastards pay for every hour they had left him stranded in this place.

In the meantime, he had no choice but to live among the natives.

He was given a hut of his own, a round shelter of branches and grass with a hole in the roof for the smoke. So while he waited for ships to come, Godfredo tried to learn what he could about these people because this was why he had left Spain and the graves of his wife and children in the first place, to travel the globe and see the new lands that were being discovered.

Through gestures and drawings in the dirt, he and Marimi managed a rudimentary sort of communication, and after a while Godfredo picked up Topaa words, and Marimi, Spanish. He learned that she had several titles: Guardian of the Sacred Cave; Mistress of Herbs and Keeper of Poisons; and Reader of Stars, which she performed at childbirths to fore-tell a baby's future and to give it its name. He also learned that she was never allowed to marry for fear sexual intercourse would sap her power, and that to lie with a man would not only cause her to sicken and die, but the whole tribe as well.

Don Godfredo thought this a terrible waste.

The people readily accepted him in their midst and the men invited him to join in their games of chance. The Topaa were nearly fanatical about their gambling and could keep a game going for days. Godfredo soon learned how to read the sticks, or knucklebones, or whatever the players tossed, rolled, threw into the air. He learned the strategy of betting his shell-bead money, and that a bad loser was frowned upon. He also quickly adapted to their habit of smoking a clay pipe and found he liked tobacco. But they didn't ferment and therefore drank no liquor to lift their spirits. When he made wine from wild grapes and got riotously drunk one night, the Topaa shied away from him, refusing to share a drink that made him possessed by a spirit, and so he did his drinking in solitude after that. He also grew to appreciate and even look forward to the sweat baths in the lodge, where he sat with the other men in the heat and smoke of a fire perfumed by various barks, scraping his skin clean and emerging refreshed and invigorated. He much preferred it to his annual bath, which he had always disliked.

Other times the practices of the Topaa profoundly disturbed him. The women with their jiggling breasts and the men as naked as Adam! There was no sense of shame in them. And Godfredo thought their perplexing laws only encouraged promiscuity: if a husband caught his wife in adultery, it was his right to divorce her and take the other man's wife. The Topaa held ritual fertility dances beneath the full moon and then retreated to their grass huts, where it was no secret what was going on. Unmarried girls were encouraged to choose partners, and on several occasions married women gave their favors to men who were not their husbands. While Marimi tried to explain the principle to a shocked and disapproving Godfredo—that sexual union between men and women awakened the earth's fertility and ensured that the tribe was blessed with fecundity, that intercourse was in fact holy—he clung steadfastly to his belief that they were an immoral race.

One night, when a language had grown between them, Marimi told him the history of her tribe, all the way back to the First Mother. "How do you know this?" he asked. "Nothing is written down."

"We tell our story every night. The elders tell the young. This way our story keeps going."

"That doesn't sound very reliable. The story is bound to change in the telling."

"But it *has* to be reliable. We believe in the exact word of the story. Children memorize it from their grandparents, so that when it comes their turn to tell the story, it will be the same. How do *you* remember your ancestors?"

"We have paintings. Birth records. Books."

They talked about their gods. He showed her the crucifix and told her about Jesus. She in turn tried to explain to him about the Creator Chinigchinich and the seven giants who began the human race. She also told him about Mother Moon, to whom the Topaa prayed, and Godfredo thought this very naive as everyone knew the moon was simply a heavenly body that orbited the earth, just as the sun and all the planets did.

The first few times he shared a meal with the tribe, he would find them staring at him not a little disapprovingly. Don Godfredo was the first to admit that he was a man of appetites. He gulped his food and guzzled his drink without apology, and broke wind without pardoning himself. But apparently among this people it was considered impolite to show gusto. And each night, when he sat down to yet another meal of acorn gruel or rabbit stew or clam soup, he would think longingly of meals back home: feasts of partridge and pheasant, sausages and bacon, quince jam, Florentine cheese, and marzipan from Sienna. He sorely missed beef, mutton, pork, poultry, pigeon, goat, and lamb; biscuits and breads, meat pies and tarts, crystallized sweets and sugared almonds; mushrooms and garlic, cloves and olives. He would close his eyes and dream of cheese, eggs, milk and butter. Who would have thought a man would have missed such common fare so? He recalled heated but amiable dinner arguments on the excellence of a particular cheese—Brie, Gruyère, Parmesan. He wanted to describe to the Topaa chief the delights of a good Roquefort or a sharp Swiss. But the man wouldn't understand. The Topaa didn't use animal milk. They were excellent fisherman, however, and food from the sea was always plentiful—although any civilized man knew that fish went better with a good sauce. Most of all Don Godfredo missed a cask of fine Bordeaux wine.

When not eating or sleeping or gambling, Godfredo maintained his vigilance at the beach, each dawn and dusk, through sunshine and rain, in fog and wind, a lone figure on the dunes, or perhaps with a group of children following him, still fascinated by the stranger in their midst. He would talk to himself in his foreign tongue, and pause to squint out to sea. If they could understand his language, the Topaa would learn that Don Godfredo was a man of science and learning and that he missed his books, his calculating instruments, his beakers and vials of alchemy, that he yearned for his astrolabe and quadrant and maps, his clocks and hourglasses and sundials, his quills and parchments, his inks and letters and words. They would also learn that Don Godfredo, being wealthy, was a man of comforts and that he missed castles and chairs, dinner plates and handkerchiefs, feather beds and fireplaces. He also missed politics and court intrigue, and knowing who was currently in favor, who was out. His tongue yearned for intelligent debate. He wanted his horse! All the things he had taken for granted he now longed for with a poignancy that was as real as physical pain.

And then one morning when the mist was gray and the gulls subdued, and not even the hunting canoes set out on the tide, Don Godfredo stood miserably in his layers of clothes heavy with the damp and recalled a novel that was currently the rage in Spain, called *Sergas de Esplandian*. It was the story of a knight named Esplandian who, during the siege of Constantinople, led the defense of the city against the attacking pagans. Suddenly, among the besiegers there appeared a queen, who had come from a fabulous island far away "on the right hand of the Indies, very near to the terrestrial paradise." This island was inhabited by ebony-skinned women whose weapons were of gold, and in the mountains lived fabled griffins. When the griffins were young, the story went, the Amazon women captured them and fed them on male babies the women had given birth to and men they had taken prisoner. Later in the novel, the queen was converted to Christianity, gained respect for men, married Esplandian's cousin, and took him back to her wondrous island.

Everyone who read the book or heard the story wondered, even though it was fiction, if that fabled island really existed. And so when Cabrillo had set sail from Mexico to explore this northern coast, he and his men had anticipated finding a land where the only metal, as in the book, was gold. But when they anchored in the bay to the south and saw how simply the natives lived, that there was no gold, no beautiful Amazon women, no fabled griffins, they named this place after that island—California—out of derision and disappointment.

Recalling this, Don Godfredo now grew somber with new realization. These people possessed nothing of worth to the Spanish Crown. It could be years before another ship came! And while the savages of this place could feed his body, they could not feed his soul. It would wither and die, and he would go insane.

In his new despair, he looked down the beach and saw Marimi watching him, her tall figure swathed in seal skins, a mournful look in her dark eyes. How could he convey to her this hell his fellows had landed him in, that a man needed occupation, that he would go mad if left only to eat and gamble and smoke a pipe? "I am a learned man!" he cried to the wind. "I have a mind, I have curiosity! And I have been left to rot in this place!"

Marimi came up to him and took his hands in hers, turning them up so that she could see the palms. She said something but he could only shake his head. "I don't understand you."

She pointed to the canoes on the beach, the harpoons and fishnets. She named fishermen whose acquaintance he had made. She pointed to the hut of the man who made flint knives, then to the shelter of the elderly woman who fashioned shell-beads. She lifted Godfredo's hands before his face and asked a question.

"What do I do? Is that what you are asking?" Godfredo had tried, over the weeks to explain to her his profession, but how to explain to a girl who had no concept of the alphabet or of writing that he was a diarist?

And then it struck him. "Christ's blood! Now I know what you are telling me! This is what I set out to sea for! To chronicle the journeys and discoveries of exploring men! And what am I doing? Sitting on my backside waiting to be rescued!"

He could have kissed her right there and then, and almost did were it not for a sudden look in her eyes, as if she had understood his intent, for she quickly drew back, beyond his reach.

Godfredo's somber mood changed to one of excitement as he set upon his new endeavor, trading his fine velvet hat for a handful of the chief's headdress feathers to fashion quills from them. When a hunter brought a deer down from the mountains Godfredo traded his padded jacket for the hide, and for days, while the tribe feasted on venison, people watched him work away at the deerskin, scraping it, stretching it, rubbing it with chalk and pumice until he had something he called parchment. Finally, out of squid juice, he manufactured ink.

He was ready to begin his chronicle. But first, he needed to know where he was.

When the Spaniards had seen this plain as they sailed northward, they had named it the Valley of Smoke. It wasn't just the many campfires dotting the plain, but also the purposely set brushfires. The Indians had a habit of continually burning off the brush, which Marimi explained helped new growth and prevented major disastrous fires. Godfredo had witnessed one such devastating fire that had raged for days because the old undergrowth was so thick and dry. But the Indians knew that to prevent major fires it was necessary to cause fires periodically. The result was that with mountain ranges embracing the basin, holding the smoke in, the basin was filled with smoke almost all the time; there were even days when one couldn't see the mountain peaks above the brown air.

Godfredo decided to make a map.

Marimi was his guide. She went ahead of him on trails, her generous hips swaying before his eyes, and once in a while, through the grass skirt, he glimpsed a smooth, bronze thigh. Then she would pause on hillcrests and point out places, naming them. On the north side of the Topaangna Mountains were the Chumash, who called their village Maliwu, which Godfredo mispronounced as Malibu, making Marimi laugh. The Topaa and Chumash were enemies and did not commingle. Their border was Maliwu Creek and they had different languages, which at first Godfredo found odd. "But they live just over the mountains there." And then he remembered the French living just over the mountains from Spain. Marimi pointed out other settlements: Kawengna and Simi. They trekked over the peaks to where Godfredo saw a valley filled with oaks. It had no name so he called it Los Encinos.

During his exploration, as they passed through other Topaa villages and then through the settlements of other tribes, Don Godfredo noticed the absence of a warrior class. Spears and arrows seemed designed mainly for hunting rather than for war. Disputes between tribes, Marimi explained, were small and usually resolved quickly. The inhabitants of this Valley of Smoke, it seemed, were generally peaceable and unaggressive, unlike the Aztecs, with their advanced civilization who, before their conquest, had been an aggressive, bloodthirsty race. And then Godfredo thought of the history of his own people, the Europeans, written in blood. And a new thought occurred to him: did knowledge breed aggression?

Godfredo noticed how the girl showed constant etiquette toward the land. Everything was treated with respect and with ritual. Taking fruit from a tree or drawing water from a spring was prefaced by some sort of ceremony, however simple, in the form of a request or an acknowledgment. Godfredo had seen how the Indians apologized to the animals they killed. "Spirit in this rabbit, I ask pardon for eating your flesh. May we together complete the circle of life that was given to us by the Creator of All." Marimi explained that they believed the hunted animal submitted to the hunter willingly if the people made the proper respectful observances.

Their mapmaking sojourn was brief because Marimi did not want to travel far from her tribe, nor Godfredo from the ocean. And when they returned and his map was done, Godfredo began in earnest to write his chronicle, which he envisioned as being the talk of Spain, of all Europe, upon his return. He inscribed at the top of the parchment: *Here Beginneth The Chronicle and History Of My Sojourn Among The Savage Indios Of California*. And he set to with quill and ink in the deadly earnestness of a man so intent upon his task that there was room in his head for no other thoughts. Godfredo did this in the hopes of saving himself from a fate worse than being put to sea on a wooden plank: he was starting to lust after a girl vowed to chastity.

*

He wanted to begin with science, but as science here was nonexistent, he chose medicine as the next best thing. Godfredo recorded such healings and rituals Marimi allowed him to witness. For teething babies she took the petals of wild rose, dried them, then boiled them, and then applied the petals to the baby's gums. In treating jaundice, while the acorn soup was still boiling from the hot stones, Marimi combed her hair over it, dropping lice into the soup. Godfredo was impressed for this was a remedy commonly used in Spain, where everyone knew that drinking water containing lice was the best cure for liver ailments.

But he witnessed healings that were not so clear-cut or scientific, when herbs and medicines did no good and magic must be invoked. Godfredo knew it was not the "power" in the eagle feather that cured, or the coyote fangs, or the rattlesnake skin, rather it was the combined power of the belief of the sick person in the healer, and the healer in herself. They both believed she could cure him and somehow the patient's own will effected the cure. Godfredo almost admired the system. Would that such belief were found in Europe, where most doctors were charlatans! And if not the patient, then the will of the clan caused the healing, because Godfredo witnessed such a miracle himself when one day an injured seal hunter was brought ashore. The man had been gored by a spear, and his wound was festering, causing him to burn with fever. Marimi ritualistically lighted a campfire next to the dying man while his first family stood in a tight circle around him, and then his second family, which consisted of cousins, uncles, aunts. Marimi shook rattles to the four cardinal points, invoking their power. She sang up to the moon. She scattered powdered seaweed on the man's body, and drew mystical symbols with seal fat and pigments upon his burning skin. Then she held up a stone upon which images of centipedes had been etched. She showed it to the moon, to the four winds, and then she splashed a dollop of hot asphalt on the stone, obliterating the images, "killing" the centipedes, which were symbols of death. At once the man started to breathe more easily, the fever left his face, and after another round of songs from his family, opened his eyes and asked for water.

Godfredo declared it magic while Marimi said it was simply the work of spirits. And what Marimi did consider magic, Godfredo said was simply science. When he finally persuaded her to try his spectacles, she cried out that the magic in them caused her to see a different world. When he tried to explain about glass and lenses, Marimi would not hear of it. Especially when he demonstrated how he could make fire with his spectacles, just holding them in the sunlight without needing to drill a stick into a piece of wood.

He recorded their religious practices. At the winter solstice, the Topaa gathered in a sacred canyon where the whole tribe waited for Marimi to come out of a cave. When she did, she tapped the stone on her sun-staff three times and then lifted the staff to the sky and "pulled" the sun back northward, signifying the end of winter and the commencement of the sun's return. Everyone cheered and Godfredo wrote it down.

Godfredo recorded their social customs. When he watched Marimi cook acorn mush in a basket, dropping hot stones in the watery meal and stirring vigorously to keep the basket from burning, Godfredo said, "Why don't you use a pot?"

She looked at him blankly and he realized he had seen no pottery in the village. Aside from a few pieces of stoneware, which Marimi explained had been traded from the island people for asphalt, the Topaa created no clay pottery of any kind. They cooked their meals, stored their seeds, and carried water all in baskets.

Don Godfredo noted in his chronicle that, among the elderly, the teeth of the Topaa were all worn down to the gums—not broken or missing, but worn down. He found his answer after his first meals: there was grit in the acorn gruel, and stone powder which found its way into the ground-up seeds, and dirt that adhered to roots and bulbs that were eaten raw.

Don Godfredo recorded that there were no crops growing anywhere, just small plots of tobacco, the only plant the Topaa cultivated. The tobacco was gathered, dried on heated rocks, and then pounded up in small mortars for smoking in pipes.

But mostly his chronicle was about Marimi, who was growing in his heart. He observed her duties to the gods, her interaction with the tribe, the way she laughed, her lively intelligence, and a monthly mystery when she would retire for five days to a small hut at the edge of the village where she lived in solitude, speaking to no one, seeing no one, receiving food and water from female relatives. Godfredo learned that this was the practice of all menstruating girls and women in the tribe, the monthly flow containing tremendous moon power that needed to be curbed. If a woman spoke to another tribal member during her time, or touched their food, or walked across their shadow, she could cause them to sicken and die. Women were also considered to be vulnerable to sickness at this time and so were forbidden to wash their hair, to eat meat, to exert themselves at work, to sleep with their husbands.

Finally, the day came when Godfredo could no longer keep silent the question that burned in his heart. He asked Marimi what would happen if she should sleep with a man. "It would cause me to sicken and die, and the whole tribe as well."

"And what of the man?"

"The tribe would put him to death."

*

He awoke to the sounds of industry and the smell of smoke.

Stepping outside, he saw the settlement alive with activity as people piled fish into baskets and tied otter skins into packs. They were also setting their huts on fire. Marimi explained that it was their annual journey inland to trade with other tribes, a time also to burn down their dwellings and build new ones upon their return, on fresh ground.

When Godfredo saw men bearing heavy loads by laying baskets on their backs and hooking the straps across their foreheads, Godfredo said to himself: I will teach them how to make wheels and carts. And as they started walking eastward, like common peasants, he wondered if there were horses anywhere in this land, or possibly donkeys, anything that he could tame to use as beasts of burden. The journey took two days, and in that time Godfredo gave his thoughts wing.

During his time among the Topaa his hair had grown. There was nothing to cut it with since the Topaa didn't have scissors or razors or combs. Their flint knives could only do a hack job. Also, his beard had started to grow wild and so he learned to shave it off every day with sharpened clam shells. Now, in his daydream during the trek eastward he imagined teaching the Topaa how to extract metal from the earth and fashion it into useful objects such as knives and razors and stewpots.

He fantasized about many things as they followed the ancient animal trail, a mass exodus of people on foot with not a single animal among them. They passed other settlements, some of which were also being dismantled for the great gathering up ahead on the trail. They were now farther east than Godfredo had traveled, roughly fifteen miles inland, and although he found tribal customs similar, the languages were as varied as any in Europe. Marimi explained that the track they followed was the path the First Mother had followed when she first came to this plain many generations ago. The people believed it had been here since the beginning of time.

Finally, they reached their destination, the massive encampment of many tribes, all with shelters pitched on a flat plain. Marimi told God-fredo that this was where they obtained the substance they used to waterproof their canoes and water baskets. "*La brea*," he said, giving her the Spanish name of the pools of black, bubbling tar in the midst of the encampment.

Marimi explained that they were here to deal with traders from tribes in the east, from as far away as the village of Cucamonga and even farther. When Godfredo saw that the ancient path continued due east, he asked where it went. "Yang-na," she said, and by her gestures he surmised she had never been there.

Marimi had never been farther than these tar pits.

"Don't you want to know what lies beyond?" Godfredo asked when they erected shelters from boughs and sticks they had brought with them.

"Why?"

"To see what is there."

She looked at him. "Why?"

For the first time, Don Godfredo, who had journeyed thousands of miles to this place, was astonished that this girl had no idea of the vastness of the world, was unaware that she lived on a globe spinning in space, that man-made cathedrals rose up and pierced the sky in lands far across the water. These miserable pools of stinking tar were the eastern-most border of her world. To the north, her land was bounded by a ridge where sacred oaks grew and she did not traverse it, and to the west and south lay an ocean which she believed supported the sky!

But we have known now these fifty years, he wanted to cry, that the world is not flat. And it certainly is not the size of a common dishpan as is *your* limited world, but is vast and terrifying and awesome in its wonders. He tried to tell her, drew sketches in the earth, described grandeur with his hands, but it was no use. Marimi only laughed at his antics and thought it was a nice myth.

In that moment, Godfredo knew what he had to do. As Marimi's people engaged in bartering acorns, soapstone, seafood, otter and seal skins for fired clay pottery, mesquite seeds and deerskins, rattling their strings of shell-beads, which was the universal currency, Godfredo formulated his secret plan. When Spanish ships returned, as he was certain they someday must, he was going to take this girl back with him and show her the splendors of his world. He was going to delight her with the feel of silk and pearls against her brown skin, show her the towering monuments of man, the works of art, the perfumes and tapestries and plates of silver and gold, and take her for rides on his horse and astonish her with marvels that her primitive mind could not even begin to dream of.

That night, he watched her over her grinding stone, breasts swaying seductively. Marimi had spread herself with red ochre paint, giving her body a glossy look, highlighting the delectable hills and valleys of her lush form. The sight of her filled him with growing lust. What was it about this savage creature that enchanted him so? For one, she had saved his life. When he had first washed ashore, many months ago, no one had wanted to touch him. But Marimi bravely did. But there was more to her allure than that. There was something in the way she moved so graciously among her people. He had seen women of similar status in his own society, nuns with power, ladies with money and connections, but few were gracious and many abused their rank and privilege.

There was also a vulnerability about her. Those strange spells that occasionally struck her down. It could be anywhere at any time, and the first time he witnessed it it alarmed him. She had cried out in pain and crumpled to the ground. The men drew back while women rushed forward to gather her up and carry her to her hut. There, Godfredo had stood in the doorway while he had watched her head roll from side to side in silent agony. She then went into a deep sleep and later reported seeing visions. The women told him it was a holy sickness and that it enabled her to communicate with the gods. He had seen such people in Spain, holy monks and nuns. But those were Christians who spoke to saints, and this heathen woman was no Christian.

Finally, there was her loneliness. Even though Marimi was an integral part of the tribe and was in fact the focal point for a lot of their religion, she was also at the same time separate from the tribe, living alone. In the evenings, in the other huts Godfredo heard talking and laughter, the music of flutes, the sound of sticks as games of chance were being played, men laughing as they competed vigorously. Women's laughter, the squeals of children. But Marimi's hut was always silent. Her solitude reminded him of his own, the one he had carried in his heart after leaving the three graves behind in Spain, his wife and sons taken from him when fever had swept through the town.

"Oh, maiden," he cried in silent agony, "dost thou not know how I burn for thee?"

*

On the final night of the encampment at the tar pits Godfredo finally found the courage to tell Marimi what was in his heart. He told her of the wonders of his world and how he longed to take her to see them. To his astonishment, she wept bitterly, and confessed that the same desire was in her heart. She would like nothing more than to be his wife and go where he went, but it could never be. She had been dedicated to her people, she must keep her vow of chastity.

Godfredo reeled from this unexpected declaration. In all his carnal achings for the girl it had never occurred to him to wonder how she might feel about him. That she should desire him had not entered his mind. But now that the confession was out, his desire seemed to burn out of his skin and up to the stars. "I cannot bear to go without you," he cried, "but if I stay I can't have you either! Marimi, if you come with me the rules that keep you celibate will no longer apply. We will be free to marry."

She could not go, she said tearfully, and he must never again speak of his desire for her, for it was taboo and would bring bad luck to the tribe.

A wildness entered Godfredo that night, and when sleep could not keep him on his mat, he struck out into the foul-smelling night and paced the black beach of the stench-ridden tar pits, mindless of a few insomniacs who watched him. He paced and gestured and occasionally cried out in a language none of his casual audience understood. The people from Cahuilla and Mojave and the pueblos and beyond tended their fires and watched the tortured white man wrestle with demons.

That was when the idea came to him: he was going to teach the Topaa about the modern world. By teaching them how to make paper and mine metal, the use of the wheel and the draft animal, to build houses of stone and live by clocks he would open Marimi's eyes and make her see how benightedly she was living and make her want with all her heart to go back with him.

*

His plan failed.

Each project, though drawing an interested audience at first, soon lost its novelty and the people drifted away. Don Godfredo managed to make candles, which the Topaa marveled at, but when the candles burned down, Marimi's people had no desire to make more. When he manufactured a crude soap, they happily lathered themselves in the surf but lost interest when the soap was all gone. He planted a small garden of sunflowers and showed them how they could have seeds all year round, but when the flowers died because of lack of care, so did interest in them. Why should they change, the people asked Godfredo, when they had lived this way since the beginning of time, and their ways had always been good for the Topaa? "Change is progress," he tried to explain. But to his exasperation, progress was a concept they could not understand.

He went to Marimi's hut and asked her again if she could be released from her vows.

She said, "In your land, are there women who have dedicated themselves and their virginity to the gods?"

"Yes, the convent sisters."

"And if you desired one of them, would you try to persuade her to give up her vows?"

He took hold of her shoulders. "Marimi, celibacy is man's law, not God's!"

"Do you speak to your god?"

His hands fell away. "I do not even believe in him."

She reached for the gold crucifix around his neck. "And this man Jesus. Do you believe in him?"

"Jesus is a myth. God is a myth."

Marimi's black eyes filled with sadness then, and she regarded him for a long sorrowful moment. The sickness that gripped Godfredo's honest soul was no mystery: he needed to believe in something.

✳

It took two days to follow the ancient animal trail from the tar pits to the canyon in Topaangna.

When they arrived at the mountains, Godfredo and Marimi followed a trail through thick chaparral and wild lilac. Here, they came upon a patch of open ground, where they saw a female coyote performing a crazy dance: she lowered herself to the ground, muzzle turned up, and then with a sudden upward and sideways lunge, snapped her jaws and then landed to suddenly madly dig into the dirt. As she did this over and over, Godfredo drew back, fearing they had come upon a mad dog. But Marimi laughed, explaining how the coyote was simply hunting for rain beetles. Her people called the coyote "The Trickster" because he was known to lie down and play dead to lure vultures close enough to snatch and eat them.

When they reached a cave in a small canyon, Marimi paused, and said, "It is forbidden for anyone but me and other medicine people to enter this cave. This law applies to all Topaa, and members of other tribes. But you are different, your ancestors dwell in a faraway place, and I think, Godfredo, that with your spectacles that make you see things others cannot, and which cause fire to miraculously appear, that you must be a shaman in your own world. So it is not taboo for you to enter this sacred cave."

As she led him inside, her voice dropped to a reverent whisper. "Our First Mother sleeps here."

Godfredo saw that the grave was ancient, perhaps a thousand years or more, and when Marimi laid flowers upon it, she said, "We always bring a gift to the First Mother." Then she showed him the painting on the wall and told him the story of the first Marimi.

"I tell you this, Godfredo, because you have an emptiness here." She laid her hand on his chest. "This is not good for a man, because without faith to fill the emptiness, evil spirits will find a home here. The spirits of sadness and bitterness, jealousy and hate. I brought you here to fill this emptiness, Godfredo, with the wisdom of the First Mother."

Godfredo looked down at the copper-skinned hand against his shirt that had once been white. He looked into the innocent yet wise eyes of the Indian girl, felt the weight of the mountain all around him, heard strange whisperings in the darkness, felt shadows shift and move, watchful and waiting. The cave reminded him of a grotto he had visited as a child, where it was said a saint had found healing waters. Perhaps there were such things as magical caves after all, perhaps Marimi's First Mother truly was here.

Godfredo had learned to carry implements with him as the Topaa men did, and he now brought out of the leather pouch that hung from his waist a piece of obsidian, black and shiny. With its sharp edge he carved into a clear, clean space on the rock wall: *La Primera Madre*. Then he said with a smile, "Now all future generations will know who sleeps here."

Marimi gazed in wonder at the strange shapes. While Godfredo had drawn his map and written his chronicle, he had tried to teach her to read. But the symbols remained only symbols. Now, as she gazed at the freshly engraved letters, a light dawned in her mind. Reaching out, she touched the carvings with her fingertips, and traced each one, pronouncing each in sudden understanding.

As Godfredo watched her, listened to her soft voice whisper the words, he was overcome. Here was the miracle he had longed for, the realization of his daydreams: he had taught Marimi something from his world. And in that instant he felt his lust turn into a more tender emotion. He fell in love with her.

Taking her hands, he drew her around to face him. "You are a virgin because of this first mother?"

"Yes."

"Just like the sisters in Spain who dedicate their virginity to the Mother of God. Marimi, I cannot believe in your first mother any more than I can believe in another first mother named Mary. But I respect your belief and your vows. I will no longer ask you to come away with me, for I see now that it is wrong. Nor can I live any longer with you among your people. The pain is greater than any mortal man can bear. I will leave."

When she started to cry he drew her into his arms and held her, shuddering within as he realized this would be the last he would ever see of her.

He drew back while he still had the willpower, and said, "You said that we never visit the First Mother without leaving a gift." Removing his spectacles and handing them to her, he said, "This is my gift to her." And suddenly he had a vision of the future. "Men will come and destroy you," he said with passion. "I have seen this happen to the empires in the south. They will come with their scribes and their priests and their learned men and their soldiers, and they will take what little you have and give you nothing in return except subjugation, as they did the Aztecs and the Incas and all other places civilized man has set foot. So I am going to walk south to Baja California and I am going to tell them that there is nothing up here for them, and with luck, you and your people will be left alone, for a while at least."

Marimi stayed in the cave after he left, feeling her heart break in two. For the first time in her life, she did not want to be the chosen servant of the First Mother. She wanted Godfredo.

She looked at the spectacles in her hand, these marvelous eyes that allowed one to see into other worlds. Wedging them onto her nose, she looked first at the letters that spelled First Mother, and then at the painting. She gasped. The pictographs had grown! They filled her vision and now revealed tiny details and imperfections she had never seen before. And when she moved her head, the symbols seemed to move!

Suddenly a pain shot through her skull. She cried out and fell to her knees, and then collapsed onto her side as the familiar sickness swept over her, first engulfing her in blackness and then in deep unconsciousness.

In her brief sleep, the First Mother came to her, an indistinct, shimmering vision that spoke silently, communicating through meanings rather than words, and what she told her servant Marimi was that celibacy was a law of men, not of gods. The First Mother wanted her daughters to be fruitful.

When Marimi awoke, the pain gone from her head, she removed Godfredo's magical eyes and, realizing in excitement and awe that they had enabled her to travel to the supernatural world where she had received a message from the First Mother, ran out of the cave and down the canyon, catching up with Godfredo where the boulders were carved with the symbols of the raven and the moon. "I will be your wife," she said.

*

Because the First Mother had spoken to Marimi, and because Godfredo was no ordinary man, having come from the West over the ocean where the ancestors dwelled, the chiefs and subchiefs and shamans believed that they should be permitted to marry. But because this was taboo, the spirit world must be consulted. The shamans stayed in the sweat lodge for five days, consuming jimsonweed and interpreting their visions, and in the meantime, Marimi and Godfredo fasted and prayed and kept themselves pure. When the elders came out, they declared Godfredo a reincarnated ancestor, a special man sent from the gods to be partner to their medicine woman and that sexual union with him would in fact increase Marimi's power and therefore the tribe's.

The tribe celebrated the wedding for five days, feasting and dancing and gambling, and when the final night culminated in a fertility ritual beneath the full moon, with all tribal members participating in ways Godfredo had once thought immoral, he lay in Marimi's arms and knew contentment for the first time in his life.

*

The day came when runners from the coast exclaimed that sails were seen on the horizon. Godfredo quickly gathered up his maps and his chronicle and ran excitedly to the beach from where he saw the distinct outlines of canvas against the blue. Marimi joined him, their first child in her arms. Soon the whole tribe stood on the dunes and Marimi brought out her fire-starter to light the bonfire. But as her hands spun the spindle, Godfredo stopped her. He suddenly realized something that had not occurred to him before: that if he took Marimi with him to Spain she would be a novelty, as Columbus's savages had been in Isabella's court, an object to examine, perhaps to laugh at. They would rob her of her dignity and her soul. And she would wilt and perish, a flower away from its native habitat. Nor, he realized in sudden clarity, could he go either. He could not leave his beloved Marimi and their son.

Godfredo tossed his maps and chronicle onto the unlit bonfire, where the parchment would eventually dampen and rot and be carried away by the tide, and then, taking Marimi's hand, Godfredo turned away from the sails on the horizon and led her away from the beach, back to their home.

Over the weeks and months that followed, and finally the years, a strange thing happened to Godfredo: he began to feel a curious comfort in listening to the stories around the campfire at night, tales that had been handed down from generation to generation, thrilling an audience who sighed and smiled and clapped with glee to hear the brave exploits of their forebears, to hear how Tortoise tricked Coyote, how the world was made, how the stars enabled the souls of the dead to look down upon their sons and daughters. Don Godfredo saw in the storyteller's words an invisible thread that ribboned back in time, weaving the present with the past until it became unclear whether the teller of tales was recounting something that had happened long ago or only yesterday. It didn't matter. The stories were good. They entertained. And they created a feeling of belonging and connection, both to the others in the audiences and to those who had come before.

He also came to see the uselessness of his European finery, that they were no symbol of status here among naked people, that in fact the padded velvets and constricting cotton were impractical in a land where the summers were hot and dry, the winters mild. Godfredo had become as comfortable in his skin as the Topaa men were, so he put away his doublet and jerkin and hose and walked as Adam had, so long ago.

Don Godfredo also realized he no longer missed his timepieces and days of the week or the number of the year. He began to feel a new rhythm of time in his bones. No longer did he look for a sundial to tell him the hour of day but to the sun itself, arcing the sky. And the names of days weren't important, nor were the months, only the seasons, which a man knew instinctively, he discovered, as if his own inner body were turning with the seasons, waxing and waning with the moon, ebbing and flowing with the tides. The man of science was beginning to understand the Topaa's connection to the land and to nature. He saw that humankind wasn't separate from the beasts and the trees as he and his friends back home had thought. There was a universal net, woven by a cosmic weaver, and every man, every woman, every deer and hawk and mollusk, every bush and flower and tree were inextricably intertwined.

Where he had once felt alone and cut off, Godfredo was beginning to feel more belonging than he ever had before. His home in Castile became a dream. His books and instruments, clocks and quills lost importance. And ultimately he did not teach the Topaa of the wheel and metal, nor did he give them an alphabet and mathematics. If it was God's will to keep them as innocent as Adam and Eve in the Garden of Eden, then who was Don Godfredo to offer them fruit from the Tree of Knowledge?

Don Godfredo de Alvarez lived among the Topaa as Marimi's husband for twenty-three summers. He gave her twelve children and when he died they dressed him in his original clothes, with the gold crucifix about his neck, and cremated him with great ceremony. Then, in a magnificent canoe, they took his ashes out to sea to scatter them upon the waves whence he had come. His second pair of eyes, which had given Marimi a magical look at the world and which he had bequeathed to her as a reminder of his love, she buried with the First Mother in the cave, a gift from the man who had come from the sea.

Chapter Five

Footsteps. Heavy breathing. The sound of shovels digging into dirt.

Erica's eyes snapped open. Holding her breath, she listened to the stillness of the night.

Metal striking earth. A pickax clanging against stone. A whispered curse. Labored respiration. One—no, two people.

"Oh my God!" she cried, jumping out of bed and reaching in the darkness for her clothes. She flew out of her tent and ran across the compound to where Luke slept in an old Army camouflage shelter. Pushing her way inside and nearly falling over him as he slept in his sleeping bag, she shook his shoulder, and hissed, "Luke! Wake up! There's someone in the cave! People! Digging!"

He rubbed his eyes. "Wha—? Erica?"

"Alert the others. *Hurry!*"

He sat up. "Erica?"

But she was already gone.

✳

"Wait!" whispered one of the men, putting a hand on his partner's arm. "Listen! Someone's coming."

"Impossible," growled the other, his face glowing from the sweat of his labor. "No one can hear us in here. Keep digging."

But before his pickax could make the next solid contact with stone, a light suddenly flooded the cave, and a woman shouted, "What are you doing in here?" And then, before they could react, she was flying at them with a shovel, bringing it down on their heads as she screamed at the top of her lungs.

One of the intruders managed to push past her and get out of the cave where he scrambled down the scaffolding, away from the sounds of footsteps now thudding toward the excavation site. But the other man was still inside, crying, "Hold it! Jesus!" as he tried to ward off the blows from Erica's shovel. When she raised her arms again, he charged at her with his head down, knocked her off her feet, then spun around and bolted for the entrance.

"Stop!" Erica shouted, scrambling after him. "Someone stop them!"

There were other shouts now, and the sound of feet on the scaffolding outside. When Erica came running out, she collided with Jared who, like everyone else, was only half-dressed and looking bewildered from having been startled awake.

"Those two men!" Erica said breathlessly, pointing down into the crater of the Zimmerman pool. "Don't let them get away!" Jared took off down the scaffolding.

Security lights snapped on around the compound. Figures were seen running in the darkness: people in pursuit of the trespassers.

Luke came scrambling down the ladder, long blond hair wild about his head. "I called the police, Erica. What happened? Did they get away?"

But she was already going back into the cave, the beam from her flashlight sweeping the floor and walls.

She stopped and stared in disbelief. The skeleton—

She dropped to her knees and reached out with a tremulous hand. Skull crushed. Bones shattered. Pelvis cracked like an egg.

"Holy shit," Luke whispered. "What the hell were they doing?"

"Get Sam," she said in a tight voice. The Lady's skull. In pieces. Jaw-bone snapped. "He's a heavy sleeper. Go wake him up."

"Erica—"

"Go!"

She rose shakily to her feet and lifted her flashlight to the painting. Obscene gouges in the rock. The intruders had hacked away at the pictographs.

Erica was barely aware of the sound of boots coming up the ladder outside, the heavy breathing of someone who had run a distance. She heard him come inside, sensed him standing there. And then she heard Jared say, "They got away."

She closed her eyes in blind fury. *She* would find them. Somehow, she would find the men who did this.

He came all the way in, stood in the semidarkness for a moment, then he said, "I hope you're satisfied."

She spun around. Through tear-filled eyes she saw the smears of dirt on his bare chest, the sheen of sweat from having chased after the vandals. There was no mistaking the fury in his eyes as they took in the terrible destruction in the cave.

"What do you mean?" Erica said.

"You exposed this woman when she should have been left alone," he said. "Before you arrived with your shovels and your brushes, she was safe in her grave, where she expected to rest for eternity."

She stared at him. He was blaming *her* for this? In the blackness of the cave, Erica saw red.

"Yes, look at her!" she shouted. "And I'm the one who stopped the desecrators! I don't recall seeing *you* doing anything to ensure the security of this site that you supposedly hold so sacred, Mr. Commissioner. But *I* did something." She pulled an object out of her pocket and thrust it in his face. "This is just an ordinary baby monitor. I hid the transmitter in the cave and put this receiver by my bed. Sounds of the intruders woke me. I *did* something! What did *you* do?"

Jared stared at her, his mouth partly open, and it looked for a moment as if Erica was going to throw the monitor at him. Instead she shoved it back in her pocket and marched past him to the cave entrance where she found Luke just returning from the camp. "You were right, Erica. Sam was fast asleep."

She could barely speak. "Luke, I want you to photograph everything inside the cave, exactly as it is, don't touch or move anything. And don't—" She began to shake. "Don't let anyone else in. I am going to have to write up a full report on this mess before I can start to restore order."

"Hey," he said. "Are you all right?"

"I just have to get out of here before I kill that man!" And she jerked her thumb over her shoulder toward the cave.

She met Sam at the top of the ridge, one suspender hooked over a shoulder, the other dangling down. His hair looked as if he had been struck by lightning.

"You're not going to believe it, Sam, when you see what they did."

"Luke gave me a pretty good idea. The skeleton, how bad?"

Tears streamed down her cheeks and she shook so badly she had to wrap her arms around herself. "Bad. I wish we had done more to protect her."

Sam looked as stricken as if they were talking about a living person. "Did they get away with much?"

Erica ran the sleeve of her sweater over her face. She sniffed back tears. Then she looked at Sam. "What did you say?"

"Could you see if they got away with much?"

She frowned. She pictured the cave, the vandalized wall and skeleton. Then her look turned to one of surprise. "Sam! They didn't take anything! They weren't carrying any sacks or bags when they ran out, and I didn't see any they might have left behind."

"That's odd."

"No it isn't," she said grimly. "Because they weren't relic hunters. Sam, you've seen pillaged sites. The thieves just grab the artifacts and run. They don't stop to trash the site, any more than a jewel thief would pause to trash a victim's home. This was intentional vandalism."

The senior archaeologist squinted in the direction of headlights approaching. The police. "But why? What does vandalism achieve?"

"It renders the cave useless to archaeologists and it gets Native Americans angry enough to have the cave sealed so the homeowners can get their properties back."

His wiry brows shot up. "You think Zimmerman is behind this?"

"I would bet my credentials on it." She turned in the direction of the cave, where people were standing at the edge of the cliff, milling uselessly about, like ants whose hill had been kicked. She saw Jared among the crowd, talking to the Native American construction crew. Most of them, like Jared, were shirtless, long black hair streaming down their naked backs. They were angry, some raising fists, like braves preparing for war, Erica thought.

She returned her attention to Sam. "The homeowners want nothing more than to close down the dig. Our excavation is standing in the way of their move against the completion bond. If the court finds in their favor, this canyon can be filled in and their properties restored to them. But not while this is a vital archaeological dig. So what better way to eliminate the obstacle than to trash the cave beyond all usefulness to us? We need security, Sam. I have a feeling we haven't seen the end of this."

✳

Jared had a headache that not even aspirin could touch.

It had been twelve hours since the break-in and his mood was as black as his hair. He hadn't gotten any more sleep—no one had gone back to sleep after what happened. There were questions to answer for the police, vague descriptions of the vandals, an accounting of damage done inside the cave, a brief talk with Sam Carter, who had conveyed Erica's theory that the homeowners were behind the attack, followed by Jared's barely controlled impulse to march over to the homeowners' camp, drag Zimmerman out by his Adidas, and wring a confession out of him.

Jared had returned to his RV to find his phone lines already ringing— television news stations, reporters, and Native American groups in an uproar over the desecration of a sacred Indian burial site. They accused the Anglo archaeologists of negligence, even though Jared had pointed out that it was Dr. Tyler who had thought to put a monitor in the cave and that it was she who had stopped the vandals before they could do more damage. It didn't matter. Desecration had taken place. Bad medicine was now at work.

As Jared swallowed another aspirin and wished he could go to the Club, even though his regular nightly session was hours away, he couldn't stop mentally replaying the scene in the cave when Erica's tears had stopped him cold.

He had thought she was a hard woman. When he had gone into the cave she had had her back to him. He had said, "I hope you're satisfied." But when she spun around and he had seen the amber eyes filled with tears, it had floored him. Erica had unleashed a tirade then and he had been too rooted to the spot to react. All he could think was that she was suddenly exposed and vulnerable, no longer an adversary but a victim, revealing to him a defenseless side that made him wish in that moment he wasn't a part of all this, that he'd never gotten involved in the activist movement, that he'd never met Netsuya, that he was back in his office in San Francisco, working with his father on deeds, land grants, and contracts.

And then she had marched out and he had still been too stunned to go after her and retract his words. He hadn't meant to hurt her. His words had come from the anger he carried with him day and night. Netsuya was buried in a Native American cemetery. When he had seen the smashed skull and bones of the medicine woman—

He looked across the sunlit compound at Erica's tent. *A baby monitor.* She hadn't gone to Radio Shack and bought high-tech surveillance equipment or impersonal electronic detection devices. She had purchased a simple baby monitor, as if she expected to be wakened during the night by the ancient woman's soft weeping.

"Commissioner Black?"

He turned and saw a man standing at the screen door of the Winnebago. The day was sunny and mild; Jared had latched his door open. "Yes?" he said, not recognizing the visitor.

The man held out a business card. "Julian Xavier, attorney. May I come in? I have something of a confidential nature I would like to discuss with you."

After he made himself comfortable in one of the leather club chairs, the tall thin man with gold-rimmed glasses carefully placed his eelskin briefcase on his knees and explained that he was there to speak on behalf of an elite group of medicine men and shamans from various Native American tribes. "They fear that what is happening here at Emerald Hills, Commissioner, is a symptom of the sickness in the world today. They say calamity will befall humankind if the cave is not sealed."

Jared, who remained standing, waited.

Xavier examined his perfect manicure, a man measuring out his words. "I know you already represent various Native American groups, Commissioner, and that as a member of the NAHC you no doubt have your hands full. But my clients would like to retain your services."

Jared folded his arms. "But you already represent them, Mr. Xavier. Why would they want to retain me?"

The visitor tugged at French cuffs heavy with gold links. "For one thing, you are closer to the issue than I; your involvement is well-known; you have all the facts, the contacts in Sacramento, and so forth. Advantages, Mr. Black, that my clients feel will help their cause. They also appreciate the way you feel about the archaeologists, since it is their feeling as well."

"And how do I feel about the archaeologists?"

Xavier cleared his throat. "Well, you believe they are desecrating a sacred site and you would like to see them gone as soon as possible. You have been very public about your opinion, Commissioner."

"And what exactly is it these clients want me to do?"

"As I said, you are very close to the issue and have certain inside advantages that an outsider like me would not have. Let me hasten to add, Commissioner, that my clients are not without funds for such a special case and are prepared to pay whatever you ask."

Jared stared at the man. "And who did you say these people were?"

A quick, dry smile. "Well, I'm not at liberty to divulge their identities. Frankly, it isn't something I totally understand myself. It has to do with tribal laws and taboos, that sort of thing."

Jared nodded slowly. "But if I should decide to take their case, then I would have a list of their names?"

"Well, ah, no, I'm afraid not. They can't risk their involvement in this being known because of tribal rivalry and oaths taken. It is very complex, believe me. But again, let me assure you, the funds are in place and can be moved as soon as you say."

"What exactly is it they want me to do?"

Xavier blinked at him. "Why, to get the cave closed, of course. Cease the desecration by the white archaeologists and protect the body and burial objects of the woman in the grave. This is sacred business, Mr. Black. My clients are holy men who operate at the very top echelon of Native American affairs. You might say they are the Indian equivalent of a college of cardinals."

Jared thought for a moment as sounds from the camp drifted through his open window. "Well, Mr. Xavier," he finally said, "you can tell your clients that my services won't be necessary. The state is most likely going to claim eminent domain, in which case the homeowners will be offered fair market value for their properties. The houses will be torn down and the cave will then come under the protection of the Environmental Protection Agency and in all likelihood will be turned over to tribal representatives. If this doesn't happen, I am going to petition for a permanent injunction against the canyon being filled in, in which case the homeowners will also lose. In either case, Mr. Xavier, the cave will be protected."

A quick, nervous cough. "Well, you see, my clients don't want the cave just to be protected, they want it sealed . . . permanently." He spread his hands on his expensive briefcase, as if to hint of precious contents inside, and said, "Let me emphasize, Mr. Black, that money is no object to my clients, not when it comes to the prevention of sacrilege being committed in their burial grounds. It has happened too many times in their history. And of course, they are aware that you have a personal interest in these matters. Your wife . . . ?" He let his meaning hang in the air.

"Yes," said Jared. "My wife was Native American, and the preservation of burial sites was one of her causes." He thought for another moment, frankly sizing up his visitor while the man kept a fixed smile on his face. "Mr. Xavier," Jared said, going to the screen door and pushing it open, "could you come with me for just a moment?"

Xavier's smile fell. "Go with you? Where?"

"Just to help me clarify a few points. It won't take long."

✳

"By looking into the historical record," Erica dictated into her cassette recorder, "I have been able to determine that the owner of the spectacles was most likely a crewman sailing with Juan Cabrillo who, in 1542, anchored somewhere around Santa Monica and Santa Barbara and had brief contact with the Chumash Indians. But why had the man's eyeglasses been buried in the cave? Was *he* buried there, too? Why would a European be buried in a sacred Indian cave?"

Hitting the stop button, Erica closed her eyes and massaged her temples. She couldn't concentrate. The destruction to the skeleton. Even though Sam had praised her for having prevented a truly disastrous calamity, she felt responsible. She had had a premonition that something bad was going to happen and all she did was put a simple baby monitor in the cave. Sam had said that was smart thinking. Luke and all the others were patting Erica on the back for her foresight. She was a hero to everyone involved with the Emerald Hills excavation.

With one exception. *"I hope you're satisfied."*

Her thoughts shifted again to Jared and how he had looked last night, his bare chest smeared with dirt and sweat. Slender but muscular, which made her wonder again where he went every night for two hours, out of reach by phone or pager. But more than that was the look she had seen on his face when he had said, "I hope you're satisfied." First there had been fury—the same dark anger she had seen when he had stood out beyond the gazebo in a silent argument with the ocean—but in the next instant he had looked dumbfounded. Was it because of what she had said? Erica could barely remember the words that had poured from her lips as she had lashed out at Jared Black and his arrogance. She was surprised she hadn't thrown the baby monitor at him, she was that angry. And then, to her amazement, he hadn't said anything in retort. What had made him stand there so mutely and let her march out without trying to get in the last word?

She was still furious with him. Erica rarely stayed mad at anyone or any situation for long. Anger was a waste of energy and time and accomplished nothing. But in this instance, the demon had hold of her. *"I hope you're satisfied."* Blaming her for what she alone had tried to prevent from happening! Whatever she had said in her tirade, it wasn't enough. Erica had half a mind to march back over to his RV, and shout, "And another thing, *Mr.* Commissioner—"

When she heard footsteps nearing her tent, she set aside her work, thinking it was Luke coming to give a damage report on the cave. Erica had tried earlier to go back in and make a thorough evaluation of the vandalism, but she had been so overcome with emotion that she had had to leave and put Luke to the task. *Just don't say you found more broken bones.*

To her shock, she heard Jared calling her name.

She went to the doorway and squinted out into the sunshine. He was dressing more casually these days, she noticed, thinking that the chambray shirt and blue jeans suited him, and immediately wishing they didn't.

"Dr. Tyler?" he said. "Can we interrupt you for a moment?"

She looked at Jared's companion, a stranger who had a puzzled expression on his face. Erica noticed that the man tugged nervously at his shirt collar.

She didn't invite them in. "What is it?"

"This is Mr. Xavier, an attorney representing a Native American group who wish to retain my services."

Erica waited.

Jared looked at the man. "Mr. Xavier, would you mind repeating to Dr. Tyler what you told me a few minutes ago?"

A red tide flushed from the man's collar right up to his receding hairline. "Well, I—"

"Just repeat what you said to me. Something about money being no object, I believe?"

Xavier stood flustered for a moment, and Erica thought he was going to collapse from apoplexy right there. Then he abruptly turned on his heel and hurried away.

Erica looked at Jared. "What was that all about?"

"Some hireling sent by the homeowners. Offering me a bribe to get the cave sealed."

When she started to go back inside, Jared said, "Dr. Tyler, I want to apologize for what I said last night. I was out of line and had no business talking to you that way. I was just so upset when I saw what the vandals had done."

She looked at him for a split second, taking in the honest, open expression in his smoky gray eyes and remembering Sam's words: "Jared's wife? You mean you don't know?" So she said, "I was just about to make some coffee, if you'd care to join me."

He followed her inside.

"I was upset, too," Erica said as she took a bottle of cold Evian from the fridge and poured it into the coffeemaker. "And I probably said some things to you I shouldn't have, although I don't really remember what I said."

He smiled. "You put me in my place, is what you did."

"Mr. Black, we both care about the woman who is buried in that cave. You and I should not be adversaries."

But he shook his head. "I still think what you are doing is wrong. You can call it excavating in the name of science. But it is still robbing graves. And for what? A display in a museum?"

She faced him, hands on hips. "I'll tell you what I'm doing. When the Spaniards first arrived and established the missions here 230 years ago, the Indians were rounded up from their villages and either bribed or frightened into converting to Christianity. They weren't allowed to practice their old religion or continue their traditions. And then most of them died of white men's diseases. The conquest happened so swiftly that within two generations the customs, history, and even languages of these tribes were lost. But archaeology is starting to reconstruct those lost cultures. And if you take all those artifacts away from the museums, like the Native Americans want to, and bury them again, it will be a step backward. When we take school groups to museums, we teach children how the people who were here before us lived. If we don't do that, children will grow up ignorant of what went before."

Her words hung in the air as Jared's eyes met hers.

Then she turned to her coffeemaker, which had finished brewing, and filled two mugs with cartoon characters on them. "Shamelessly expensive amaretto," she said as she handed him the Daffy Duck mug. "My only extravagance," she added with a smile, trying to dispel the tension.

It was Jared's first time inside her tent, and he looked around now, trying not to be obvious about it, looking for clues that might shed some light on this woman who continued to be a mystery to him—hard one moment, vulnerable the next, hard again, but always passionate about her work. What he saw surprised him. This tent looked as if it had been lived in for years. She clearly had an ability to move into a place and make it instantly her home. He thought of his own RV, which he was leasing and was only temporary. The Winnebago was filled with luxuries and conveniences but lacked the personality he saw here: a foot-high Statue of Liberty with a clock in her stomach; a miniature Eskimo totem pole; a theater lobby card from the movie *King Solomon's Mines*; a "Malibu Lifeguards" calendar; what looked like a flowering cactus in a pot but which was in fact a candle; an open box of Oreo cookies; finally, an autographed picture of Harrison Ford: "To my favorite archaeologist." It was signed "Indiana Jones." He looked at her computer. The mousepad was a Ouija board. When he finally stared at a shelf crammed with Beanie Babies, Erica said, "My pets. I take them with me everywhere." He saw name tags on them: Ethel, Lucy, Figgy. "They all get along well," she added with a smile. "Most of the time."

But there were no family snapshots, no pictures of parents or brothers and sisters. Then he saw the pile of mail on the bed—magazines, bills, letters, circulars—all addressed to Erica at a post office box in Santa Barbara.

When he caught her watching him he reddened slightly and stirred his coffee in a self-conscious way. "So your home is in Santa Barbara?"

She leaned against her worktable and sipped the fresh brew. "That's where my mail is delivered. I don't have a permanent home. Actually"—she held out her arms—"this is my home right now."

He drank his coffee, watching her over the rim of his cup, trying to hide his perplexity. This was *it*? Everything she possessed was contained in this small space? "I visited a friend once who was on a dig in New Mexico. His tent was full of artifacts. His own private collection. He never traveled without it." Jared looked around the tent. "I guess I expected to see the same here."

"I don't collect artifacts. I don't believe in private antiquities collections."

He gave her a surprised look. "But you said a minute ago—"

"I believe in *museum* collections, because they are shared with the public and because they advance learning and understanding. I am opposed to the private collecting of archaeological objects. It promotes pilferage. As long as there are collectors who will pay top dollar for tomb objects, then tombs will be forever ransacked. Trafficking in relics only encourages the very grave robbing that you denounce."

Jared found himself suddenly thinking of the few items in his house in Marin County, genuine pre-Columbian artifacts for which he had paid top dollar. It had never occurred to him to wonder at what cultural expense those objects had been obtained.

As he was about to remark on the desperate tactics of Zimmerman and the homeowners, and that everyone was going to have to be extra-vigilant in the coming days, they heard boots thumping on the dirt outside, and suddenly Luke burst in, saying, "Erica, you've got to come see this!"

She put her cup down. "What is it?"

"In the cave! I started doing a bit of cleaning up—no no, I haven't touched anything but—Erica, you have got to see this!"

The three hurried to the edge of the canyon and climbed down the scaffolding. Inside the cave, Erica dropped to her knees and gently brushed soil off the newly exposed object. "It looks like it might have been wrapped in some sort of cloth," she murmured. "Rotted away, but microscopic analysis of the fibers . . . Good heavens!" she said suddenly. "It's a reliquary!"

Jared bent for a closer look. "A reliquary?"

"A receptacle for relics. Usually the bones or hair of a saint." She gently brushed more dirt away, exposing a hand and forearm made entirely of silver. "Definitely a reliquary. Well, it looks as if someone other than the Lady is buried in this cave."

"Which saint is it, Erica?" Luke's voice was electric with excitement. "Whose bones are they? Can you tell?"

"And how did it get here?" Jared wondered aloud.

Erica chose a softer brush. "After Cabrillo in 1542 there was no further contact for the next 227 years. I am guessing that whoever brought this to America, didn't bring it earlier than 1769."

She brushed away more dirt and brought the light closer. When she read the name inscribed in the silver, she gasped. Then she looked up at the others, utter disbelief on her face. "I'm afraid our little excavation is about to become an international issue."

"Why?" Jared said.

"Because I am going to have to report this," she said, pointing to the half-buried silver arm, "to the Vatican."

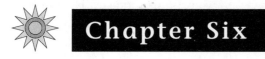

Chapter Six

TERESA
1775 C.E.

Teresa had two wishes: that she could learn what troubled Brother Felipe so, and that she could find a way to ease it.

"We harvest only the leaves of the foxglove plant," Felipe was saying in his voice that always sounded to her like a summer wind whispering through a canyon, calming and soothing. Everything about Brother Felipe was calming and soothing—the way he walked, so unhurried as some of the Fathers were, his manner as serene as the garden he moved through. The way he ate, taking minutes between bites as if savoring the bounty of the earth. When he would pause at his labors, hands folded into the voluminous sleeves of his robe, and bend his shaved head for a moment of prayerful reflection. But the most soothing aspect of him was his eyes, Teresa thought, gentle and doelike, doorways into a quiet, faraway place where there was no anger or violence, no pain or death. Sometimes, when

Teresa could no longer bear the suffering of her people, who were falling sick at a frightening rate, she would look into Brother Felipe's moss green eyes and feel her spirit fly away into them, into that precious, peaceful solitude.

At least, this had been so until recently. But a disturbing change had come over Brother Felipe of late, a change perhaps so subtle that only Teresa, who worked daily at his side in the herb garden, could sense it. It was not so evident in his mannerisms and speech, but there were new shadows beneath his eyes, and a strange haunted look that had not been there three years ago, when he had first arrived at the Mission.

Teresa ached with love for the young friar but she could never tell him so. Brother Felipe was a holy man whose life was dedicated to his god and to the purifying of spirits. Like the Fathers at the Mission, he did not think upon matters involving man and woman, love and sex. He had even sworn an oath of celibacy. Although there was no celibacy among Teresa's people, there was a wonderful Topaa myth that told of a hero who came out of the sea one day and fell in love with the clan medicine woman. This was generations ago, and the medicine women of that time were not allowed to marry but had to remain chaste all their lives. After the hero married her, however, all subsequent medicine women were permitted to take husbands, which was why Teresa's mother had married, and why Teresa herself hoped someday to marry, even though she was destined to be the clan medicine woman. But it could not be just any man. She wanted Felipe.

"The foxglove," he was saying, and Teresa detected a new tension in his voice that surely had not been there yesterday! Was he homesick? Was he yearning for the land of his ancestors? Teresa had never known anyone, Topaa or stranger, to be happy for long away from his tribe. Yet the Fathers had been here for six years already, building their strange huts and growing their strange food and grazing their strange animals, and they were giving no indication of leaving soon. But Brother Felipe wasn't like the Fathers, who seemed made of sterner spirit. Felipe was a gentle man, barely out of his youth, with a pale complexion that was quick to blush, and a smile that was shy and sweet. There were times when Teresa thought Brother Felipe wasn't a real human at all but a guiding spirit sent from the ancestors to watch over the Topaa while the Fathers were here.

Teresa had come to the Mission three years earlier when the people of her village had been enticed by the offer of food. Teresa and her mother had expected to return to their village by the sea afterward, but her mother had taken unexpectedly ill and, despite the kindly ministrations of the Franciscan Fathers, had died. When Teresa, only fourteen years old, grief-stricken and filled with pain, had prepared to return to her village, and Brother Felipe had invited her to stay at the Mission, as the Fathers were inviting Topaa, welcoming any who wished to live with them, she had looked into his gentle green eyes that made her think of forest pools and misted glades, and accepted.

It was because of Brother Felipe that she had allowed herself, a few months later, to be baptized.

Teresa didn't really know what the water on the head meant, like the other baptized Topaa who lived at the Mission, learning to grow and harvest crops, to milk cows, to weave blankets and make pottery. They had found Mission life easier than life in the village, where people had to fish for food or go into the woods to gather acorns, often coming away empty-handed. At the Mission the Fathers provided plentiful food and a roof to sleep beneath, as long as the people said, "Our Father," and "Jesus," and "Amen." They followed the priest during the morning ritual, standing, sitting, kneeling, touching their foreheads, chests, and shoulders when he signed a cross in the air, taking the little piece of bread on their tongues and reciting words that they didn't understand. Brother Felipe said that those who had been baptized were now saved. From what, Teresa wondered?

Was it because they had been "saved" that they could never leave the Mission? Although many of the people liked staying at the Mission, many also wanted to return to their villages, but the Fathers said they couldn't once they had been baptized. Which was why they were locked up at night, and why soldiers were sent to bring back the runaways. A lot of the people said that if they had known that the water on their heads meant being prisoners at the Mission, that they were to have been kept from the traditions and their religion, they would never have submitted to it.

Teresa wondered if this was why her people were falling sick and dying.

After her mother's death, Teresa was to have taken over the care of the cave at Topangna, but she had never completed her initiation into the secrets, the myths and spells, the proper prayers and rites. Was it because the First Mother had not been visited in three summers that the people were dying? But Teresa was afraid to attempt the cave rituals without guidance. Some taboos were so strong that the slightest mistake could bring calamity, such as an earthquake or flood.

But wasn't her people dying also a calamity?

"We must be careful not to bruise the leaf," Brother Felipe was saying in his mellifluous voice.

Teresa tried to pay respectful attention. She had been chosen to help Felipe in the medicinal garden, where he grew healing herbs, because she had knowledge of such plants herself. Unfortunately, neither she nor Brother Felipe was able to find curative herbs for the sickness that was claiming more and more Topaa lives.

"Like this," Brother Felipe said as he delicately harvested the foxglove leaves. He spoke in his own language, Castilian. Teresa had learned the Fathers' language, as all the Topaa and Tongva and Chumash were required to do. The language was new, as was the flower Felipe was showing her, which contained a spirit that eased heart ailments. This garden was full of new flowers brought from a place called Europe—carnations, hellebore, peonies. And beyond the fence there were new animals—cattle, horses, sheep—grazing on grass also brought from across the sea. The fields where her people and members from other tribes now stooped at bent-backed labor, hoeing, weeding, planting, were filled with strange new plants—wheat, barley, corn. All this new brought into a place of old made Teresa feel vaguely troubled. She hadn't seen the Fathers ask the land permission to plow it up, or to bring heavy beasts to tread upon it, or to alter the course of the river by digging canals where no canals had been. Would order break down and chaos come in its place?

Teresa remembered the day the strangers first came. She had been eleven summers old and word had spread through the villages that travelers from the south had entered ancestral land and were not paying the proper respect. The intruders were helping themselves to water without first asking permission from the river, they plucked fruit without asking permission from the trees, they cut branches and lit campfires without any of the proper respectful ritual. It was agreed among all the tribes that the strangers must be made to understand the Peoples' ways.

But when the multitude approached the newcomers, showing them their spears and arrows to let them know the people intended to protect the spirits of the land, the strangers suddenly lifted a woman into the air and held her up for all to see. Thinking she was a medicine woman, the people fell silent, waiting for her to speak. But she did not. Neither did she move. Was she dead? they wondered. But her eyes were open and she smiled. Thinking that the intruders were presenting a holy lady, the chiefs laid down their bows and arrows out of respect, and their mothers and sisters came forth to offer beads and seeds. And when the strangers built a shelter for their lady, and laid flowers at her feet, the Topaa and Tongva and others likewise came and left offerings for her. Teresa had wondered at the time how the lady could remain still for so long, but she had since learned about paintings, and that it had not been a real woman at all but a representation of one on something called "canvas." However, they all agreed on one thing, intruders and people alike: that she was called the Lady.

After six years, Teresa and the Topaa were still wondering why the intruders were here. Surely it couldn't be for much longer, the chiefs and medicine men and women speculated, because no people can stay far away from their ancestors for long. And according to the Fathers, they had traveled a very great distance. But there was something about the visitors that, despite their generous ways, troubled Teresa. In the spring, the chief of the Fathers arrived for a visit. A very short man—the Topaa towered over him—he called himself Junipero, after the juniper bush. And Teresa overheard this Father Serra discussing a people called Indians who had revolted at a Mission called San Diego, and that this was a very disturbing thing. Then Teresa heard Junipero say to the Fathers: "The spiritual fathers should be able to punish their sons, the Indians, with blows."

So much about the Fathers' way of thinking confused her. For example, when the priests discovered that the women used concoctions of herbs to prevent conception, they were severely punished. But everyone knew that controlling conception was vital to the health of the tribe for otherwise the tribe would grow beyond the capacity for the land to feed the people. It was what the gods had taught the Topaa generations ago: that too many people meant not enough food and therefore famine. But the Fathers' answer was to grow more food. They showed the Topaa how to plant seeds and water them and care for them, and then harvest the corn and beans and squash that they had brought with them from their faraway world. As there was now enough food, women should no longer prevent conception. But Teresa saw chaos in this, undoing a pattern the gods had woven at the beginning of Creation. Food and population growing until not a handspan of space was left in the land.

And anyway, the Fathers' plan *wasn't* working because they weren't growing enough crops to meet the demands of the soldiers in the presidios, and now in the villages the people were dying of starvation. Every day, more and more Topaa, Tongva, and Chumash arrived at the Mission, their empty baskets held out for food. The Fathers gave food if the Indians stayed and became Christians. And so Teresa's people filled their bellies with Jesus and wheat, and allowed their names to be changed to Juan and Pedro and Maria.

Her thoughts returned to Brother Felipe and her growing worry that a sickness was eating his spirit.

If Teresa could look into the young man's soul, she would see a yearning so great that it was consuming him like fire. Felipe had come to the New World for one thing: to experience rapture. So far, it had eluded him.

Like Blessed Brother Bernard of Quintavalle who lived five hundred years ago, Felipe thought now as he stared at the bell-shaped flowers in his hands, having forgotten for the moment what he was supposed to do with them. Ever since Bernard took the habit of St. Francis, he was often rapt in God through the contemplation of celestial things. Oh Blessed Grace, to experience that sublime gift from God! Felipe dreamed of it often, wondering how it must have felt for Brother Bernard when, in church one day hearing Mass, his mind had been so lifted to God that he had become transfixed and enraptured, remaining motionless, his eyes gazing upward from Matins till the hour of Nones! For fifteen years afterward, Brother Bernard was rewarded with this celestial treasure, his heart and countenance raised daily to God. So completely was his mind detached and withdrawn from all things earthly, that Bernard soared like a dove above the earth, and remained sometimes thirty days at the top of a high mountain contemplating things divine.

Felipe dreamed of being rewarded as Brother Masseo, companion to St. Francis, had been when, after shutting himself in his cell and punishing his body with fasts, whippings, and prayers, he entered a forest and asked the Lord with cries and tears to grant him divine virtue. Whereupon the voice of Christ called from Heaven, "What wilt thou give in exchange for this virtue thou seekest?" And Brother Masseo replied: "Lord, I will willingly give the eyes out of my head." And the Lord said, "I grant thee the virtue, and command that thou keep thine eyes."

To hear the voice of Christ! Felipe shuddered beneath his heavy woolen robe. This was what he had come to this savage land for—to be blessed with divine revelation, to gaze upon The Sacred Countenance. When God had called him to missionary service, Felipe had eagerly answered. What rejoicing there had been in his village back home, when it was announced he had been chosen to join the mission to Alta California! How proud his father had been. How everyone had crowded into their small church to offer prayers for Felipe's safety and for the success of his mission. And how Felipe's heart had beat with hope and the sure knowledge that in that distant land his lifelong dream of meeting the Savior in person was certain to come true.

All during his long sea journey halfway around the world Felipe had imagined what it must have been like that first day of contact six years ago, when the Fathers had arrived at the River of Porciuncula and were threatened by a multitude of savages brandishing their war spears and bows and arrows. Fearing that they were about to be killed, the Fathers had produced a canvas painting of Our Lady of Sorrows and had held it up for the savages to see. God's blessed miracle! The heathens instantly recognized that they were in the presence of the Virgin and had laid their weapons down.

It was a sign, Felipe was certain, that here was where humble men might find grace.

Grace . . .

Forgetting the flowers in his hands and the Indian girl at his side, Felipe lifted his eyes and stared for a long time out to the horizon. A voice sounded in his head: *Blessed St. Francis, who spoke with the Lord on a daily basis, as he lay dying at Porciuncula in Italy begged to be buried in a criminals' graveyard. I wish for the same. I want my body to be laid in the humblest grave in the most detested piece of ground.*

Saint Francis had called himself the "vilest of God's creatures." Felipe ached to humble himself so, to degrade himself as the Blessed Saint had. He wanted men to spit upon him and rain him with dirt as he welcomed the humiliation as St. Francis and his brethren had. But . . .

And now Felipe's heart lurched with the new pain that had invaded him and was growing within him each day, the pain of doubt and guilt and self-loathing. Because he had had a revelation one night in the stable, as he had lain prostrate in the cow dung, praying for rapture, and his inner voice had suddenly whispered: Arrogant man! Isn't the wanting of humility an act of pride? How can you be humble and proud at the same time?

Most Blessed Lord, Felipe wanted to cry out right here and now, in this garden where he toiled and in the presence of the heathen girl so recently come to Christ. Look upon me as your most wretched servant! Witness the punishment I inflict upon this miserable corpse which is called Felipe. Observe my loathing of food and drink. See these marks of daily wounding of my unworthy flesh! And reward me with but a glimmer of Your Blessed and Divine Countenance!

His shoulders slumped. It wasn't enough. After three years of denial and hard work and humbling himself, Felipe realized in utter misery that he had not done enough to be rewarded with the vision of Christ. He had to do more. But what? *If only I could go home, back to Spain, I would crawl upon my hands and knees across Europe to pay homage at Porciun-cula, where my Blessed and Perfect St. Francis died.*

Wondering what had Felipe's attention so, Teresa looked out past the garden and the pastures and wheat fields to where the river meandered across the plain. "What do you see, Brother Felipe?"

"Porciuncula," he said in a strange voice. "We named it that, to keep the memory of Blessed St. Francis."

"Named what? Do you mean the river?"

She waited. Her alarm grew. "Brother?" she said, lightly touching his arm.

As if beholding a vision that no one else could see, he said in a distant voice, "There is a humble little church near Assisi, called Porciuncula, which means 'little piece.' It was named so because it was such a small structure, standing forsaken and in ruins. Blessed St. Francis came upon it one day, and when he learned it was named for the angels who lifted Our Lady to the heavens upon her Assumption, he decided to repair the church and live there for a while. It was while St. Francis was at Our Lady of the Angels of Porciuncula, in the Year of our Lord 1209, that he experienced a divine revelation and his way of life was revealed to him. Years later, when he was in his final illness, he asked to be taken to Porciuncula so that he might die there. And now we have come here, to this place, five hundred years after his death, and we have named a river for that church St. Francis bore so much affection for."

He closed his eyes and swayed slightly.

"Brother Felipe?" Teresa grasped his arm and was shocked to feel its thinness beneath the woolen sleeve. "Are you not well?"

When he opened his eyes he had to bring himself back to earth. He looked down at the strong brown fingers clasping his arm. Then he re-membered: Teresa. He was harvesting foxglove with Teresa. He squinted at her with pain-filled eyes, finding curious relief in her tranquil round face, her soul of patience that made him think of centuries. There was something about this girl—his first convert. But he couldn't put his finger on it. She looked not quite like the other Indians at the Mission. The larger nose, the hairline across her forehead as it came down in a peak, the limpid black eyes waiting for his questions. She stood there like the embodiment of an answer, but she was as beyond his reach as the stars and the sun and the moon.

＊

The Mission was built around a square, four long thatch-roofed huts with an inner arcade that connected the chapel, workshops, cooking and dining facilities, storerooms, the priests' quarters, and a room called the *monjerio*—nunnery—where the females over the age of six were locked every night and not released until morning. Through one small window the imprisoned women could hear the men of their tribes enjoying life beneath the stars as they smoked their pipes and tossed gambling sticks into the air. The Fathers had tried to discourage these games of chance but with little success, and in the end allowed the men their recreation— as long as they adhered strictly to the daily regimen of prayer, work in the fields, more prayer, more work.

It was late, and the door to the nunnery was locked. Teresa moved among the women stretched out on mats, each with one blanket. The number of sick was higher tonight. They coughed and wheezed and burned with fever. None could eat and few could take water. The flesh was melting from their bones as their lungs spewed blood. No matter how hard Teresa tried to help them with Brother Felipe's teas and decoctions, and her own Topaa remedies, the sickness was spreading. A sickness like none her people had ever known. It was because of spirits, Teresa knew, brought by the white men, spirits that did not belong here but in another world far away. The white men did not die when these spirits entered their bodies. Some never even got sick. But the Topaa and the other tribes had no power against the invading spirits.

Many of these women had come to the Mission for the protection of the Fathers because they were afraid of the soldiers—lawless men who liked to get drunk and ride on horseback after defenseless native women, lassoing them like animals and raping them. The women's husbands and brothers, with spears and arrows, were helpless to protect them against the soldiers' musket balls. And so it was safer to leave the villages and seek safety at the Mission. But at what sacrifice? Teresa wondered as she looked around the crowded hut and heard the babel of dialects as Tongva tried to talk to Chumash, and women tried to quiet babies crying in their arms, and young girls sat with haunted looks as they wondered how they were going to find husbands, who was going to study the family lines? In another era, another life, the words "breakdown of the social order" might enter Teresa's mind. But all she understood on this night of many questions was that things were suddenly not right in the world.

She came to the farthest bed and knelt quietly beside the woman who lay on her side, facing the wall. Her baptism name was Benita and she had been raped by soldiers, to later discover that she was pregnant. When she suffered a miscarriage, the Fathers suspected her of having committed an abortion because she was unmarried. And so they had punished her by strapping irons to her legs, publicly flogging her, shaving her head, forcing her to dress in sackcloth and cover herself with ashes, and to carry a wooden image of a child, painted red to symbolize abortion, as she went about her daily duties. At Sunday Mass she was made to stand before the Mission church to receive the taunts and jeers of churchgoers. This punishment was designed to force Indian women to keep unwanted children because the Fathers said abortion was a sin. But what the Fathers couldn't seem to understand was that it was the sicknesses that were causing so many miscarriages among the Topaa. Like the evil spirits that tormented the women with fevers and lung congestions, a sickness the Fathers called "pneumonia," there were spirits that caused sores and rashes, which Teresa had heard the Fathers call "syphilis" and "gonorrhea." These were new spirits to the Topaa, like the new grasses and the new animals and the new flowers. And the people had no resistance to them.

Benita was dying. Her sickness was not of the body but of the spirit. She had not caused the unborn child to leave her body. But the Fathers did not believe it. She must be set as an example, they had said. Just as they set examples with baptized husbands and brothers who wanted to return to the old life: they were hunted down by soldiers and brought back, and locked in something called a "stock" for people to make fun of them.

Teresa sat back on her heels and thought about the women and girls crowded into this cramped shelter, with no ventilation, no warm fire, no shaman to keep the spirits from jumping from one body to another. It took only one woman to be possessed by the measles-spirit, or the typhus-spirit, to make all the women ill, as the evil spirit took possession of them, one after another.

The Fathers didn't seem to understand. But there was so much they didn't understand.

Why did they insist on sweating in the summer heat in their itchy woolen robes when it made more sense to go about naked? Why did they make the women cover up, saying that their breasts were shameful? Why did the Fathers call the people "Indians"? There were many tribes, their languages and myths and ancestors different. That woman there, Teresa thought, she is Yang-na. She and I descend from different bloodlines. I do not know her ways, she does not know mine. And those women over there, they are Tongva, no relations to my own race. But the Fathers do not understand this.

Teresa had tried to keep up the tradition of telling stories at night, the tales and myths that linked the generations all the way back to the first ancestors. But the Fathers divided the clans and even families, taking brothers to one mission, sisters to another, grandparents were separated from grandchildren, cousins from cousins, so that the stories that were told at night weren't always those of one's own tribe. Teresa was worried that if this continued, the elders would die without having passed the stories on to the younger ones. So she sat with her fellow prisoners and told them about the First Mother coming from the east, how she caused an earthquake when she stepped on a tortoise burrow. She told the story of the stranger who came from the sea, how he brought magic eyes to the Topaa. But Teresa's myths meant nothing to many of these women because they had their own. And when she told the story of the man who came from the sea, one of the little ones asked, "Was that Jesus?" The people's myths were becoming mixed up with the Christian ones, and worse, some of the little ones were having a hard time understanding Teresa at all because they were learning to speak only Spanish. And when they were baptized they had all been given Spanish names so that the young ones were starting to forget their tribal names.

Teresa curled her hand around the leather pouch that hung from her neck on a cord. It contained the ancient spirit-stone handed down from the First Mother.

Was this why there was so much illness among the people? Her own mother had died of the lung disease, and others were now coughing and burning with fever. Was it because the stories weren't being told? When she looked at the sick and frightened women, Teresa blamed herself. *I should not have stayed here. I should have gone back and taken care of the cave. Who is looking after the First Mother? No one, and that is why this curse has fallen upon us.*

She knew what she had to do. To save her people she must go to the cave, even though it was forbidden and her punishment would be severe. She would simply have to make certain the soldiers didn't find her, for surely they were going to search, as they did for all runaways. She wasn't as fearful of the punishment as of the fact that she would never again have a chance to return to the cave.

Finally, Teresa thought of Felipe. It tore her heart to think of leaving him, because once she ran away she could never come back. But her people were sick and dying. To help them she must leave her beloved Felipe and never see him again.

The window opening was just wide enough. Her friends helped her up, and spoke blessings and good wishes to her, in Topaa and in dialects Teresa did not understand. She promised that she would not get caught. She promised that she was not going to let the old ways be forgotten. And then she dropped down, silently and catlike, into the night.

❊

Teresa went first to the medicinal garden, moving in and out of shadows, each darker than the last, her way lit by stars and moon. Among the herbs and plants she plucked flowers and dark green leaves. Then she hurried past the stable, toward the east, where she would find the ancient track that led to the mountains.

She stopped when she heard a strange sound.

Peering through a crack in the stable door, she could not at first make out what she was looking at. And then suddenly she drew in a sharp breath. In the pigsty between two stalls, Brother Felipe was on his knees, stripped to the waist, and whipping himself with six knotted leather strips tied to a wooden handle. His back was streaked with blood.

Flinging the door open, Teresa rushed in and dropped to his side. "Brother Felipe! What are you doing?"

He didn't seem to hear her as he continued to flagellate himself.

"Stop!" she cried, seizing the whip and pulling it away. "What are you doing, Brother?"

Felipe stared down at his empty hand, then he brought his head around and looked at her with hollow eyes. "Teresa . . ."

When she saw how badly his back was torn, and scarred from old wounds, she started to cry. "Why are you doing this?"

"I . . . want God to find me worthy."

"I do not understand! If your god created you, then are you not worthy? Does he create unworthy beings?" She reached out and gently touched the red welts on his white skin. She wanted to lay herself across his back and let her tears heal him, let her love pour over him like a balm.

Felipe began to sob. How to explain to her that he yearned for rapture? He wanted to be afflicted with the stigmata as Blessed St. Francis was. He wanted to tame wild doves and preach to the fishes in the sea. He longed for a vision—the Lord and Mary had appeared to St. Francis and his companions, why not to him?

Fetching water from the trough, Teresa did the best she could to bathe his wounds. She tore off the bottom half of her skirt and dried the blood, gently patting the places where the skin was broken. She wept the whole time, seeing Brother Felipe's abused body through tears.

He remained kneeling, submitting to her ministrations like a child, his bony chest racked with bitter sobs.

Finally, when she had washed away the blood and his skin was dry, Teresa helped him to his feet and drew the sleeves of the gray robe up his arms, restoring to him a portion of his dignity. Then, in the darkness of the crude stable, she looked into his eyes, and said, "Tell me what it is you want, Brother Felipe."

His throat was raspy, his voice dry. "I seek perfect joy."

"And what is that?"

"I will tell you. One winter day, St. Francis was traveling with Brother Leo from Perugia to Our Lady of the Angels, and both were suffering from the bitter cold. St. Francis called to Brother Leo, who was walking ahead of him: 'If it were to please God that the Friars should give a great example of holiness and edification in all lands, this would not be perfect joy.' After another mile passed, St. Francis called out a second time: 'Brother Leo, if the Friars were to make the lame to walk, give sight to the blind, hearing to the deaf, speech to the dumb, this would not be perfect joy.' A little while later, he cried out again: 'Brother Leo, if the Friars knew all languages and were versed in all science, if they could explain all Scripture and possessed the gift of prophecy, and could reveal all future things, the secrets of all consciences and all souls, this would not be perfect joy.' After another mile, he cried out again with a loud voice: 'If the Friars could speak with the tongues of angels and could explain the course of the stars and knew the virtues of all plants, if they were acquainted with the qualities of all birds, of all fish, of all animals, of men, trees, rocks, and waters, this would not be perfect joy. And if the Friars had the gift of preaching so as to convert all infidels to the faith of Christ, this would not be perfect joy.'

"So Brother Leo stopped on the road, and said to the saint, 'Father, teach me what is perfect joy.' And St. Francis replied, 'If, when we arrive at Our Lady of the Angels, drenched with rain and shivering with cold, plastered with mud and weak from hunger, and if when we ring the gate bell and the porter comes and we tell him that we are two of the brethren, and he says angrily that we do not speak the truth, that we are impostors deceiving the world so we can rob the poor of their alms, and he leaves us outside in the snow and the rain to suffer from hunger, and if when we knock again the porter drives us away with blows, and if, urged by cold and hunger, we knock again, entreating the porter with our tears to give us shelter, and if he knocks us on the ground, rolls us in the snow, and beats us with a stick—if we bear all these injuries and cruelties and iniquities with patience and joy, thinking of the sufferings of our Blessed Lord which we would share out of love for him, this then, Brother Leo, is perfect joy.'"

Teresa was speechless.

"When St. Francis died," Felipe added miserably, "he was nearly blind from having wept so much during his life."

"Your god wishes for you to cry all your life?"

"St. Francis was called by God to carry the cross of Christ in his heart, to practice it in his life, and to preach it by his words, truly a crucified man both in his actions and in his works. St. Francis sought shame and contempt, out of love for Christ. He rejoiced when he was despised, and grieved when honored. He traveled the land as pilgrim and stranger, carrying nothing with him but Christ crucified. I wish to be like him. And I wish to be like Brother Bernard who, when he arrived in Bologna and the children in the streets, seeing him dressed so strangely and so poorly, laughed and scoffed at him, taking him for a madman, accepted their derision with great patience and with great joy for the love of Christ. Seeking to be despised yet more, Brother Bernard went to the marketplace, where he seated himself, and when a great number of children and men gathered round him and seized his robe and assaulted him, some throwing stones and dirt at him, Brother Bernard submitted in silence, his face bearing an expression of supreme joy, and for several days he returned to the same spot to receive the same insults until one day the townspeople grew thoughtful, and said, 'This man must be a great saint.'

"I wish to be like that," Felipe cried "But to be a great saint I must have humility in my heart. How can I wish for greatness and possess humility at the same time? This is my torment! My sins of pride and vanity are going to rob me of that sublime joy."

In alarm Teresa thought: the sickness is not only among my people, it is afflicting the white man, too. So it was in the land and the air and in the plants and in the water, and needed to be rectified. The world must be put back into balance.

She held out her hand.

*

Felipe went submissively. They took a mule and followed the moonlit track eastward from the Mission, past the tar pits and marshes, until they arrived at the foothills of the mountains the Fathers had named for St. Monica. Through the darkness they went until they reached an outcropping of boulders marked with ancient symbols of the raven and the moon, and from where Teresa said they must continue on foot. Feeling impelled by a power beyond his own, Felipe followed obediently, too steeped in his own pain and misery to question why he placed one foot ahead of the other.

When they encountered a rattlesnake in the canyon, Felipe recoiled but Teresa told him to walk softly, that the snake would not hurt them. "He is our brother and will allow us to pass if we show him the proper respect." Indeed, they tiptoed past and the snake slithered away.

When they approached the cave, Teresa said quietly, "This is a holy place. You will find healing in here."

She first placed the offering of flowers on the ancient grave, explaining to Felipe that one always brought gifts to the Mother. Then she built a small fire, lighting it with her fire-starter tools. When she dropped the dark green leaves she had obtained from the garden onto the flames, instantly a pungent smoke rose up, stinging Felipe's nose with the familiar aroma of marijuana, which he cultivated for his medicines. As the fire illuminated the symbols painted on the wall, Teresa told Felipe the story of the First Mother, as it was told to her by her mother, and by her mother's mother, all the way back to the first story.

Felipe listened quietly, his eyes on the strange symbols on the wall, and after a while the pain did seem to recede a little, and he felt a small easing of his anguish.

As smoke filled the cave, and the interior grew warm and close, and Teresa, who now called herself Marimi, kept up the soft litany of her tribe's history, reciting the myths as had been told to her, she slowly removed the clothes the Fathers forced her to wear: the blouse and skirt, the underdress, the shoes, until she stood before the First Mother in her natural state.

The young friar was not shocked as he might once have been. As the incense filled his nostrils and head and lungs, and the healing power started to work, he began to see nothing strange at all about standing in this ancient cave with a naked Indian girl, listening to tales he would once have called heathen and vile.

And after a while, as he listened to the rhythm of her voice, he began to feel a rhythm within himself, as if his pulses and respirations, even his nerves and muscles were responding to Teresa's steady chanting. Without knowing that he did so, Brother Felipe began to divest himself of robe and sandals and loincloth, until he, too, stood before the First Mother in humble nakedness.

With the shedding of the heavy wool, he felt a shedding of scales from his eyes and shackles from his soul. He experienced a sudden lightness that he had never thought possible. He felt himself start to smile.

And then something was touching his skin, like wings, like whispers. He gazed in fascination at the bronze fingers caressing the scars of old wounds in his flesh. Teresa's eyes were filled with tears as she saw the shocking state of Felipe's body, the ribs and bones, evidence that in his quest for rapture he had starved himself, inflicted abuse upon himself. How mistreated these poor limbs! How battered this frail skin!

"My poor Felipe," she wept. "How you have suffered."

Her arms went around him and drew him to her warm bosom. He buried his face in her hair, encircled her with his arms, and held her to him. He felt her tears on his chest. His own tears dropped onto her head. They cried together, holding each other in the heat of the mystical smoke.

And then something began to happen. Felipe began to drift upward out of his body. It was as if angels were transporting him, lifting him up on their wings until he found himself high up in the ceiling of the cave and looking down, where he saw two of God's creatures, embraced in their natural state, holding each other, filling each other's hearts with love. He saw the man draw the girl to the ground and lay her on a bed made of flowers and a Franciscan's gray robe. The girl's long black hair fanned out around her; there was a look of ecstasy on her face. Felipe saw the man's bruised and scarred back, and the hands of the girl caress the wounds. They kissed, long and lovingly, making Felipe smile. And then, to his amazement, he started to laugh. His ethereal form felt warm and moist all over, a sublime sensation that made his heart rise to his throat until he thought he was going to perish with desire and joy and fulfillment. He heard the man cry out in rapture, and saw tears like diamonds glisten on the girl's black lashes.

And suddenly the cave was filled with wondrous bright light and Felipe saw people everywhere! As if the stone of the mountain had melted away, Felipe could see as far as the horizon, a vast multitude of humanity stretching off into a blazing infinity. He realized in blinding revelation that these were the souls of all who had lived before him and who now dwelled in the Beneficent Light of God. At the head of this great multitude stood the prophets Elijah and Moses, in resplendent robes. And between them was Jesus, transfigured into a column of light. Soaring above them all was the Blessed Mother, now a radiant dove, now a beautiful woman, glowing and luminous, bestowing her love and grace upon all below.

Felipe gave a great shout and felt his body come apart and his soul shoot free to the heavens.

And then the angels brought him gently back down to earth, back to the cave and the warmth and the girl, where Brother Felipe slipped into the deepest sweet sleep he had ever known.

✳

When he awoke, he was at first surprised to find that he was naked. But then, remembering, he knew it was his natural state, that this was how God had created him, and all men and women, and that there was no shame in nakedness. Had not Blessed St. Francis removed his own clothes, and declared, "Our Father who art in heaven"?

Felipe looked at Teresa, slumbering sweetly. Here was the answer he had sought, the mystery of the girl that had been puzzling him. He had watched her talk to the plants, whisper to the wind and sing to the rain. She wasn't afraid of animals but understood them and practiced a kinship with them the way St. Francis had but that Felipe had not. She did not consider herself above nature as men did, but equal with it. This was the true definition of humility! She had been there all along to tell him so, yet he had been too blind to see.

He sobbed with joy, his tears flowing as freely as those of St. Francis had once flowed. Brother Felipe had come to California to find rapture, and he had found it.

✳

They reached the Mission before dawn, wordlessly, both filled with wonder and knowing that a healing magic had taken place that night. Teresa climbed through the window back into the nunnery, and Felipe went to his cell.

But he didn't stay at the Mission. Before the sun reached its zenith the next day, he was on the track westward, carrying nothing but a loaf of bread and a small bundle concealed in his sleeve. He was filled with awe and glory and joy. There was no pain, no more questions. Suddenly everything fell into place, and he *understood*.

When St. Francis died in the year 1226 he was buried in the Church of St. George in Assisi. Four years later his body was secretly removed to the great basilica built by Brother Elias. During that clandestine reburial, a brother in the grip of religious fervor removed the saint's little finger from his right hand and hid it away in a small monastery in Spain. Over the years, the relic was housed in various containers, each more precious and worthy than the last, until the blessed bones came to final rest in a silver reliquary fashioned into a human hand and forearm. When the Fathers prepared to set sail for New Spain to take up their mission in Alta California, the reliquary was secretly entrusted to their care, that the saint's presence in the far-off savage land ensured their mission's success.

This was Felipe's gift to the First Mother.

Inside the cave, he stripped down to his loincloth and gently wrapped the reliquary in his robe, after which he buried it in the floor of the cave. Then, recalling the forty-day and forty-night fast of St. Francis, during which he had eaten half a loaf of bread out of reverence for the Blessed Lord, who had fasted forty days and forty nights without taking *any* food, Felipe left the cave with only his rosary and loaf of bread and, instead of turning downward toward the mouth of the canyon, which ultimately led back to the Mission, continued upward into the canyon, his face to the sun, a radiant smile on his lips, upward and upward until he vanished between wilderness and sky.

Chapter Seven

If Los Angeles had a heart, Erica thought, Olvera Street would be it.

As she walked along the block-long passageway, she felt her spirits lifting in this colorful tile-paved street where vendors sold puppets, leather goods, serapes, sombreros, statues of saints and authentic Mexican food, while a mariachi band played a lively rendition of "Guantanamera." Erica had just lunched on spicy chili relleno in a quaint patio restaurant that made one forget one was in the middle of a metropolis of five million inhabitants.

She had been on her way back from the San Gabriel Mission when she had impulsively pulled off the freeway. She didn't know why except that she needed to think. The visit had been unsuccessful. Although Mission records went all the way back to its initial founding in 1771, there was no mention in the archives of the Indians or the Fathers having ever engaged in the manufacture of such an object as Erica had found that morning in the cave and which she had hoped someone at the Mission could explain. So now, because of her impulse, she walked happily among throngs of tourists and locals who were visiting the historical places that were part of LA's hidden, romantic soul. The Church of Our Lady of the Angels, built in 1818 by Indian laborers who hauled beams from the San Gabriel Mountains, and where, on Saturday mornings, *quinceañeros* were held, festivities marking the coming-of-age of fifteen-year-old girls, a high-spirited celebration believed to have descended from ancient Native American rites and which the Catholic Church was trying to suppress. The Sepulveda House, a beautiful old Victorian built in 1887; the Pelanconi House, built in 1855, the first brick building in Los Angeles; and of course the Avila Adobe, believed to be the oldest building in Los Angeles, built in 1818, thirty-seven years after the founding of the city. All vibrating, Erica was certain, with the passions and stories of the past.

As she emerged into the sunlit Plaza, a Mexican-style park dominated by a huge fig tree, she was glad she had pulled off the freeway at the last minute. Solitude had its merits but sometimes the soul yearned for crowded places. The benches were all occupied by tourists resting their feet, or local citizens with noses deep in the *Los Angeles Times* or *La Opinion*.

And then she saw the ghosts, transparent people in old-fashioned attire, and horses and wagons, mangy dogs, ramshackle adobe buildings, wooden sidewalks. Erica was used to seeing ghosts, even in downtown Los Angeles at the peak of noon. The dead never really went away. Archaeology proved that. She saw women with parasols, a bowlegged man wearing a sheriff's badge, fur trappers on horseback, and tough hombres looking for a saloon. People thought Los Angeles was wild today. They should see it 150 years ago. Here was the terminus of the Wild West.

She saw a young, modern-day Hispanic couple with their arms around each other, heads together, the look of honeymooners. Erica had never thought of Los Angeles as a place to spend a honeymoon, but the Plaza, with its ambience of Old Mexico, the flowers, the music, the good food, people in costume, and the merry atmosphere, seemed a perfect place for two people in love.

When she spotted an Asian restaurant worker in a stained white apron leaning against a lamppost and reading that morning's edition of the *Times,* she was brought back to reality. Emerald Hills was on the front page—again. This time with the word "haunted" in the headline. A supermarket tabloid had dredged up old news accounts of Sister Sarah and some of the strange goings-on in the Haunted Canyon. Sister Sarah had even declared that the idea to build her Church of the Spirits where she did had come to her when she was visited by a vision of a "woman in robes." Erica suspected the vision had more to do with theatrics than reality. Nonetheless, the story had triggered a rash of "sightings" at the cave and workers were now claiming to have odd feelings around the place.

There was another big story in the press. After finding the reliquary containing the remains of St. Francis, Erica had contacted the Vatican. They reported that the reliquary had been brought to California in 1772 and was listed in Mission records as missing in 1775, along with a Brother Felipe, who vanished mysteriously and was believed to have been killed by grizzly bears. Erica wondered why a Franciscan friar would bury the bones of St. Francis in a cave so far from home. In an Indian cave at that.

The Vatican had immediately sent a representative. Erica was not surprised at the swiftness with which they had acted. It wasn't because the reliquary was so important per se (there were thousands of them around the world) or because St. Francis was a major saint. It was politics. Junipero Serra had been beatified, the first step toward sainthood, but a lot of parties were protesting his canonization, rendering it a touchy issue. More and more of the Mission Friars' treatment of the Indians was coming to light, and the Catholic Church was coming under criticism. The finding of a saint's bones buried with those of an Indian raised some significant questions.

Although the reliquary was on its way to Rome, it had received so much press that people were lined up at the Emerald Hills security fence, hoping to be allowed in to pray at the spot where the bones of Blessed St. Francis had been buried. People with sick children or loved ones in wheelchairs, reciting their rosaries as they waited to be let in. Latinos were claiming that La Primera Madre referred to a sighting of the Virgin Mary in the cave, causing the media to liken it to the cave at Lourdes. A photo in the newspaper of the protective clear plastic cover that had been put over the skeleton and the heavy iron gate that now guarded the entrance to the cave, bestowed on the cave an air of religious mystery—it did indeed look like the site of miracles.

That morning, when Erica had driven down the hill, she had seen at the bottom, where the road joined the Pacific Coast Highway, policemen arresting two young men who had apparently erected a barrier across the road with a sign that said: *Emerald Hills Excavation Site—$5.00 per person*. It had made her smile. Los Angelenos were, if nothing, enterprising.

Bringing herself back to the modern world that hurried past her in high heels and wing tip shoes, Erica reached into her purse and withdrew a small cloth bag and emptied the contents into her palm: a homely crucifix made of tin and stamped with a date: *Anno Domini 1781*. "Perhaps it commemorated a special event," the priest at the Mission had said when Erica explained that the crucifix had been buried with care and reverence, in a hole lined with flowers. "A birth, perhaps," he said.

A birth? But whose?

"Were you born here, Dr. Tyler?" Jared asking when chance had thrown them together at the same table in the cafeteria. He had quickly added, "You have such a passion for California history."

The question had surprised her. It also surprised her that he was that observant, and she had been flattered for a moment to think that he was curious about her. But then she had thought: it isn't out of friendly interest that he's asking, he's studying me, just as I have been studying him. Isn't that what adversaries do, search for each other's strengths and weaknesses? She had given him the standard answer: "I'm from San Francisco." At least that was the place of birth written on her birth certificate. The truth was a little harder to explain.

The kindly hospital social worker, saying, "So your name is Erica? Don't you have a last name? All right, Erica, can you tell me if the man who brought you here is your daddy?"

Erica saying, "I don't think so." She was only five, but even then she recognized perplexity on an adult's face.

"What do you mean you don't think so?"

"I have lots of daddies."

The social worker writing something down and Erica fascinated by the long fingernails with pretty color polish, and the gold ring flashing on the nice lady's hand. "And the woman who was brought in with you, was she your mother?" Quickly correcting herself: "Is she your mother?" Because they hadn't told Erica yet that the woman had died in the ER.

Jared had then asked: "Is your family still in San Francisco?"

"I have no family," she had replied. "Just me." Not exactly a lie, since Erica didn't know.

Later, in another room, the kindly social worker saying, "Any luck?"

And the baldheaded man, unaware that little Erica could hear them:"My hunch was right. I figured the kid most likely came from one of the hippie communes. The woman's drug overdose, the guy that brought her in, the way he was dressed. Well, I found the commune. Apparently the kid was abandoned. They said her mother took off with a biker. As for the biological father—the mother arrived at the commune pregnant and had the baby there. She never mentioned the father. I doubt she was married."

"Did you get the mother's name?"

"She went by Moonbeam. That's all I could get. I don't think you're going to find her or the father. I doubt they were even married. Probably don't even have a birth certificate for the kid."

"I've had one drawn up. We recorded the place of birth as San Francisco."

"What now?"

"Well, she's going to be hard to adopt, being five years old."

"You think so? Some couples want older kids, especially a pretty little girl like that."

"Yes, but there's something strange about her . . ."

It was growing up knowing that her mother had abandoned her, being moved from foster home to foster home, her social workers changing with frightening regularity, that made Erica retreat into fantasy. Stories became her life raft, fiction her sanity.

In the fourth grade she had fantasized about a handsome man in a military uniform striding into the classroom and saying in a commanding voice, "I am General MacIntyre and I've come from a field of battle to claim my daughter and take her home." They would hug in front of all those kids—Ashley and Jessica and Tiffany, the barracudas of Campbell Street Elementary—and go off hand in hand, Erica's arms full of new toys. In the fifth grade she saw herself lying in a hospital bed after brain surgery, on the brink of death because she needed a blood transfusion that only a close relative could give, and her parents rushing to her bedside, saying they'd been searching for her and then they saw her picture in the paper and the headline that said, "Can Anyone Help This Little Girl?" They were very wealthy and donated money for a new hospital wing that was to be named after their daughter.

In the sixth grade Erica started a family album of other people's photos. She labeled them: "Mom and me at the Beach," and "Daddy teaching me to ride a bike." In the seventh grade, when puberty brought a new sense of urgency into her life, she began calling child welfare services on a regular basis to see if her mother had contacted them.

The social workers came and went, the foster homes changed, the schools, the neighborhoods. Erica felt as if she lived in a pinball machine, bouncing off bumpers and flippers and never stopping. She grew resilient, imaginative, affable. Some group homes were filled with tough delinquent girls. But Erica survived because they liked her stories. She pretended to read palms and tea leaves and always predicted happy futures.

She never stopped believing her parents would come for her.

Looking at the crucifix in her palm, she thought: *did* it commemorate a birth? But whose? And then, as she looked around at the restored buildings, wondering again why she had come to this old heart of Los Angeles on an impulse, she saw a bronze plaque that read: *Pueblo de Los Angeles Historical Monument—1781* A.D. And suddenly Erica knew.

The crucifix commemorated not the birth of a person but of a *place. . . .*

Chapter Eight

ANGELA
1781 C.E.

What kind of place was this to found a settlement? Captain Lorenzo thought in ill humor. The river was leagues away, there was no harbor, no natural defenses along the shore. All the world's great cities were built on rivers or defensible harbors. But this place was in the middle of nowhere!

Lorenzo knew that Governor Neve had in fact purposely chosen this area to establish his new pueblo. It didn't matter that there was no harbor, no navigable river. The settlers were here to plant crops and raise cattle, and this flat, smoky plain was perfect for the purpose. Lorenzo thought that Neve was looking very satisfied. As well he should, having accomplished his mandate to establish two settlements in Alta California, one in the north and one in the south, one named for St. Francis and the other for the Virgin Mary.

Dios mio, Lorenzo thought philosophically. To name the town after the river here, which was itself named after a chapel in faraway Italy! Such a grandiose name, such a mouthful that a man could not say it and eat his beans at the same time. *El Pueblo de Nuestra Señora la Reina de los Angeles del Rio de Porciuncula*. The Town of Our Lady the Queen of the Angels of the River of Porciuncula. People were already making fun of it. They laughed and said Porciuncula was ironic because it meant "little portion" and wasn't that what the government was granting them for settling here? And what of the Angels? Nobody saw angels here, just a ragtag group of colonists brought up from Mexico, a mere eleven families of racial mix: Indian, black African, mulatto, mestizo, even a Chinese from the Philippines! Lorenzo's Mexican soldiers, plus the Spanish Fathers with their gaggle of Mission Indians, completed the total audience for Governor Neve's founding of a new city. But there were no angels.

Lorenzo had been one of the recruiters assigned to bribe men from Mexico to settle in Alta California. Each colonist was to receive a house lot, two fields of irrigable land, and two fields of dry land. Each was also to have rights to the common pueblo lands for grazing and the storage of firewood. Each family would receive a three-year salary of ten pesos a month plus clothing and tools, two cows and two oxen, two ewes, two goats, two horses, three mares, and one mule. The colonists, in return, had to work the land for a minimum of ten years.

Although Lorenzo thought the enticements were generous, nonetheless he and Captain Rivera had found it impossible to recruit the required number of colonists. What was there for them in that godforsaken place? people asked. And surely communication with home would be impossible. Ultimately they had fallen short of their quota and had struck north on an arduous journey with only twenty-three adults and twenty-one children, one of whom, Lorenzo's own daughter, had died along the way.

And now here we are, he thought as he waited for the speeches to end, setting his squinting eyes out to the distant mountains and the ocean, where a smoky haze hung perpetually in the air. A lonely place, he thought, cut off from civilization, and where we are outnumbered by the natives thousands to one. Although himself a *criollo,* being of Spanish descent born in Mexico, Lorenzo did not scorn the Indians the way some of his fellows did. In fact, he admired their penchant and skill for gambling and thought that the only saving grace in his promise to settle in this untamed place. He had accepted the assignment to recruit colonists because his compensation was release from military service, and Lorenzo, once he established his homestead here, planned a leisurely retirement engaged in cattle breeding, hunting, and gambling.

Lorenzo's mood darkened. What sort of a life was it going to be now? His wife, Doña Luisa, couldn't stop grieving over the loss of their daughter. Worse, she would not allow Lorenzo into her bed.

He brought his thoughts back to the ceremony taking place beneath the blazing sun while a pair of red-tailed hawks circled overhead. The new plaza had already been laid out with boundary posts fixed to mark the building lots that faced it. A formal procession, headed by the Governor of Alta California, with Mission Indians bearing a large banner of the Virgin Mary, had marched solemnly around the periphery of the plaza while, from a distance, the Indians of Yang-na, whose land this was, watched passively.

"We are here on God's errand to save souls," the padre from the Mission was now saying. Souls! Captain Lorenzo thought cynically. It is the concern of the Crown that the Russians are increasing their hunting in Alta California and are settling in the north that we are here. It is because the British have their greedy eye on the California coast that we need a notable Spanish presence in this place. For is it not our mandate to create as many Catholic Spanish citizens as possible in the quickest time, to encourage conversion among the heathen and encourage them to be fruitful, because the more Catholic Spanish citizens there are here, the harder it will be for another nation to lay claim to this land? Captain Lorenzo had been at court in Spain thirteen years ago when the Spanish ambassador to Russia had reported that the Russians were planning to occupy the Monterey Bay area. The King of Spain took immediate action.

And we are the result of that action, Captain Lorenzo thought as the Father said a prayer over the new plaza. Lorenzo didn't care a whit about bringing Jesus to the heathens. His interest was in cattle and horses. All this land, as far as the eye could see, free for the taking. A man could get rich . . .

His gaze fell upon his wife, Doña Luisa, seated with the Governor's wife and the wives of the other officers beneath the shade of a thatch roof on four poles. A beautiful woman, he thought with a pang, possessing an inner fortitude that would be needed in this wild frontier. Creole like himself, Luisa descended from Spanish nobility. It was apparent in her stiff posture, the reserved expression on her face. She saved her weeping for the privacy of their quarters. If only they had had more children. But Selena had been the center of Luisa's universe, and now that center had been snuffed out like a candle. What was a highborn lady going to do here, where all labor and occupations were performed by Indians? Not that Luisa would put her delicate hands to the tasks of cooking and sewing. Her role was to raise her husband's children, to teach them and guide them. But there were no children. Nor did it appear there were ever going to be.

Lorenzo tried again to pay attention to the ceremony, after which there was to be a feast commemorating the founding of the pueblo. He would make his exit then, with as little offense as possible, he prayed, to the governor and the padres.

Across the new plaza, standing on a plot of ground where someday an adobe church would be built, the Mission Indians paid respectful attention to the ceremony. They wore the tin crucifixes stamped with the year and strung on hemp strings that had been given to them as an incentive to join the nine-mile procession from the Mission to the site where the new Pueblo was going to be built. Teresa had asked permission to be part of the festivities, even though she was ill and needed to rest, because it was an opportunity for escape.

She had brought with her her five-year-old daughter Angela, so named because she was the daughter of a saint and because she had been conceived in the cave of the First Mother.

Teresa's thoughts often went fondly to Brother Felipe, who had vanished nearly six years ago and who, it was whispered, had stolen the bones of St. Francis from the Mission. He had gone back to Spain, everyone said. He had turned his back on God and gone home to sell the blessed relics and live the life of a rich man. But Teresa knew the truth. Brother Felipe had gone to join his god.

As she tried to draw shallow breaths because of the pains in her chest from the white man's illness, she looked at the soldiers and the new colonists, who were impressed with their achievement of having "claimed" this land, while the Yang-na stood off to the side, uncomprehending, not realizing that their ancestral land was being taken from them. Teresa was appalled. *We thought these people were our guests. But now they will build homes on land belonging to someone else's ancestors.*

Teresa kept a keen watch for an opportunity to escape.

From the moment they had realized she was pregnant, the Mission Fathers had kept an eye on the errant girl, assigning a dutiful baptized Indian woman to watch her at all times. They knew she had somehow gotten out of the nunnery, but they couldn't prove it. If one Indian could get away with it, the Fathers said, they would all try it, and there would be a mass exodus back to the villages, leaving the Fathers with no one to toil in the fields or to build their churches. In the six years since Teresa's visit to the cave the rules had gotten stricter, the punishments more severe. There had been several violent outbreaks among the Mission Indians, rebelling against their subjugation by the Fathers. Soldiers with guns were brought in and the Indians, having no defense against such weapons, were again subdued.

And so Teresa had realized that this would be an opportunity, when the Fathers were distracted with the soldiers and the colonists. Despite the fever that burned her skin and the pain in her lungs, Teresa was determined: she and Angela were going to escape once and for all.

❋

Armed with his deed from the Spanish Crown, Captain Lorenzo rode the boundaries of what would one day be his new rancho: south to the creek which had no name and which he christened Ballona after his father's hometown in Spain, east to the marshland, identified as *la cienega* on the deed, and north to *la brea,* the tar pits, with an ancient path running east and west along the northern border. He hadn't been given the land right off, but rather grazing rights with the proviso that in a few years, if he had improved the land and occupied it, he could petition for and receive a full grant in his name. When that day came, he had already decided, he would call his new home Rancho Paloma.

It covered four thousand acres and already teams of Indian laborers were making adobe bricks, one group in a massive mud pit, stomping the clay-and-straw mixture with their feet, another group pressing the compound into wooden molds, while a third was breaking sun-dried bricks from the molds and stacking them in readiness for building. The Indians worked cheaply, mainly for food and for beads, which they gambled away in their interminable games of chance. They had left their villages and built huts on the border of Lorenzo's property. He wondered if, once the homestead was completed, they would return to their old life. He hoped not. He was going to need hands to take care of his cattle and horses.

What a fine rancho this was going to be! Soon there would be a house here, with stables and other outbuildings, shaded by trees, which Captain Lorenzo was having shipped from Peru. He pictured the rose arbors and fountains, the tiled walkways and breezy arcades. Inside, there would be polished wooden floors and Luisa's big heavy furniture, which had been hauled up from Mexico on sledges drawn by oxen and currently waiting, under canvas tarps at the Pueblo settlement, to be moved into their final home: ornately carved four-poster beds, dressers, armoires, tables. Luisa had brought silver and tapestries, pewter and quilts, candlesticks for the fireplaces, platters for the kitchen. It was going to be a home fit for a queen, Lorenzo thought in pride.

But then he recalled how he had left Luisa, back at the settlement, snapping orders at her Indian servants as they worked with oil and cloths to polish and preserve their mistress's furniture. Ever since they had buried their little girl in the Sonoran desert Luisa had become fanatical about the care of her chairs and chests. Were these to become her children? Lorenzo wondered bleakly. Was she going to worry more about the condition of her precious writing desk than her husband's comfort?

Suddenly he had a grim vision of the future: Doña Luisa, childless and friendless—the colonists' wives were hardly fit companions for a high-born Spanish lady—growing more and more bitter as the years passed, moving silently among her furniture, inspecting for tarnish and dust, resenting her Indian maids for their fecundity and taking it out on them in unseen smudges and specks. Lorenzo saw himself ignored, forgotten, seeking comfort in the arms of brown-skinned women but finding no joy in his own home which, *Dios mio*, every man was entitled to! This was not what he had come to California for.

Another baby was needed. But Doña Luisa was spurning his advances and, being a gentleman, Lorenzo would never force her, nor was it to his liking to make love to a woman who lay still as a corpse.

His good mood ruined, Lorenzo decided that he would go hunting. As he steered his horse in the direction of the Mountains of Saint Monica, he thought: something big. Only a deer or a grizzly bear would satisfy him today.

*

While the Fathers and the governor were celebrating, and the new colonists began looking around at their new land, talking about what they were going to build here and plant there, Teresa quietly took a mule and, with her daughter riding in her arms, followed the ancient track to the mountains.

By late afternoon they reached their destination, where they dismounted and, with each breath a labor, causing sharp pain in her chest, Teresa led Angela past the markings of the raven and the moon, up the small canyon and into the cave.

The setting sun was at such an angle that it sent slanting rays of light upon the painted wall. "Here is the story of the First Mother," Teresa said. The stories were being lost. Fewer people lived in the villages so that someday the villages weren't going to exist at all. The tribes were all mixed together at the Missions: Tongva with Chumash, Kemaaya with Topaa, and the Fathers were calling them Gabrielino and Fernandeño after the names of the Missions. The wrong stories were being told at night, or they were not being told at all. Instead the stories were about Jesus and Mary so that the ancestors of the Topaa would soon be forgotten. But Teresa was going to teach Angela the stories, and tell her that she must continue to pass them on so that their story was not forgotten.

"You will not live by the ways of the intruders," she said as she lifted the crucifix on its string from around her neck. "They do not understand our people." The looks on the Fathers' faces when she had told them she was pregnant, the hours of interrogation—who was the man?—their insistence that whoever the father was he be brought to the Mission to be baptized. But Teresa had proudly kept her silence. What she did with her body was her own concern, as every Topaa woman knew. These men who called themselves "father," even though in their celibacy they could not sire children, tried to dictate to the native women how they should act, how they should conduct themselves sexually. No Topaa man would dare such impertinence.

Explaining to Angela about leaving a gift for the First Mother, Teresa buried the crucifix in a bed of petals. In her fever and illness, it did not occur to her that her act was symbolic as well, that she had buried her new religion in the bosom of the old.

Removing the spirit-stone from around her neck, she placed it around Angela's. Then she knelt before the child, and, taking her by the shoulders, said, "Your name is Marimi. You are no longer Angela. I am going to take you to a village where the people have not heard of the Spanish god who instructs his people to steal land belonging to others. You will be raised in the ways of the Topaa and the First Mother."

She laid her hand along the girl's cheek, this angel who had been given to her by a saint, and said, "My precious daughter, you are a special and chosen one. The sickness that you sometimes feel in your head is not an affliction but a gift, and someday you will come to understand this. But before that time—"

Teresa suddenly coughed and doubled over with the pain.

"Mama!" the child cried.

Teresa held her breath until the pain subsided. The ride from the new plaza had weakened her. She had not realized she was so ill. "Listen to what I have to say, my daughter. Your new name is Marimi, do you understand? You are no longer Angela, for that is the name of the Christian strangers who do not belong here. You are Marimi and you will be the new Keeper of the Cave. Do you understand?"

"Yes, Mama."

"Say it, daughter. Tell me your name."

"I am Marimi, Mama."

"Good . . . And now we will go. There are villages west of here where the intruders have never walked. We will be safe there. The soldiers will never find us."

But when Teresa turned toward the cave entrance, her legs suddenly gave way and she collapsed to the earthen floor. "I can go no farther," she said breathlessly. "Marimi, listen to me carefully. You must get help. Go down the canyon and turn toward the sea. Can you do that?"

The child nodded solemnly.

"There is a village . . . some of our people still live there. Tell them that I am in this cave, the cave of the First Mother, and that I am ill. Say it for me, my child. Let me know that you understand."

Angela repeated the instructions and Teresa settled back against the wall. "They will have medicines. They will restore my health. And then we will live among our own people. Go now, child. To the sea. To the village. And bring them back. I will wait."

The little girl scrambled down the canyon, intent upon her errand, but in time she became lost. Whichever way she turned, there were more canyons, more rocks, and no sea, no village. She started to cry.

Suddenly a half-naked man appeared before her, his hair long and matted, his skin burnt red from the sun, his expression wild.

Angela turned and ran, but she was boxed in. The wild man stood between her and the opening of the canyon.

He towered over her, staring down at her with a bewildered expression, emaciated, with scars and sores on his dirty body and only a tattered length of cloth around his loins. But he had intelligent green eyes and after a moment a kind of light dawned in them. "Why are you crying, my child?"

His voice was surprisingly gentle, which made her stop crying. "My mama is sick and I can't find the village."

He blinked. And then he looked around. "Where is she?"

"In the cave."

The man stood stock-still. The cave. He remembered a cave . . . had it been years ago or only yesterday? The cave where he had experienced his rapture and he had been touched by the Hand of God, and since which he had walked daily with Jesus in these mountains.

He frowned as he looked more closely at the girl. The hairline, the shape of her eyes, the fullness of her lip. Teresa!

And something else. A small mole on the right side of her jaw. His own mother . . . his mind struggled with the memories he had long put aside. And a sister. The same mole.

"Do not cry, little one," he said, smiling now to reveal broken teeth. "I know where your mama is. I know the cave. We will help her. We will make her well." He stretched down a gnarled hand and Angela took it.

"Stop!" cried a voice suddenly, echoing off the canyon walls.

Angela and the wild man turned to see a Spanish officer at the base of the canyon. "Let her go!" he commanded.

Brother Felipe took a step forward, hands outstretched, ready to explain. But the trigger was quicker, and the musket ball hit him square in the heart, knocking him off his feet.

Angela started to scream. Lorenzo rushed up and swept her into his arms to hurry her away from the sight of the dead man. When he was out of the canyon and back where his horse was tethered, he put the girl down and tried to soothe her. "He cannot hurt you, little one. The wild man is gone."

She fell silent and stared at him. *"¿Habla Español?"* he said.

She nodded. And then she started crying for her mother.

A beautiful child, he thought, intrigued by the way the widow's peak on her forehead gave her face a charming heart shape. Almost the age of his own daughter when she died.

Her clothes indicated she was a Mission Indian. Runaways? *"¿Cómo te llamas?"* he asked.

"I have to go to my mama," she replied in Spanish. "She's sick."

"Sick?" He looked around the canyon, growing dark now with long shadows and a chill in the air. So the mother had absconded with her daughter and come to these hills to hide from the Fathers. And she was sick. When night came on, the woman would be defenseless against the mountain lions and grizzly bears that lived in these mountains.

An idea began to form in Lorenzo's mind. "I will take you to your mama if you tell me your name," he said with a smile.

She rubbed fists in her eyes. Her head was starting to hurt. Mama had told her something about her name, but she couldn't remember. So she said, "Angela."

He put the girl on his horse and she rode silently for a while in his arms, but when she saw that they were riding away from the mountains, she began to scream and call again for her mama, so Lorenzo put his hand over her mouth, spurring his horse to go faster, knowing that in time she would forget, being so young, especially once his wife welcomed her as her own daughter and smothered her with love.

As he galloped across the plain, away from the mountains and the sea, the child pinned and silent in his arms, and thinking how Luisa was going to come out of her mourning and accept him into her bed again, Lorenzo decided that the day's hunting had gone well indeed.

Chapter Nine

"He went crazy after his wife died, you know."

Erica spun around, startled. Ginny Dimarco was wearing a hard smile beneath hard eyes. She had followed Erica out onto the pool deck, away from the noisy guests and the Gypsy Kings singing "Hotel California" through enormous stereo speakers. Despite the cold night air, a few guests were swimming in the heated pool. But the beach beyond the deck was dark and deserted.

Erica knew that Jared Black had been invited to the cocktail party at the Dimarcos' beach house and that he had declined. She suspected that Ginny Dimarco was now resorting to the revenge of the stood-up hostess: spiteful gossip about the offending guest—especially as the guest was the head of the Native American Heritage Commission and the hostess, a wealthy socialite patron of the arts, was on a personal crusade to create an Indian museum with her name attached to it.

Five minutes earlier, inside the Dimarcos' fabulous Malibu beach house that was a showcase for Pueblo pottery, West Coast basketry, Zuni fetishes, kachina dolls, Eskimo totem poles, and Kwakiutl masks, Ginny had cornered Erica, her eyes strangely feverish. "What is it like to be working with Jared Black again?"

Erica hadn't wanted to come to the Dimarcos' party, but Sam had reminded her that it was good PR and important to make nice to the rich people who funded their grants. So Erica had put on her only cocktail dress—a plain black number with spaghetti straps—and combed her hair up in some semblance of salon style. The high heels and nylons felt strange after weeks spent in socks and work boots. "I'm not working *with* him."

"*Fighting* with him then." A sharp, brittle laugh. And then, Ginny's eyes fast on Erica and a pause before adding, "It's unfortunate Mr. Black had a previous engagement tonight. There are people here who would have liked to meet him. Important people." Erica caught a flicker of hostility in Ginny's eyes. "The invitation went out weeks ago," Mrs. Dimarco had added, her tone full of meaning.

Erica knew she was expected to fill in the missing information, the excuse Jared had for this unforgivable slight. She wondered if in fact Ginny had used Jared's name as a draw, if there were guests who had come with the intention of meeting and mingling and hoping to make connections in Sacramento. While Erica had struggled to curb her tongue—she was tempted to say that Jared was back at the camp watching *I Love Lucy* reruns on TV—another guest had interrupted to tell Ginny what a fabulous party it was. Erica had seized the opportunity to escape out onto the pool deck to fill her lungs with fresh ocean air and get away from the talk and gossip of the party, to be alone and try to make sense of her jumbled emotions.

Jared had been slowly invading her thoughts and her dreams, whispering to her: *What you see is not who I really am.* Erica needed to fathom this growing preoccupation with Jared, to find its roots and understand it. But her hostess, like a predator, had followed her out. "You *do* know he went crazy after his wife died?" she repeated now, raptorial eyes watching Erica.

Why this relentless attack? Erica wondered. And then it occurred to her that Ginny was hoping Erica would go back to the camp with tales to tell, to let the rude Commissioner know what an unforgivable faux pas he had committed.

"Right after the funeral," Ginny continued, as if Erica had prompted her for more, "he vanished. His family launched a manhunt, they were frantic. Well, I don't suppose they really thought he would commit suicide, but there was speculation."

Erica blinked at the woman. Jared? Suicide?

"You didn't know?"

"I was in Europe."

"Well it was simply one of the major stories of the day, how Jared disappeared and the police couldn't find him. It was only by accident that a team of marine biologists found him four months later on one of the Channel Islands. He had gone native. They found him completely naked and fishing in a lagoon with a spear. His hair was long and he'd grown a beard and he was as brown as a nut, they said."

Dark figures were starting to materialize now on the dunes—families arriving in droves to park on the shoulder of the Pacific Coast Highway and launch themselves onto the beach with flashlights and sacks for the annual grunion run. Erica, her mind filled with the image of a forlorn figure alone among driftwood and sandpipers and kelp, was only vaguely aware of them.

"They had to chase him," Ginny went on, seeing how she had captivated her guest, and relishing it, "and then he hid in some caves. They actually tracked him like an animal. The way they finally caught him was by waiting until nightfall and they saw the light from his campfire."

Erica rediscovered the glass of wine in her hand and took a long sip, her eyes set out to the far horizon where stars met ocean. She was suddenly consumed with a burning fury.

"There was a big news brouhaha, of course," Ginny continued, "when the biologists brought him home. The senior Black demanded a psychiatric evaluation, he even wanted to put his son in an institution for observation. But Jared simply cut his hair, shaved off the beard, and went back to work as if nothing had happened. But still, it isn't normal, is it? Certainly a man is supposed to grieve after a wife dies, but to go to such extremes?" She laughed and the diamonds at her throat flashed with moonlight. "I should hardly expect my Wade to become an aboriginal simply because I had died!"

Erica's grip tightened around her glass. She wanted to throw her wine into the woman's face. Instead she forced her attention on the campfires that were now flaring up along the beach.

Grunion are a species of coastal fish, eight inches long with small mouths and no teeth. Every year, from March to August, they make nocturnal spawning runs on Southern California beaches—thousands of grunion riding the waves with the females frantically burrowing into the wet sand, laying their eggs while males circle and fertilize them. Afterward, they all ride the waves back into the sea until the next run. Unless, of course, they are seized first by the humans waiting at the surf's edge to snap up the unsuspecting grunion with their bare hands and throw them into sacks.

Erica had been on grunion hunts before, had held the flashlight or the sack, and had then sat at the midnight barbecue and happily feasted on the hapless spawners. Tonight, however, the spectacle filled her with inexplicable sadness.

He went crazy. Erica imagined the shrine Jared must have constructed to his wife in the bedroom of his RV. It would consist of Netsuya's portrait and fresh flowers that he changed every day, maybe even candles. Jared would talk to Netsuya every night before retiring and she would be the first person he spoke to in the morning.

Erica put her hand to her chest. She suddenly couldn't breathe. Yards away, foamy breakers crashed onto the shore, and a pair of children, running along the beach, their squeals like the cries of gulls, swung flashlights. A beam of bright light stabbed Erica's eyes.

The blinding sunlight of the wild and windswept Channel Islands.

In the next instant, something slammed against her chest, like an invisible shock wave. She gasped.

"Look at that," Ginny said with a brittle laugh. "The grunion don't stand a chance." She shook her head. "Where else but in Southern California would the fish throw themselves ashore? One doesn't even need a fishing rod! No wonder our Indians were so unwarlike."

Erica stared at her. Then she set her glass down on a patio table, excused herself, and went inside.

She pushed her way through well-dressed people and waiters in red jackets offering trays of champagne and hors d'oeuvres, plunged blindly through, feeling a pressure grow around her heart. She found Sam, convinced him she needed to leave, and when he gave her the car keys, saying he could catch a lift back to the camp later, Erica was out of the Dimarco house and speeding away on the Pacific Coast Highway faster than the tide that was bringing the doomed fish to shore.

✳

Erica sat for a long moment after she killed the engine and the headlights. Resting her perspiring forehead on the steering wheel, she closed her eyes and tried to examine herself internally.

What had happened out on the Dimarcos' pool deck? Was it a heart attack? A panic attack? The pain was still there, behind her breastbone, aching, catching her breath short. *"They found him on one of the Channel Islands, naked and spear fishing. . . ."*

Erica felt an overwhelming impulse to cry. But the tears wouldn't come. As she drew in slow breaths, trying to restore herself, she felt the heaviness settle in her chest, as though something new had lodged there. It was dark and ponderous, like an unwanted bird that had come to roost, its fusty wings tucked in for the long haul.

Erica managed to get out of the car and head for the lighted compound, her bare skin rising in bumps. The moon played peekaboo through the overhead branches, an eye watching Erica, like the eyes of ghosts she imagined inhabited the Topanga woodland. She looked over at Jared's RV. It was dark. He had not yet returned from his nightly escape to God knew where. And if he *were* here, what would she say to him?

When she neared her tent she saw that the doorway flap wasn't secured the way she had left it earlier.

Entering cautiously, she turned on the light and looked around. Her first concern was for the find she had made that afternoon at Level IV. But the object was still there, exactly as she had left it on her worktable. Checking her metal file cabinet, she found it still locked. Since she didn't keep money or jewelry in her tent, she couldn't imagine why anyone would have broken in. And yet she was certain someone had been there.

Then she saw it. On her pillow.

It was an ordinary handax, found in any hardware store, except that it had been wrapped with strips of rawhide and decorated with feathers to make it look like an Indian tomahawk. Erica knew what it meant.

It was a declaration of war.

She began to shake. Someone had violated her privacy, just as Ginny Dimarco had violated Jared's. For a moment, Erica literally saw red. Then she flung herself back out into the cold night and, heedless of the fact that she was still in cocktail dress and high heels, marched across the compound to the cafeteria tent, tomahawk in her fist. The Indians weren't in their usual corner playing darts, as if they had known she would be coming after them. Going back outside, she saw them at the edge of the camp, illuminated by a campfire, a circle of warriors throwing darts at the board nailed to a tree.

As she approached, she saw a giant of a man, his graying hair in long Indian braids, dominating the game. He wasn't familiar to her. He wore a nylon bomber jacket with a fierce Asian tiger embroidered on the back and beneath it, in crimson-and-yellow letters: *Vietnam, June 1966*. When he turned, Erica saw the military insignia of a flaming spear on one shoulder, labeled, *199th Infantry Brigade*. He had a thick browridge and a heavy jaw, his stance was aggressive and his smile a sneer, as he said, "Well well, if it isn't our friend the anthropologist."

"Who are you?" she demanded, going up to him. Despite her heels, he was still a head taller than Erica. "You're not one of our crew."

He brought a beer can to his lips and took a long drink, his narrowed eyes fixed on her.

Erica held up the tomahawk. "Is this yours?"

Running a big hand across his mouth, the giant said, "You know? I remember when I was growing up on the reservation, you white bitches would come from the nearby university and spend the summer studying us."

She raised the weapon higher. "I said, is this yours?"

"You'd walk around with your cameras and notepads, wearing short shorts to show off your long legs to the horny Indian boys while you clung defensively to your pasty, geeky anthro boyfriends in their fake bush jackets and backpacks. You thought we all had the hots for you, didn't you? When all we were really doing was laughing at you as you earned semester credits writing down the stories we told you because you didn't know we made them up since we sure as hell weren't going to give away our real, sacred stories."

When Erica opened her mouth to respond, he stepped closer, menacingly. "We heard you're gonna run DNA tests on the skeleton. But you've got a surprise coming. You're not going to be scraping any cells off my ancestor and putting them under a microscope. We don't need no laboratories to tell us who our elders were."

He took another step closer, and when Erica glanced back toward the camp through the trees, he laughed, and said, "Ain't it awful how there's never a cavalry around when you need one?" Except he pronounced it "calvary."

Then they heard footsteps crunching over twigs, and a newcomer emerged into the circle of campfire light. Jared, carrying his nightly gym bag. "Charlie, what the hell are you doing here?"

The giant's eyes went flat and mean. "The name's Coyote, man."

"You don't belong here. You're trespassing."

"It's a free country. Indian country. From sea to shining sea."

When Jared gave Erica a questioning look, she handed him the tomahawk. "This was in my tent."

"Any of you recognize this?" The men ignored him and resumed playing darts. Jared hefted the tomahawk in the air, leaned back, and flung the ax with such ferocity that when it hit the bull's-eye it split the dartboard in two. He turned on Coyote. "Breaking and entering is a felony. Just remember that."

"White man's laws, not ours." Coyote jabbed the air with a thick finger. "You Anglos have done your best to deny us California Indians our land and our identity. The treaties of the 1850s were never ratified by the Senate so we weren't allowed to keep our territories. California Indians have been systematically undercounted by the Bureau of Indian Affairs so we have the smallest per capita funding rate of all BIA areas. Shit, man, half our tribes don't even have federal recognition so we don't get the money, like other Indians do. California Indians are suffering economic and federal aid losses because of our historical dispossession of land, which is the worst in the nation. So go screw yourself with your felony."

Jared grabbed the big man by his shirt, and said in a low voice, "Whatever it is you're up to, I suggest you pack up and leave right now."

Coyote pulled back, smoothing his shirt. "You just remember this, man. We ain't gonna take this lying down anymore. We're getting organized, we're mobilizing. You think we're just a bunch of dumb Indians but you've got a big surprise coming. You let those people come and pray here," he flung a massive arm toward the security fence on the other side of Emerald Hills Drive, where a group of New Agers were holding hands and chanting a mantra. "This offends us, those Christians with their fake new religion, coming to *our* place of worship and pretending to be pious. How would you like it if we put on our feathers and our beads and performed a rain dance in the middle of St. Peter's Cathedral? Times are changing, man. We've got lawsuits against publishing companies that print dictionaries with the word 'squaw' in them. This word is insulting to our women. We're making botanists change the names of plants you Anglos call squaw-weed and squaw-bush. We're telling zoologists to come up with another name for squaw-fish. We're even going to do away with the word Indian, because we don't come from India, man. And we aren't Native Americans, we are the *First* Americans. So you keep your eyes open, Mr. White Lawyer, and witness the power of the sons of Sitting Bull and Crazy Horse."

Jared took Erica by the elbow and walked her quickly away. "We're going to have to watch our backs," he said quietly. "Coyote isn't here for social reasons, he's here to agitate. While our guys are generally apolitical and nonmilitant, interested only in earning a paycheck, Coyote can be very persuasive. He's a core member of the Red Panthers."

Erica felt a jolt at Jared's unexpected touch on her bare skin. In that instant she no longer cared about Coyote and the tomahawk, the Indians or even the cave. Jared was here, touching her, and the impact of Ginny Dimarco's story came rushing back. "The Red Panthers?" she heard herself say. She wanted to ask about the Channel Islands. Had he found what he was looking for there?

"They're a radical offshoot of the American Indian Movement, and ever since Alcatraz and Wounded Knee they've been looking for a new place to showcase their grievances. They have their eye on our cave."

The pressure in her chest increased. "Who is that Coyote person?"

"His real name's Charlie Braddock. Tried to affiliate with every tribe you can name, from the Suquamish in Washington to the Seminoles in Florida. None of them would take him because he couldn't prove blood. So he decided to affiliate with a nonfederally recognized tribe because then he wouldn't have to prove ancestry."

"You mean he isn't really Native American?"

"If Charlie has Indian blood, he got it from the Red Cross. Before he joined the Indian movement he tried a stint as a mercenary in Africa, and before that he was an ambulance driver until he got arrested for impersonating a doctor. All that talk about living on the reservation is fabricated. Charlie was born and raised in the San Fernando Valley, went to an all-white high school. And that jacket he's wearing—he never served in Vietnam. When the draft was called, Charlie quietly slipped across the border into Canada and waited it out. Luckily for him his number never came up. But don't underestimate him. He's dangerous, to both whites and to the Indians."

When they entered the lights of the camp, Jared switched his gym bag to his other hand and suddenly grimaced, clutching his side.

Erica looked at him in alarm. "Are you all right?"

"I'm okay." But he didn't look well. He was pale, Erica saw now, and perspiring despite the chill night air. "It's okay, really. Just an injury. A stupid injury."

"What happened?"

He attempted a smile. "I zigged when I should have zagged."

"Shall I go find the nurse?"

He shook his head. "I just need a drink. It's been a long day." His eyes roamed over her hair, which was still pinned up with rhinestone clips, and then explored her bare shoulders. "Nice dress," he said.

Her lungs contracted. "I just came back from the Dimarcos' party."

He remained standing there, in the middle of the oak trees and tents, with people passing by, as if he and Erica were alone at the top of the world with no one to think about but themselves. "It's still a nice dress," he said quietly.

Her heart skipped a beat. *He went crazy after his wife died.*

"That was a brave thing you did just now, standing up to Charlie and his crew like that."

"I've learned to deal with his type." *"There is nothing more powerful than direct eye contact. Always remember that, Erica. When confronted by a bully, stare her down. If confronted by a group, single one out and stare her down. She will back away and the others will follow. And when you are in the courtroom, meet the judge's eyes. Do not look anywhere else. Do not look at your lawyer or the bailiff or the court reporter. You will be amazed how much strength there is in your eyes."*

The voice from the past had referred to bullies as females because the bullies Erica had had to face were tough girls in Juvenile Hall who pulled her hair and called her "poor Valley trash."

"I'll alert security to keep an eye on Coyote, *and* your tent," Jared said. "Come and have a drink with me and tell me what I missed at the party."

✳

Erica had been inside Jared's RV only once, at the start of the project. She remembered the "living room" section behind the driver and passenger seats consisting of a leather sofa and two leather club chairs with a TV/VCR nestled between. There had been an impressive "business center" consisting of fax and phones and computer, stacks of legal papers, correspondence, law books, and beyond that, the kitchenette, impressively furnished with a refrigerator, dishwasher, stove and oven, microwave and a state-of-the-art cappuccino machine. Through the bedroom door, Erica recalled, she had seen a king-size bed.

But as she now followed Jared inside and he turned on the lights, she saw that a startling change had taken place.

The office desk had been replaced by a drafting board. Sketches of houses and offices buildings were tacked up on the bulletin board, covering up legal memos and press releases on the Emerald Hills Project. Where she remembered boxes of pens and a stack of legal pads was now a supply of drafting tools and pencils. Most astonishing of all: the small dinette table, designed to fold up and out of the way when not in use, now supported a scale model of a fabulous contemporary-style house, complete with landscaping and swimming pool. "Are you designing this for someone?" Erica asked in amazement.

"It's just a hobby," he said, but there was pride in his voice and he was clearly pleased by her reaction. Jared had devoted many late-night hours to the careful design and meticulous construction of the cardboard-and-balsa-wood model—down to the tiny brass knobs on all the doors.

There was furniture inside, Erica saw, and tiny people. "Who are they?" she asked.

"The people? They're just there for scale."

She thought a moment, her eyes roaming the spacious little rooms, constructing the lives that were being lived in them. "They're the Arbogasts," she said. "Sophie and Herman Arbogast, and their kids Billy and Muffin. Sophie doesn't work but fills her time as a volunteer at St. John's Hospital and as a docent leading groups through the Getty Museum." Erica peered down into cutaway upstairs rooms, where stairways led to nowhere. "Herman is a cardiac surgeon going through a midlife crisis. He is considering starting a love affair with his office nurse. He thinks Sophie doesn't know, but she does, and she hopes he has the affair because she's been having one for the past year with Herman's partner." She bent low to peek into the spacious kitchen and adjoining family room. "Billy is excited because he's about to graduate from Cub Scouts to Boy Scouts, and Muffin's walking on air because her pimples have finally cleared up and she thinks a certain boy in her history class likes her." Erica straightened and looked at Jared. "It's a beautiful home."

When she saw how he stared at her, she blushed, and said, "It's a nasty habit I have, making up stories."

He smiled and shook his head. Then he slid open the partition and disappeared into the bedroom.

Erica looked around at the curious metamorphosis that seemed to be taking place in Jared's private world, law books giving way to drafting pencils, legal briefs to blueprints. It was as if the architect were taking over the lawyer, reclaiming his former life. As if something within Jared were trying to get out, trying to give itself shape and meaning.

He emerged from the bedroom, hand pressed to his side, and went into the bathroom, where he gingerly pulled off his shirt to inspect his ribs. Erica saw his reflection in the mirror: a nasty bruise was already forming.

"Is that where you got injured," she said, "at your tomahawk-throwing class?"

He stuck his head through the doorway. "I beg your pardon?"

"That *is* where you go every night, to take tomahawk-throwing lessons?"

He gave her a puzzled look. Then he laughed, wincing. "Fencing." He came out carrying a first-aid kit.

"Fencing! Picket? Post and rail? Wrought iron?"

"Foils, epées, swords," he said, sweeping his arm in a swashbuckling gesture that made him flinch with pain. "I wasn't concentrating and my very worthy opponent got me."

Erica suddenly pictured him in the *en garde* stance, declaring, "For France and the Queen!" and then dodging and feinting, light and swift on his feet, rapier slicing the air with a singing sound, cries of "Touché!" A nobleman's sport. A deadly sport.

As he retrieved an Ace bandage from the kit and removed the plastic wrap and metal clips, Erica became acutely aware of the small space within Jared's RV, that they were just a few feet away from each other, both half-dressed—or half-naked as an optimist might say, Erica thought giddily—he shirtless, she in the barely there cocktail dress. When he tried to wrap the bandage around his chest, with no success as it was awkward and he kept dropping it, Erica stepped up, and said, "Let me help."

She anchored one end of the bandage on his sternum and had him hold it while she unwound the bandage around his rib cage. He tried not to grimace, but she could tell he was in pain.

As she unrolled the Ace bandage, bringing it across his chest, then reaching around to pull it snugly across his back, she noticed that he smelled faintly of Irish Spring and that the ends of his black hair were still curly from shower steam. But his skin was warm and dry, and beneath, hard muscles quivered. Every night without fail, Jared Black engaged in a vigorous, physically demanding sport. Why? For physical fitness? Or were there deeper reasons that compelled him to take up swords against other men?

When he suddenly gasped, Erica stopped, and said, "Sorry. Do you think it's broken?"

"No. It's not really as bad as it looks. It only hurts when my heart beats." She resumed wrapping. He asked, "Where did you learn such a light touch?"

"From handling brittle objects."

Their eyes met. "I'm not brittle."

She didn't believe that. There was something inside Jared that was very breakable because he worked so hard to protect it. She wanted to know, but you just can't say to someone, "I hear you went crazy one day." So instead she said, "We missed you at the party."

"I'd rather have a root canal."

"But I thought you would like the Dimarcos. They do a lot for Native causes."

"They're pseudointellectual liberals who pump investment money into movies like *Dances With Wolves* but wouldn't dream of having a Native American at their dinner table. Were there any Indians at the party?"

"There was one, I believe, a chief from one of the Coachella Valley tribes."

"And I'll bet you he wore an Armani suit and arrived in a Porsche. Those casino chiefs are rich. Very little of the gambling profits trickle down to the people on the reservation. Did Ginny give you her no-soap-on-the-reservation speech? It's her favorite ladies' luncheon shocker, guaranteed to open checkbooks. The poor Indians, no soap on the reservations."

Erica brought the bandage snugly across his chest, then carried it around back, reaching for it with her other hand so that she briefly encircled him in her arms. Their faces were, for an instant, close together. "I didn't hear that one but Ginny did offer a theory about the grunion being the reason why the Spanish found California such an easy conquest."

She continued unrolling the bandage, around and front, arms encircling but not touching. Jared said quietly, "I like your hair that way. Wait, you have an escapee." He reached up and lifted the errant curl from her neck, tucking it back up into the rhinestone clip.

Erica wanted suddenly to collapse against him, lay her head on his shoulder, hold on to him, give up her struggle and be weak with him. But she kept at her labor until finally she came to the end of the wrapping, and as she fixed the clips into place, Jared, staring at her, murmured, " 'For the love of God, Montressor.' "

"I beg your pardon?"

"Your eyes are the color of amontillado sherry." He smiled. "And now your cheeks are the color of Washington apples."

"I hate it when I blush. I envy women who can coolly conceal their reactions." She stepped back. "You're done. In the future I would advise you not to play with knives."

"Swords."

"Whatever." She hid her smile.

"I don't like women who can coolly conceal their reactions. Blushing becomes you. Like that dress."

Her cheeks grew hotter. His eyes met hers for one heartbeat, then he turned away to tear the string off a dry-cleaner's box and retrieve a clean shirt, ironed and folded in a plastic bag. "Do you prefer wine or scotch?"

Erica hesitated for only a split second. "Wine. White, if you have it."

She watched him put the shirt on—it looked silk and tailored and expensive—and appreciated how the fabric fit snugly across his broad back. He did all the buttons except the top one, leaving his collar open, then he tucked the shirt into his pants.

As he poured drinks, they suddenly heard a soft, whispering sound. The *tink-tink* of raindrops hitting the roof of the RV. They both looked up, as if the ceiling were transparent and they could see the unexpected rain clouds in the night sky. The intimacy within the small space intensified. Erica cleared her throat. "Do we really have something to fear from the Red Panthers?"

"They think I should have shut down your operation weeks ago." He held out her drink to her. "Did you know that there are now nine tribes claiming possession of the cave?"

Her eyebrows rose. "I didn't know anybody wanted it!"

"There are eighty California tribes currently fighting for recognition by the federal government. The problem is in proving a legitimate historical bloodline. A local tribe that can claim connection to the cave and therefore to the skeleton has a stronger case for getting on the federal Indian tribe register, and therefore qualifying for funds." He dropped ice into his scotch. "Unfortunately, the rest of the tribes don't want new tribes to be recognized because then there would be fewer federal dollars to go around. Which puts you and me in the middle of a very nasty battle."

They tasted their drinks in silence.

"So why fencing?"

He leaned against the kitchen counter. Neither seemed to want to sit down. "It's for anger management. It's an outlet. If I didn't cross swords with someone, I might do something I would regret."

"What are you angry at?"

"Me."

She waited.

He looked into his drink and listened for a moment to the rain, weighing his thoughts, coming to a decision. Finally: "Netsuya was like no one I had ever met before." His voice was soft, like the rain. "She was exotic, angry, passionate. But she was not easy to be married to. She didn't like Anglos and had a hard time reconciling her love for me with her crusade. She often went to meetings that I was barred from."

He drew in a deep breath that made him grimace, then he sipped his scotch. Erica had the feeling he was about to open a very private door. "When Netsuya suspected she was pregnant," he said, "she didn't go to a regular doctor. Among her circle of friends was a Pomo woman who was a midwife. Netsuya wanted to have the baby at home, which I agreed to, but it wasn't until later that I learned I wasn't to be taking part in the birth. Something about women's secret rituals and men not being allowed. I had to respect that."

He took another sip of his drink, but he wasn't relaxing into his story. Erica heard the tension in his voice. "I wanted her to see a medical doctor but she wouldn't go. She said that white men took over the practice of obstetrics two hundred years ago when they were jealous and took it out of the hands of white women. She said that her people had been having babies for thousands of years without the intervention of white male doctors. When I suggested a female physician, she still refused. We argued. I told her it was my baby, too, and that I had a voice in this. But Netsuya argued that ultimately it was her body and, therefore, she got the final word."

Jared took another drink, his eyes grazing the roofline of the house model as if wondering how the Arbogasts had handled the births of Muffin and Billy. "When her labor began, she called the midwife who arrived with an assistant, also a full-blood Indian. The three women went into the bedroom and closed the door."

Jared paused long enough to add another splash of scotch to his glass, another ice cube. "The labor went on for hours. Once in a while I was allowed to go in and sit with Netsuya while the midwife made herbal tea and the assistant filled the room with sacred smoke and chanted native prayers. When the baby came, I was barred from the room because my presence was taboo. So I waited outside the door and listened. Netsuya screamed, and then she was silent. I kept listening for the baby's cries. When there was only silence I went in."

The ice rattled in his glass. The rain on the roof intensified.

"There was—" He clasped the crystal tumbler and looked into it, like a man about to fall. His voice grew tight. "There was too much blood. And the midwife—I'll never forget the look on her face. She was terrified. I bundled Netsuya into blankets and drove her down the hill to the hospital. I don't remember the drive. I know I had my hand on the horn and I ran red lights. The doctors did what they could to save my wife and son, but it was too late."

Silence rushed in behind his words while Erica stood immobilized. "I am so sorry," she finally said.

A vein stood out on Jared's forehead. He choked out the words. "There isn't a day goes by that I don't think about my son and wonder what he would be like now, three years old. I can't forgive Netsuya for what she did. I can't forgive myself."

"But it wasn't your fault, it wasn't anyone's fault. These things happen."

"These things do *not* happen." He turned a furious look on her. "It was preventable. That's what the attending physician told me afterward, when he asked me if Netsuya had been taking drugs during her pregnancy. I told him she wouldn't even take an aspirin. She wouldn't let people smoke around her. Netsuya was so health conscious that she drank only herbal teas and took herbal supplements. Then the doctor asked me about the supplements.

"I remembered that Netsuya had gone regularly to the midwife to get a compound of ginkgo biloba, garlic, and ginger, which the midwife had prescribed to prevent blood clots. It turns out these herbs also prolong bleeding. The doctor said that that was what had most likely caused the hemorrhaging."

Jared turned haunted, shadowed eyes on Erica. "He said that people think that because they're taking natural herbs they're doing something healthy when in fact they could be doing something lethal to themselves. He said it's a growing problem as more and more people are taking herbal supplements, and it has now become a routine question for surgeons to ask their patients preoperatively, because certain herbs cause bleeding problems, and that if Netsuya had gone to a licensed physician, she would have been warned about this. She and the baby would not have—" He turned away, and for a moment Erica thought he was going to dash his glass against the wall.

Now she understood his nightly appointment with swords, his ordained rendezvous with sharp blades and points. Of course he would wear padding and a face mask and the swords would be blunt, but that didn't matter. It was the fight itself that was needed, cutting the air with his fury and grief, slaying his demons over and over in an endlessly repetitive dance of guilt and anger and self-recrimination.

"Dear God," his voice broke. "I killed them—"

She took a step toward him. "You didn't. Jared, it wasn't your fault."

He spun around. "It was! I should have intervened. He was my child, too. He deserved the best medical care. Instead I left him at the mercy of ignorance and superstition."

Erica searched for words, desperate to help. "Netsuya was educated, she knew the facts, and that was what she chose. You did the right thing in respecting her wishes."

Jared looked into his scotch, fist clenching the glass as if to crush it. "I have nightmares," he said quietly, "I'm running, trying to get somewhere, always arriving too late. I wake up in cold sweats."

They fell silent then, listening to the rain. Erica's emotions were raw, as if they had been peeled and left exposed to the elements. She didn't know what to feel. Jared and his pain, his guilt. And her own demon, hunched malevolently behind her heart. She wanted to comfort Jared, ached for him, wanted to feel his arms around her, his mouth on hers.

"In three years I haven't discussed this with a soul," he said. "You're the first."

Erica wanted to comfort him but didn't know how. Foster mothers telling her to stop crying because she wasn't the only person with troubles, teachers telling her that if she stood up for herself the kids wouldn't tease her, social workers accusing her of whining and sniveling. If Erica had ever been comforted by someone, she couldn't remember. Perhaps in the hippie commune, when her mother still loved her. Children needed to be taught how to comfort, just as they were taught how to love and hate. They needed to be let in on the secrets of these skills.

"Well," Jared said, suddenly aware of his empty glass. "I've kept you too long." A ragged sigh. "I hadn't intended to tell you my life story."

Erica realized in horror what she had done. She had hesitated. *That* was the secret to comforting someone—you did it without thinking, you didn't stand there wondering what to do next. She wanted a second chance. She wanted to roll the clock back a mere minute, back to when he said, "You're the first," and then go to him, slide her arms around him, press her warmth to him and let him know that someone cared.

Instead the moment had stretched too long, it became cold and hollow, Jared with his back to her now, his hand reaching for the scotch bottle. "I'd better go," she said, putting her glass down. "I left my windows open."

She waited.

And then she let herself out into the rainy night.

✳

By the time Erica changed out of her evening clothes and into comfortable sweats, the storm had increased, creating a muffled roar inside her tent.

She pictured the grunion hunters running for their cars—and the fish riding the waves as they had done for thousands of years, unthreatened by capture. Then she turned her attention to the object on her worktable, the astonishing find from Level IV that afternoon.

At the time of discovery, she had been overwhelmed by it, her mind centering on the object like a dog on a bone. But now she almost wondered what the thing was and why she had attached so much importance to it. All she could think of was Jared.

She forced herself to address the task at hand. It was what she had done all her life, it was what kept her from drowning in her own pain. *Don't think of the demon that haunts you and it won't exist.* "The hair is black with no signs of gray," she dictated into her recorder in a voice that sounded a little too loud, "plaited into a fourteen-inch braid which appears to have been cut off at the nape of the neck. I am surmising that it is a woman's braid." Using tweezers she plucked out what looked like a pink flake. "The braid appears to have been buried with petals," she said, turning the brittle flake over in the light, examining it under a magnifying glass. "Bougainvillea," she pronounced after a moment.

She swallowed hard. The heaviness in her chest was still there, like a sinister black-feathered creature that had been waiting for her in the shadows beyond the Dimarco pool deck, watching for a moment of weakness when Erica's guard was down and it could fly in and take roost inside her rib cage.

"As the bougainvillea plant wasn't introduced into California until after 1769, and since the braid was found at a lower level than where we found the American one-cent coin, but at a higher level than where we found the tin crucifix, whatever strange ritual took place in the cave involving the severing of the braid happened between 1781 and 1814." She paused, her eyes went out of focus, her hands froze over the specimen, and she thought, *We're coming closer in time.*

She picked up the braid in both hands, felt the heavy hair in her fingers, tresses that had once crowned a young woman's head, and she wondered why such a brutal act had been committed—for surely shearing off a woman's hair in a century when all women wore their hair long had to have been a punishment, or an act of discipline or humiliation. The victim wasn't American, Erica knew that for certain. Not at the level where the braid had been found. So she had been a Spanish lady who had been dragged to the cave by morally outraged brothers, where they had cut off her hair for soiling the family honor. Or perhaps they were the Mexican sisters of a young man who had committed suicide when she scorned his love. Or had she been a martyr in a forgotten Indian sacrifice?

Erica closed her eyes and felt tears run down her cheeks. This hair had once lain warm upon a woman's back, had bounced when she ran, flown free in the wind; had been brushed, washed, caressed, perhaps kissed. And finally, lovingly braided with bougainvillea petals to be hacked off in a savage act.

Pressing the braid to her chest, she thought of Jared lifting the curl off her neck and tucking it back into its rhinestone clip. Such an intimate gesture, powerful in the responses it evoked. Pain suddenly washed over Erica like a tide of cold, hard grief. A sob escaped her lips. The heaviness expanded inside her chest. She pictured Jared alone on the island, running from his rescuers, wanting to be left alone. And earlier, in a mad drive to the hospital, guilt and fear stabbing him like swords. *"It was preventable . . ."*

And suddenly she knew what it was, the thing roosting behind her heart like a malevolent hobgoblin. It was reality. Jared's. And her own. Now she knew why she had been thinking about him lately. It was because of his aloneness.

We all need someone to watch over us, but not all of us are so lucky as to have someone. Me. Jared. The Lady in the cave. We are alone and vulnerable to those who would attack us.

She suddenly wanted to protect Jared from the Ginny Dimarcos of the world, just as she was protecting the Lady from vandals. But she had no idea where to even begin.

Chapter Ten

LUISA
1792 C.E.

They were going to run away. Doña Luisa and her daughter, Angela.

Except that Angela didn't know it. Nor did Captain Lorenzo, Luisa's husband. Neither did the padres at the mission nor the other colonists living in and around the village of Los Angeles. Luisa alone harbored the secret, and she planned to keep it thus until she and Angela had reached Madrid in Spain. Once there, they would stay, never to return to Alta California and their life of bondage there.

It occurred to Luisa that people might consider what she was planning a sin because she was deserting her husband. But this was not so. She intended to write to Lorenzo once she reached Spain and ask him to join her there. If he refused, then the sin would be upon him for deserting his wife and child.

And anyway, the Blessed Mother, who saw into everyone's heart, would see that Luisa was doing the right thing. That was all that mattered.

She was in her garden harvesting botanical herbs, and because the sea voyage was going to be long and perilous, she was gathering more than her usual amount of opium. The medicine was for Angela.

The sixteen-year-old girl had suffered from debilitating headaches and fainting spells ever since the day Lorenzo had brought her, a foundling, out of the mountains. The opium was not so much to ease the pain during the spells as to keep her from talking. The first time Angela was stricken, she had cried out suddenly, clutched her head, and fainted. In a strange delirium that alarmed her new parents, the little girl had screamed, "They are on fire! They are burning up!" And then she had cried hysterically. When she awoke later, Angela had no memory of the incident and Luisa had dismissed it as a bad dream. But when a fire broke out in the Saint Monica Mountains that evening, and had raged for seven hellish days until it was extinguished by a summer storm—and it was later learned that several Indio families had perished in the inferno—Luisa had looked at her adopted child in alarm. Because Angela had been wearing Mission clothing and spoken Spanish when Lorenzo found her, Luisa had assumed she was a baptized Christian. But all the holy water in the world, Luisa knew, could not wash away a person's race. If the child was Indio, then might not there be accusations of witchcraft should her gift of prophecy be known? Although witches were no longer burned in Spain, who knew what the Mission Fathers, who had a penchant for severely punishing their Indios, would do? So Luisa had begun to keep a supply of opium on hand to sedate the girl whenever she had a spell. As a consequence, although the headaches still came, there had thankfully been no more prophetic utterances.

Luisa paused in her garden of bright pink poppies and, laying a hand on her lower back, stretched. Stiffness in her joints reminded her that she had recently celebrated her fortieth birthday—her nineteenth year away from Spain. Luisa had gone with her family to Mexico City in 1773, when she was twenty-one. Her father had been appointed Professor of Sciences at the University of Mexico, a very prestigious post, and because her uncle also happened to be the Viceroy of New Spain, and another uncle the *alcalde* of Guadalajara, Luisa had enjoyed the privileged life of the upper class. Less than a year later she met the dashing and handsome Captain Lorenzo, married him, and gave birth to their first child. Luisa had thought her life was perfect.

And then they had left New Spain to come north to follow an insane dream and had buried their daughter along the way. That was when Luisa had begun planning her escape from this godforsaken colony. Now, eleven years later, her dream was about to come true.

She had had to obtain Lorenzo's permission to travel, and he had at first refused to grant it. Who would run his household while she was away? Who would supervise the Indian women and make sure he and his men got fed? Luisa had told Lorenzo he could choose from among the women, one he trusted, even hinting that he could bring such a woman into the house, because Luisa knew Lorenzo had Indian mistresses. Luisa had then sought the support of Father Xavier, offering to bring back rosaries and prayer books, and saying that she would be happy to carry objects from the mission to be blessed by the bishop in Compostella, where the bones of blessed St. James were buried. But it was when she promised Lorenzo that she would bring back money from her brother and cousins in Madrid to invest in Lorenzo's rancho that he had finally consented. Next had been the problem of finding a ship captain who would take two female passengers. The master of the *Estrella* had agreed only when he heard the price Luisa was willing to pay. So Luisa and her daughter now had written permission to travel, they had paid for their passage, and tomorrow they would set sail on the *Estrella*, currently anchored off the Palos Verdes peninsula.

As Luisa turned to the next row of poppies, she saw Angela on her silver-gray Arabian, Sirocco, galloping across the fields, her black hair streaming back. Wearing a divided skirt so that she could ride like a man instead of sidesaddle, she rode with her arms around the stallion's neck, her flying black hair mingling with his silver mane. Angela and Sirocco were inseparable. Every day at daybreak, before her morning chocolate, Angela would saddle up the horse and ride into the rising sun. Together they would gallop, horse and girl, for an hour before coming back, breathless and elated, Sirocco to his stall, Angela to her breakfast and lessons with her tutor. When informed of the impending journey to Spain, Angela had asked if they could take Sirocco with them. But Luisa had explained that such a journey would be unpleasant and possibly harmful to the horse, and had assured Angela that he would be well taken care of while they were gone. It pained Luisa to know that her daughter would never see her beloved horse again, but the sacrifice was worth their freedom. In Madrid, she would offer her daughter the choice of any horse, hoping that in time she would forget Sirocco.

Luisa watched Angela finally bring the horse into the compound and dismount, handing him over to a groom. As Angela walked toward the house, tall and willowy, carrying herself with dignity and grace, Luisa thought what a beautiful young girl she was. Well educated, too, in reading and writing, and history and even basic mathematics. But Angela was innocent about the ways of the world. Perhaps too innocent, Luisa thought in concern. The power of the Mission Fathers was strong in the colony, and their dictum that women should be submissive and sequestered in the home was followed by most families. As a result, Angela had rarely ventured from her father's land. Except for visits to the Mission to attend Mass on holy days and brief rides through the small village of Angeles, Angela knew a world that was restricted to four thousand acres.

Luisa wanted more for her daughter. The Angeles Pueblo consisted of a mere thirty adobe buildings surrounded by a wall. Angela had never seen a city, or cathedrals and palaces, universities and hospitals, fountains and monuments, or crowded narrow streets that opened suddenly upon sunny plazas. And people everywhere, in the marketplaces and on the roads! Here, one could ride for miles and not encounter a soul. Well, Indios roaming about, but that wasn't the same thing.

Luisa wanted Angela to have experience, culture, knowledge of independence, and free will, and power in her own right and not just through a husband. Such was not possible in this backwater colony where, in Luisa's opinion, the padres wielded too much power.

Look what happened to Eulalia Callis, wife of Governor Fages, who had publicly accused her husband of infidelity. Fages denied it, and when

Callis continued in her accusation against the advice of her priest, she was arrested and locked in a guarded room at Mission San Carlos for months. While she was a prisoner there, Father de Noriega condemned her from his pulpit and repeatedly threatened to punish her with shackles, flogging, and excommunication. Although the rest of the colonists denounced the woman for scandalizing her husband's good name, Luisa had privately believed Callis's petition for divorce was a strategy for survival. Pregnant four times in six years, Eulalia first gave birth to a son, miscarried a year later, made the perilous journey to California while pregnant again, fell seriously ill after the birth of her daughter, and buried a baby only eight days old just a year later. Luisa knew what had prompted the woman's drastic action: Eulalia Callis had hoped to be allowed to return to Mexico and thus ensure her own survival and that of her two remaining children.

In Alta California a woman did not have sovereignty over her own person. Both civil and church law gave male family members authority over a woman's sexuality. Apolinaria del Carmen, a widow on a neighboring rancho, had been nearly beaten to death by her son when he found her in bed with one of her Indian *caballeros*. Apolinaria was ostracized by the colonists and excommunicated from the church; her son inherited the rancho when she died a year later.

And then there was the sad tale of Maria Teresa de Vaca, betrothed on the day she was born to a man named Dominguez, a soldier serving escort duty at the San Luis Mission. On the day she turned fourteen, Maria was forced to wed Dominguez, by then a man of nearly fifty and almost toothless! It was the talk of the Pueblo how the poor girl ran away three times until, beaten at last into submission, she resigned herself to her fate and was now pregnant with their fourth child.

Luisa vowed that these fates were not to be for Angela. The Blessed Mother did not intend for Her daughters to be sold and owned like cattle.

Angela entered the garden, shining black hair tumbling over her shoulders and down her back, her eyes bright with the excitement of having just ridden Sirocco. "Good morning, Mamá! Look!" She was carrying a basket of the first of the jicama she had been growing. A tuberous root with the texture of a potato and the flavor of a sweet water chestnut, the large turnip-shaped vegetables were produced on underground stems of vines bearing beautiful white or purple flowers. Angela had planted the seeds six months earlier and was clearly proud of her first harvest. As Luisa took the basket, she decided she would serve the jicama raw with lemon, chili powder, and salt—a popular snack back in Mexico City.

"And I found the perfect spot to plant my new orchard, Mamá. I hope Papá will let me have it. It's only a few acres, down by the marshes."

Luisa had no idea where this notion of Angela's had come from, to plant fruit trees on the rancho. The Mission Fathers were introducing oranges to Alta California, and Angela seemed quite taken with the idea of covering Rancho Paloma with orchards. There were a lot of things, mysterious things, about her daughter that she didn't understand. Such as the inexplicable restlessness that came over her every autumn. Angela would ride for hours on Sirocco, not talking to a soul, just galloping as if to fly off the ends of the earth. And then she would suddenly stand very still and stare off in the direction of the mountains. These strange actions usually coincided with the time of the Indians' annual acorn harvest. They would be seen for days tramping along the Old Road, coming from villages far away, carrying babies and all their worldly goods, a strange, savage parade.

"By the way, Mamá, I encountered Father Ignacio. He asked if we could bring back paper for him. And books to write in."

Everyone was asking for something from home. In this remote outpost, where it sometimes took a year to receive supplies, the people tried to manufacture needful items such as candles, shoes, blankets, wine. But they couldn't make paper. Or silk. Or objects made of silver and gold. Some of the colonists had given Luisa letters to take home, and gifts for families in Spain.

Angela gratefully accepted her morning cup of hot chocolate from an Indian servant and, after taking a sip, said, "Oh Mamá, a flock of seagulls appeared in the sky from out of nowhere! They circled overhead, making a great noise. And after I had watched them for a moment, they all turned as a body and flew westward to the ocean. It is an omen that our journey is going to be a safe one, I am sure of it, Mamá!" Luisa felt a sudden pang of fear. If Lorenzo found out she was planning never to return, he would lock her away for the rest of her life. She prayed that Angela's seagulls were indeed a good omen; however, she didn't trust solely in signs or portents but relied also upon prayers for the intercession of saints and the Blessed Mother.

When Angela slipped into the house to finish her breakfast, Luisa returned to her work, feeling the benevolent California sun warm on her back. These were special poppies, grown from imported seeds since the poppies native to Alta California did not produce opium. Luisa cultivated them with great care, always planting after the autumn equinox, feeding the young plants with plenty of water and manure, pinching back the first flower stalks so that many buds flowered instead of just one. And then she inspected them daily since it was vital to begin milking the seedpods at precisely the moment when the gray band where the petals had been turned dark. Luisa always began the milking in the morning, incising the pods with a sharp knife and then returning the next day to scrape off the white ooze and leave it in the sun to dry.

The secret to a plentiful opium harvest lay in the precise incising of the capsule: cut too deeply, and the plant quickly died, but cut just sufficiently, and the plant could continue to manufacture milk for another two months. Doña Luisa of Rancho Paloma was known for having the most delicate touch in the Los Angeles Pueblo. Her laudanum—a tincture of alcohol and opium—was in constant demand.

As she gently scooped the sticky white substance off the seedpods and deposited it in a small leather bag, she thought about how back home in Madrid if a person needed something for pain, he or she would simply go to the neighborhood apothecary. But there were no apothecaries in this distant outpost of the Spanish empire. Medicinal supplies had once come up from Mexico along the overland route from Sonora, but the bloody uprising of the Yuma Indios on the Colorado River, eleven years ago, had closed the land route. And since foreign ships were not allowed near the California coast, the colonists were forced to rely upon the occasional, undependable supply ship from Mexico. So they turned to their own gardens for remedies. Some secretly visited Indio shamans and healers, but many came to the home of Doña Luisa, where her solarium was always well supplied with fresh herbs, ointments, salves, tinctures.

As she neared the end of her morning labors, having also harvested pennywort stems to go into wound ointments and henbane leaves for rheumatism poultices, Luisa saw men arriving on horseback from the direction of the Old Road. A cloud crossed the face of the sun, briefly casting the landscape in shadow and sending a ripple of fear through Luisa's bones. She knew why the men had come.

Lorenzo did very little work around the rancho. Most of the rustling and herding was done by Indios trained to be *vaqueros*, leaving Lorenzo and his friends to spend their days gambling, hunting, and lounging in the sun. But the men arriving today had come not to roll dice or to hunt deer, but to bargain with Lorenzo for possession of his daughter.

Angela was a prize to be fought over.

As word of Los Angeles spread south toward the lower Mexican provinces, more settlers were coming to the Pueblo in search of a better life. The problem, however, was most of the newcomers were unmarried men. The governor, anxious to tame this wild frontier by providing wives for the men, had sent several desperate requests to the Viceroy of Mexico to send *doncellas*—"healthy maidens"—to California, but with no success. Then he asked simply for "a hundred women." When this produced no results, the governor resorted to accepting foundlings—orphaned girls— who were rounded up in Mexico and brought to California, where they were distributed among families.

These men today, whom Lorenzo was welcoming with happy shouts and cups of wine, wanted Angela not so much because she was available or beautiful, but because she was *hispana*. By marrying a woman of pure Spanish blood a man of mixed blood could apply for an official decree of *legitimidad y limpieza de sangre*—"legitimacy and purity of blood"—for his children, a decree certifying that the bloodline was untainted by Jewish, African, or any other non-Christian blood, thus assuring them of prominence and high social standing in the colony.

No one knew the truth: that Angela wasn't *hispana* at all, but Indio. Luisa's "gift from God."

Luisa remembered the day, the hour, when Lorenzo brought the angel home. Luisa's knees had been raw from kneeling in prayer to the Blessed Virgin. Her child, buried in the Sonoran desert, was gone but her love was not. She had needed an outlet for her maternal love. Luisa hadn't even had the comfort of a grave to visit, to tend and weed and nurture, no headstone upon which to lay flowers, no gentle mound of grass to go to when the soul needed solace. Lorenzo, being a man and having his duties, filled his hours with work. Luisa had only Selena's little dresses that would never be worn again. As she spoke her vow to the Blessed Mother—*help me to have another child and I shall devote myself to good works in thy name*—there was Lorenzo with a child in his arms. The girl was crying, "Mama! Mama!" And as soon as she put her arms around the child, Luisa felt the dammed-up love flow from her heart like a cleansing brook. She knew that this was Blessed Mary's answer to her prayers, and while she would always grieve for the little one buried in the desert, Luisa would love this angel with all her heart and devote her life to good works as she had promised.

No one had questioned the sudden appearance of a child in Captain Lorenzo's small adobe house. Everyone in the colony was too busy trying to survive to wonder about the private affairs of others. If people remarked upon Angela's dusky coloring—Luisa being fair-skinned—Luisa simply said that the girl favored Lorenzo's mother, who was olive-complected. Luisa did not consider this lie a sin because she believed it to hold a kernel of truth. Luisa secretly believed Angela wasn't a full-blooded Indio. While the girl did bear a resemblance to the natives who lived at the Mission, her skin was lighter and her face wasn't as round. Luisa wondered if perhaps the child was the offspring of a Spanish soldier.

The voices of Lorenzo's visitors drifted on the breeze and swirled around the garden where Luisa toiled. She held these men in contempt. Arrogant braggarts, and yet not a drop of pure racial blood ran in their veins.

Luisa was a highborn Spanish lady who had been raised in a country where the lines of social class were clearly drawn: there was the noble class, the wealthy merchant class, and the peasants. Rarely did they mingle. Bloodline meant everything. Even in New Spain, where the Spanish had ruled a bare two hundred years since conquering the native populations, strict racial boundaries were maintained. The new aristocracy in Mexico were the *peninsulares*—whites born in Spain—which caused resentment among the whites born in Mexico—the *criollos*. Only *peninsulares* could be addressed as Don and Doña, and they did not marry outside their class. Next came the *mestizos*, those of mixed Spanish and Indian descent—a large, amorphous class of people who were shopkeepers, artisans, servants. Comprising the lowest social stratum were the *indígenas*—the native Indios—used mainly for hard labor. So strict were the rules of race and class that an *indígena* caught wearing European clothing was punished by the lash. Luisa, being a *peninsulara*, had been very comfortable with Mexico's class structure.

But in Alta California there were no clearly drawn social lines. Nearly everyone here was of some sort of racial mix, with very few white Europeans. It was hard to know one's station. Although Doña Luisa had no doubts about her and Lorenzo's place in this frontier society, there were wealthy rancheros of Indian and Spanish mix who had been peasants in Mexico! It was like a soup in which all the bloods were being stirred. It troubled her sense of class. Lorenzo, as a *patrón* with five hundred head of cattle, a member of the Spanish aristocracy, *and* a retired military officer, was treated with respect. But in the insanity of the frontier mind, the same respect was accorded to Antonio Castillo, a man of Mexican and African blood, married to a local Indian woman, simply because he was the blacksmith at the Pueblo! Here a person's occupation counted as more important than his ancestry, which to Doña Luisa was backward thinking and unhealthy for a young society.

Feeling her fears prick her anew at the sight of Lorenzo's visitors—her flight from California was less than twenty hours away—Luisa left the garden and delivered herself into the coolness of the solarium, where she kept her vast store of herbs and medicines.

Her home was not as grand as Lorenzo had promised a decade ago, but sufficient to reflect their higher station. Made of adobe with a thatched roof, the structure consisted of four sleeping chambers, a dining room, a hall for entertaining visitors, and a massive kitchen that fed not only the captain and his wife and daughter, but the Indian women who laundered and sewed and cooked and made candles, and their husbands the *vaqueros* and *caballeros*.

Men and their empty promises, Luisa thought contemptuously as she sorted leaves from stems and separated them into storage baskets. Not only had Lorenzo not given her the grand house he had promised, but the struggling pueblo was not conforming to Governor Neve's original vision. Here was an opportunity, he had declared at the dedication ceremony eleven years ago, to plan a city unlike any in Europe, for it would be a planned city before the first inhabitant even took up residence. He had drawn up a blueprint for the Pueblo, showing the layout of plaza, fields, pastures, and royal lands. There would be no unfettered growth for the Los Angeles Pueblo, Neve had promised. And yet already new arrivals were building where they pleased! Luisa could see the sprawl this homely town would someday be.

As she laid the opium out to dry—later it would be rolled into a sticky black ball and stored in a leather case—Luisa examined her conscience once again and found no reason to feel guilty about running away. Hadn't she fulfilled her promised to the Blessed Virgin?

Luisa was proud of the number of Indian women she had converted to Christianity. They attended chapel every Sunday, dressed modestly, and when one wished to marry, the prospective husband was required to convert. Because she was a fair and generous mistress, most of her servants were loyal. Many even emulated her. Doña Luisa wore her long black hair in a braid pinned in a coil at the back of her head, covering it with a small mantilla of black Spanish lace which she removed only at bedtime. And so her servants covered their hair with scarves. They recited the rosary and named their daughters Maria and Luisa. Only rarely did one run away back to an Indian village and the old life. More and more camps were springing up on the ranchos, built by Indios who had left their native life to work for the colonists, becoming expert horsemen, cattle wranglers, silversmiths, and carpenters. With beef provided at every supper, they saw no need to make the annual trek into the mountains to gather acorns. A few still went, to hear the stories and to arrange marriages, but the gatherings in the forests were growing smaller each year. The five-day festival that for generations had been held in honor of Chinigchinich, the Creator, was being replaced by Christmas holidays and the Feast of Santiago, patron saint of Spain.

The solarium was filled with baskets made by Luisa's Indian women.

Some were quite exquisite and supposedly the patterns told stories. The women who wove the baskets had cheerfully told these myths to Luisa—explaining to the Señora how the world was created and how Grandfather Tortoise caused earthquakes. Little Angela had told the same stories at first, about coyotes and tortoises and a First Mother who came out of the east to start a new tribe, but Doña Luisa had replaced these heathen tales in Angela's mind with Christian stories and Spanish fairy tales: the story of two sisters, Elena and Rosa, who lived in the Kingdom of Sapphires and how they were transformed by their godmother, the Fairy of Happiness; the tale of young Gonzalito, who, with the help of magical animals, saved a princess and her kingdom from a wicked dwarf; and the adventure story of four princes on a quest for the hand of Princess Aurora. Stories Luisa herself had grown up with and which now were Angela's.

She looked through the open window and saw that Lorenzo and his guests were still drinking in the shade of the rose arbor. One man, a head taller than the rest, caught her attention: Juan Navarro. Luisa didn't like him. There was something strange about his eyes. They lacked warmth, making Luisa think of the eyes of a cold sea creature. And his smile was not so much a natural smile as a drawing back of his lips to bare his teeth. Rumor had it that Navarro was in Alta California fleeing the Inquisition, who had brought him up on charges of reading forbidden books. He made his living off the dead. Navarro had plundered the tombs of the Aztecs and found fortunes in gold, silver, turquoise, and jade. Granted, they were heathen tombs he robbed so no desecration had taken place. Nonetheless, it seemed ghoulish to Luisa to take a ring from a corpse and wear it on one's own hand. She knew what his ambition in California was: Navarro was a man of low birth who wanted to marry into aristocracy.

Fear stabbed her again, and she quickly suppressed it. Let Navarro ask Lorenzo for Angela's hand. Luisa wasn't worried. She would readily agree to the betrothal—on the condition that the wedding take place *after* their return from Spain.

Leaving the solarium, Luisa made her way through the house where women were polishing furniture and scrubbing tile floors, and delivered herself into her private chambers, where trunks stood packed and ready for the journey. This was Luisa's private sanctum, where Lorenzo had not set foot since the house was built. He kept to his own quarters at night, seeing his wife and daughter only at the evening meal. Luisa knew he would not miss her for long. Perhaps at first he would feel outrage when he realized she was never coming back, but then his fellows would come over for a game of dice, the wine would flow, and the two females who had once taken up space in this house would eventually be forgotten. Lorenzo would not be without consolation. Luisa not only knew about his Indian mistresses, she knew about his Indian bastards as well.

Sitting at her dressing table, Luisa raised the lid of a small wooden box and lifted up the velvet lining. Under it was a brass key. As she held the key in her palm, curling her fingers around it, she felt fresh hope flow from the metal into her flesh. The key was to a small casket which was currently in the safekeeping of Father Xavier.

The secret cache had begun by accident, ten years ago, when Antonio Castillo, the blacksmith, had ridden frantically from the Pueblo to tell Luisa that his child was ill with fever and they needed the señora's help. With special herbs Luisa had brought the child back from the brink of death and Señora Castillo had been so overjoyed she had insisted upon giving Luisa a gold ring as a token of the family's gratitude. Luisa had tried to refuse but the ring was pressed upon her, and her acceptance of it sent the señora away a happier person. And then when Luisa had helped a young wife through a perilous childbirth with potions she had learned from an old Indian woman, the grateful husband had humbly offered Luisa the gift of a small silver brooch. After a while, Luisa stopped refusing. She didn't see why one could not do good works in the name of the Blessed Mother *and* receive payment as well. Did not the Mission Fathers pass the collection plate during Mass?

Lorenzo did not know about Luisa's secret cache. When she had collected the first few valuable items, she had feared he would find them and gamble them away. With the colonists and soldiers Lorenzo played cards and dice, and with the Indians, the wager could be on the number of fingers a player was holding up behind his back. Lorenzo would even lounge with his fellow rancheros under a tree, watching *El Camino Viejo*, and they would wager on the color of the next horse that would come trotting by. So Luisa had taken her little casket of treasures to Father Xavier at the Mission and entrusted it to his care. Over the months and years, whenever Lorenzo was away gambling or hunting, Luisa would pay a visit to the Mission and deposit the latest with Father Xavier, as if he were a banker. There was coinage in the casket, too: silver pieces of eight, Mexican pesos, Spanish *reales* and even some gold doubloons. A king's ransom.

It was all to go to her daughter. Angela was to be independent even should she marry. If Luisa had had the money when their daughter died in the Sonoran desert, she would have turned around and gone back to Mexico. But she had been dependent on Lorenzo. This was not to be so for Angela. She was going to give it all to Angela in Madrid, where she planned to have legal documents drawn up stating that Angela's husband, whoever he might someday be, could not touch the money.

When she heard a knock at her door, she quickly restored the key to its hiding place, returned the box to its drawer, then bid the person to enter.

To her astonishment, it was Lorenzo. And she could tell, even though he stood across the room, that he had been drinking. She clasped her hands tightly in her lap. With less than a day to go, she dared not risk ruining their plans now. But when she saw his eyes roving over the trunks filled with clothes and gifts for family back home, her heart leapt. He had changed his mind!

She kept her back ramrod straight. It didn't matter if he had found out about her plan to stay in Spain. Lorenzo never woke before noon. She and Angela would slip out before dawn and make their way to the coast. . . .

"Perhaps things have not been right between us," he said in a thick voice, as if unused to speaking to her, "certainly not the way of husband and wife, but I have loved you, Luisa. *Dios mio*, I have loved you."

Although there was gray in his hair and his skin was sun-weathered, Lorenzo was still a handsome man with military bearing. But he did not move her as he once had, back in Mexico when they were young and in love. The day they buried their daughter, Luisa had closed her body to him. And when, eleven years ago, she had prayed to the Virgin for another child, she had been praying for a miracle, for even then, even for the sake of having another baby, Luisa would not allow Lorenzo into her bed. Instead, the Virgin had delivered a grown child to Luisa, sparing her the indignity of having to suffer a man's intimate embrace and the pains of childbirth.

She remained silent. He was speaking like a man about to make a confession. She braced herself for it.

"You cannot go to Spain."

She remained calm. "The *Estrella* is not sailing?"

"The *Estrella* will sail, you will not."

"I do not understand."

"We haven't the money for the passage."

"But I have already paid Captain Rodriguez."

"I took it back."

She blinked at him. "You took it back?"

"The money was owed to other men. As well as a great deal more." Lorenzo shifted uncomfortably, feeling out of place in this room filled with flowers and colorful rugs and small portraits of saints. "I've had a run of bad luck. Debts I owed. And there was a ship I heavily invested in. Loaded with furs, bound to China to trade for spice, but it sank off the Philippines." He paused, looking everywhere but at his wife.

"All of our money is gone?" she asked, trying to keep the fury out of her voice. The fool! What right had he to squander their fortune? But Luisa kept her head. She must not get angry. Humor him. Stall him. Anything, until she and Angela could get to the *Estrella*. "Then we shall sell something."

He hung his head. "We have nothing to sell."

"But we own much, Lorenzo," she said softly, spreading her hands to encompass the beautiful furniture, the bedding, the silver and hangings.

"Wife, you don't even own the buttons on that dress." There was no rancor or impatience or anger in his voice. He was merely stating a fact, as if commenting on the weather.

She looked down at the pearl buttons on her bodice. She lifted a perplexed look to him. "How can you have lost everything?"

"I did and that is all there is to it. I've tried my best."

She saw defeat in his eyes, bewilderment and disillusionment. Where was her brave military captain who had promised her so much? Had he also gambled away his pride? "We have lost . . . *even the rancho?*" she whispered.

He brightened. "That is the beauty of it, Luisa! I have arranged with a man of means to erase my debt. In return, he will hold title to the rancho and everything in it, but we shall continue to live here!"

She frowned. "But how? He pays your debts and you give him our home. Why should he allow us to live here?"

"Because . . . I have given him Angela as well. As a bride."

Luisa sat stock-still.

"You will both thank me for it later," he added quickly. "Times are dangerous in Europe what with revolution fever burning like a brushfire. Peasants lopping off the heads of kings. Best you and the girl stay here where it is safe."

"Who," she began, but already knowing in her heart and with terrible dread the name of the man, for there was only one man in the Angeles Pueblo who had that much money. "Who is to marry my daughter?"

"Navarro."

She closed her eyes and crossed herself. "*Santa Maria,*" she whispered. The man who robbed the dead.

"I am sorry, but this is how it is to be."

She thought about this, then slowly nodded. "So be it. Angela will marry Navarro. *After* we return from Spain."

"But I have already explained that you cannot go. We haven't the money for your passage."

"I have money of my own," she said, prepared for his look of surprise, feeling also a moment of triumph. But then the moment stretched on, and there was something in Lorenzo's eyes, and suddenly a jolt of panic shot through her. "What is it?" she demanded.

He sighed raggedly. Lorenzo suddenly felt every single day of his fifty years. "That money is gone, too."

She tipped her chin. "You do not know what money I speak of."

"By God, I do," he said, some of his pride returning, a flush of indignation in his cheeks. "The day you sought to enlist Father Xavier into your secret scheme he came to me and told me. I have known these eleven years."

She stared at him in shock. The casket! "He had no right to tell you!"

"He had every right!" he boomed. "You are my wife, by God, and everything you own belongs to me. It is all gone," he added more quietly, suddenly uncomfortable beneath her gaze. "I took the gold from you long ago, wife, and that is the end of it. We shall speak no more of this."

Luisa shot to her feet. "I will not let you have Angela!"

"Woman, have you forgotten?" he bellowed. "Angela is mine! I found her! Therefore, I can do with her as I please!"

As he stormed out, slamming the door behind him, Luisa's mind raged with panic as she tried to think of solutions. She and Angela must escape. But they had no money! No ship captain would aid them. If they tried to run to another town, they would be found and brought back.

Suddenly she was thinking of Angela's newly harvested jicama and how extremely poisonous its seeds were. It would be so simple. Steep the seeds in water to extract the toxin, and then add it to Lorenzo's evening wine. By morning she would be free.

Just as quickly, the nefarious thought fled. She could never murder Lorenzo.

Her shoulders slumped as she saw how utterly without power she was. And then she realized in the next instant the horrible mistake she had made in rejecting Lorenzo, years ago, punishing him for bringing her to this remote place. She saw the past eleven years in the snap of two fingers and she knew that if she could somehow go back she would forgive him, she would take him into her arms and give him more children, making him a doting husband and father who would think first of his family instead of his precious games of chance and investments in ships that sank.

But Luisa knew there was no going back. No escape. No prayers to the Virgin that were going to save her now. And she had no one to blame but herself.

Moving woodenly, Luisa once again brought the small box out of its drawer, but this time she wasn't interested in the lining and the useless key hidden there. Now she lifted out the object she had placed in the box eleven years ago.

It had been around Angela's neck when Lorenzo found her in the mountains, a small black stone wrapped in soft deerskin. Luisa had not been able to bring herself to throw it away. Perhaps she had known that someday it would remind her of the truth—that Angela *wasn't* her daughter, that she belonged to another woman.

All these years Luisa had somehow managed to put it from her mind that Angela was a Mission Indio. But this stone reminded her now. And this stone must have had some value or importance for the mother to place it around her daughter's neck. For the first time, in the sharp noon of this land that Luisa had never come to love or feel part of, she wondered about the mother of that child. Why had they been in the mountains? Why did the mother never go back to the Mission to look for her daughter? Was the mother dead or had she been mourning these past eleven years, the way Luisa had mourned for the child buried in a small grave in the desert?

Luisa tried to picture the woman who gave birth to Angela. Although many Indian women worked at Rancho Paloma, Luisa never really *looked* at them. And whenever she went riding and sometimes encountered a small village of unbaptized Indios, walking about naked and smoking their peculiar pipes, she had thought they were creatures barely a step above dumb animals.

But animals do not hang protective talismans around their daughters' necks.

Blessed Mother of God, her heart cried out. Did I commit a wrong in taking another woman's child? Lorenzo brought the girl to me when I was out of my mind with grief, and my knees were raw from hours of kneeling in prayer, and I saw the child as a gift from You. But was she really? Was she in fact a test of my strength and my honesty and I failed?

God forgive me for what I have done! I forsook my marriage vows and turned my husband from me. I stole another woman's child. This is my punishment. Angela must marry Navarro and I shall never see Spain again.

✳

Captain Lorenzo galloped away down El Camino Viejo, anxious to put distance between him and the look in Luisa's eyes. Did she think it was so easy, turning a wasteland into a profitable ranch? It was a lot of damned hard work. Never mind the searing summers and the rains that flooded the basin, and fires that raged out of control, and diseases that swept through his cattle, and crops that died, there were the wild Indios to contend with! First there was their tradition of gathering annually at the tar pits that Lorenzo had had to contend with. They had set up a massive encampment right where Lorenzo had planted corn. The destruction to his crop that first year had made him mad enough to want to wipe out the whole savage lot of them. He put up fences and the Indios would tear them down. They would come tramping for miles along the Old Road, which ran along the north border of his property, build their shelters out of branches ripped from his trees, and help themselves to lambs and goats from his herds. The Indios couldn't be made to understand that this was *his* land now and that the animals they killed and ate weren't wild but belonged to *him*.

Then there were their nightly raids on the cattle, not for food but out of rebellion. The padres weren't converting and absorbing the native population fast enough; there were still pockets of resistance among the unbaptized Indios, strong leaders who tried now and then to organize a major revolt against the colonists. One had even been led by a woman! A young one at that, of the Gabrielino tribe, inciting the chiefs and warriors of six villages to revolt against the soldiers and the Mission Fathers. So Lorenzo and other rancheros were forced to hire guards to ride the borders of their land, and he was tired of it.

Luisa just couldn't see this. Sheltered in her house, waited on by servants, living a life of ease. And hiding money away for a frivolous journey to Spain! She had no right to make him feel guilty for having tried to make himself rich. Was it his fault he was unlucky? She should be thankful Navarro wanted their rancho and their daughter. Now life could go on as it had been, they would not be reduced to poverty.

Women! Lorenzo thought in exasperation. But then, as he slowed his

horse to a relaxed canter and headed in the direction of the village of Los
Angeles with its population of two hundred souls, as he felt the warm dry
sun bake his bones, and as he smelled the dust of the road and heard
the drone of insects, he felt his mood begin to mellow. He was glad
Navarro was going to take over the rancho. The problems would all be
on Navarro's shoulders from now on.

Cheerfully anticipating the coming afternoon spent in the good company of Francisco Reyes, the *alcalde* of the Pueblo, rolling dice and drinking fine Madeira wine and leaving the worry of the rancho to Juan
Navarro, Captain Lorenzo decided that, sometimes, going bankrupt could
be a blessing.

✳

"The marriage duty is not pleasant," Luisa explained solemnly to her
daughter, "but thankfully it is brief. Your husband will go quickly about
his business and then he will fall asleep." Luisa thought she was describing all men, not stopping to consider that she had been a virgin when
she married Lorenzo and had never been intimate with another man.

They were in the bedchamber that had been prepared for the newlywed couple. The vows had been exchanged before the priest, the marriage
recorded in the official register, and when a respectable time had passed,
Luisa had taken her daughter by the hand and led her from the wedding
feast. Now Luisa and an Indian woman were helping Angela out of her
wedding dress while outside, in the warm summer evening, the festivities
continued.

Angela wasn't thinking of the marriage bed, where bougainvillea petals
had been sprinkled on the pillows. Her mind was filled with visions of
the lemon and orange orchards she was going to plant. "I have told Señor
Navarro my ideas and he likes them. He even thinks a vineyard would be
nice."

On the day the *Estrella* sailed without its two female passengers, three
months ago, Navarro began courting Angela under the watchful eye of a
female chaperone. He came every day to sit with her beneath the bottlebrush tree that Lorenzo had imported from Australia at great expense.
They would comment on the weather, on Father Xavier's latest sermon,

on a new breed of horse, politely addressing each other as Señor and Señorita. Sometimes they sat in silence. After three months, they remained courteous strangers.

Luisa sighed wistfully as she laid Angela's petticoats aside. "You are lucky. Navarro is a very generous man." She tried not to think of the long gold earrings she was wearing, a gift from Navarro to his new mother-in-law. He had taken them, he said, off the mummy of an Aztec princess. The man has brought ghosts into this house, Luisa thought. For surely the spirits of the Mexican Indians would come back for the treasure stolen from them.

She glanced at the brass-studded box on the dressing table. It contained Navarro's wedding gift to Angela. Neither she nor Angela knew what was in it; it was to be opened later, when the newlywed couple were alone.

And then a small comfort occurred to Luisa: that Navarro would always be faithful to Angela. Luisa knew that he was interested not in conquest but in acquisition, that he was a man not of heart but of mind, that no heat burned within him but instead a cold mind that was forever calculating. His wife would provide sexual release, he would need no other women.

Angela took her mother's hands, and said, "I will be all right, Mamá."

Luisa was struck by the irony of the daughter consoling the mother when it should be the other way around. As she looked into Angela's calm eyes, she wondered if perhaps the wisdom she sometimes thought she saw there was simply patience. "Perhaps in time, little one, you will love Navarro."

"All that matters, Mamá, is that we are able to keep the rancho. Here is where I belong; here is where I wish to die."

Luisa was shocked. That a sixteen-year-old bride should speak of death on her wedding night! But perhaps this was the Indian blood in her speaking.

Angela wished she could convey to her mother the deep joy she felt in this place, how much she loved Alta California and Rancho Paloma. Her heart was here. Sometimes, when she went out riding, she would tie Sirocco to a tree and lie down on the grass to watch the sky. And she could almost feel the earth reaching up to embrace her. It was as if she were part of this land, even though she had been born in Mexico. But she had no memory of Mexico or the long trek she and her parents had made along with the other colonists to found the new pueblo. It was almost as if her life began when she was five years old; that was as far back as her memories went.

Although, there were times—in dreams, or sometimes when she caught a scent on the wind, or heard a sound—strange images would flash in her mind and for just an instant she would have the odd feeling that she was someone else.

Because the wedding had been such a big affair, Indian women had been sent from the Mission to help out. One of them now was assisting Angela out of her wedding clothes and carefully laying them in storage. Angela saw the plain tin cross on a string around the woman's neck and suddenly strange images flashed in her mind that almost felt like memories. A cave. A woman telling her to remember stories. Had Mamá taken her to a cave when she was small? But for what purpose?

When she had completely removed her wedding dress, which consisted of a tight bodice of rose-colored silk and a full skirt of white silk embroidered with tiny roses, Angela put on her long cotton nightgown and sat down to let her mother brush out her long, thick hair. There was sadness in every brushstroke, and in Luisa's dark eyes as they took on a faraway look.

Finally, Luisa and the Indian woman left, leaving Angela to await Navarro's arrival.

He knocked at the door, just as her mother had said he would, but instead of turning down the lamp and undressing in the dark, Navarro surprised her by leaving the light on as he removed his jacket and boots. While Angela sat demurely on the edge of the bed, hands folded in her lap, feeling her heart start to pound, Navarro poured himself some brandy and settled comfortably into a chair by the fire, where the flames cast his skin in a curious pallor.

He held out his hand. "What are you doing over there? Come here and let me see you."

He had brought the box containing her wedding gift to the small table between the chairs, and as Angela stood self-consciously before him, he lifted the lid and Angela saw the fiery glint of gold. Then he looked at Angela, gazing at her for a protracted moment, his eyes moving slowly up and down her body, resting for the longest moment on her hair.

Finally, he said, "You can take that thing off."

" 'Thing,' Señor?"

"That thing you're wearing." He flicked his wrist. "Take it off."

She frowned. "I do not understand."

"Didn't your mother tell you anything?" he said impatiently, rising from the chair. "We are married now. Husband and wife. The nightgown will not be necessary."

Cheeks blushing a fierce red, she turned around and started to undo the buttons at her throat.

"No," he said. "Face me."

He sat back in the chair and tasted his brandy while Angela's fingers clumsily undid the buttons. Then she slid each shoulder down, hesitating, noticing for the first time a strange coldness in his eyes. She slowly drew her arms out of the sleeves, her heart thumping wildly, and finally stepped out of the gown, bringing it up in front of herself for modesty.

Navarro rose from the chair and snatched the cotton gown away. "You will have no need of this from now on."

Despite the heat from the fire, Angela shivered violently. She crossed her arms protectively over her breasts but an incisive look from Navarro made her drop them. His eyes brashly devoured her, leaving her not a shred of modesty. Finally, he opened the small chest and lifted out a pair of gold earrings more magnificent than the ones he had given to Luisa.

"When I visited Peru," he said as he gently clipped each one to her earlobes, "I found an ancient city in the Andes that no one knows about. I and my men dug for months until we found tombs containing hundreds of mummies. Strangely, they were nearly all women, and all of the nobility or royalty judging by the wealth of gold buried with them."

Angela stood frozen as he brought out silver bracelets encrusted with emeralds and fastened them on each of her wrists, saying, "The women were mummified in a sitting position, and then the corpses were covered in straw, and then dressed in magnificent fabrics, and gold and silver and jewels."

Lastly, he brought out a breathtaking platinum necklace heavy with gold beads, jade, and turquoise inlay. As he reached under her hair and clasped the necklace at the nape of her neck, Navarro said, "I will tell you who I am. When Cortez conquered the Aztecs 240 years ago, there was a Navarro among his men who helped burn the cities to the ground. The son of that Navarro, and then the grandson, subsequently saw the natives of New Spain fall victim to the pox, fevers, and influenza. Millions of Indios died, wiping out entire villages and towns."

With long tapered fingers he arranged the necklace on her breasts, and Angela shivered as much from his touch as from the feel of the cold metal on her skin.

"My ancestors," he said, tracing the fullness of each breast with a fingertip, "took over the deserted land and we became prosperous. We owned mines and slaves, we ruled New Spain. This is what is in my blood, Angela, the legacy of the strong to take from the weak, the living to take from the dead. It is my destiny, and the destiny of the sons you will give me, to have power and dominion over others."

He stepped back to regard his handiwork, Angela standing naked before him, her young body glowing in the firelight, her dusky skin a seductive backdrop for the precious metals and gems he had draped upon her.

"I am incapable of love, Angela. Do not look to me for tender sentiments. What I *am* capable of is making you the most envied woman in Alta California."

He came close to her again and reached behind for her thick hair, drawing it over her right shoulder, arranging the luxuriant tresses as he had arranged the gold and jewels. "My mother was a great beauty. Men were always looking at her. One day she ran off with a lover. It took my father five years but he finally found them hiding on the island of Hispañola. He killed them both, as was his right. That will never happen to me." He drew the long hair over her breasts, touching her nipples, watching her face for a reaction. "You have great beauty, Angela, and it belongs to me. This hair, this body, they are mine."

His breathing began to quicken. A film of perspiration appeared on his forehead. "This hair is what I first noticed about you, as rich as the finest velvet, as rare as the blackest opal. It was this hair that I first determined to own." He ran his fingers through it, lifting it up and draping it back over her shoulder. "Now that you are a married woman, you will wear this hair up. But when you are alone with me, you will always wear it down, like this."

He walked behind her, standing so close that Angela could feel his breath on her neck. "Bend over," he whispered harshly.

Her voice caught in her throat. "Señor?"

She felt rough hands on her shoulders. "Do it!"

As she did as she was told, Navarro suddenly gathered her hair and pulled it back. "Hold still!" he ordered.

She started to struggle, and when she felt the painful, unexpected thrust, she cried out. When he commanded her to be quiet, reminding her of the wedding guests in the courtyard, Angela bit her tongue to keep silent. He pulled harder on her hair, as if it were the reins on a horse, drawing her head back so far that she could hardly breathe.

Angela squeezed her eyes shut and clenched her jaw as he continued his assault, pain and humiliation flooding her. When she whimpered, he yanked harder on her hair, pulling her head so far back she thought her neck would snap. A red cloud began to form behind her eyes. She gasped for breath. His thrusts were brutal, knifelike. Hot tears stung her eyes.

When he finally released her, she slumped to the floor gasping.

Navarro buttoned his trousers and poured himself another brandy. "All your silly plans for orchards and vineyards, you can forget. I own this land now and I alone will say what is to be done with it. I will bring in more cattle and sheep, and plant more grazing grasses. Your domain, wife, will be in the bedroom and the kitchen."

She blindly grabbed on to the edge of the bed and started to pull herself up, but Navarro ordered her to stay where she was, on her knees. "And there will be no more riding. It is unseemly for the wife of Navarro to gallop over the fields like a *caballero*. I have a buyer for Sirocco. The man will be here in the morning to collect the horse."

"Oh no! Please, Señor—"

He strode back to the brandy bottle. "I cannot have you calling me Señor. We are married. It will not do. In front of others, you may call me Navarro. When we are alone in this chamber, you will call me Master."

She gave him a shocked look. And then she saw the cold flat eyes and saw in them her future, and how utterly powerless she was going to be. Her mind worked quickly. "I will do as you ask, Señor," she said with a dry mouth. "I will do anything you ask of me, if you will do one thing for me. Send my mother to Spain."

He shook his head. "Your mother's presence here is my guarantee of your obedience. Both she and your worthless, contemptible father will live here for as long as I desire."

She began to cry. "Then I shall grow to hate you," she whispered in hard, bitter sobs.

He shrugged. "Hate me now, it means nothing to me. I do not want your affection. I want only that you give me sons and that you keep your beauty. That I insist upon, that you never lose your beauty. Now, call me 'Master.'"

She remained silent.

"Very well. I shall evict your parents this very night. I wonder how long will they survive on their own, penniless."

"No! Please! I beg of you."

"Then do as I say and I shall continue to give your father an allowance to cover his wagers and your mother will continue to live in comfort. Am I understood?"

She stifled a sob. "Yes. . . . *Master*. . . ."

He stroked her hair as she knelt before him. "Very good. And now, my dear, the night is yet young. What shall we try next?"

✳

When she awoke she found herself in bed, naked under the blankets, in pain. Navarro was snoring at her side, deeply asleep. As she lay for a long time trying not to think about the humiliating acts he had forced her to submit to, Angela saw the marriage road that lay before her, all the years and dark nights to come.

A sob escaped her throat. She quickly stifled it and looked anxiously at Navarro. He continued to sleep.

When she crept softly out of bed and stole into the next chamber, he still did not stir. Angela bathed herself, knowing that she would never again be clean, and when she dressed, it wasn't to put on the nightgown but her riding clothes for what she knew would be the last time. She moved mechanically and without emotion. She braided her hair, unaware that fragile bougainvillea petals from her pillow were trapped there. Then she stole out of the sleeping house and, quietly saddling Sirocco in the stable, led him out of the compound and out into the fields from where she rode westward down El Camino Viejo, past the tar pits, past the marshes, onward toward the low, jagged mountains silhouetted against the stars. She didn't know where she was riding to or why. She was driven by instinct, and fear and humiliation. What happened tonight could never be told to anyone. She rode even though it caused her pain, or perhaps because of it, each gallop reminding her of what Navarro had done to her and was undoubtedly going to do to her for the rest of their married lives. Angela felt her helplessness turn to fury. She rode as if to send herself and her beloved Sirocco off the edge of the earth.

When she reached the foothills, skirting the village where unbaptized Indios still lived the old ways, she picked her way along a trail until she came to a curious formation of boulders scarred with strange carvings, which she somehow knew represented a raven and the moon. Here she found the entrance to a narrow canyon and, not knowing what had drawn her to this place, guided the horse up the rocky incline.

She found the cave without knowing how she knew it was there, and when she went inside she was overwhelmed with feelings of familiarity. *I have been here before.*

Angela had come only to rest. She knew now that she was going to run away, she was just going to keep riding until she found a safe place in the wilderness, far from Navarro and his cruelty.

Finally, all the tears and sobs that she had been forced to keep inside, burst forth in a fury of weeping. As she collapsed to the earthen floor and cried as if her heart would break, she prayed to the Virgin Mary, and after a while a voice whispered in her mind: *You cannot run away, daugh-*

ter. You have duties now which you cannot shirk. But there is courage within you, the courage of those who came before you.

Sitting up, her tears subsiding, Angela pondered this. And she realized she couldn't abandon her mother. It would not only cause her mother pain, but running away would only bring shame upon the family. Possibly, Navarro would cast Lorenzo and Luisa out.

In the silence and solitude of the cave Angela felt her thoughts and emotions suddenly settle down, like birds once excited now coming to roost for the long, dark night. It left her with a strange and unexpected clarity of thought.

She knew what she must do.

Returning to Sirocco, who was nibbling greenery at the cave's entrance, she unsheathed a knife from her saddle, returned to the silent darkness and, taking hold of her long braid, severed it at the base of her skull. Feeling the rope of hair lying like a quiescent snake in her hands, and the cool air on her bare neck, Angela thought: I have taken away his power.

As she buried the braid in the cold earth of the cave, she experienced no moment of triumph, no feelings of victory, for she knew Navarro would punish her for what she had done. But she had needed to commit this one act of defiance in order to save her spirit, because she knew it would be the last act of defiance she would ever be able to commit against her husband, and the memory of this moment, she knew, would sustain her in years to come.

Chapter Eleven

The men who gathered in the posh executive board room on this crisp morning exuded a relaxed confidence. Comfortable with their power and secure in the knowledge that they ran the show, they wore expensive suits and discussed golf scores. Three were talking on personal cell phones, two exchanged stock tips, Sam Carter was giving instructions to the woman who would be recording the minutes of the meeting, while a seventh man, his long white hair plaited into Indian braids, sat stoically looking out the window of this thirtieth-floor conference room high above prestigious Century City. On a mahogany sideboard stood a silver coffee urn and rows of china cups in china saucers. There were crystal glasses filled with water and a slice of lemon, and platters of cold cuts, bagels, fresh fruit. The napkins were linen and the forks and spoons silver. It was an atmosphere of wealth and clubbiness, and as Sam Carter consulted his watch and saw that everyone was here, he felt extremely pleased with himself. It was he who had called this meeting, and he had no doubt as to its outcome. Handshakes and off-the-record promises practically guaranteed it.

"All right, gentlemen I think we can get this meeting under way. I'm sure we all have appointments for this afternoon."

Wade Dimarco, who was to present his proposal to build a museum on the Topanga site, said quietly next to Sam, "We're not going to have any trouble from Dr. Tyler, are we?"

"Erica is my employee, Wade, she does what I say." Besides, Erica knew nothing of this meeting. Sam had made sure of that. By the time she found out, it would be too late. "Don't worry," he added as he clapped Dimarco on the back. "I can almost guarantee we'll all be walking out of here today having arrived at a very amicable agreement."

As they took their seats, with Sam instructing the members to consult the printed agendas that had been set before them, there came a knock at the closed door. The seven men at the conference table were surprised to see a woman enter, her manner and attitude businesslike. Sam and Wade Dimarco exchanged a glance and Harmon Zimmerman looked instantly displeased, while three of the men stared blankly at the stranger, and Jared Black smiled.

Erica ignored the smile. "I trust I am not too late, gentlemen," she said as the door closed behind her. "I was not informed of this meeting until a short while ago." She wore a navy blue business suit that consisted of a tailored jacket over a white silk blouse, a skirt that stopped at the knees, and sensible pumps. Her glossy chestnut hair brushed her shoulders in a soft pageboy.

Without invitation she took the only available seat, at the opposite end of the oval table from Sam. Several of the men rose politely. Sam glowered at her. "This is Dr. Tyler, my assistant. She is here to *observe*."

Erica folded her hands on the table and tried not to let her anger show as Harmon Zimmerman started off the presentations. She avoided looking at Sam for fear she would lose control and say something she would regret. She avoided looking at Jared for the same reason.

Harmon Zimmerman represented the homeowners and backed up his analysis of their situation with charts and graphs that he passed around, a flurry of paper to support his case. None of the report pages reached Erica. The men had not expected an eighth member sitting in. The white-haired man with Indian braids, seated on her right, shared his materials with her.

Erica barely listened to what Zimmerman had to say, she was so angry. Sam and Jared had conspired to keep this meeting a secret from her.

The morning after the Dimarco cocktail party, Erica had been surprised to see Sam showing Ginny and Wade Dimarco around the camp. There had been other people with them, one man taking pictures, another jotting notes on a clipboard. Erica had asked Sam what it was about, and he had said, "They're just curious, like everyone else." The Dimarcos weren't the first notable persons Sam had taken on a tour of the site; it was something of an honor to be granted access to a project that was off-limits to the general public. However, what made the Dimarcos' visit different was that not once did they go inside the cave. Wasn't the cave the whole point? Erica had started thinking, and when she reviewed the night of the Dimarco cocktail party, when she had left so abruptly, she saw something she hadn't been aware of at the time. Sam and Wade Dimarco with their heads together like conspirators.

That was when her suspicions had been born. Sam was up to something. In the days that followed, he acted a little too cheerful, a little too spirited, as if to cover up nervousness. And then, just that morning, Erica had seen Sam leaving the compound, dressed in his best suit and whistling merrily. A few minutes later, Jared had also driven out, dressed to the nines and carrying a briefcase. Luckily, the temp secretary was still at Jared's RV. Explaining to the woman that she had lost the address for the meeting and that she hoped she wasn't going to be late, Erica had learned that Jared and Sam were headed for a building in Century City where the secretary's law firm was offering the use of their conference room for a meeting.

While Zimmerman outlined the loss of income to the homeowners because the excavation was holding up litigation against the builder and insurance companies, Erica finally looked at Jared. And she wondered: the night of the Dimarco party, when she was binding his injured rib and he was telling her about his wife's tragic death, had he known then about this secret meeting? As he was drawing her into a false confidence, had he already entered into a covert alliance with the men in this room? Because Erica had a strong suspicion of what they were up to here today.

Barney Voorhees, the developer and builder of Emerald Hills Estates, was next, with a slide show of maps and surveys, grants and deeds and permits, all proving he had developed the canyon properly and legally and that it wasn't his fault City Hall hadn't had sufficient soils and geological surveys on file. He, too, argued that the continued excavation held up any progress toward a resolution that would be financially satisfactory to all concerned. The archaeologists, he stated bluntly, were bankrupting him.

Next, the man from the U.S. Bureau of Land Management erected an easel and gave a well-prepared presentation, complete with graphs and charts, speaking as Zimmerman and Voorhees had in dollars and cents, recommending that the state of California cease the archaeological work at Topanga and instead develop a conservation and protection plan for Emerald Hills Canyon.

When Wade Dimarco's turn came, he impressed them all by dimming the lights and causing the center of the table to rise, so that each member was faced with a monitor. His ten-minute video was a masterpiece of computer modeling and special effects, as the audience was taken through a virtual tour of the museum he proposed to build at Emerald Hills. The narrator used the phrase "revenue to the taxpayers of California" more than once. Again, the implication was there: the sooner the excavating of the cave was stopped, the sooner the new Indian museum could bring profits to the state treasury.

The next to speak was Chief Antonio Rivera of the Gabrielino tribe, whom Erica recognized as the man Jared had brought to the cave in the early days of the project, hoping he could make a tribal identification of the painting. Of advanced age, his face mapped with a million lines and creases, coppery and weathered with small, alert eyes, he spoke softly and solemnly about the holy places of the American Indian. He spoke in the curious hybrid accent of LA's barrios: the result of growing up in a Spanish-speaking home and neighborhood laced with years of watching American movies and TV. Chief Rivera handed out folios containing color photographs of sacred sites around the Southwest, all of them in various stages of neglect, decay, and vandalism. "Because no one protected them," he said sadly. "My people are poor, and we are few in number. These were our churches." He lifted with a shaking hand the photograph of a cluster of boulders engraved with mystical petroglyphs defaced by obscene words in spray paint. "The cave in Topanga was our church. The stone walls, the earth floor, sacred symbols painted there are all holy to us. We would like our church back, please."

Jared spoke next. The Indians he represented wanted the project stopped so that they could get their ancestor properly and respectfully buried in a Native American cemetery. His handouts consisted of a petition containing thousands of signatures, and letters from tribal leaders calling upon the good consciences of all religious men, Indian or white.

He gave a moving speech: "As some of you here know, the Native American Heritage Commission was established in 1976 in response to California Native Americans requesting protection of their burial grounds. Ancient human remains uncovered during construction for housing and roads were ignored and left rotting in the sun by the workers. Archaeologists and amateur collectors came along and collected the human remains without any care or concern for what the Native people were feeling or the religious beliefs of these people. In addition to the insensitive wholesale destruction of burial sites, human remains were being warehoused by archaeologists at locations across California for future research projects."

He swept his dark eyes over the faces of his audience, settling a split second longer on Erica. "The taking of these remains was a continuation of the behavior toward Native Americans between 1850 and 1900, during which time ninety percent of the California Indian population perished from disease, starvation, poisoning, or gunshot wound. Alive, or dead, California natives were not treated with common decency and respect.

"I am here to see that this does not happen in the case of the Emerald Hills Woman. We wish for her immediate removal from the cave for reburial in a designated Native cemetery."

While Jared spoke, Erica felt her body and her heart react to the sight and sound of him. As a woman she desired him. But her brain rejected him. She was riding an emotional roller coaster, a ride she had sworn long ago she would never take again. *The foster mother, whom Erica had allowed herself to grow very fond of, saying: "We want to adopt you, Erica. Mr. Gordon and I, we want you to be our daughter." Hugs and kisses and tears and promises. And eleven-year-old Erica spinning dreams and fantasies, giving her hopes wing knowing that she would be part of a real family at last, with a little brother and a dog and a room of her own. No more visits to Dependency Court, no more trying to keep up with social workers who changed jobs faster than the seasons. And then: "I'm sorry, Erica, it isn't going to work out after all. And given that we can't adopt you, Mr. Gordon and I think it would be best if you were placed in another foster home."*

The high hopes, she had decided, like falling in love, were not worth the bitter disappointments that invariably followed.

Sam was the last to speak, presenting his own graphs and columns of figures to demonstrate the financial cost of the continued excavation to the taxpayer and projected financial loss compared to historical gain. "It's a money drain." He looked at each seated man in turn. "A drain," he said again, as if he'd finally found the word he'd been searching for.

So Erica's suspicions were confirmed, the purpose of this secret meeting. Every man in this room wanted the Emerald Hills Project stopped for one reason or another: the homeowners to be handsomely recompensed for their loss, the builder to avert bankruptcy, the Indians to have control of the cave and possibly a lucrative tourist attraction, the Dimarcos to build their self-named museum. She wasn't sure what Jared's personal motive was, maybe he didn't have one, and she told herself she didn't care. She was here for one reason only and that was what she must focus on.

"Gentlemen," Sam said, bringing the agenda to a close. "We have heard all the facts presented and we all seem to be in agreement, so I call the question. Is there a second?"

Zimmerman raised a hand, but before he could second the call, Erica said, "Point of order."

Seven faces turned to her.

Sam frowned. "What is your point of order, Dr. Tyler?"

"I haven't been given a chance to present *my* case."

His bushy eyebrows shot up. "Dr. Tyler, you work for the state and I have already presented the case for the state. All sides have been heard. We are ready to take a vote."

"May I ask where this agenda was published?"

He blinked. And then a flush rose up from his collar.

Erica pressed on: "Surely, Dr. Carter, you are aware that in the state of California, if a commission or an agency is going to take action on something, it must publish the agenda in advance. I found no such public notice in the local newspapers or in the lobby downstairs. Did I miss it?"

He squared his shoulders. "There wasn't one. This is just first reading. No agenda has to be published for first reading."

"Then no vote and no action can be taken today. Am I right?"

Their eyes locked across the length of the table while the other participants waited in silence. "Yes," he said.

"Therefore, I have something to say."

She rose with dignity and spoke in a strong, clear voice. "This morning we have heard figures and statistics. We have spoken of ecology and native rights, environmental impact studies, financial losses and gains. We have heard from representatives of the people and of the environment. One man"—she nodded respectfully toward Chief Rivera—"even spoke on behalf of the cave. I am here to speak on the behalf of someone who cannot speak for herself. The Emerald Hills Woman."

"What!" Zimmerman blurted. "Lady, weren't you listening to *him?*" he said, gesturing toward Jared. "The man said the Indians want the bones back. They're going to be buried in a proper cemetery."

"That is not sufficient. The woman in the cave was once known by her people, and by her descendants. She has a right to get her name back. This is what I—"

"It's a pile of bones, for Chrissake."

Erica leveled a cool gaze on Zimmerman. "Sir, I did not interrupt you while you were giving your presentation. May I please be afforded the same courtesy?"

Zimmerman turned to Sam. "I thought we were finished here. You gonna let just anyone come in and keep this meeting dragging on?"

Before Sam could speak, another voice intervened softly. "I would like to hear what the young lady has to say."

Erica looked at the Indian elder. "Thank you, Chief Rivera."

"I, too, would like to hear what Dr. Tyler has to say," Jared said with a smile. Erica did not return the smile.

"Very well, Dr. Tyler," Sam said, not looking happy. "Please proceed, but keep it short." He made a point of looking at his watch.

She squared her shoulders. "Gentlemen, I have no charts or graphs, no slide show or video, no fancy binders filled with expensive words. All I have is this." She reached into her bag and brought out a nine-by-eleven manila envelope. Handing it to Mr. Voorhees on her left, she said, "Would you please look at this and then pass it around?"

The others waited—some impatiently, some with interest—while Voorhees opened the envelope and drew out its contents. "Good God!" he blurted, staring in shock at the black-and-white photograph. "Is this a joke?"

"Please pass the picture around, Mr. Voorhees."

He quickly handed it to the man from the Bureau of Land Management, who took one look and said, "What the hell is this?"

"Erica?" Sam said. "What have you got there? What did you bring?" He held his hand out, but the picture was passed first to Jared, whose shocked reaction matched those of the other two.

"What you are looking at, gentlemen," Erica said, "is a photograph from the City Morgue. You will find the official stamp on the back. The subject is a Caucasian female in her mid-twenties who was found in a field three days ago, the victim of suspected foul play. Her identity is unknown. She is tagged currently as Jane Doe #38511. The police are trying to find out who she is."

Erica had considered making copies of the photo, one for each member of the meeting, but then had decided that a lone photo would have more impact, each man having to face it and deal with it, the lone victim being passed around the table without even the company of cloned sisters. The photo was brutal and frightening. The young woman's eyes were closed, but she did not give the appearance of sleep. She had clearly not slipped from life peacefully; shadows of the struggle she must have suffered haunted her once-beautiful face. Strangulation marks on her throat stood out in savage relief.

Jared handed it to Sam, who barely gave it a glance before thrusting it upon Zimmerman. "Jesus!" the movie producer shouted, and jumped as if Sam had put a snake in his hands.

Erica continued: "This young woman lies naked and exposed on a morgue table. She was once someone's daughter. Perhaps she was someone's cherished sister or wife. She deserves to be mourned and remembered."

"I still say it's just a pile of bones," Zimmerman muttered.

"Beneath that flesh, Mr. Zimmerman," Erica said, pointing to the morgue photo in his hands, "is also a pile of bones, as you put it. That woman is three days dead. The Emerald Hills Woman is two thousand years dead. I fail to see the difference. I propose we submit the Emerald Hills remains to DNA testing for tribal—"

"DNA testing!" Wade Dimarco said. "Do you realize the cost of such a procedure? To the taxpayer, I might add?"

"And how long would it take?" Voorhees the builder groused.

Dimarco, his expression stormy, said, "Sam, you yourself said the project was already a drain. How much more money and time are we going to waste on it?" He turned to Jared. "You said you've already made arrangements for reburial of the skeleton, right?"

Jared nodded. "The Confederated Tribes of Southern California wish to assume guardianship of the remains."

"We have no right to just sweep that woman under the bureaucratic carpet because of a few dollars," Erica countered. "The historical evidence in the cave indicates that her descendents intended for her to be remembered. Mr. Commissioner"—she turned to Jared as she brought a piece of paper from her purse—"may I read something to you?"

The others made a sound of impatience but Jared gave her the go-ahead.

She read out loud: " 'The mission of the Native American Heritage Commission is to provide protection to Native American burials from vandalism and inadvertent destruction; to provide a procedure for the notification of most likely descendants regarding the discovery of Native American human remains and associated grave goods; to bring legal action to prevent severe and irreparable damage to sacred shrines, ceremonial sites, sanctified cemeteries and places of worship on public property; and to maintain an inventory of sacred places.' This is the mission statement of your own Commission, Mr. Black."

"I'm familiar with it."

"I thought you might need to be reminded that your primary objective is to find the most likely descendent. Don't you think that immediate reburial of the skeleton is in direct contradiction of that goal?"

She lifted the morgue photo, which had made its way back to her. "Gentlemen, let me put it to you this way. Would you prefer that the authorities make no effort to find out who this woman was?" Erica met the eyes of each man at the table. "If she was your wife, Mr. Zimmerman, or your daughter, Mr. Dimarco, or your sister, Sam, wouldn't you want the authorities to handle her remains with respect and dignity, and do everything in their power to restore her to her family?"

Erica placed her palms flat on the table and leaned forward. "Let me finish my work in the cave. It can't be much longer. Once DNA testing is approved, we should have at least a tribal identification of the skeleton. And maybe that tribe, whoever they are, have a story in their mythology about a woman who came across the desert from the east. They might even know her name."

Sam Carter's small, acute eyes roved Erica's face, saw the familiar passion and earnestness. He wished he had sent her back to Gaviota and the abalone shells. "You'll never get approval, Dr. Tyler. What you're proposing is spending a big chunk of taxpayer money on something the public is going to consider a waste of time and resources."

"But I plan to get taxpayer support." Erica reached into her purse and pulled out a newspaper clipping. "This woman has agreed to help." She sent it around the table until it reached Sam. He scowled when he saw what it was. Sam was familiar with the columnist for the *Los Angeles Times,* a woman who was also the founder and president of the League to Stop Violence Against Women. She was famous for occasionally running a Jane Doe morgue photo in her column with the caption: *Do you know me?*

"She has agreed to run a photo of the Emerald Hills Woman," Erica said.

✳

Downstairs in the lobby, Jared caught up with her. "Quite a persuasive presentation, Dr. Tyler."

She turned on him. "Did you really think you would get away with this?"

His mouth dropped open. "I beg your pardon?"

"You and your cronies holding a secret little meeting—"

"*My* cronies! What are you talking about? The meeting wasn't a secret."

"Then why wasn't I told about it?"

He gave her a blank look. "I thought you had been. Sam said he informed you of the meeting but that you couldn't make it."

The elevator doors opened and Sam Carter, in the company of Zimmerman and Dimarco, stepped out. Erica blocked his path. "What's going on, Sam? What was that all about?"

He gestured to his companions to go on ahead. "I called the meeting in the interests of the other parties, not that I have to explain myself to you."

"Damn it, Sam, that was no first reading. You were going to vote today, weren't you? You violated the standards of the Little Hoover Commission. You met behind closed doors to vote on a decision that is going to affect the public and yet the public was not informed."

He started to push past her but she stood her ground. "It's the Dimarcos, isn't it? What did they promise you? Curatorship of their museum?"

He narrowed his eyes. "What are you implying?"

"When I saw you with the Dimarcos I thought something was up. But you know, I might have let it go if I hadn't gone into your tent one morning looking for you just as a fax was coming through on your machine. I'm not a snoop, but when I saw that the letter bore the official seal of California, I knew it wasn't personal and so I felt within my rights to read it. But you know, Sam? The memo was puzzling. It was signed by the Secretary for Resources and it was essentially a letter of permission for you 'to move on your proposed action.' Naturally I wondered *what* action. Wasn't what we were already doing—excavating out the cave—our official action? What more would you be wanting to do?

"That was when I remembered you once telling me that you would like to retire from fieldwork and find a nice office or museum job somewhere. What a coincidence that the Dimarcos should happen to want a museum with their name on it."

"So you went to the City Morgue and got a picture that was sure to shock."

"Can you tell me any other way I can fight all of you? We're going to run the column, Sam. And I'm betting I get public support on my side."

"Why does it mean so much to you, to the point of risking your job, your career?"

"Because once, years ago, I was as vulnerable as the Emerald Hills Woman is. I was going to be steamrollered over just as she is. I was a case number, Sam; they didn't even refer to me by my name. I was about to be dropped through the cracks of a heartless and soulless child welfare system when a stranger stepped in and stood up for my rights. I vowed that someday I would repay the favor by doing the same for someone else. Sam, one way or another I am going to do this. If I have to go to Washington and lobby the United States Congress, I am going to succeed."

✳

"Despite the objections of local Indian tribes," came the newscaster's voice over the car radio, "the federal government said yesterday that DNA testing of the Emerald Hills skeleton will go forward. The decision follows days of discussions involving representatives from Southern California tribes and officials from the Department of the Interior, and the Department of Justice, as well as the California State Native American Heritage Commission. Experts on ancient DNA analysis have pointed out that the procedures will be complex and time-consuming and may not provide conclusive data for determining the skeleton's tribal identity. The Confederated Tribes of Southern California have criticized the decision and continue to demand that the bones be reburied."

Jared clicked the car radio into silence. He was just getting back to Topanga after five days in Sacramento, where he had attended an emergency session of the Native American Heritage Commission. The session had been called because Coyote and his Red Panthers, protesting the continued excavation of the cave, had staged a "human landslide" on the Pacific Coast Highway, backing traffic up for miles. They swore to escalate their fight until the cave of their ancestor was sealed. Sam Carter had also been at the emergency meeting—Sam had changed his tack, as had the Dimarcos, calling for the archaeologists to be allowed to continue working in the cave until the most likely descendant could be found. The Dimarcos claimed their change of heart had nothing to do with the negative press and pressure from feminist groups that had resulted from Erica's crusade to keep the project going. The morgue photo, printed in the *Los Angeles Times* alongside a photo of the Emerald Hills skeleton, had made its intended point.

As Jared got out of his car something caught his eye—a flash of crimson and yellow through the trees. An Asian tiger embroidered on a jacket.

He frowned. What was Coyote doing back here? A court order had been issued keeping him and his group away. As Jared watched him, he realized Charlie's actions were furtive, sneaky. The giant kept looking over his shoulder in the direction of the cave. Then Jared saw him toss something into the back of a pickup truck.

"Hey—" Jared began.

But Charlie was behind the wheel and speeding out of the parking lot in a shower of dirt and dust.

Jared started off toward the cave, his steps going faster until suddenly he was running. Every instinct told him Charlie had been up to no good and that whoever was in the cave was in danger.

✳

"It resembles sacred fetishes carried by medicine men and women. A very powerful object," Erica explained to Luke as they knelt at the excavation pit, examining the small black stone they had found tucked inside a leather pouch.

"It looks very old," Luke said. "Two, maybe three hundred years."

"Yes, but strangely we found it on the same level as the American one-cent coin, which means this spirit-stone can only have been left here in or after 1814. Which is to say"—she lifted her eyes to meet Luke's—"*after* the founding of Los Angeles, an indication that this tribe was still practicing its rituals in the first part of the nineteenth century."

"Erica? *Erica!*"

She turned toward the cave entrance. "Was that Jared?"

"Sounded like him. Frantic, too."

Erica shot to her feet and dashed the dirt off her jeans. Jared was back from Sacramento! Once he had convinced her that he hadn't been in on any secret plot with Sam and that he had honestly thought she knew about the meeting in Century City, Erica was back on her emotional roller coaster. As she followed Luke toward the entrance to the cave, eager to hear Jared's news, to see his smile, to share space with him, to relish the secret thrill his nearness sparked, the air rocked with a sudden, deafening *bang*. A shock wave slammed into Erica, knocking her off her feet. Then came a tremendous roar and the cave shook and trembled as dirt and rocks came crashing down.

"Luke!" she screamed.

The electricity went out, plunging the cave into unearthly darkness. The air suddenly filled with dust. On her hands and knees, Erica crawled blindly in the dark. "Luke?" she said, coughing.

She stretched her eyes wide, but there was not even a pinpoint of light. She had never known such utter blackness. She crept cautiously forward, one hand out, groping at air. Finally, she met a rock wall where there shouldn't be one. She listened. Dust continued to sift down from the ceiling. She blindly explored the blockage. More rocks came tumbling down.

"Luke?" she said. "*Luke!*"

But all she heard was her own raspy breathing in a sudden stillness that made her think of a tomb.

Chapter Twelve

MARINA
1830 C.E.

Please God, Angela Navarro silently prayed. *Let everything go smoothly tomorrow. Let the wedding take place without incident.*

Her favorite daughter was marrying for love, a phenomenon nothing short of miraculous. But Navarro could spoil it. Even at this late date, he could still ruin everything.

Angela was forever vigilant—it was how she and her children had survived, by her cunning and by never once letting down her guard. She would read her husband's moods, watch the signs, and then act accordingly. Navarro tasting his soup, his eyebrow arching, Angela quickly calling for the serving girl to take this horrible soup away—even though Angela herself had secretly thought it delicious. Or mud tracked onto the polished tile floors by one of her young sons, and Navarro scowling down at the dirt, Angela declaring how careless of her to not have wiped her feet, and the back of Navarro's hand landing on her cheek instead of on the boy's. Luckily, most of the time Navarro didn't know he was being manipulated. But it required Angela to be constantly on her toes. The few mistakes she had made had cost her, and the children, greatly. A misplaced word, a look he didn't like, and he would reach for his strap, raining blows on wife, children, servants alike.

And so she had learned over the years to detect just the right moment to remove the children from his presence, when to scold just before Navarro did, when to head off an angry outburst, when to criticize herself before Navarro could, how to take the blame for everything so that servants and children were spared his wrath. She knew when submission on her part calmed him, or when it angered him, and how to quickly adjust to his mood. It was as if they played an elaborate game, except that Navarro didn't know it. But it had been wearisome over the years, to shield her children constantly from his violence, to head off disasters, to never be herself but only a reaction to Navarro's whims. But now, once Marina was gone, Angela could finally relax. Although what she was going to do with her time with no more children to rear, she did not know. She had long since set aside her old dream of growing citrus and cultivating grapes on the rancho. Her children and their survival, as well as her own, had always come first.

As she anxiously oversaw the chaos in the kitchen which, being much larger than the modest kitchen of Doña Luisa's day, was hot and smoky from meat being barbecued on great open grills and bread and stews baking in massive beehive ovens, she took a moment to look out the window. With so much yet to do for the wedding tomorrow, Angela had barely had time to finish her morning chocolate, and so she paused now to sip it slowly, savoring the richness of the thick drink made of cocoa, sugar, milk, cornstarch, eggs, and vanilla, to calm herself and to tell herself that everything was going to be all right.

Gazing out the window, she let her spirit fly across the pastures and fields, as she had done many times over the years, to relish memories of the days she had ridden Sirocco in freedom and joy. There had been fewer trees on the landscape then, fewer cowboys and people. *El Camino Viejo* was busier now, with wagons and horses and mules. She recalled the Indians' curious annual migration westward along the Old Road as they had headed for the autumn acorn harvest in the mountains, thousands of natives carrying their worldly goods, tramping to the sea as though responding to an ancient call. It had been a long time since Angela had seen any Indians heading west in the fall. She wondered if they went in search of acorns anymore.

When her gaze fell upon the vast cattle herds as far as the eye could see, the clouds of dust raised by their hooves, Angela's peaceful thoughts became troubled.

Navarro was overgrazing. He wasn't allowing the land to rest and rejuvenate itself. He seemed to forget that cattle, having been brought from across the sea, were not natural to this place and that therefore special care must be taken to keep the balance of nature. But Angela had not dared suggest he cut back on the herds and leave some acres untouched, for her words would only earn her a quick, sharp slap.

Reminding herself that this was supposed to be a joyful day, she forced her worries aside once more and turned to find Marina still holding vigil at the window in the southeast wall of the kitchen.

Eighteen years old and deliriously in love, Marina was intently watching *El Camino Viejo* where wagons and horses came and went in their treks from the village of Los Angeles to the coves of Santa Monica, stopping at the tar pits along the way. Angela knew her youngest daughter was watching for her fiancé, Pablo Quiñones, a skilled silversmith born in California to Mexican parents.

Angela had never seen a girl so in love! Marina yearned toward the open window like a flower to the sun, her slender body nearly trembling with anticipation. And her face! Eyes wide and staring, lips parted breathlessly, watching for the moment her beloved Pablo appeared on the road. How many times had Marina come running into the house blushing and starry-eyed after sitting in the shade of the pepper tree with Pablo! They would spend hours together there, under the watchful eye of an elderly chaperone, chatting away, laughing, animated with youthful life. So unlike Angela's own brief courtship with Navarro, when they had sat in silence. And Marina would say, "Oh Mamá, Pablo has been to so many places. He has been to San Diego! Imagine that."

But Angela could not imagine it. A town two hundred miles away might as well be two *thousand* miles away. What allure could it possibly have for a girl of eighteen when her home and all that was familiar were right here?

Of course, Angela didn't know what it was like to be in love. There might have been a time, once, when she could have fallen in love with Navarro, but that was long ago, when she had been another Angela.

She was startled by the sound of the children suddenly screaming. Going to the window that opened onto corrals, sheep pens and stables, she saw her grandsons and granddaughters climbing a fence in order to watch men on horseback bring a wild grizzly bear into the corral.

The *vaqueros* had captured the beast in the Santa Monica Mountains and had dragged it, alive, to Rancho Paloma where, tomorrow night, it was going to be pitted against a bull as part of the wedding festivities. The grizzly was putting up a ferocious battle, baring its fangs and claws and roaring with fury while the riders held on to their ropes, horses rearing and whinnying and kicking up clouds of dust, and the children clapped their hands and squealed with delight.

As Angela watched her grandchildren scale the fence like puppies to watch the spectacle—a healthy little mob ranging in age from sixteen to toddler years—her thoughts returned to Marina and she felt a mixture of sadness and joy grip her soul. Sadness because her youngest daughter was to be married tomorrow and leave home, but joy because the house she was moving to was not far away.

It was to be the last wedding in this house, her own having been the first, thirty-eight years ago, when she had been forced into union with a man of cold mind and colder heart. Nearly four decades had passed since Angela had hacked off her braid in the cave in the mountains and yet she could still feel the bruises from the beating she had received the next morning, when Navarro had wakened to find she had cut off her hair. The punishment had not ended there. Navarro had kept it up, devising different ways to remind Angela again and again who was her master. He would make her take off her clothes and then he would tie her to a chair and leave her there all night. He would force her to perform lewd and debasing acts, all of which she suffered silently because it happened only at night and when they were alone. When the sun rose in the morning Angela could almost think Navarro's acts of cruelty had been but bad dreams. He took care that marks of his brutality never showed so that not even Angela's lady's maid, who helped her to dress in the morning, knew. And when there were times when Angela thought she could take his torments no longer, she would remember her children, how well Navarro provided for them, and this beautiful home he had built.

Angela did not hate Navarro. She pitied him, for there was no love in him and therefore no joy, and no one loved him in return, not even his children. And in a way Angela could not explain, she was also grateful to him—for the children he had given her, for having kept his promise to allow her parents to live in this house until they died, and for making her precious rancho the most beautiful and prosperous in Alta California. In return she had fulfilled her end of the bargain: at fifty-four, Angela still had her beauty.

The noise and chaos in the huge kitchen brought her out of her thoughts. All these women busily grinding flour, making tortillas, preparing vegetables, kneading dough, chattering and laughing, and there was still much to do! The hacienda had been making preparations for weeks. First there would be the grand wedding procession on horseback with the bride and groom, dressed in their finest, leading the pageant through the village of Los Angeles and back, Marina in a broad-rimmed plumed hat and bright velvet skirts, Pablo in his embroidered jacket and pants, his horse laden with silver. And then the wedding feast, to be held among the imported jacaranda, bottlebrush, and pepper trees, complete with mariachi band, dancers, and fireworks.

The entire Navarro family was gathered for the occasion, Marina's brothers and sisters, all older than she and married, and all having arrived with their spouses and children. Even Marina's sister Carlotta, older by eighteen years, had made the long journey from Mexico City with her second husband, the Count D'Arcy, and their six-year-old daughter, Angelique.

Angela paused to inspect the cook's red chili sauce in a large skillet, the onion, garlic, chili pulp, oregano, and flour sizzling in fat. She tasted it and frowned. Selecting a small fresh tomato, she rapidly chopped it up and scooped the pieces into the skillet. Now the sauce would be perfect. As she turned away from the stove, Angela saw through the window a tall, fiercely visaged man stride over to the corral and pluck one of the little girls from the railing. He was Jacques D'Arcy, Carlotta's second husband and doting father of Angelique, sweeping her away from the cruel spectacle of the bear and taking her into the shade of a rose arbor, where he sat her on his knee and plucked a blossom for her hair.

Angela's thoughts grew troubled again. Navarro detested Carlotta's second husband. When her first husband, a *Californio* selected by Navarro, died in Mexico City, Navarro had expected his eldest daughter to return to Alta California and marry a local ranchero. Instead she had met and fallen in love with a man whose family had fled the revolution in France and found haven in Mexico City. Navarro hated the French and refused to speak to Jacques D'Arcy, and D'Arcy, affronted, had declared that he was willing to stay only for Carlotta's sake.

Feeling a chill despite the warm day, Angela quickly scanned the compound for signs of Navarro. It would take very little—a few cups of wine, an imagined insult—for him to decide to challenge D'Arcy to a duel. Navarro had done it before. His opponent had lost.

As she watched how D'Arcy now doted on his little girl, Angela suspected his motives for coming to the wedding were less to please Carlotta than to amuse his little "princess." Named for Grandmother Angela, the six-year-old was watched over by a dour-looking *Azteca* who was more than just a nanny, she was a *curandera*—a healer—possessing ancient Aztec medical secrets. The dour-faced woman wore strange clothes: a long colorful skirt and a sleeveless tunic of another colorful fabric that reached to her thigh. Her long hair was tied up in two fabric-wrapped bundles that looked like horns over her forehead. Her earlobes, inserted with gold plugs, were so long they brushed her ears. Carlotta had explained that the woman came from a village where they still lived the way their ancestors had, before the arrival of Cortez, and where they kept secrets of healing which they had never shared with their conquerors. Carlotta and D'Arcy had hired her because of Angelique's falling sickness, the same affliction that plagued Angela. And Marina.

Of all her children, only Marina had inherited the fainting curse. Poor little Marina! The first time it happened and she had seen frightening visions. How she had cried and clung to her mother. It was their special bond. No one else could understand what it was like. Pablo Quiñones had assured Angela that he was ready to take care of Marina during her spells. But Angela felt she was the only person who could help. And that was why she was thankful the girl had fallen in love with a local boy, so that she would not be far from home.

A mother shouldn't have favorites among her children, but Angela's heart had a mind of its own. Here were her two most loved daughters, the eldest and the youngest. Carlotta had been her first, born when Angela was only eighteen years old. There were many in between, some of whom had not survived and now slept in the small family burial plot beneath a pepper tree. There were the strong and sturdy boys, men now, three of them arrogant like Navarro, one shy, one who never stopped laughing, and there were the other girls, two sensible women who had made good marriage matches. Nine surviving children out of fourteen pregnancies. Marina was the youngest, born to Angela when she was thirty-six years old. Three more had been conceived after that but two had not made it to their first birthday, and the third Angela had lost in miscarriage. After that, Angela could no longer get pregnant and so Marina remained her precious "baby," especially after the others had grown up and married and moved away.

Marina's name had come to Angela in a dream while she was still pregnant with her and before she could possibly have known the baby was a girl. A special name. But she couldn't hear it clearly in the dream. She saw herself in a frightening dark place, a strange painting on the wall, feverish hands burying a crucifix in the earth, and a muffled voice calling her—Was it Marini? Mamiri? They didn't sound like names. Marina! Yes, that was it, the name in the dream. A beautiful name.

Unable to stand the bear's shrieks of terror and outrage any longer, she turned away from the unsettling spectacle—the poor beast was on his back trying to break free from the ropes—and an unexpected thought entered her mind: *the bear did not give permission to be lassoed and dragged here for our entertainment.*

Where had that come from? Strange notions entered her mind at the most unexpected moments. A quick flash of thought, like a fish jumping in a stream to be seen in a bright glint only to disappear back into the water. Sometimes these errant thoughts were so fast that she couldn't remember them, couldn't hang on to them. Occasionally they were words, other times images.

Shrugging off her strange thoughts, Angela brought herself back to the monumental task of feeding so many guests and workers on this festive occasion.

Rancho Paloma was now a grand hacienda: an economically diversified estate that employed a huge labor force, combining agriculture, grazing, and other production. Navarro had made good his wedding night promise to become very wealthy. The village of Los Angeles was also prospering. There were now farms everywhere, with orchards, gardens, and vineyards. Rancho Paloma had neighboring ranchos now: La Brea, La Cienegas, San Vicente y Santa Monica. And farther out, the larger ranchos of Los Palos Verdes, San Pedro, Los Feliz—hundreds of thousands of acres owned by families with illustrious names: Dominguez, Sepúlveda, Verdugo. The population of the Pueblo had grown to nearly eight hundred.

When Angela saw Marina abruptly put her hand on the window frame, a sudden, anxious gesture, Angela looked out to see what had caught her daughter's attention. Had Pablo arrived? But no, the rider coming through the gate was not Quiñones but an Americano Navarro had lately been having dealings with.

Daniel Goodside, a ship's captain, who made Angela, for reasons she could not name, uneasy.

Navarro's dealings with the *Yanquis* used to be illegal, when he had met secretly with American traders in the coves of Santa Barbara to exchange beef hides for gold. But now it was all legal and done in the open. Ironically, Navarro despised *Americanos* even more than he despised the French, but he deemed them a necessary evil—little better than parasites but a rich source of trade and income. Angela herself thought *Americanos* a strange breed. She remembered when the first one came to Los Angeles twelve years ago, when California was still under Spanish rule. "Pirate Joe" had been captured during a raid off the Monterey coast. When it was learned that he was a gifted carpenter, he was spared from prison and sent down to Los Angeles to oversee the construction of a new church at the Plaza. Angela had been forty-two years old at the time and had glimpsed blond hair for the first time in her life. Everyone crowded around the work site as Indios hauled in timbers from the mountains and the tall blond stranger gave orders. When the church was finished, Joseph Chapman married a Mexican *señorita* and settled down in Los Angeles. Seven years later, after Spain had given up her holdings in California, a mountain man named Jedediah Smith presented himself at the San Gabriel Mission, but he had not been arrested because by then it was no longer illegal for foreigners to enter California.

Eight years ago, when the people of California learned that Mexico had seceded from Spain, they pledged allegiance to the Mexican government, which had immediately opened up the province to international trade with English and American vessels. Hide and tallow became the major economy. Steer hides from Rancho Paloma were shipped to New England where they were made into saddles, harnesses, and shoes, and Rancho Paloma tallow was melted down for ultimate conversion to candles. The booming new trade was bringing more and more *Americanos* to California so that today, the sight of an *Americano* in the streets of Los Angeles was not unusual.

Angela wondered what her mother, Doña Luisa, would think of these changes as she slept in her grave in the family cemetery plot. Luisa had died the year Mexico broke away from Spain, as if her own ties with her beloved homeland had been irreparably severed and she did not wish to go on living. Luisa had been sixty-nine years old. Lorenzo was also buried there, having been killed in a gambling dispute.

Angela watched Captain Goodside dismount from his horse and remove his hat. Like Pirate Joe, his hair was the color of ripened wheat. Then she said to Marina, "Pablo will come," when she saw the look on her daughter's face. The poor girl had been waiting all morning for her fiancé, but instead only strangers had come through the gate.

"Oh, Mamá," Marina sighed, turning away from the window to dash impulsively from the room.

After exchanging a glance with Carlotta, who was supervising the preparation of *dulce de calabaza*—candied pumpkin—and who remembered what it was like to be eighteen and impatient, Angela left the kitchen and entered the outer colonnade, where graceful arches opened onto gardens filled with flowers and shrubs and the low-hanging branches of willows and pepper trees. She paused to inspect a row of chairs hidden beneath a protective blanket.

A surprise wedding gift for Marina and Pablo, they were a set of four upholstered antique armchairs crafted back in 1736 and styled after a suite of chairs made for the Royal Palace at Madrid. Influenced by the French Louis V style, the pieces were veneered in rosewood with ebony inlay and upholstered in crimson silk brocaded with gold thread and trimmed with gold fringe. Doña Luisa had brought them to Mexico in 1773 and then had had them hauled by oxen along with her other furniture to Alta California after she married Don Lorenzo. They had been declared the most exquisite pieces of furniture in the province, and now they were going to pass to Marina.

As Angela continued along the arcade, she espied three men standing by the stables, admiring a horse Navarro had recently acquired. Although in his sixties with silver hair, Navarro was still as robust as a bull. Angela saw that her future son-in-law was with him, Pablo with a boyish face, short and tending to stockiness. She wondered if Marina knew he had arrived. Then she saw that the third man was Captain Goodside, standing slightly taller than Navarro, his curious wide-brimmed straw hat shadowing his features.

As she observed the men, Angela tried to read Navarro's mood. He had canceled one wedding before, on a whim at the last minute, making their son smolder with silent fury and the bride's family threaten violence. But Angela could detect no dark currents in her husband's behavior. In fact, Pablo Quiñones was making him laugh.

Then she saw Marina, hiding in the shade of an arbor, watching the men. Angela tensed. She knew her impulsive daughter wanted to run to Pablo, but there would be plenty of time for that after the wedding. Be careful, my child, she silently cautioned. Do not let your father see you.

There was something in Navarro that detested other people's happiness, even that of his children. Too much joy soured him.

Angela noticed that the Yankee had the square, thin box with him again. He carried it everywhere, slung over his shoulder from a leather strap. What was so important that he could never be parted from it? Even though Americanos were now permitted in California, she still did not trust them. After years of illegal trading, a man did not turn honest overnight.

As she was about to go into the house, her eye caught a figure approaching along the path from the Old Road. Recognizable by his gray Franciscan habit, he was a padre from the Mission, arriving on his mule. And when she saw how he slowed his animal and searched the faces of the *vaqueros,* she knew why he had come. Some of his Indios must have run away again.

It was easy to find willing workers for Rancho Paloma's four thousand acres. The Indios found life on the rancheros preferable to that in the Missions, and many were even starting to leave the Missions for town life. There were now several hundred residents in the Los Angeles Pueblo, many of them needed servants and hired workers. To keep the Mission Fathers from losing their Indios—for then who would be left to tend the cattle and vineyards belonging to the Church, and weave the cloth and make the candles that the Fathers needed?—the Governor of California had prescribed ten lashes for any baptized Indian caught in town without permission from the Fathers.

As Angela watched the visitor dismount, she wondered if he and his religious brothers were fighting a losing battle. There was talk that Mexican officials were going to abolish the Mission system, which the Spaniards had revered, and sell the land to private parties. Where, then, would the Indios go? Most had lived at the Missions all their lives and knew no other way of life. Although, Angela had to admit, she didn't really understand the Indios. They were just figures that blended into the landscape— men in sombreros and blankets, women in long skirts and shawls. Yet there were still brutal fights between the *Californios* and the Indians over the land. Recently a rancho in San Diego had been attacked, the daughters kidnapped and never seen again; there had been a Chumash uprising in Santa Barbara, and the Temecula Indians had gone on a pillaging spree in San Bernardino.

She saw by the way the padre looked into the face of each Indio that he was searching for a particular one.

Shading her eyes from the sun, she scanned the gardens where men were pulling weeds and spreading fertilizer, swept her gaze over the corrals and animal compounds, the dairy and granary, the tanning and laundry sheds—all bustling with human activity. When she came to the olive press, she watched the old man who was patiently urging the burro to go round and round as the big stone crushed the olives into pulp and oil. Bent and white-haired, he was not familiar to her. And when he moved from shade to sunlight, she saw his distinct Indian features.

Before she could react, the old man looked up and saw the padre. He froze. Then he broke into a run.

The priest, lifting his robes to reveal bare feet in sandals, gave chase, shouting at the man to stop, and immediately a crowd of workers, family members, and visitors ran to see what had the padre in such a state.

Angela was the first to reach them, the priest having cornered the Indian under the archway that led to the *lavanderia*. The old man had fallen to his knees and was raising his clasped hands imploringly to the padre.

"Please, Father!" Angela said breathlessly. "Do not handle him too harshly."

"This man is a baptized Christian, Señora. He belongs at the Mission." The padre softened. "They are like children, Señora, and must be corrected. When you raised your sons and daughters, did you not punish them when they needed it?"

"But this man is old, Father, and he is frightened."

She was startled when the old man began frantically tugging at her skirt, begging for help in a mixture of Spanish and his native tongue. He was clearly terrified.

"Perhaps, Father, he can go back to his village."

The priest sadly shook his head. "When the Sepúlveda family received the San Vicente y Santa Monica land grant, they cleared the land for grazing. This man was found scavenging among the ruins of a deserted village near the foothills. He was naked, Señora, and near starvation. He was brought to us so that we could feed him and clothe him and bring him to Christ."

Angela looked at the priest and thought, He is not a bad man.

Then she looked down at the old man and thought: He just wants to be free.

It occurred to Angela that she had the power to save him. If she told the padre she wanted the old man to stay here, he would listen to her. After all, she was the wife of Juan Navarro.

But in the next instant she saw Navarro approaching, fury in his stride. He had already assessed the situation and Angela's role in it. Giving the padre permission to take the old Indian away, Navarro barked at everyone to disperse. When they were momentarily alone beneath the archway, Pablo having gone to Marina and the Americano having tactfully returned to the stable, Navarro gripped Angela painfully by the arm and said in a low voice, "I make the decisions on this rancho, not you. You have humiliated me."

*

As Marina silently made her way across the yard, her slender body casting a tall shadow in the moonlight, she soundlessly felt her way along the stone walls, taking care not to trip on the uneven ground or stumble over a tool. She dreaded to think of what her punishment would be should her father find out what she was up to. But Marina wasn't thinking with her head, it was her heart that had driven her out of the house at this late hour, her young body feverish with love, her mind dizzy with thoughts about the ceremony tomorrow night and the bridal chamber afterward.

She skirted the slaughter yard where, by day, cattle were skinned and butchered, their skins scraped clean of meat and stretched to dry in the sun. The smell wasn't as bad at night, and the flies were asleep. The only evidence of the day's bloody enterprise were the great stacks of stiff hides—"Yankee dollars"—waiting to be taken to the holds of trading vessels. Outside the tallow room were the enormous iron pots where fat from slaughtered steers was melted down for the manufacture of candles and soap, and stored as tallow in large skin bags to be traded with foreign ships. Marina slipped inside the tallow shed, where hundreds of long, thin tapers hung in rows on the walls and from the ceiling. In the center of the room stood the ungainly candle-dipper, its wooden arms draped with strings coated in various thicknesses of tallow. The contraption was still and silent now, but during the day its creaking never ceased as, hand-cranked by an Indian, it turned, dipped, turned, and dipped, producing hundreds of candles at a time.

Marina thought it ironic that a room with so many candles should be so dark. "Are you here?" she whispered in the darkness. "Did you come, my love?"

Bootheels scraped on the stone floor. A moment later, a match flared and then a lantern came to life in a soft glow.

Marina gasped when she beheld who stood there—the Americano, Daniel Goodside. She was held momentarily transfixed by the sight of him—the pale light casting a halo around his blond hair, the blue of his eyes as bright as the noon sky, his lips parted as if in surprise. And then she was flying across the small space between them and delivering herself into his arms, receiving his kiss and holding desperately to him never to let go.

She would never forget the day, three months ago, when she had gone out riding and had come upon a stranger at the edge of the property, sitting on a stool and sketching in a large book. His jacket was folded neatly on the grass, his shirt shone blazingly white in the sun, and a large straw hat had concealed his features until, hearing the sounds of her approach, he turned, slowly stood, and then swept his hat off his head to reveal hair the color of ripened wheat and eyes the blue of cornflowers. And his beard! Like fleece it was, closely cropped and framing a secret smile. His cravat was loosened, revealing a sunburnt throat, and the fabric of his breeches strained against strong, well-muscled legs. He had looked like a young god.

And then he had greeted her in Spanish! Marina had thought Yankees spoke only English. And with what ease he spoke her tongue, and almost without accent. More than a god—a magician, a wizard. A magnetic si-lence had captured them that day in a speechless moment as the summer breeze ruffled his sunlight-colored hair, and Marina felt her heart expand within her chest like a morning glory opening to the sun. And then the stranger had said, "Forgive me for staring, Señorita, but when I visited your village of the Angels, I wondered what angels it had been named for. Now I know."

As she held tightly to him now, inhaling his scent, feeling his strong hands on her, hearing the deep timbre of his voice as she pressed her ear to his chest, Daniel was saying, "What are we to do?" Marina felt a sob gather in her throat and stay there to stop her from breathing. For three months she had known joy and misery, uncertainty and dreams. She had thought she loved Pablo, and then she had met Daniel. But she was promised to Pablo and the miracle she had prayed for nightly, to be released from that promise, never happened. And now Daniel was leaving, to sail away on tomorrow's tide.

"I shall die," she murmured against his chest. "I cannot live without you."

"I, too, dearest Marina," he said as he stroked her hair and marveled at this angel in his arms. "I have been called by God to take His word to foreign lands and I will need your strength and gentleness to help guide me on that difficult path. Before I met you, I knew fear. I would look out to sea and my soul would tremble at the thought of delivering myself into barbarian hands. And then you, kind and gentle soul, came into my life and calmed me. You remind me daily of God's grace and that we are never alone. I see days of trial before me, and I fear that without you I shall fail."

For three golden months they had spun a beautiful dream together, walking hand in hand by the marshes, where they would not be seen, Daniel talking about the wonders of the world, Marina seeing them behind her eyes. When he had told her all the things he was going to show her, Marina had believed it. For a while, they had lived in a fantasy. But reality was inevitable, as was her marriage to Quiñones. And now the day was upon them and the fantasy was at an end.

Marina held her breath. She knew what was coming next—the forbidden words as yet unspoken but which she knew Daniel must now utter. "Run away with me," he said. "Be my wife."

Love washed over her like an ocean wave, but pain as well, and fear and sorrow. She wanted nothing more under God's sun than to be

Daniel's wife and to travel the world with him. But she knew the price that would be paid for such a selfish act.

She drew back, hating to leave the shelter of his arms, but knowing she needed distance between them, if only a little, for what she had to say. "I cannot go with you, my Daniel. My father is a proud and angry man. His wrath would know no limits if I were to defy him and bring dishonor to the family."

"But you would be far from him, Marina."

"It is not for myself that I fear. He would punish my mother for my transgression. He would punish her severely, and for the rest of her life. How could I be happy with you, my Daniel, knowing this?"

He took her face into his hands and murmured, "Love, such a mystery, it never asks permission to happen." He kissed her again, more deeply, and her body responded.

"God in Heaven," he said hoarsely, knowing that they had reached a dangerous brink. It would be so easy. There was straw on the floor. And no one would know.

"I cannot," he whispered against her ear. "I will not have us be like this. If it cannot be as husband and wife, then I shall be satisfied with only your kiss."

They held each other again and heard through the night the mournful roars of the grizzly bear in his compound, and the rattle of chains as he tried to free himself.

Marina wept softly for another moment, then she drew back, detaching herself completely from Daniel, filling her eyes with him one last time. "I must go. Father might catch us."

But he took her by the shoulders and said with passion: "I will be at the house of Francisco Marquez until midnight tomorrow, and then I must sail with the tide. I pray with all my heart and soul, my beloved, that you will find the strength to come to me. But if I do not hear from you, I shall take it as God's will that we are not meant to be together. And if you marry Quiñones, I will wish you a long and happy life with him. I shall never forget you, and I shall never love another as I love you, my dearest, dearest Marina."

✳

"Mamá, you must come quickly! Something is wrong with Marina. I think she is having one of her spells!"

Carlotta needed to say not another word. Angela flew out of the kitchen, where servants were busy filling wine goblets for the arriving guests. The wedding ceremony was to begin in an hour.

Entering Marina's chamber she found her daughter lying supine across the bed, sobbing her heart out. She had not yet put on her wedding dress! Dismissing the others, including Carlotta, who had been there to help Marina dress, Angela lifted her daughter by the shoulders, and said gently, "Are you ill, my child? Shall I fetch the laudanum?"

"I am not sick, Mamá! I am unhappy!"

Angela wiped the tears from Marina's face. "This should be the happiest moment of your life. How can you cry? Tell me what is wrong, child."

Marina flung herself against her mother's breast and let the words tumble out. Angela listened to the story in astonishment. Marina was in love with the *Americano*? When had they had time or opportunity to fall in love?

"Marina," she said sternly, lifting her daughter up and searching her face for deceit. "Tell me truthfully, have you have been alone with him?"

Marina bowed her head. "During siesta, while everyone slept."

"You were alone with an *American*?"

"He is very much the gentleman, Mamá! All we did was talk. And such wonderful talk!" The words rushed out, tumbling so rapidly from her lips that Angela was left speechless. "Daniel isn't a trader like other Yankees, Mamá, he is an explorer. He travels around the world and sees fabulous wonders and strange new places. He paints them, Mamá, as a record, a memorial to the various peoples he encounters. He told me of a place where the people ride great big animals with humps on their backs and a land where people live in houses made of snow."

"What nonsense, Marina."

"Oh no, Mamá! These aren't fabled places, they are real. And I want to see them. Oh how I long to go to China and India and Boston. I wish to drink tea and coffee, and wear capes and turbans, and dance at a campfire and ride in a snow sleigh. You and I have only *seen* snow from a distance, Mamá, on the mountain peaks. But Daniel has *walked* in it, he has slept in it."

Marina seized her mother's hands between her own feverish ones. "Daniel has described to me buildings so tall they disappear in clouds, churches as big as cities and palaces with a hundred rooms. He has walked on roads that are two thousand years old, Mamá, and there is a river called the Nile where there are gigantic stone lions that were built by mythical beings at the beginning of time."

Angela didn't understand half of what her daughter was describing, but the words were not important. What stunned her was the light in Marina's eyes, the luminescence of youth and optimism, and yearning for knowledge and adventure. A light that Angela had never seen in her own eyes in a mirror, nor in the eyes of her other children.

And then the brutal truth of what Marina was saying struck: the *Americano* wanted to take Angela far away! "What is in these other places that we do not have here?"

"Mamá, when you look at the horizon, don't you wonder what lies beyond?"

Angela was suddenly angry at Goodside for filling Marina's head with nonsense. "There is nothing beyond the horizon. There is only here, this world, *our* world. What lies beyond belongs to others, not to us. Here is where our hearts are, where the soul yearns to be."

"*Your* soul, Mamá, not mine."

Marina's words struck her like a blow, and she thought: *Am I the only one who hears the poetry in the trees when the wind whispers through them? Am I the only one whose heart answers the cry of the red-tailed hawk overhead? Am I the only one unafraid of earthquakes, imagining them simply to be a sleepy old giant turning over in his bed?*

"Look, Mamá," Marina said, dropping to her knees and pulling a box from under the bed. She lifted large squares of heavy paper from it, on which Angela could see colorful pictures. "These are called watercolors, Mamá. Look at the beauty Daniel creates."

Angela was spellbound. The American had captured not only the look of California in his paints, but also the feel. As she went from vista to vista, she could smell the heat of summer, hear the drone of insects, taste the dryness in the air. He had painted a pair of quails, their topknot feathers nodding toward each other. And the peaceful blue Pacific, white sails on the horizon. Gentle paintings, she thought, executed by a heart of love.

"Daniel says the sunlight in California is unlike anywhere in the world. He says it is sharper and purer, and the colors are alive." Marina added softly, "My Daniel is an artist."

Angela gave her a startled look. *My* Daniel? As they heard the musicians outside tuning their instruments, and voices raised in greeting as guests arrived, Angela felt a terrible foreboding steal over her. "But think of Pablo. He is a nice boy. You will have a good life with him." She heard the note of panic in her words, and she realized her heart was racing. If Navarro were to hear of this—

Marina bowed her head. "Yes, Mamá, I know. I will marry Pablo."

"You will? After all this?"

Marina's uplifted eyes swam with tears. "I will marry Pablo because I have promised to do so. I will not dishonor you, Mamá."

"But . . . you will not be happy."

Marina bent her head. "My heart will always belong to Daniel. But Pablo is a good man and I shall try to be a good wife to him."

Angela beheld her daughter's bowed head and marveled that this beautiful, strong spirit should have sprung from her and Navarro.

"Then you must get dressed, before the others start to wonder." As Angela moved aside the dressmaker's sewing box which had been brought out for last minute alterations to the wedding dress, memories from long ago suddenly came to mind—her mother packing for their trip to Spain, and how it had destroyed her when they couldn't go. Now that Angela thought back on it, perhaps the trip hadn't been solely for Doña Luisa's benefit after all. At the time, sixteen and in her own world, Angela had thought the journey was for her mother. But hadn't her mother said, "I want you to have a better life"? How Luisa had grown quieter and quieter afterward, as if her soul were shrinking, like a candle flame growing smaller until it was out.

Angela realized now in shock that her mother had never planned on coming back from Spain. But deserting a husband was against the law of man and Church. She would have been excommunicated, a devout woman like Luisa. Perhaps imprisoned. *She was doing it for me.*

And then another memory: Navarro scoffing over Angela's choice of name for their baby. "Marina? You name our daughter for a fleet of ships?"

But to Angela, Marina was more than just the Spanish word for navy. It also pertained to the ocean, to the sea, and it conjured images of marine creatures swimming in freedom. And how ironic that Marina should fall in love with a sea captain! Perhaps the dream had been a prophecy.

She continued to look at her daughter's bowed head, the slumped shoulders, the attitude of resignation. It was the way the old Indian had looked when he had gone away with the padre. And through the open shutters, over the music and the laughter, Angela could hear the cries of the grizzly bear, who had not asked to be brought here, roaring pitifully in his pen to be set free.

"This Daniel," she said as her heart began to break in two, "he is a Protestant?"

Marina lifted her head, light shining again in her eyes. "He is a good and devout man, Mamá. He wants to take the word of God to people who have never heard of Jesus Christ. But . . ." She frowned. "Why do you ask?"

Angela listened to the sounds of merriment drift through the open shutters, she sensed the warm evening, balmy and sweet, and knew that in years to come she would remember every small detail of this moment: the musician hitting a wrong note, a firecracker going off, the booming laugh of Pablo's father, how the small painting of Santa Teresa, hanging on the wall, winked in the candlelight. "You cannot go into the town," she finally said. "You must arrange for a place to meet Daniel."

Marina gave her a puzzled look. "What are you talking about?"

"Where is Daniel Goodside? Can you send word to him, before he leaves at midnight?"

"I will not go," Marina said firmly, although tears rose in her eyes and fell freely, and her voice broke with a sob.

Angela took her by the shoulders. "Child, you have something rare and beautiful. So few of us find such love in our lives, you cannot let it slip through your fingers." Angela suspected that such embers of passion might even glow somewhere in her own heart, but no man had come along to fan them into flame, and perhaps never would. But Marina must be allowed her chance to know deep and abiding love.

Marina averted her eyes. "I will not go," she said softly.

"But why? Surely you will be miserable if you let Daniel go away."

Marina faced her squarely, and Angela saw the fear and regret in her eyes. "What is it, child? What aren't you telling me?"

"I can't leave you, Mamá."

Angela gave her a bewildered look.

"Father," Marina said. "I cannot leave you alone with him."

Angela's hands flew to her mouth. "What are you saying, daughter?"

"Mamá, I know. About you and Father. How he treats you."

"You do not know what you are saying!" Angela felt a pain rip through her, as if her body had been torn in two. Dear God, do not let it be so. Let my secret have been safe all these years!

But she saw in her daughter's eyes the dreadful truth. Marina knew of Navarro's abuse. Perhaps the others knew as well. The sudden shame and humiliation of it made Angela clutch her stomach and turn away.

"Mamá," Marina said, reaching for her.

When Angela turned around it was to present a pale face to her daughter, chin held high, pain masked behind her eyes, as she had learned to do for so many years. "Then this is all the more reason for you to go," she said as she fought back the tears. "What unhappiness I have known since the day I married your father would only be made a thousand times worse if you were to stay now. It is only by your going away with a man you love that I will be able to live with it."

Marina fell into her mother's arms and they both cried softly, even though the walls were three feet thick and no one could hear them. They wept tears onto each other's shoulders and clung to each other for what they both knew would be the last time. Then Angela drew back, and said, "Can you send Daniel a message for him to meet you somewhere?"

"He is at the house of Francisco Marquez. He said he will be waiting for word from me, but that he must sail at midnight."

Angela nodded. "Then we must act quickly, we haven't much time." She went to the door that led to the outer colonnade and looked out. As she had hoped, Carlotta was waiting outside, pacing nervously. Gesturing for her to come inside, Angela closed the door and explained briefly about the turn of events.

"Santa Maria!" Carlotta whispered, looking at her younger sister with new admiration.

"I need you to find someone to carry a message to the house of Francisco Marquez," Angela said as she went to Marina's small writing desk and withdrew notepaper and a pen. "It is important this message is delivered before midnight." She folded it and sealed it, then handed it to Carlotta. "Who can we trust?"

Swept up by the romance and intrigue of the moment, Carlotta said with a feverish smile, "There is no one better than my own dear husband, Jacques! D'Arcy is the first to volunteer to ride with love letters to a forbidden lover, and the last to tell the secret!"

"Hurry then, and do not let anyone see you. After D'Arcy has left, tell everyone that Marina has a headache and that the ceremony will be delayed."

After Carlotta left, Angela returned to the writing desk. "I know of a cave where you and Daniel can meet." She hastily sketched a map on another piece of notepaper. "The cave is in a canyon, where you will find a formation of rocks with these carvings on them." She handed the piece of paper to Marina.

The girl looked at it in wonder. "How do you know of this place, Mother?"

"I went there years ago when I, too, was afraid. And . . . I think, before that, although I cannot remember. I'm afraid I have no money to give you but you must take this." She reached into a pocket in the folds of her gown. "Your grandmother, God rest her soul, gave this to me the night she died. She said it was very special, a good luck piece." Angela fell silent. The night her mother died, Doña Luisa said strange things. She had seemed remorseful, penitent even about something which Angela could make no sense of. Did it have something to do with the strange dreams Angela had had all her life—of the cave with mysterious paintings and a wild man coming down out of the mountains to be killed by rifle shot? Had these things really happened or were they the fantasies of a child, stories she had heard?

She folded Marina's fingers over the spirit-stone, and said, "Go now. You will be safe there until Daniel joins you."

They embraced quickly and wiped tears from their cheeks, but as Marina was fastening her cape and reaching for her gloves, the door flew open to reveal Navarro standing there like a wrathful god. "What is this? I overheard Carlotta tell D'Arcy that there was something wrong with Marina." Then he saw the cape and traveling bag. "Have you lost your senses?" he boomed.

"She is not going to marry Quiñones," Angela said.

"Shut up, woman. I will deal with you later." He turned on Marina. "Get into that wedding dress."

"I cannot, Papá."

"*Dios mio*, I raised you better than this!"

"You did not raise her," Angela said, "*I* raised her. And I say she can leave."

His arm shot out so fast Angela did not see it coming, and he struck her with such force that he knocked her nearly across the room. Then he reached for Marina.

As Angela struggled to her feet, shaking her head to clear it, her eyes focused on the seamstress's shears on the dressing table. Angela moved swiftly. The shears were in her hand, rising high in the air, plunging deeply into Navarro's back.

He roared like a grizzly bear, turned slowly, and blinked at Angela in frank surprise. Then he fell forward, landing on the floor facedown, still and silent.

The two women stared at him for a moment, then Marina dropped to her knees and placed her hand on her father's neck. She looked up at her mother with big, frightened eyes. "He is dead," she whispered.

Kneeling at his side, Angela wordlessly went through Navarro's pockets, finding a handful of coins, which she dropped into Marina's bag. Then, thrusting it into her daughter's hands, she said, "Go now. Hurry.

Do not let anyone see you. When the Quiñones learn of this, they will ride after you."

"But Mamá—"

Angela pulled her daughter to the door that led to the inner courtyard, through which Marina could escape unseen. "Go, and you must make sure they do not find you." With tears in her eyes, she added, "You can never come back here, for once you set foot on this road, you must follow it to its end. Your brothers, and possibly the Quiñones, will say you have dishonored our families. But I say it is worse to dishonor one's heart. When you are safe, my daughter, send word to Carlotta in Mexico and she will find a way to let me know. But your whereabouts must not be known, not for a very long time. Go now. Go with God and with my love."

Marina paused to watch her mother draw a chair next to Navarro's body. "What will you do?"

"I will wait here until I am certain you are safe," she said. And she sat down, hands folded in her lap, to wait.

*

Marina rode like the wind, her way guided by the full moon, her heart galloping in cadence with the horse's hooves as she prayed frantically that Daniel would receive the message and come for her.

Her father lying dead on the floor! And Mamá, sitting there, grimly awaiting her fate.

As she neared the end of *El Camino Viejo* she followed her mother's instructions until she found the little canyon and, hidden behind boulders, the cave. Inside, while she waited for Daniel to join her, she sat near the entrance, in a pool of unearthly moonlight, and counted her money in her lap. Coins taken from Father's pockets—pesos, reales, and an American one-cent piece. Her fingers trembled with fear and her heart leapt at every sound. A cold wind blew through the canyon and rushed into the cave like the icy breath of a ghost.

The hour grew late and Marina's fear mounted. What time was it? Had D'Arcy made it to Marquez's house? Or had he been stopped?

Suddenly—hooves picking over the rubble outside.

Marina held her breath.

A rider dismounted.

Hastily putting the coins back in her purse, she stood up, a coin falling to the earth along with the spirit-stone.

"Daniel?" she called out. "Is that you?"

Chapter Thirteen

Darkness.

Erica couldn't tell if her eyes were open or closed. Where was she? She tried to remember, tried to assess her situation. Her head felt funny and there was a pressure on her chest making it difficult to breathe. Her hands hurt.

She realized after a moment that she was slumped on a dirt floor. Then she remembered: she was in the cave. There had been an explosion, a cave-in. Luke buried in the rubble. And she had started frantically digging her way out. That was why her hands hurt. She had cut and torn her fingers. How long had she been lying there unconscious? The air was dangerously thin. How much was left? And how close were the rescuers who were surely digging on the other side of the cave-in?

She tried to sit up but found herself shockingly weak. So she remained on the floor, the scent of dirt and dust filling her nose. "Help . . ." she whispered, but there was little breath in her lungs.

Suddenly she saw someone standing over her, purse-lipped and wagging an admonishing finger. Mrs. Manion. Erica's fourth grade schoolteacher. What was she doing here in the cave? *I must be delirious. Or is my life flashing before my eyes? But doesn't that only pertain to drowning persons?* Other faces joined the teacher, characters from Erica's past, people who had been both real and fantasized. They were trying to tell her something.

And then she passed out.

*

When Erica regained consciousness again she listened carefully. All around was deathly silence. Was no one trying to dig her out? Had they given up?

More faces materialized, ghostly, beckoning. "No . . ." she whispered, thinking they had come to escort her to the land of the dead. Or were they taking her someplace else? Back in time . . .

His name was Chip Masters and he was one of the Bad Boys of Reseda High. When he invited Erica and her girlfriend to go for a ride with him and some other kids in his dad's new car, how could she resist? At sixteen Erica chafed against the strict rules of the girls' home she currently lived in. Chip was mystery and adventure.

There was beer in the car. Although she didn't like the taste, she took a few sips, to fit in with the crowd. They took turns driving—Ventura, White Oak, Sherman Way. Onto the freeway. Off at Studio City. It was during Erica's turn at the wheel that a police cruiser turned on a siren and ordered her to pull over. Erica was suddenly scared. She didn't have a driver's license. And then like lightning, the other kids jumped out and ran while Erica, puzzled, stayed in the car.

At the police station she tried to convince the cops that she hadn't known the car was stolen. How did she get the keys? they asked. Whose car did she think it was? Who were the companions who ran off when she pulled over? But Erica had learned in group and foster homes the code of teenage ethics that dictated one never ratted on friends.

She was charged with grand theft auto and sent to Juvenile Hall until her hearing. There she encountered tough kids who told her horror stories about California Youth Authority camps. "You're pretty and you're white. You'd better watch out for yourself in the showers."

Being in court was not a new experience for Erica. As a ward of the state, whenever her status changed, she had had to face a judge in Dependency Court. Except that now she was in Delinquency Court, and if they found her guilty and sentenced her to CYA, then her "ass was toast," as the Juvie kids warned.

It was September, the worst month to be in the San Fernando Valley, when heat and smog were at their peak, and Erica was more frightened and depressed than she could remember. Not only had Chip Masters and the others not come forward in her defense, the woman who ran the group home declared she didn't tolerate bad girls and refused to offer a good character witness for Erica. She was the most alone she had ever been in her life, and facing a hard sentence behind chain link and razor wire.

Erica was in one of the hallways at Superior Court waiting for her case to be called. The hearing was to determine if she should be tried as a juvenile or as an adult. A kid ran past an elderly lady and knocked her purse off her arm. Others came to the woman's aid, helping her up, taking her to the elevator. Erica, sitting on a bench, saw the coin purse that had slid under a chair. She picked it up, looked at the money inside, then ran after the lady, catching her just before the elevator doors closed.

The hearing had a disastrous outcome. The judge determined Erica to be streetwise and mature and therefore should be tried as an adult. While her social worker was escorting her out of the courtroom, Erica had suddenly gotten sick. She went into the ladies' room while the social worker waited out in the hall. And it was in the white-tiled bathroom that smelled of disinfectant, while Erica was sobbing her eyes out and thinking that her life had come to an end—for surely, since no one believed her story, she was going to be sent to prison on a felony charge—that a well-dressed lady carrying a briefcase came in and asked her what was wrong. Erica blurted out her story and to her surprise, the woman said she would help. "I saw you return that woman's money to her this morning. You could have kept it. No one was watching you. You didn't see me on the other side of the newsstand. That tells me something about your character. A girl who returns a purse full of money is not going to steal a car."

The lady, it turned out, was a lawyer who was on good terms with the judge. She took Erica straight back into the courtroom and explained to the man on the bench that this minor had been represented by a panel attorney and therefore had had inadequate representation. She asked to be appointed guardian ad litem and sought an immediate rehearing for the girl. The judge looked at Erica, and said, "This person has taken an interest in you. Are you comfortable with that?"

"Yes."

"Then I am going to strike my previous order, appoint this woman as your guardian ad litem, and refer you back to juvenile court. You are being given one last chance, young lady. I hope you realize how lucky you are."

❊

When Erica regained consciousness again she listened to the unearthly silence. Had the rescuers given up? Did they think she had been buried in the cave-in? She felt something in her hand, hard and stonelike. How had it gotten there and why was she clasping it so tightly?

And then: Sounds! Thumping. Digging. Muffled voices. "Yes . . ." she whispered with a dry throat. "I'm here . . . don't stop . . ."

❊

"Come on!" Jared shouted. "Hurry up! She's running out of air!" Erica had been trapped in the cave for nearly eight hours.

The teams madly dug away at the rubble and earth that had sealed the cave entrance. They used shovels, buckets, hand trowels, and bare hands. Paramedics were standing by.

"Wait!" Jared said suddenly, holding his hands up for silence. "I thought I heard—"

A faint sound from the other side of the cave-in. *"Hello? Can anyone hear me?"*

"It's Erica! She's alive! Keep digging!"

Finally: a small opening in the dirt. And then Erica calling weakly, "Can you see me? Jared, is that you?"

He attacked the earth until he had an opening large enough to reach in and haul her out and help her to her feet. She was badly shaken and covered with dirt. "Luke! Is Luke hurt?"

"He's all right. He managed to jump free before the cave-in caught him. But what about you? Are you okay, Erica?"

"Yes, yes," she said weakly. She unclasped her fingers and looked in surprise at the small pink statue she had been holding. "I was digging my way out . . . I don't know what level it was at—is it Aztec? How did an Aztec god get so far north—"

Suddenly Jared's mouth was on hers in a hard, breathless kiss.

Erica held on to him for a moment, then she went limp.

"Are you okay?" he repeated.

"Oh yes. I'm fine," she said.

And she fainted dead away.

Chapter Fourteen

ANGELIQUE
1850 C.E.

They were auctioning off the women. Again.

Seth Hopkins thought it a revolting practice. Slavery was supposed to be illegal in California, yet the San Francisco authorities could do nothing about it because the ships' captains were within their rights to claim unpaid fares, even if it meant selling the female passengers to the highest bidders.

It seemed to Seth that the number of abandoned ships in the harbor had multiplied since he was last here. As soon as a boat came into port, captain and crew jumped ship and headed for the gold fields. A few enterprising men had hauled some of the clippers onshore and turned them into hotels, but the forest of spars and masts of some five hundred deserted vessels still extended halfway into San Francisco Bay. Which was why the *Betsy Lain* had had to anchor far out, requiring cargo and passengers to be brought ashore by launch. Seth paused in the packing of his wagon to watch the obscene stampede of men to the *Betsy Lain*'s landing stage. Word had spread that the Boston clipper was bringing *women*.

After being processed through the customs shed, some of the women left immediately, many of them, Seth knew, to go in search of husbands who had abandoned their families when they caught gold fever. The rest, because they had not paid their fare, would be offered to any person on the dock who would pay what was owed, forcing the unfortunate woman into legal bondage.

From all over the world the women came to California, as did the men, in the hope of starting a new life. Some were hiding from a husband, some were hoping to catch one. Some came to lose themselves, some to find themselves. In California anything was possible. The land and resources were limitless, and there was gold for the grabbing. Most important of all, there were no social rules to keep a person in his or her place. Here a peasant was as good as a king, if he had money. And here no one asked questions. A man could even, Seth thought darkly, escape the stigma of being an ex-convict.

Seth watched in disgust as the *Lain*'s female passengers were herded like cattle into a roped-off area on the dock, penning them in among cargo bales, luggage, and crates while the growing crowd of men pressed around the perimeter, anxious for the auction to begin. Many were owners of bordellos and fandango houses, gambling joints and dance halls. These would choose the youngest and the prettiest and force them into a life of prostitution until the debt was paid. But there were also decent, hard-working men in the crowd, miners and trappers who were lonely and craved the gentling touch of a female. Honest marriage was what these men offered.

Seth Hopkins, at thirty-two years of age, had never been married, nor did he ever intend to be. Experience had taught him that the matrimonial state was just another form of bondage. The solitary life was what called to him, with trees and green pastures as far from the Virginia coal mines as he could get.

He turned away, securing ropes over the supplies piled in the back of his wagon. He disliked the mayhem of the Port of San Francisco, where squealing pigs were being off-loaded, cattle were bellowing and dogs barking, carriages and wagons creaked by, people shouted, argued, haggled, and horses with their loudly *clip-clopping* hooves randomly dropped manure. Smoke filled the air, as well as the stench of stagnant water and rotted fish, which the midday summer heat made worse. Seth was anxious to get back to the mining camp in the mountains, where the air was clean and pure, and a man could hear his own thoughts.

The captain of the clipper, a short, stocky man in a blue mariner's uniform, climbed up onto a block and started the auction. He pointed to the first woman in line, a stout lady in her forties who was looking both angry and frightened. "This one owes fifty dollars. Who'll pay fifty dollars?"

Mrs. Armitage, whom Seth recognized as the owner of the Armitage Hotel on Market Street, shouted, "Can she cook? I need a cook!"

"Got any seamstresses?" another woman called out. "I'll pay top dollar for anyone who can use a needle!"

A horse-drawn trolley pulled up and a group of twelve colorfully dressed women, who had been standing off to one side, happily climbed on board. Seth knew they were headed for Finch's Fandango Club and its upstairs bordello.

A man with the grizzled look of a forty-niner pushed through, and said, "How much for that blonde! I need a wife and I need her fast!" The crowd roared with laughter.

The women started to go quickly, as money changed hands and men stepped forward to claim their prizes. Some women went willingly, others reluctantly, a few were even weeping. As Seth was about to climb up into his wagon, his eye caught on a woman who was somehow different from the rest. Refusing to stand in the auction line, she sat primly on her big traveling trunk, hands folded in her lap. Her face was shadowed by the brim of the big feathery bonnet she wore, tied under her chin in a bow. But it was her gown that had caught Seth's attention. He had never seen silk of such a color before—or rather *colors*, for it shimmered and changed as the lady moved, or as a breeze from the harbor rippled the fabric. When she breathed, the bodice shifted from sea green to turquoise, and when she stood up, the skirt went from aquamarine to sapphire blue. It made

Seth think of peacock feathers and butterfly wings or tide pools on a summer's day. The effect was hypnotic.

He realized that she was trying calmly to explain something to the ship's purser, and when the breeze shifted Seth could hear her words, spoken in a thick Spanish accent. "I have said, Señor Boggs will pay my fare."

The purser, a red-faced man with a dyspeptic scowl, scanned the crowd. "Don't see Boggs. Might be outta town. Sorry, lady, I gotta get your fare. I'll have to let one of these men have you."

"What is this, 'have you'?"

"Anyone willing to pay your fare gets to take you away. You become his property till you work off your debt."

She tipped her chin and Seth caught a flash of dark eyes. "I am not that kind of a lady, Señor, and if my husband were alive, he would challenge you to a duel to defend my honor."

The pursuer was unimpressed. "Rules of the shipping line, lady. I gotta collect a full fare for every passenger we carry. Where it comes from is none of my concern. But I gotta enter it in this here ledger."

"Then my father will pay!"

The purser wrinkled his nose. "And where be he?"

"Well . . . I do not know just now. He is here."

"Where?"

"In California."

He made an exasperated sound. "Look, Boggs ain't here so I gotta collect the fare from one of these men. That's the rules." He took hold of her arm.

"But you cannot do this, Señor!"

"Look, I don't see Boggs and I don't have time. Gotta have the receipts to the shipping office by noon."

"Remove your hand from me!"

The purser looked at his passenger list. "Your name D'Arcy? Listen up, gentlemen! This one's a genuine Frenchee. Name of *On-zhay-leek*. Who'll start the bidding?"

"That's the one I've been waitin' for," said a man nearby. "Here, girlie," he shouted. "Lift up your skirt and show us an ankle."

Seth climbed up onto his wagon and reached for the reins. One thing prison had taught him was that life wasn't fair. It had also taught him that smart men kept out of other people's business. Besides, the woman already belonged to Boggs. She knew what she was getting into.

But as he started to get his horses going, something made him stop. He looked back at the woman. The purser had left her for a moment to settle a fight that had broken out between two customers. Boggs, Seth thought. He knew the man. Cyrus Boggs had come out as a preacher two years ago but had found a more lucrative enterprise. He currently owned a brothel on Clay Street and was known to lure unsuspecting women to San Francisco with newspaper ads for teachers and nursemaids, offering to pay their fare when they arrived, and then imprisoning them in his cribs—small, windowless rooms where the helpless women were expected to service up to thirty men a day.

With a sigh, Seth dropped the reins, jumped down to the ground, and went back to the ropes. "Pardon me, lady, did I hear you say Boggs?"

"Sí," she said as she dug into her purse. Her hands were small, he noticed, her gloves made of soft kid. "After my husband dies," she explained, "the government takes our farm for taxes. I have little left. But then I see this." She handed a newspaper clipping to him.

"Sorry, I don't know Spanish. What does it say?"

"It is, how do you say, *anuncio*. This man says he wishes for teachers of young ladies. Here is his name and address. I write him a letter." She produced a folded sheet of paper. Seth read the false promises it contained.

He handed them back. "This letter and advertisement are a fraud. Boggs got you here under false pretenses."

She gave him a puzzled look. He saw dark lashes framing dark eyes, black curls escaping from under the bonnet.

He cleared his throat. He didn't know how to put it delicately. "Boggs is a criminal. He isn't going to help you. Did I hear you say your father is here?"

"Sí! He is why I come. He is wealthy. He will pay my fare."

Seth saw how the men were eyeing her, and then he remembered that just last week a vigilante group, mostly disbanded American soldiers with nothing to do now that the war with Mexico was over, had raided a tent community on Telegraph Hill called Little Chile, and raped and murdered a mother and daughter. People of Spanish descent were not safe in San Francisco at the moment, especially a Spanishwoman on her own. If the woman's father didn't show soon, then Boggs surely would, and if not Boggs, then one of these men would pay for this D'Arcy woman and enslave her God knew where.

"Hey, you!" the purser shouted, coming back. "Get away from there!"

Despite his hard-and-fast rule not to get involved, Seth couldn't stand by while an injustice was being done.

He offered to pay the fare, reaching into his pocket for a roll of banknotes. When another man immediately raised the bid, the purser accepted it. Seth grabbed his arm and said close to his face, "Friend, I don't want trouble. But you asked for the price of the lady's passage, and I offered to pay it."

The purser looked down at the fingers digging painfully into his arm, then into the unblinking eyes of the tall stranger. He pulled away. "Awright, settle with the captain over there."

"Thank you, Señor," Angelique said as Seth moved her trunk from behind the ropes. "I am in your debt. How do I pay you?"

He squinted up at the sun. He was anxious to get going. "I'm at Devil's Bar, north of Sacramento. When you find your father, you can pay me back." Touching the brim of his hat, he started for his wagon.

As he started to climb up, he looked back. She remained standing beside her trunk, looking lost. Men were starting to crowd around her, saying, "You really French? You need a place to stay? I can guarantee you'll make lots of money here."

Seth went back, pushing his way through the protesting men. "Do you really have nowhere to go?"

"Only Señor Boggs . . ."

"Now see here—" began one man.

"And you have no idea where your father is?"

"I come to look. This is why I answer Mr. Boggs's *anuncio*. I come to California to look for my father. And while I look, I work as a teacher, you see?"

"Your father a forty-niner?"

When they recognized the stranger's proprietary manner with the woman, the men drifted back to the auction, where a woman with a baby was being offered for thirty dollars.

"No, no," Angelique explained to Seth Hopkins. "After my mother dies my father goes to New Orleans, to his brother there. They come to California, he says in a letter, for the fur trapping." She produced another folded piece of paper. Seth squinted at it then handed it back. "I don't know French either. You say he's a trapper? He'd be up north, then. Unless he's gone for the gold. In which case he could be in one of a thousand mining camps." He rubbed his jaw. "Look, you'll probably have a better chance of finding him if you go to Sacramento." He sighed, wondering why he was getting himself into this. The heat must have addled his brain. "I can take you there."

"Oh! You have already been too kind, Señor. These men will help me."

"These men—" he began. "Never mind. Sacramento is what you want, believe me, it's closer to gold country. You can put the word out on your father. The camps get traveling preachers, circuit judges, entertainers, trappers, miners, and all sorts of assorted folk passing through. Word of mouth travels very quickly among the mining camps. Your father'll soon hear you're looking for him. What's his name?"

"Jacques D'Arcy. He is a Count," she added proudly.

Seth would have liked two bits for every "Count," "Baron" and "Prince" there was in San Francisco, and phonies the lot of them. He doubted half the men on this wharf were even going by their real names.

"Oh," she said when she saw the wagon. "Is Sacramento far?"

"We aren't taking the wagon to Sacramento. Just along to the terminal to pick up the steamboat to take us upriver."

✳

As Seth guided the wagon up and down the streets of Sacramento in search of a respectable place where Miss D'Arcy could stay, Angelique was thankful to be off the steamboat. When Mr. Hopkins had said they were to take an overnight steamer upriver, she had pictured a cabin and the opportunity to loosen her corset and perhaps bathe, have tea brought.

The trip from Mexico had been horrendous. Boarding the *Betsy Lain* at Acapulco, Angelique had found the Boston ship already overcrowded with passengers. But the overnight passage on the steamboat had been an even more appalling experience. Because the cabins were all taken, she and Mr. Hopkins had had to sleep on the deck among their belongings, along with hundreds of other people—most of whom had been men—even with horses, donkeys, and pigs! Thoughts of finding her father had sustained her. Papá was going to make everything all right. He had always taken care of her, and he would take care of her again.

Sacramento was a new town, sprouting up at the convergence of two rivers. Angelique, who had been born in a three-hundred-year-old city that was itself built upon the ruins of a city far older, marveled that only the year before Sacramento had been a tent city, and before that an Indian village. Now there were brick buildings, wooden houses, church spires, and properly laid out streets. But finding a hotel or boardinghouse where she could stay was turning out to be a challenge.

After riding around for an hour in the rented wagon, finding fault with each boardinghouse and hotel he found, Seth began to realize that he could no more leave Miss D'Arcy on her own here than he could in San Francisco. Signs in windows read NO MEXICANS OR FOREIGNERS NEED APPLY. And people stared openly and rather rudely, Seth noticed, at the highly mismatched pair—he in homespun shirt and blue jeans, the lady at his side in a shimmering blue-green gown that couldn't make up its mind on a color. He had a good idea what was on people's minds, and he suspected that Angelique's respectability, an attractive young woman on her own, would come under question. He couldn't just abandon her, any more than he could have back in San Francisco. Even though it was she who owed *him*, he felt responsible for her. There was only one solution. She would be safer at Devil's Bar, and, after all, he told himself, she would be closer to the word-of-mouth grapevine that would lead her to her father.

"There are several decent ladies at the camp," he offered. "I'm sure one of them will gladly take you in."

Angelique graciously accepted and as she rode primly at Seth Hopkins's side, looking forward to a hot bath at last, a proper meal, and a good night's sleep between clean sheets, she peered anxiously into the face of every man they passed, anticipating the joyous reunion with her father. She thought about the birthday parties when she was little, and Papá had made a crown for her to wear and a special throne to sit on. And when she had grown up he had even chosen her husband for her, as no ordinary man would do. A D'Arcy, a distant cousin, who had had to promise that he would continue to treat Angelique in the manner she was accustomed to. Pierre had done just that, right up until the day he had died at the hands of American soldiers.

"Will you go to your family in Los Angeles?" Father Gomez had asked the day she left Mexico City.

But Angelique had no intention of looking up her mother's family. She had heard so many times when she was growing up how shabbily Grandfather Navarro had treated her father that she wanted nothing to do with them. It had felt strange when the *Betsy Lain* stopped at Los Angeles and she had looked out at the smoky plain and wondered if the family was even still there. She only vaguely recalled her last visit to Rancho Paloma, twenty years before, when she was six years old. There was to have been a wedding, and then something happened—Auntie Marina disappeared and everyone was sent home. There had been no communication with her mother's family after that.

As the wagon carried them through countryside that was flat and parklike and dotted with oaks, Angelique sneaked surreptitious looks at the man at her side. Mr. Hopkins had an interesting face, she thought. Sunburnt and creased, with a large straight nose and deep-set thoughtful eyes. When he removed his hat to mop his forehead, she saw thick, wavy hair, warmed by the sun to a golden brown. She liked the sound of his voice, it possessed a mellow quality, and he always spoke carefully, with measured words. There was something solid and sincere about him. She decided she felt safe with Seth Hopkins.

Seth, on the other hand, was entertaining thoughts of a different nature. As they rode in silence through the sunshine, their road gradually diminishing as they left the settled areas behind, he tried not to stare at his unexpected traveling companion. She sat on the wagon seat like a queen, her back straight, her parasol perfectly angled against the sun. In all his thirty-two years he had never beheld a sight so exotic. She also baffled him. It was hard to believe she was as naive as she had appeared back at the Port of San Francisco. He placed her age around twenty-five, and she had been married, so she must know something of the ways of the world. Yet her response to her situation had seemed almost childlike.

But this woman was no child, he reminded himself as he tried not to take too long a look at the small waist flaring into feminine hips, and the breasts that strained against the green-blue silk. There must be a hundred petticoats under that frilly skirt. A light sheen of moisture had appeared across her brow and above her pink lips. And she smelled faintly of roses. He tried to identify her coloring. She wasn't Anglo so her complexion wasn't white. But she wasn't brown either, or dusky like a gypsy. Honey-colored, he decided, and it brought bile to his throat to think of how the "Reverend" Cyrus Boggs had intended to use her.

When he saw her produce a small medicine phial from her purse and take a delicate drink, he gave her a questioning look. She slipped the phial back into her purse and said, "It is a medicine that is my great-grandmother's recipe. A chemist in Mexico City mixes it for me for the journey. When I feel a headache coming, I drink and I am fine."

"And if you don't drink it?"

"Do not be worried, Señor, I am fine." She wasn't going to tell him about the visions or the voices she experienced during her spells. He would think she was a lunatic, or worse.

"Listen," he said in a lowered voice, even though they were on a lonely road with only the horses to hear. "You'd better drop the 'Señor.' Folks around here don't cotton to Mexicans. The war is still fresh in people's minds."

It was still fresh in Angelique's as well. Her husband had been killed in the battle at Chepultepec, and she would never forget the fear she had felt when American troops had marched triumphantly into Mexico City. "But I am Spanish," she said. "My family on my mother's side is *Californio*. My family in Los Angeles were the first here." She reached into her purse and brought out a daguerreotype in an oval frame. "My mother was a beautiful lady, as you can see."

Seth took in Carlotta Navarro D'Arcy's high cheekbones, the leaf-shaped eyes, the sensuous lips and olive complexion. There was more than just Spanish blood there. It would take a blind man not to see. And the daughter took after the mother. He wordlessly handed the picture back, understanding something now about her exotic features that maybe the girl herself didn't realize—something to do with her family coming to California when there were only Indians here.

Finally, they entered a land of tall pines, deep ravines, and high mountain ridges, the air sharp and pure. They reached Devil's Bar just before nightfall.

Angelique leaned forward on the seat, anxious to see this town in the mountains. During the long ride she had composed a mental image of what it would look like—brick homes and shops lining cobblestoned streets, with a church facing the plaza, a fountain in the center, paved sidewalks, private courtyards shaded by trees. Since gold miners—rich men!—lived here, it might even be more splendid than she could imagine.

The wagon rounded the bend and the forest gave way to a hillside cleared of trees. And covering the hillside were—

Angelique's jaw dropped.

Tents.

Rows of canvas tents with an occasional log cabin or wooden structure in between. The streets, if they could be called such, were dirt with garbage strewn about, dogs scavenging, flies buzzing in the heat. There were no sidewalks. No fountain or church. No shady courtyards where a lady could retire for tea. Not a brick or adobe structure in sight.

And the people! Men in dusty work clothes with battered hats pulled over their eyes, and women in plain cotton dresses dragging in the dirt. Everyone, including the women, seemed to be carrying something—heavy sacks, or shovels and picks, buckets of water, armloads of firewood. If they were so rich, why did they live so poorly? She saw men hammering boards together to make a coffin. And up the slope of the hill, an area cleared of trees and dotted with wooden crosses and grave markers.

Her spirits sank as she took in the vista that was painted in tones of gray and brown, the bare hillsides dotted with tree stumps, the patches of yellow grass, the scrawny wildflowers. The smell was almost as bad as the heat. A pall of thick smoke hung over the little valley. Angelique drew a perfumed handkerchief from her purse and held it to her nose.

A couple of men on horseback suddenly came galloping through, shouting "Eureka!" and shooting pistols into the air, horses' hooves sending up clods of dirt, one of which landed in Angelique's lap. "Oh!" she said in alarm. "They are *banditos*?"

Seth laughed. "Just a couple of forty-niners who made a lucky strike. There'll be free drinks at the saloon tonight!"

At the sound of a wagon entering the camp, people came out of their tents to see. "Hoy there, Seth Hopkins! Back are you then?"

As Seth brought the wagon to a halt in front of a wooden, two-story structure with a sign that said DEVIL'S BAR HOTEL, ELIZA GIBBONS, PRO-PRIETOR, a crowd quickly materialized, eyes going wide at the sight of the young woman at Seth's side. Angelique remained seated while he unloaded crates and boxes, and people came up to claim purchases he had made for them in San Francisco. They happily took their goods and told Seth they were glad he was home. No one said a word to Angelique as they gawked at her.

A woman emerged from the small hotel, smiling broadly as she dried her hands on a towel. She went up to Seth and said something Angelique couldn't hear. Seth laughed, and Angelique saw how the woman beamed. Medium-sized and around thirty, the woman wore her hair parted and drawn severely back in a bun. Her dress was plain and she wore what looked like men's boots. There was something familiar about the way she touched Seth's arm.

When the last of the goods was claimed, Seth brought the woman around to introduce her as Eliza Gibbons, owner of the hotel. Eliza nodded curtly, and although she smiled, Angelique saw a hardness in the look that startled her.

"I was hoping," Seth began, and then stopped. He suddenly saw how the men were eyeing Miss D'Arcy, no different from the way they had in San Francisco, and he realized she wasn't going to be any safer here after all. He hadn't thought it through, back in Sacramento when he had decided to bring her to Devil's Bar. He had reckoned he could find a place for her with one of the women, but he realized now his plan had been poorly conceived. None of the married women would take her in, not the way their husbands were looking her over. And she couldn't be on her own, not with the way the men were devouring her with their eyes. So that left the single women. But the only unmarried females were the ladies who lived above the saloon, and Eliza Gibbons, owner of the four-room hotel. And if Seth knew Eliza, she would take one look at Miss D'Arcy's expensive gowns and triple her usual rent. Which Seth would have to pay until Miss D'Arcy found her father. It suddenly occurred to him that rescuing a lady in distress was not as simple as he had thought.

There was only one place in all of Devil's Bar where he could be sure she would be safe—in his own cabin. Waving good-bye to his friends, he climbed up onto the seat, picked up the reins, and said to Angelique, "Listen, I work my claim from morning till night and have no time to keep house, so I pay a woman to help. Do you think you could keep house for me? I would pay you the same as I've been paying Eliza Gibbons for one of her maids."

She brightened. "Señor Hopkins, in Mexico I manage a large hacienda while my husband is away fighting in the war. I am very capable."

They pulled away from the hotel, leaving the crowd behind to murmur and to speculate—and Eliza Gibbons to stare enigmatically at the retreating wagon.

Seth's log cabin was farther down the ravine and nearly the last dwelling on the dusty road. He helped Angelique down, then pulled aside the canvas flap that served as a door to allow her to enter. The cabin consisted of just one room, and Angelique stood speechless in the center of it as she took in the rough log walls, the blackened fireplace, the bare dirt floor, the sooty potbellied stove, the narrow bed, and a table that looked as if it hadn't been cleaned since it was a tree. There were no windows, just another door at the back.

"You can stay here tonight and I'll bunk with Charlie Bigelow. We'll work arrangements out tomorrow." He started for the door.

"You are leaving?"

"That wagon and horses aren't mine. They're rented by the day. Help yourself to anything here. Food in the pantry over there. Fresh water well's out back, just through that door." He paused, cleared his throat in embarrassment, and said, "The, um, is under the bed. You empty it down by the creek."

She turned to look, and just glimpsed in the darkness, under the bed, the white enamel chamber pot. Shock rendered her speechless.

Seth went out, closing the canvas door, and Angelique was engulfed in darkness. She continued to stand there bewildered as she heard voices outside: "She's a respectable widow lady." Seth explaining to the small crowd that had followed him to his cabin. "She's come looking for her father. Anyone know of a Jack D'Arcy, Frenchman fur trapper? Pass the word, we need to find him."

"You missed some excitement while you were gone, Seth. A vigilante mob from Johnston's Creek rode through chasin' after Injuns that raided their camp. Came back a week later and said they'd cornered the thieving lot on Randolph Island, 'twas like shooting pigs in a pen, they said. Won't be having no more trouble from that band."

Angelique heard footsteps tramp away and voices fade until she was alone in the crude cabin, where she could see the last of the dying daylight through cracks in the walls.

✳

Too numb with shock and too exhausted to do anything else, Angelique had curled up on the bed, wrapping the single blanket around herself, and had spent a night filled with dreams and nightmares until she was awakened at dawn by Seth presenting himself outside the door, announcing his presence.

It took Angelique a moment to remember where she was. Her first thought, before opening her eyes, was that she would have the maids change all the bedding throughout the hacienda, as her blanket smelled musty. She would also give all the rooms a good airing, and set the women to the furniture with oil and cloths. Fresh flowers in each room, too, would help to dispel the fustiness. And who was making all that noise outside, people calling to one another in English, riding horses too closely by? And where were the birds that always greeted her every morning from the bottlebrush tree outside her window?

"Miss D'Arcy? You awake?"

Reality shot back like a bullet. Angelique quickly got up and smoothed back her hair. She looked down at her gown in dismay. She had slept in her clothes and felt itchy all over from the straw mattress. "Come in, Señor."

Seth pushed the canvas door aside and a milky dawn struggled to come in with him as he filled the small cabin with his height and masculine presence. Casting Angelique a quick, self-conscious smile, he frowned at the table and then at the cold stove. "I came for my breakfast but I reckon you didn't know the hour I would be here. And you don't know my preferences. I head off to my claim at the river as soon as the sun is up. I like coffee, eggs, and biscuit for breakfast. Bacon when it can be afforded. I'll take my breakfast at Eliza's this morning. Tomorrow we can start our routine."

He took a minute to show her the creek out back, and the well and how to use it. He pointed out the wooden storage bin containing potatoes, onions, turnips, and carrots. Acorns, too, he said, from last fall. Back inside the cabin he showed her the two lamps, asking her to trim the wicks and refill them daily. She would also be cleaning out the ash from the cookstove, making the morning coffee, doing the laundry, and ironing. Angelique followed him wordlessly. Since waking up and realizing that no servants were going to bring her hot water for bathing or her breakfast chocolate, and that she must handle the chamber pot herself, she had moved in a kind of stunned torpor.

Now Seth was opening a small ledger book and turning to a fresh page where he wrote "Angelique" at the top. "The going rate for washing and ironing shirts is a dollar apiece," he said as he pointed to the pile of dirty clothes in the corner. "I was going to take them to Eliza today, but now the job is yours. I'm an honest man, Miss D'Arcy. I won't cheat you by a single penny." He closed the ledger and returned it to the drawer. "I have to go check on my claim now. Charlie Bigelow's kept an eye on it for me. I'll be back for supper. Whatever you cook will be fine with me."

And then he was gone.

She remained rooted to the spot. When he had asked her if she could keep house, she had thought he meant could she give orders to servants.

Having no windows, the cabin was dark. She pushed back the canvas that covered the front door and the one covering the back door, but still not enough of the early-morning light poured in, so she decided to light the lamps. But as she regarded the two lamps, Angelique realized she had never had to light her own before and had no idea how it was done. She decided to just leave the doors open and make do with daylight.

Next there was the question of food. Angelique was ravenous.

She contemplated the crusted frying pan Seth had pointed out. What was she supposed to do with it? In a cupboard she found sacks of rice and flour, salt and spices, olive oil, coffee beans, baking soda, sugar, a jar of beef fat, a few canned goods and fruit preserved in jars, salted fish in a large crock pot. She had no idea what to do with any of it. Breaking off a piece from a loaf of bread and slicing a block of hard cheese, she ate ravenously and eyed the filthy clothes heaped in the corner. Did he really expect her to wash them? At home she had only to oversee the collecting and later the storing away of laundry. Angelique had no idea what happened in between. As she devoured the bread and cheese, wishing for her morning chocolate, Angelique listened to sounds of the camp coming to life, strange, foreign sounds, rude and crude, she thought, not at all like the gentle mornings on her hacienda outside Mexico City. When she wondered again why she heard no birds, she remembered the barren slopes surrounding the little valley, and the tree stumps covering them.

The birds have retreated, and so should I.

Standing in the middle of the tiny, dirty cabin belonging to a man she did not know, in the middle of a miserable mining camp in the middle of a godforsaken wilderness, Angelique began to realize the horrific mistake she had made. Not in coming to California. She had had no choice but to come. Upon her husband's death, the Mexican government had confiscated her estate—the hacienda, fields, livestock—to cover back taxes, leaving Angelique with only a trunk full of clothes. The mistake had been in coming to Devil's Bar.

Her first thought was that she must find a way to get back to Sacramento, find a hotel, and wait for her father to find her. But then she reminded herself of the debt she owed Seth Hopkins. Not only the hundred dollars, but he had rescued her from a man of criminal intent, or so he had said.

Stiffening her spine and squaring her shoulders—D'Arcys honored their debts—she thought: How difficult can this be?

First, she hauled water up from the creek so she could bathe, discovering as she did so that she had had no idea water was so heavy. She withdrew fresh clothes from her trunk, carefully choosing the right outfit, spending extra time on selecting earrings that went with the red hues of the gown. Dressing herself proved a small challenge. Angelique had never had to do it by herself before. How was she to tighten her corset? She took pains with her hair, brushing it out and fixing it up on her head with combs. She applied cream to her face and hands, polished her shoes, brushed out her traveling gown and hung it up, laundered her undergarments and hung them out to dry.

By the time she was done with her personal business, it was noon and the cabin was still dark inside so she worked on the matches and lamps until she figured out how to light them and keep them burning for the rest of the day. But once there was illumination, she saw how filthy the floor was, so she found the broom and as she swept debris from the earthen floor she came across a curious thing at the base of the wall beside the cookstove. A cone-shaped mound of unidentifiable substance rose from the floor several inches. Bending low to scrutinize it, she let her eyes travel upward until she came to the hook the fry pan hung from.

"*¡Santo cielo!*" she declared. Apparently Seth Hopkins didn't bother to wipe out the pan when he was done, but hung it straightaway on the hook and let the fat drip to the floor!

She found few personal things belonging to Seth: aside from the shaving mug, brush and razor, there was a daguerreotype of a woman to whom Seth bore a resemblance, and four well-worn books. Picking up *A Treasury of Poems,* Angelique flipped through Burns and Keats, Shakespeare and Coleridge until the book fell naturally open to a page of Shelley, as if Seth had turned to it many times: "I arise from dreams of thee/In the first sweet sleep of night." The three other books were *Animal Husbandry, The Life of Napoleon,* and *The Sketch-Book* by Washington Irving, a scrap of paper marking the page for "The Legend of Sleepy Hollow."

With her hands on her hips, surveying the crude little dwelling that in her opinion wasn't fit to house pigs, Angelique decided she must do something about it. She worked for an hour, and when she satisfied herself that the cabin was a little more habitable, she confronted the task of cooking an evening meal.

When Seth Hopkins arrived home shortly after sunset, he called out to her first before walking in, and when he entered the cabin, he came to an abrupt halt, his mouth dropping open. Colors assailed him. From a Spanish shawl embroidered in brilliant colors draped across the bed, from little painted saint statues, from a small painting of the Virgin Mary and the Christ child framed in gold. Votive candles flickered in little red glass jars. A lady's fan was pinned to the wall, opened out to reveal eye-catching yellow flowers. Hanging on a hook, a pale blue bonnet decorated with bright pink ribbons and flamingo feathers. On the upended powder keg that served as a night table: an Aztec figurine carved out of pink jade, a large rock crystal of the deepest blue azurite, a small vase painted with pink roses. The keg itself was hidden beneath a lady's scarf of shimmering emerald green silk. Propped against the foot of the bed, a turquoise parasol with pale green ruffles. Blood-red hyacinths, which he had seen growing by the stream, in a jar of water.

Seth had to blink several times to make sure his eyes were all right. What had the woman done to the place?

Then he saw wisps of smoke curling out of the stove.

"What happened? Where's my supper?"

Her hands fluttered helplessly. "I try, Señor. But I do not know how."

He stared at her. "How can you not know how to cook a simple supper?"

"How should I know?"

"Because you're a woman and—Good Lord, you've used nearly all the kerosene!"

"This is *un calabozo* in here. It is a dungeon! I must have light!"

"Keep the doors open."

"And then in come the flies!"

He looked her up and down. "Why are you covered in soot?"

When she explained how she had tried to light the stove and instead clouds of smoke had billowed out, he showed her how she first had to sift the old ashes down and scoop them into a bucket, and then how to adjust the vent.

"Don't you have an apron?"

She shrugged helplessly.

"We'll need coffee for supper," he said with a sigh, and showed her how to use the pot. Then he got a fire going in the stove and left. He returned a few minutes later with meat pies and fried potatoes. "From Eliza's kitchen," he said as he put the food on the table. "Cost me four dollars."

"Is that a lot of money?" Angelique hadn't the faintest idea of the cost of anything.

He sat down without waiting for her to sit first. "It's an arm and a leg! It isn't the gold miners who get rich here, it's those with goods to sell. A handkerchief back in Virginia goes for five cents. Here it's fifty cents!"

He poured coffee first into his own mug and then into hers. As he brought the brew to his lips, he frowned into his cup. He tasted it, made a face, and said, "What did you do to the coffee?"

"I do as you say, Señor. Put coffee in the basket, put the pot on the stove."

Seth lifted the lid and gaped in astonishment. "You used whole beans! You're supposed to grind them first. Never mind. It's an honest mistake. You'll know better from now on."

As they started to eat, a terrible noise rent the air. Angelique jumped to her feet, but Seth kept on eating. Outside, in the twilight, she saw a man playing Scottish bagpipes.

"That's Rupert MacDougal," Seth explained when she came back. "He likes to sign off the end of the day with a playing of the pipes. Unfortunately, he only knows 'The Campbells Are Coming.'"

She watched him address his food in a most singular manner, elbows on the table, fork held as if it were a shovel. She had been unable to find any napkins or tablecloth, and supposed he hadn't any since he seemed quite at home wiping his mouth with the back of his hand.

Biting into a potato and finding it surprisingly delicious, she said, "Where is your gold mine, Señor Hopkins?"

"I don't have an actual mine. The kind of gold hunting I do is called *placer* mining. I just sift through the silt in streambeds and pick up what gold is lying there. I don't have a taste for gouging holes in the earth, looking for the veins as some men do. I had enough of that back in Virginia, where the coal mines were killing the earth and the men. I reckon if nature leaves gold lying around, then we've a right to pick it up. But I don't like to tear up land that God created."

She eyed the little glass jar he had come home with. It contained gold flakes floating in water. "What will you do with the gold you find?"

He wiped his mouth with his fingers and dug into the second meat pie. "I think I would like to own a farm. Not animals. I don't think I want that. Something peaceful and green. Growing something, maybe."

"Have you experience with a farm?"

"I come from a family of coal miners. But I can learn how to farm."

"We grew avocados in Mexico," she said wistfully. "But they are very sensitive trees. Too much wind and too much sun is not good. Perhaps oranges, yes? Lemons would be nice. It will depend on where you will have your farm. Tangerines and grapefruit grow best in heat, but lemons love fog. And I know of an orange that is sweeter when planted away from the coast."

He looked at her. "How do you know all that?"

She shrugged. "It is just something I know."

After supper, Seth opened the tin box that contained the ledger, ink bottle and pens, and assorted scraps of paper. On the back of a flyer advertising a circus, he wrote a list with a stubby pencil, saying, "Take this to Bill Ostler in the morning. Tell him to fill this list and charge it to my account. I'll stay at Charlie Bigelow's again tonight and probably all the while you're here."

When he appeared the next morning for his breakfast—eggs and toast which Angelique had ruined beyond recognition—he said, "I'll go on to Eliza's for coffee and biscuit. Make rice and bacon for tonight's supper. You can't ruin rice. You boil it in water over the fire." He pointed to the fireplace where a big black pot hung on a hook. "And you'll find the bacon in that barrel there. Packing it in bran keeps it from spoiling in the heat."

He paused. "Can you bake bread? All right, ask Ostler, he'll give you what you need."

Ostler's general store was up the dusty road, past tents and cabins and lines of laundry. The store consisted of four log walls with a canvas roof and was crammed inside with shelves of jars, cans, boxes, bottles, tools, dishware, utensils, medicines, and even bolts of cloth. For the occasion Angelique had carefully chosen a gown of dove gray silk with rose pink lace. The plumes in her bonnet were of a darker pink and matched her gloves and parasol. When she entered Ostler's, where three women were sorting through a box of buttons and thread Seth Hopkins had brought up from San Francisco, she paused to adjust her eyes to the interior darkness.

Bill Ostler, recognized by his shock of red hair and paunch above his belt, blurted, "Oh my goodness!" and rushed around the counter so fast to greet her that he nearly knocked over the pickle barrel. "Mrs. D'Arcy! What a pleasure! What can I do for you?"

Feeling the eyes of the three women on her, she handed Ostler the list. When she quietly asked him how to make bread, she heard one of the women whisper, "Imagine, a woman who doesn't know how to make bread."

Before she left with her purchases, she saw a bolt of calico and gestured with her hands how much she wanted.

In the cabin, she cut lengths of the calico and nailed them to the wall so that they covered a two-by-three-foot square. The rest she draped over the table.

Then she decided to cook the rice. She filled a pot with water and scooped rice out of its sack, using a tin cup with measurements imprinted on the side. One cup didn't look like enough. Four cups, she decided, would make a nice meal for her and Mr. Hopkins. Then she covered the pot and hung it over the fire in the fireplace and left it. While she got wood burning in the stove and managed to wedge the side of bacon into the pan, she heard a clang as the pot lid flipped over and fell to the stone hearth. To her horror she saw rice surging up and pouring over the sides, dropping into the fire.

"Santa Maria!" she cried, and flew at the pot with the knife she had been holding and, as if to kill it, began banging on the sides.

By the time Seth came home, the cabin smelled of scorched rice and burnt bacon, and Angelique was at the back door, fanning the smoke out with her new apron.

"This devil!" she shouted at him, and she kicked the side of the stove.

He peered at the mess in the frying pan. "You used the *entire* side of bacon? You're supposed to slice off a rasher or two." His eyes stopped on the calico on the wall. "What's that?"

"Curtains," she said petulantly, rubbing her nose and leaving a smudge.

"But there's no window there."

"Sí, but now does it not look like there is one?"

He eyed the calico tablecloth with a glass jar of fresh flowers on it. "Where'd you get these apples? Vendor doesn't come through here till Saturday."

"I buy them from Señor Ostler."

"What! He buys them from the fruit and vegetable vendor and then triples the price! No more buying produce from Ostler. Wait for the farmer's wagon on Saturday."

He went to the pantry and brought out hardtack and jerky. "It's all right," he said when he saw her crestfallen look. "I've had worse."

She looked around the cabin. "What could be worse than this?"

He stared at her. Anyone else would have made the question sound like an insult. But she didn't seem to mean offense. "Prison," he said as they sat at the table.

Her eyes grew round. "You were in prison?"

He peeled an apple, handing her half. "I saw a man beating on a woman. I told him to stop, but he had a rage in his eyes. I knew he was going to kill her. So I stopped him."

"You . . . killed him?"

Seth shook his head. "Broke his back. Now he sits on two useless legs. Won't be beating up on anyone again."

He chewed. Swallowed. "They charged me with attempted manslaughter. I served a year in Eastern State Penitentiary. No labor. Solitary confinement. My meals were slid under the door. For a year, I never saw or spoke to a soul."

They finished supper in silence, and when he was done, Seth stood and lifted the corner of the tablecloth. "This has to go back to Bill Ostler."

"But it is cut up. He will not take it back."

"Then I'll have to add the cost of it to what you owe me."

When he saw her chin begin to tremble, he said, "You've done the place real nice." Seeing the little Aztec figure on the upended powder keg he picked it up and examined it. "This is pink jade. Very rare, very costly."

"It is more than that, Señor Hopkins. This talisman once belonged to Montezuma's queen. It is the figure of the goddess of good fortune. It is a good luck charm given to me by my Aztec nanny and it contains great power."

"You think she'll bring you luck?"

"She will lead me to my father," Angelique said with confidence.

"Better yet, ask her if she can teach you to cook."

Although he said it with a smile, and although Angelique could see he meant no insult, nonetheless she felt her blood rise. What he was expecting of her was simply too much. This demeaning situation was not worth the hundred dollars she owed him.

But as he started to leave for Charlie Bigelow's, something occurred to her. "A moment, please. I wish to know something."

"Yes?"

"Señor Boggs."

"Yes." She saw that his jaw tensed.

"You said he was a bad man."

"Yes," he said, and she waited. After a moment, he sighed and said, "You wouldn't have lasted long with him. Women like you don't."

"He would have made me work?"

He looked into her innocent, wide eyes and didn't know how better to put it. "The ladies who live above the saloon," he said. "That is what Cyrus Boggs would have you do."

A heartbeat passed. Angelique suddenly flushed deep red, then she went dead pale. "Tomorrow," she said, "I will not burn the rice."

❊

Seth continued to sleep in Charlie Bigelow's tent but went to his own cabin every morning for breakfast, a clean shirt, and his lunch bucket, which Miss D'Arcy filled. As it turned out that she didn't know how to wash clothes, Seth's first clean shirt after Miss D'Arcy's arrival had had to be purchased at Ostler's for an astronomical sum. After that, he showed her how to boil water over the fire, fill the wooden tub outside, cut flakes off the bar of soap, and stir the clothes in the tub. He had managed to teach her how to cook breakfast, but it soon became a monotonous fare of bread either burned or half-baked and coffee too weak or too strong. And his bucket lunch invariably consisted of smoked sausage, salvaged parts of a bread loaf, and apples bought from the weekend vendor. At the end of each day Seth returned for supper, which was ruined more often than not, sending him to Eliza's for two dinners to take out. After supper, while Angelique washed the dishes, he sat down with the jar that contained the day's take—gold flakes, dust, and nuggets floating in water— which he cleaned and dried and weighed on a small set of scales, and then poured into a little leather pouch that he secured in a locked box. At bedtime he would take his leave and go to Charlie's. Otherwise, his life at Devil's Bar continued as it had been before his unexpected houseguest. He still rode into American Fork every weekend to have the gold assayed and deposited in a bank. And Saturday nights he took down the big wooden washtub, filled it with hot water from the fireplace and scrubbed the week's grime from his body. Then he dressed in clean clothes and went to the saloon, where he drank whiskey and played cards with Llewellyn, Ostler, and Bigelow, after which he went to the hotel where, once the dining room was closed, he "sat a spell" with Eliza Gibbons, as he put it. What Miss D'Arcy did in her spare time he had no idea. He suspected it wasn't learning how to cook.

As he knelt on the riverbank with the hot sun on his back, placing a mixture of dirt and gravel into his pan and then submerging it into the stream, he prayed he would find a nugget that would cover the expenses Miss D'Arcy was running up. He knew she couldn't help it. She was trying hard, and with little complaint, but she kept ruining the food and burning his shirts with the iron, and using up too much lamp oil. He sincerely hoped that when she found her father, Jack D'Arcy had made enough money trapping to take care of his expensive daughter.

He dipped the pan into the stream again, and as he brought it out of the water and shook it back and forth, tapping it against the heel of his hand to let some of the gravel slip over the far edge, he thought about the Frenchman. Every time someone new came into camp Seth would inquire if they knew a trapper named D'Arcy. He was starting to worry. He had been hearing news of Indians ambushing trappers because the trappers were depleting the Indians' food supply. There had been bloody skirmishes up north resulting in a lot of dead white men.

Dipping the edge of the pan again and again, at a greater angle each time until he had worked it down and he had almost no gravel, only black sand and gold, which he then swirled gently, Seth's eyes strayed to dark brown pebbles that lay on the streambed, flashing in the sunlight, and they reminded him of Angelique's eyes, especially the way they would flash in her quick strikes of anger and she would whisper, "Santa Maria!" and strike a blow at bread that hadn't risen or pudding that had burned. Then he noticed that the tinkling of the water over the rocks sounded like her laughter that always immediately followed such bursts of anger as she chided herself and pushed a lock of black hair from her face. When a kingfisher came to perch on a branch over the stream, looking for fish that were no longer there, Seth thought its blue-gray feathers were the same color as one of Angelique's gowns, the one she had spilled gravy on and had spent hours trying to clean.

He shook his head. The way Angelique kept cropping up in his thoughts, it was as if she had followed him to this place.

He tried to steer his mind to other matters: what changes statehood might bring to California, where he should be thinking of buying a farm, was winter going to come early this year. But his mind was its own master and seemed to want to think only of Angelique D'Arcy. Last Sunday, for instance, when the circuit preacher came to Devil's Bar and the saloon had been converted into a church, Miss D'Arcy had arrived late. When she appeared in the doorway, all heads turned and everyone fell silent.

She was wearing one of her beautiful gowns with a magnificent Spanish lace veil over her head and shoulders, and she had a prayer book and rosary in her gloved hands. When the silence stretched—Catholics were looked upon with some suspicion in this predominantly Protestant settlement—instead of coming forward, Miss D'Arcy had taken a seat at the back, with the prostitutes.

Gold being heavier than sand, it stayed in the center of the pan while the sand moved to the outside, allowing Seth to pick out the nuggets and flakes with tweezers. Then he carefully drained the last of the water and touched a clean, dry fingertip to the remaining specks of gold, lifting them out and dropping them into his glass jar. It was hard, time-consuming and backbreaking work. Sometimes a day of panning produced no gold. Other times he found nuggets that seemed as big and bright as the sun.

This lot done, he rested back on his heels and mopped his brow with a handkerchief. He looked across the stream at the ruins of the Indian village. Seth had been one of the first to stake a claim on this offshoot of the river. The day he arrived, the village was thriving. Indians had stood on the opposite bank, silently watching the crazy white man sift through dirt. And then other white men had come with picks and shovels, and built sluices and great wooden cradles for dredging the gravel from the streambed. In a short time, fish disappeared from the stream and so the Indians had left, to go in search of other food sources.

Some had even gone looking for gold because, even though they had no use for the metal themselves, they had learned they could buy blankets and food with it. Some had gone to work on white men's farms and places like Sutter's Sawmill. When he and Miss D'Arcy had stopped at Sutter's Mill to water the horses on their way from Sacramento they had seen several hundred Indians squatting in the noon sun. As soon as troughs of food were brought out and set on the ground, the Indians had swarmed over them, on their knees, madly scooping food into their mouths as if they knew there wasn't going to be enough.

Most Indians, however, were hiding in the mountains. There were some white men who felt the Indians no longer had a place here and so went after them with guns. The federal government, meanwhile, was trying to round up all the natives and confine them to reserved land. The only villages still going were inhabited by women, but even they were starting to vanish due to rampant kidnapping. When news of gold had got out, every man and woman in California had dropped what they were doing and headed for the gold fields. Farms and ranches were suddenly left without workers, rich people had no servants. So now there was a lucrative trade in kidnapped Indian women and children. They were taken south and sold for labor.

As he took a break beneath the warm sun, Seth contemplated the colors of wildflowers, the blue of the sky, things he hadn't noticed in years. Memories of Eastern State Penitentiary haunted him, with its experimental program of keeping men isolated for their rehabilitation. What the prison officials didn't know was that, for Seth Hopkins, the solitary confinement hadn't been much different from the silence of his father's cottage or the darkness of the coal mines. The day he had been released, the warden had said, "I hope you've learned something here." But the only thing that Seth had learned was that every man was on his own in this world. Each man is born alone and must survive alone. And no man can depend on anyone to help him get by.

As he reached for his pan and braced himself for another hour of backbreaking labor, a surprising image sprang into his mind: Miss Angelique D'Arcy sleeping in his bed, her rich black hair tumbling over his pillow.

❉

A spell was being cast over the folks at Devil's Bar. Eliza Gibbons was certain of it. A spell woven by the cunning Miss D'Arcy, the beautiful French widow Seth had found on the docks at San Francisco and brought home like a stray cat. Eliza was no fool, nor was she blind, which was perhaps why she was the only person immune to the creature's power. It was as if a sort of mass hysteria had gripped the people of Devil's Bar.

Eliza had first suspected that something was wrong the Saturday morning the creature had surprised everyone by showing up at Eliza's hotel while Seth was away at American Fork, paying his weekly visit to the bank. The small lobby and dining room had been busy with Devil's Bar citizens enjoying Eliza's good coffee, or picking up their mail and newspapers, which had just been brought on the morning stage. Eliza's was a place to congregate and meet, to share gossip and news, and to shed the weariness of a week in the gold fields. Seth's French widow had suddenly materialized in the front entrance and the place had fallen dead silent.

Eliza would never forget how all heads had suddenly turned and everyone had stared. And then, in the next minute, the men had done something that had made Eliza's mouth fall open: they rose from their seats and removed their hats! No other woman in the camp had ever received such treatment. Least of all Eliza herself, who was of the firm opinion that if any woman should receive royal treatment, it was Eliza Gibbons. *Wasn't I the only one to think of contracting with the stagecoach line so that mail and newspapers are delivered to my hotel? Am I not the only one who connived a way to build a cold storage so that folks can keep their hams and butter fresh, game birds to be saved for a special occasion, even Bill Ostler's secret bottle of champagne? Are my meat pies not famous all the way to Nevada? What thanks do I get? Only grumbles that my prices are too high.*

The attitudes of the men, on that Saturday morning, had alarmed Eliza. Especially when Mrs. Ostler had next greeted the creature with a "good morning," and the other ladies had followed!

Miss D'Arcy had explained that she wished to purchase something for Mr. Hopkins's supper, and so she had bought fried chicken with mashed potatoes and giblet gravy from Eliza's kitchen. Eliza had wanted to inform the creature that the food was for hotel customers only, but how could she say that when it wasn't true and everyone was standing there to witness her lie? She had had no choice but to let the girl go off with a basket full of Eliza's best cooking, which she had no doubt the creature was going to claim she cooked herself.

It hadn't ended with that. There had been the Saturday night when a group of fiddlers had come into the camp to hold an old-fashioned barn dance without the barn and it had ended up in a brawl because all the men wanted to dance with Angelique. And the day a couple of mountain men came into Eliza's hotel with their Indian women and Eliza had been about to demand that they leave when Angelique had come running in, having heard of their arrival, to ask if they knew her father and, learning they were French, to get them all prattling like monkeys in a foreign tongue with Llewellyn, that daft Welshman, asking her afterward to give him French lessons! Ingvar Swenson sending a dozen fresh eggs to Miss D'Arcy as a welcoming gift; Mrs. Ostler wanting Miss D'Arcy's opinion on the color of the yarn she had chosen for a new shawl; and Cora Holmsby asking Miss D'Arcy for advice on perfume.

But the final straw had been the incident with the peaches.

Eliza had secretly contracted with a farmer in the valley to bring a wagonload of peaches on the guarantee that everyone would buy them, with Eliza receiving a percentage of the take. As she had promised, peaches were such a rare treat that everyone crowded around, pressing banknotes and bags of gold dust upon the vendor. And then all of a sudden, Seth's creature had come pushing through, babbling something about the fruit being bad and that to eat it would make everyone seriously ill.

A fracas had erupted, with the farmer shouting angrily and waving his arms, and Miss D'Arcy trying to stop people from reaching for the peaches, and Seth Hopkins arriving and trying to calming everyone down. When asked why she thought the fruit was bad, the creature hadn't even been able to explain. She had just looked at Seth with those bewitching eyes, and said, "Please, you will all be ill if you eat."

To Eliza's astonishment, Seth had said, "Well then maybe we shouldn't buy the peaches," and everyone had replaced the ones they had selected.

While the others stood around wondering what to do, with the farmer shouting invectives in a language no one recognized, Eliza had walked up to the wagon and purchased a whole bushel of peaches. The others immediately followed suit, nearly emptying the man's wagon and sending him off with a smile.

What had burned the incident into Eliza's brain was the way Seth had acquiesced to the creature's admonition, as though she had sapped his will. That was when Eliza had realized it was time to take matters into her own hands.

And so, on this late-summer Saturday evening with crickets singing and a taste of fall in the air, she plied Seth Hopkins with a generous second helping of her peach pie. "She knows things," he said between mouthfuls, washing the sweet, juicy pie down with cold milk. "I don't know how or why, but Miss D'Arcy just somehow knows things. She said she saw the camp falling sick after eating the peaches. Like a vision." He ran his spoon around the plate, catching the last of the syrup and crust. "Some folks do have the sight, you know. Women, mostly."

Eliza didn't know anything about visions or sight, but she knew a sly and cunning woman when she saw one. After the peach vendor left Eliza had made up a batch of pies so that the folks who had missed the farmer could still have a treat. She had even sent a pie over to Seth's cabin, only to learn the next day that the creature had thrown it out! Everyone in the camp had savored Eliza's peach pies and declared them the best in the territory. Who did that creature think she was to throw one out? But Eliza knew the gesture had less to do with Miss D'Arcy being worried about the fruit than with her staking a claim on Seth Hopkins. Eliza knew what the creature was up to. Even if Seth did not.

For a few Saturday nights now, as Seth had sat with Eliza on the front porch of her hotel, he had sent conflicting signals. One minute he would tell her he was reaching the end of his patience with Miss D'Arcy and that she was costing him an arm and a leg to keep, in the next he would comment on Miss D'Arcy's perfume, or the charming way she laughed. Eliza knew what even Seth himself did not know: that he, too, was falling under the creature's spell.

Eliza hadn't expected competition for Seth. It was one of the reasons she had come out to California from the East, because women here were outnumbered by men at least ten to one. Even a woman such as herself, who had been "passed over" and was a spinster at thirty, stood a good chance of snaring a great prize like Seth Hopkins. She had been trying for eight months to get him to look at her in a "matrimonial" way, seducing him with jam tarts, meat pies, and praise of his masculine strength whenever he worked the odd repair around her hotel. She never criticized him, even when he wiped his mouth on her tablecloth instead of using his sleeve, or when he belched without pardoning himself. She never mentioned that she thought he should expand his claim onto Charlie Bigelow's since Charlie wasn't working his own spot a hundred percent. She didn't push Seth to higher ambition, like suggesting he would get more gold if he used a sluice instead of a pan—his argument being that those up-stream shouldn't be greedy because those downstream would get nothing. She bit her tongue when he declared all he wanted was enough to live comfortably while every other man in Devil's Bar was burning to be richer than Midas. Eliza felt she was drawing close to a time when she could plant the seed in his mind that here they were, good friends by now, and helping each other as neighbors should, and how he needed a woman and she could use a man around the place, which only led to a logical conclusion. But now Miss D'Arcy was seducing him with her bright gowns and feminine helplessness.

"Won't be long now," he said as he filled his pipe, "before California becomes a state."

"When it does, I hope they do something about all these foreigners coming in. I hear there are Chinamen up at American Fork now."

He looked at her. "Aren't *we* foreigners, Eliza?"

Her smile remained fixed. "Of course! I was joking!"

He nodded and went back to lighting his pipe. "Everyone here came from someplace else. 'Cept for the Indians. I reckon God created them right here."

Eliza said nothing. She loathed California's natives and thought they couldn't be gotten rid of soon enough. Thank God for men like Taffy Llewellyn and Rupert MacDougal who went on periodic purges through the countryside. If it were up to Seth Hopkins, Devil's Bar would be overrun by savages. "Is Miss D'Arcy working out any better?" she asked, reminded of another loathsome creature.

He puffed the tobacco to life. "I'm in a quandary, Eliza. She comes in a mighty pretty package but she's completely useless. I've tried to show her a few things, but it's like she's afraid of the stove. When bacon spat-ters, she jumps back. She doesn't want to get grease on any of her fine dresses. And all the raccoons and foxes love my cabin, she throws so much food out. I came home the other night and there was Miss D'Arcy running out of the cabin with the frying pan on fire. She threw the whole lot into the creek. I had to buy a new frying pan from Bill Ostler, and you know what *that* cost me!"

He stretched his legs in front of him, crossing them at the ankles. "I've never known a woman didn't know how to cook and sew. Not like you, Eliza. You're a very capable woman. You don't worry about being pretty or making yourself look nice. And you appreciate the value of a dollar."

Eliza's lips compressed in a thin line. "Maybe she won't last long and you will be rid of her."

"Can't see that happening. She's working off the debt she owes me. And she's looking for her father. Can't turn her out on her own. Not with her being so helpless."

Eliza wanted to say something about Miss D'Arcy and her helplessness, but instead said, "Are you sure there *is* a father?"

He gave her a look of genuine surprise. "Why would she lie?"

Eliza didn't respond. How could Seth have reached the age of thirty-two and not know that there were some women who would say anything to get a man to take care of them?

"In the meantime," he said, "I suppose I'll just have to put up with Charlie Bigelow's snoring, and burnt potatoes for my supper."

"You can always come here for a good meal. Fried chicken, biscuits, and gravy. Your favorite."

He laughed. "Eliza, you charge an arm and a leg for your dinners."

"I would give you a special discount, you know that."

"Nope. Wouldn't be fair to the others who are working just as hard as me. I'd insist on paying the full price, fair and square."

Eliza kept her thoughts to herself. There were times when Seth Hopkins's sense of fairness and honesty galled her. "Well, you are to be praised for doing your Christian duty and rescuing that poor creature."

"Being Christian had nothing to do with it. Couldn't leave her at the mercy of the likes of Boggs. Any other man would've done the same."

Any other man, Eliza thought, would have brought the creature home and set her up in a gilded cage and gone moony-eyed over her. But not Seth Hopkins. When it came to women, he wore blinders. He had once spoken of a sweetheart back home who ended up marrying someone else. In all of his talk of the girl, Seth never once uttered the word love. Eliza was beginning to wonder if he was one of those men incapable of love. The most a woman could ask from him was loyalty and protection. Well, that was all Eliza expected from a man. She wasn't sure romantic love even existed, the type that poets spoke of. Men could be silver-tongued when they thought a woman was coming into an inheritance, she recalled bitterly, and then vanish when they learned that she was in fact penniless. No, Eliza preferred Seth's bluntness. At least she knew where she stood with him. And if they should marry, she wouldn't even expect to fall in love.

"Would you like me to try and help? Show Miss D'Arcy some basic cookery?"

He seemed awash with relief. "Oh Eliza, I would be most grateful! I think Angelique could benefit from the help of an older woman."

The face of Eliza Gibbons, who was only five years older than Miss D'Arcy and two years younger than Seth, went hard and her eyes glinted like chips of black coal. But she managed to keep her smile, as she said, "Leave everything to me. I'll help poor Miss D'Arcy find her way around a stove."

✳

She couldn't believe it. She had ruined the potatoes again!

As she stared at the burnt mess in the cooking pot, Angelique felt tears threaten to rise. How did the other women manage it? She either made the stove too hot or not hot enough. If she paid attention to frying the meat, then the vegetables burned. If she stirred the stew, then the corn bread caught on fire. How was she to juggle everything at once? As she tossed the blackened spuds out back, knowing the raccoons and foxes would make a meal of them later, she pictured what Mr. Hopkins's reaction was going to be: when she ruined a meal or burned holes in his shirts with the iron, he was never angry or critical. He would simply say, "You'll learn and do better next time." Seth Hopkins was the most even-tempered man she had ever known. She couldn't imagine him almost killing a man. Yet he said he had gone to prison for that very thing. He didn't seem to have that kind of rage within him. Perhaps the woman he was protecting was someone he loved. Was there maybe a hidden part of Seth Hopkins, a wellspring of passion waiting for the right woman to come along, someone like herself, who understood passion?

Chiding herself for such thoughts—more and more lately she had found herself daydreaming about Seth Hopkins, his tallness, his strength, his handsome face, wondering even what it would be like to be kissed by him—she returned to the cabin with its dark shadows and musty smells and loneliness. She had driven pegs into the walls and hung her gowns and dresses from them so she could work on the stains and the small tears in the fabric. Keeping her wardrobe in pristine condition was nearly a full-time job. It was also what kept her sane.

Angelique had never thought life could be so hard. She was even starting to develop blisters and raw hands, and her muscles were sore all the time. It was work, work, work with no diversion or entertainment whatsoever. Not even the traveling circus stopped in Devil's Bar because the camp was too small to be worth their time. And the only piano was in the saloon, where women were not allowed. The only distractions came from Saturday night brawls, the occasional fistfight in the street, or the time the entire camp was wakened in the middle of the night when Llewellyn the Welshman's moonshine still exploded, or the evening Charlie Bigelow, unable to take one more rendition of Rupert MacDougal's bagpipe concert, came out with a shotgun, aimed it at the pipes, and said, "Learn ye another tune or I'll blast ye and that infernal contraption to kingdom come."

There had been one bright spot, when a baby was born to the Swensons. Children being such a rarity in this part of the territory, miners came from all around to pay their respects and bring gifts for the child, even Indians came bearing beads and feathers. Angelique had watched grown men weep at the sight of the baby, and the moment was so infused with reverence that it reminded her of the nativity of Jesus (although, later all the men got drunk and tore up the camp with fights and gunfire).

Most of all she was homesick. She craved chili peppers and tortillas. Her ears ached for the sound of a Spanish guitar. She missed strolling through the immense open-air markets of Mexico City and perusing the pottery, textiles, and unique wood carvings. She wished there were someone to speak Spanish with.

Picking up the Aztec figurine and curling her fingers around it, its familiar shape a comforting reminder of home, she recited a mental prayer to the little goddess to give her strength, then she kissed the cool jade and replaced it beside her bed.

"Hello? Miss D'Arcy?"

Angelique turned to find Eliza Gibbons standing in the open doorway. "Oh! Miss Gibbons!" She rushed forward to draw out a chair and dust off the seat. "You do me an honor. Please, come in."

Eliza took in the younger woman's green satin gown over numerous petticoats, aquamarine gemstones glittering on her earlobes. As if, Eliza thought in contempt, she were ready for a grand ball. But there were smudges of flour on her face and in her hair, and close up one could see stains on the gown that no amount of soap had been able to vanquish. No wonder the creature couldn't cook. She cared more about the condition of her clothes than feeding Seth Hopkins.

"I confess to being remiss in calling upon you," Eliza said as she remained standing. "Mr. Hopkins gave us to understand that your stay here was but temporary."

"I thought my father would find me before now."

"And now winter is coming. Once the rains arrive, travel is difficult, and communication impossible."

Winter! Angelique's thoughts grew bleak. She would never last a winter in this place.

"I have interrupted your cooking," Eliza said.

"I am hopeless at it. I have caused poor Mr. Hopkins more trouble than I have helped him."

"You are making soup, I see?"

"I try before. But Mr. Hopkins says my soup has no taste."

Eliza removed her bonnet. "How are you seasoning it?"

"Señora Ostler tells me to add two pinches of salt. And so I do, like this."

"Just that? Just that two pinches for the entire pot?"

"*Sí.*"

"Then that's your problem. Mrs. Ostler meant for you to add two pinches for *each serving*. This is a large pot, ten servings at least. Pour some salt into your hand. There you are. That is what you must put in the pot."

Angelique's eyes widened. "All of this?"

Eliza smiled. "That's what will make it tasty. Now let me tell you a little secret that I use in my own cooking," she said as she reached for the jar of molasses, "and which Mr. Hopkins declares is the best gravy he has ever tasted . . ."

Angelique's hopes were high again by the time Seth came home. He sat at the table and looked askance as Angelique set a plate before him, throwing him a wink that surprised him. He peered at the gravy. Then he brought the plate to his nose and sniffed.

"There is something wrong?" she asked.

"This gravy . . . looks different. Smells different, too."

She smiled. "I have added the secret ingredient."

He tried the soup first, delivering a generous spoonful into his hungry mouth. A split second later he sprayed it all over the table. Quickly taking a long drink of water and then wiping his hand across his mouth, he said, "What did you do to this soup?"

She stared at him. "What is wrong with it?"

"It's awful!"

Silence fell, leaving only the buzzing of the flies in the air. After a moment, pale-faced and struggling for control, Angelique placed her hands flat on the table and slowly rose to her feet. "Mr. Hopkins, you rescued me from a terrible fate and I will thank you forever. But this is not a good situation for both of us and I think I must leave."

He gave her a startled look. "Leave! I just wanted to know what you did to this soup. It tastes—"

"It tastes wrong. Everything I do is wrong. It shall never be better." She walked with straight-backed dignity to the upended keg beside the bed, picked up the pink jade goddess, looked at it for a long moment, then came back to the table and gently set the statuette down. "This is the payment for my debt," she said softly. "This is worth more than I owe you. But I pay it so we are even. I shall go to Sacramento on the stagecoach when it comes through in three days."

✻

There wasn't one of her gowns that didn't have at least one small stain. She had tried so hard to keep them nice but it had been impossible to protect them from grease and gravy, coffee and juice, soot and dirt. Aprons had been no help, and Bill Ostler's store didn't stock adequate spot removers. When she got to Sacramento, she planned to devote her energies to restoring her beautiful wardrobe.

As Angelique carefully laid each dress in her traveling trunk, she tried not to think of the man she was leaving. Seth was in her dreams and her waking thoughts day and night, sometimes he appeared as a gentle rescuer, other times he was a passionate lover. When had he crept into her heart? How could she not have seen it coming?

Seth had stayed away for the past three days, and so when she heard footsteps outside, her heart jumped. But it was only Bill Ostler, looking in. "Heard you was leaving, Miss. I would have come by sooner but the missus is down with a cold. Been up all night with her." She noticed the shadows beneath his eyes and the high color on his cheeks. "Too bad you're leaving, Miss D'Arcy. You're the best thing to happen to Seth. He could do with some good luck. Did he tell you he spent time in prison?"

"He told me. He nearly killed a man, he said, who was beating up a woman."

"Did he tell you the man was his own father and that the woman was his mother? Old Man Hopkins knocked her so hard on the head it nearly blinded her. That's when Seth decided it was time to end his father's reign of terror. He didn't repent. That's why he was given hard time in the penitentiary. Say, could I trouble you for some water? My throat is terribly sore."

She gave him a cup.

"Well, good-bye, Miss D'Arcy. It's been a pleasure."

She was just tying her bonnet beneath her chin when Seth finally appeared in the doorway. He looked like he hadn't slept in days.

He took in her traveling clothes, the bonnet and gloves, the trunk by the door, ready for the stagecoach, and he said in a tired voice, "I've been doing some thinking these past three days." Taking her hand, he placed the jade talisman in it, curling her fingers over the little Aztec goddess. Then he brought out the ledger and tore out the page titled *Angelique.* "I made a mistake bringing you here. I didn't know how hard it would be for you. I didn't know how different the world is where you come from. Well, you know where I am. When you find your father, he can come repay the debt. But I don't hold you to it." He looked around. The cabin seemed bleak. She had removed all the color, even the calico curtains from a window that didn't exist. "I'll go to Sacramento with you and make sure you find a decent place to stay." He pressed a hand to his forehead.

"Are you all right, Mr. Hopkins?" she asked in sudden concern, remembering Bill Ostler.

"To tell the truth, I've felt better. Charlie Bigelow's caught himself a cold real bad. I think I might have some of it. If I could just sit down for a minute . . ."

She pulled out a chair and gave him some water. "How long have you felt this way?"

"Two, maybe three days. I thought it would go away, but it seems to be getting worse. And now my head—"

"You should lie down."

He didn't argue, and when he rose from the chair he faltered so that she put her arm around his waist to steady him.

"I'll be okay," he said as he settled his head on the pillow. "Just need to close my eyes. You'd better go on out. The stage will be here soon. Tell them there'll be two passengers."

She watched as he closed his eyes, then she removed a glove and placed her hand on his forehead. Seth was burning with fever.

She thought of Bill Ostler and his wife. She remembered the peach farmer eight days ago, and the vision she had had of the camp falling ill.

She glanced toward the doorway. The stagecoach would be coming through in a few minutes. And then Seth groaned, and it was a sound of pain.

Removing her bonnet, she drew a chair to the bedside and sat down. Fifteen minutes later she heard the stagecoach creak and rattle down the street. She remained at Seth's side.

When he awoke after sunset she was able to coax him to drink some lukewarm coffee. But he had no appetite for the fruit and biscuits she offered. He tried to get out of bed saying he should be getting to Charlie's but he hadn't the strength. So Angelique made him more comfortable and went down to Ostler's, where she bought blankets and another pillow, coming back to fix a bed for herself on the floor.

The next morning, Seth was worse.

With her hand on his burning forehead, she felt his pulse. It was abnormally slow for such a high fever. Terror suddenly gripped her as she remembered a fever that had swept through Mexico city ten years earlier. The high fever and slow pulse had alarmed the doctors for it was a sign unique to a dreaded illness: *febre tifoidea*—typhoid fever.

She closed her eyes in fear. She had been right about the peach vendor. He was what the curanderas in Mexico called a carrier. He had brought illness to Devil's Bar. Angelique stood paralyzed with fear and helplessness. People died of typhoid, even young, healthy men.

As she frantically wondered what she should do, whom she should call for help, Seth woke up and blinked at her with fever-bright eyes. "You're still here," he whispered. "Can I please have some water?" Suddenly he leaned over the side of the bed and vomited. "Oh God, I am so sorry," he moaned as he fell onto his back. To her horror, she realized he had also soiled himself.

And all of a sudden everything that had happened in the past weeks— the voyage on the *Betsy Lain*, the auction block, Devil's Bar—rushed at her like a malevolent black tide and she could take it no more. She ran out of the cabin crying, wanting her father, hating this place, hating Seth Hopkins.

Blindly she fled from the camp, splashing across the creek and up the slope covered with tree stumps.

At the top she reached the forest where she fell to the ground and wept bitterly, all the loneliness and feelings of helplessness and home-sickness pouring out of her. And then pain filled her head and she was far from her medicine so she had no choice but to let the attack run its course, this accursed falling sickness she had inherited from Grandmother Angela.

As she lay immobilized by pain and paralysis, visions filled her mind, not prophecies or hallucinations, but memories from years ago, when she was six years old: that strange time at Rancho Paloma when there was supposed to have been a wedding but something else happened and they had all abruptly left. Angelique didn't know what it was, but she suddenly remembered now her mother's hysterics at the time. Carlotta, whom Angelique had always remembered as being strong and practical, reduced to hysteria. It had something to do with Auntie Marina vanishing mysteriously, and something happening to Grandfather Navarro. But what stood out in Angelique's mind now as sharp as the mountain peaks surrounding her, was Grandmother Angela's face—round and pale and beautiful—and her voice, as clear as the birdcall in these woods, as she said, "I have done what had to be done. You can say it was wrong, and perhaps it was wrong, but it was what had to be done." And then Carlotta, panicked: "They will come for you, Mother! They will hang you! You must run. You must hide." And Grandmother, so calm and strong: "I will neither run nor hide. I shall face whatever God has set before me. Navarro women are not cowards."

D'Arcy had taken his wife and daughter away the very next day, and the memory had faded from Angelique's mind. She wondered now, in the grip of a sick headache, what had happened that fateful night, why had her mother thought Grandmother Angela would be arrested and hanged? Where did Auntie Marina vanish to and was she ever found again?

Who went riding out that night in a thunder of hooves?

Finally, the spell began to pass. The headache subsided, the voices and visions faded like dreams at dawn. When Angelique opened her eyes she seemed to see and hear and smell the forest around her for the first time. What majesty. What beauty. She inhaled air and it was like inhaling power. Inhaling the soul of the woods. *"Navarro women are not cowards."* Angelique looked around the sylvan paradise she suddenly found herself in, and through the trees, saw the homely mining camp she had just a short time ago despised. And she thought, I will do what has to be done.

She returned to the cabin to find Seth trying to undress himself. He had poured water in a basin to wash, but he had collapsed on the floor. The sheets and blanket were ruined. Remaking the bed with the only spare sheet, she settled Seth back down, covering him with the quilt he saved for winter, then she went to Eliza's hotel where the chambermaid informed her that Miss Gibbons was ill, as were the four hotel guests. But the cook was in the kitchen, and she gave Angelique bread and soup, custard and sausage. After obtaining fresh sheets from the chambermaid, she then went to Bill Ostler who, though clearly feverish, insisted he was all right. He warned her, however: "The high fever can be dangerous if it is not brought down quickly. It can cause fits and permanent brain damage. Even death. Keep Seth's skin moist and fan him. Give him plenty of cool water to drink. And don't try to wash his sheets. Everything must be burned, clothes, bedding, everything."

Lastly she borrowed a cot from Llewellyn the Welshman to make a bed for herself.

She returned to find Seth clutching his abdomen and groaning. Angelique warmed the food she had bought at the hotel but he couldn't keep it down.

His temperature rose in steps for three days and then remained elevated. Bouts of vomiting were followed by diarrhea, so that she had to go back to the hotel for more sheets, burning the soiled ones behind the cabin. He lay limply on the bed, trying not to let his pain show, but Bill Ostler had told her what the typhoid did and how it afflicted the intestines with ulcers which caused great agony.

It was necessary to bathe him so she set aside her shyness and, reminding herself that she had been married, gave him bed baths from a basin of warm water, keeping the blanket over his loins for his own dignity. When she saw scars on his back she brought the lamp closer and examined them. They crisscrossed his flesh so many times they could not be counted. They were a few years old, so she knew they must have come from the prison lash. Scars on his wrists and ankles could only have come from shackles and irons. She began to cry. "Blessed Mother of Sorrows," she whispered as she crossed herself, her tears falling upon the scars. "You poor, poor man."

The fever stayed high, causing him to tremble violently in delirium. A rose-colored rash appeared on his chest and abdomen as he slipped into a sleep that was like coma. Fear gripped her as she desperately tried to lower the fever with cool wet cloths. She stayed at it day and night, laying wet cloths on him and then fanning him, trying to get him to drink cool water. If she dozed off, she woke abruptly and got back to work. Recalling how in Mexico, during hot summers, ladies would dab cologne on their wrists and temples, she bathed Seth in her scents and toilette water, the alcohol evaporation helping to cool him a little. When those ran out she went to the saloon, which was deserted, and took the last bottle of whiskey and bathed Seth in it.

When she burned the last bedsheet she went to the hotel for more, but there were none to be had, nor were there any at Bill Ostler's. Devil's Bar lay beneath a pall of stinking smoke from the many fires where bedding and clothing were being burned. So she returned to the cabin where she opened her trunk and brought out her petticoats. They covered the bed and were made of a soft cotton. When the petticoats ran out, she tore up her gowns, rolling Seth onto his side as she spread the emerald silk or pink satin under him, gathering up the soiled ones and throwing them on the smoldering pile out back. Angelique struck matches and watched her silks and satins blacken and vanish in flames.

As her dresses were needed for bedding, she opened the box where Seth kept his clothing and chose a pair of the strange trousers made out of something called blue jean, with the pockets attached by metal rivets, and one of his homespun shirts, which she tucked in after tying a rope around her waist to keep the pants up. No longer having time to fuss with her hair, she combed it straight out and plaited it into two long braids. When Bill Ostler saw her he was shocked. "Thought I was seein' a squaw," he said.

Seth could not eat solid food so she overcame her fear of the stove— cooking was now a matter of life and death—and, keeping the wood burning, discovered how to cook rice to just the right consistency, adding salt and sugar to strengthen Seth. A porridge of oats. Beef and vegetable broth. Cold tea.

When the food ran out she went to the hotel again where she didn't see anyone. The dining room and kitchen deserted. But she heard moaning upstairs and the sounds of someone retching. There was a pile of smoldering, stinking bedsheets out back. She went to Bill Ostler again who was now seriously ill, dragging himself to the door. "Is there anything I can do to help?" she asked

"It's in God's hands, Miss D'Arcy. With typhoid you can't say who is to live, who to die. That decision is up to the Almighty." He collapsed and she helped him to bed. She saw Mrs. Ostler, who looked on the threshold of death. She helped herself to supplies from the store and left a bag of gold dust.

Going to the Swensons' hoping to buy eggs, she found Ingvar struggling to take care of his wife. When Angelique took a look at Mrs. Swenson, she saw the baby asleep in the crook of her arm. She looked more closely. Then she crossed herself.

"Mr. Swenson, your baby—"

"I know. She won't let me bury him, poor little tyke."

The camp was deserted except for scavenging dogs. Angelique saw new graves on the hillside and wondered who was buried there and who had had the strength to dig them. The stench of sickness hung over the settlement. She remembered the smell from years ago, when typhoid had swept through Mexico. She also remembered the burials, night and day. There would be more here at Devil's Bar, before the sickness had run its course.

She stayed at Seth's side every moment. When he tossed and turned in pain and delirium, she cradled him in her arms. And when she lifted him up to feed him, and when she stroked his face, she felt a tenderness she had never experienced before.

Every night she fell exhausted into bed.

On the seventeenth night after she was supposed to have left on the afternoon stage, Angelique looked down at Seth's gaunt face, at the wasted body where little flesh remained. His eyes had sunk back into his head, his hair had fallen out on his pillow. It had been days since he had even opened his eyes. A person cannot burn with fever for two weeks, she knew, and live. But there was nothing else she could do. Exhausted and weak from hunger, thinking she would go mad from sleeplessness, she stared at the man in the bed with eyes bright with something that was not fever, but with an insanity of the spirit.

Devil's Bar was silent. No longer did she hear the honky-tonk piano in the saloon, the constant coming and going of horses and wagons, the sounds of people. She couldn't remember when she had last spoken to a soul. When she had gone to see Charlie Bigelow she had found him lying dead in his own filth, untended, uncared-for. Visitors had stopped coming into Devil's Bar. The last stage had been days ago. They had been abandoned by the world, left to die.

Near the midnight hour, when the last of her lamp oil burned low, she sat by Seth's bed and sensed a curious gathering of shadows around her. She thought at first they were the ghosts of Charlie Bigelow and the Swenson baby and Eliza Gibbons's two chambermaids. Then she realized it wasn't ghosts that were visiting her but memories coming back—memories she had long suppressed, things her mother had told her when she was a child about her family in California. That Angelique in her adoration of her father had turned herself against the Navarros because of their shabby treatment of him. But now she was remembering that Grandmother Angela had welcomed Jacques D'Arcy as a son. She recalled when an officer had come to the hacienda to inform her of her husband's death at the battle of Chepultepec, Angelique had never felt so alone in her life. Her father had already left, and her mother was dead. She had no one. But now she was suddenly remembering all the cousins. Something about a bear being brought into a corral, and Angelique was surrounded by children, all related to her. She had never thought about it before but she had a large family. And what a comfort families must be at times like this.

And now they were in fact here, in her memories, bringing comfort. And something else: aid in her most dire moment of need.

Grandmother Angela at the kitchen table, which six-year-old Angelique could only just reach, preparing something in a cup, patiently explaining to the child how the magic in the bark cooled a fever.

Without thinking, Angela dashed out of the cabin and ran down to the creek to follow it by moonlight until she came to a willow tree. She threw herself upon it, clawing at the bark with her fingers until it peeled away in her hands. Then she stumbled back to the cabin where she boiled water and put the willow bark in, letting it cool and trying to coax some between Seth's lips. He coughed and spat it out. She put the cup to his mouth again. He could not drink. So she soaked a handkerchief in the tea and squeezed it out between his lips. Hour after hour, she gradually coaxed the brew down his throat.

Finally, clutching her rosary, she knelt beside the bed and laid herself across Seth's body so that her face was buried in his chest and she prayed with all her might. She fell asleep in this position and was wakened by the feel of his hand on her hair.

The fever had broken, the crisis had passed.

✳

Although Seth was still ill, Angelique was able to leave him alone while she went out into the camp to assist others. She helped feed and bathe the victims, cooked huge amounts of beans for the well ones, assisted with the burials and the burning of clothes and bedding, and shared the secret of her willow tea. At night she sat at Seth's bedside and read to him from *Animal Husbandry*, which made him smile weakly at first to hear her recite, " 'If you wish to raise egg-laying hens, the White Leghorn is best,' " and then later, when he gained more strength, to laugh out loud when she read in a serious tone, " 'The Holstein cow produces four times more milk than the conventional beef cow . . .' "

Finally the typhoid was gone from Devil's Bar. The last burial had been days ago, people were starting to resume their lives, inspect their claims, and put the horror behind them. Seth, able to sit now in a chair, looked at Angelique with clear eyes, all shadows of illness gone, and said, "I'm starving."

She fixed him something solid to eat, and he was astonished at the perfect potato pancakes she had cooked, chewy in the center and crunchy at the edges, spiced just right. While he ate he asked how the others fared. "Ingvar Swenson lost his wife and baby. Mrs. Ostler died." She had difficulty speaking. There were thirty-two fresh graves on the hillside.

"Eliza?" he asked.

"Miss Gibbons is still very ill."

"I'll pay her my respects when I can get back on my feet. Did I talk in my delirium?"

She smiled.

"Should I apologize?"

"You woke up once and looked at me and said you didn't know there were angels in Hell. You also spoke of your mother. Will you be going home?"

"I can't go home," he said. "They don't want me."

"Your father I can understand. He is angry, yes? But certainly your mother will want you to come home."

"The day I got out of prison I went home. My mother told me to go away and never come back. She said I had saddled her with a useless cripple, that I should have either killed him outright or let him alone. She said I had made her life a hundred times worse than before."

"She will change her mind. She is still your mother."

"Last year I sent her all the gold I found in the first month, over five hundred dollars' worth. She wrote back and told me to keep my money, that all my father would do was buy liquor with it." He shook his head. "They don't want me. I'm on my own. I've reconciled myself to that."

Angelique felt a sharp pain in her heart. She wanted to take him into her arms and cry for him, and tell him that he wasn't on his own, that he was loved by someone. But she could neither move nor bring the words to her lips. "Rest now," she said instead. "You will soon be well enough to go down to the creek and work your claim."

"Why did we get sick and you didn't?"

"I didn't each the peaches."

"I'll never eat another peach for as long as I live. How did you know we shouldn't eat the fruit?"

"In Mexico, our *curanderas* tell us that there are people who carry sickness but who themselves never fall ill from it. If you eat food they cook or water they pour, you will fall ill with the fever. I had a sense that the old man was such a carrier."

His eyes moved up and down her body. "Except for the braids, you look like a boy."

"I have no more dresses," she said with a smile. Then she covered her face with her hands and burst into tears.

✳

When Seth was strong enough, he went to see Eliza Gibbons, who was now fully recovered, and then to inspect his claim at the river.

He came back to find Angelique packing. She didn't need the trunk anymore. Everything she owned fit into a small pillowcase. She said to him, "When I first arrived in San Francisco, I came with the hope of finding someone to take care of me. Mr. Boggs. My father. Or someone that I might marry. I never dreamed that I would be capable of being on my own. But now I can cook and wash and keep a house. I have even learned to speak like an American. I shall travel from camp to camp, from mining town to mining town, cooking and washing and taking care of myself until I find my father."

"You can't leave!"

She looked away, her chin quivering. "Our roads separate from here, Mr. Hopkins. You will go back to your gold mining and to Eliza Gibbons, who is in love with you, and I have to find my father."

He startled her by taking her by the shoulders, and saying, "Angelique, I need you. Before you came into my life I lived in a world without color. It was a world of brown and gray and black. But you brought me rainbows and sunsets and all the flowers that the good earth grows. Dear God, what was wrong with me? I kept you in a dark cabin much as I was once kept in a dark coal mine, and later in a dark prison cell. You were meant to live in sunshine, Angelique. Every morning I've gone down to the stream where there are rocks and trees and birds and sunlight, leaving you behind in the dark. I should have taken you for walks in the woods. I never even showed you my claim down at the river. I jailed you as I was once jailed."

He took her face in his hands, and said with passion, "Listen to me, Angelique. I'm done with gold seeking. There's still gold in the stream, but I'm not greedy, I've got what I need. I'll leave what's there for the next man. And anyway I'm a rich man. The bank in American Fork holds my fortune and I'm ready to share it with a woman I find myself to be very much in love with and in need of having at my side for the rest of my life. Please say you will be my wife. Besides, how am I going to start my farm without your help? Without you there to listen to the wind as it tells you what to do?"

But how could she answer him when he was suddenly kissing her so hard?

"Hoy, in there! Hullo?"

They turned to see a stranger in the doorway, a white man in buckskins and a fur hat. "They tell me you folks is lookin' for a Frenchy name of D'Arcy. I can take you to him if you want."

✳

As it was to be a long journey, they bought pack mules and gear for winter, and headed up into the mountains, stopping first at American Fork to speak marriage vows before a Justice of the Peace. When they reached D'Arcy's grave far in the north, there was new snow on the ground.

Angelique knelt and said a prayer. Then she strung her rosary beads on the wooden cross, the beads her father had given her on the occasion of her first Holy Communion.

The tracker who had brought them said to Angelique, "Over there, that were the squaw yer Da were living with."

She looked across through the trees and saw an Indian woman in buckskins, her long gray hair bound in braids.

"Never proper married," the tracker said. "But Jack were devoted to 'er." He clucked and shook his head. "Life is going to be hard for that one now. No man to protect 'er." He shrugged. "Ah well, nowt to be done about it. Her kind are nearly all gone anyway."

They stared at each other in the silence of the woodland, the woman of the woods and the woman of the city, both with long braids and dark, leaf-shaped eyes. The moment held a brief magic as the winter silence embraced the two. Then the older woman turned and disappeared through the trees.

Angelique slipped her hand into Seth's, and said, "I want to go back to Los Angeles. I want to see if the hacienda is still there, if Grandmother Angela is still alive."

"We'll go straightaway, my dearest. That's where we'll start our farm. In the light and sunshine, and we'll never know darkness again."

Chapter Fifteen

Erica couldn't stop thinking about Jared's kiss.

It had been so unexpected, so electrifying that for an instant she had thought she was going to catch on fire and explode. And then she had fainted. Lack of oxygen the paramedics had said. From being sealed in the cave for so long.

It was all she could think about, even after the stunning find she had made that morning as they were clearing away the last of the rubble from the cave-in. Even after she had opened the mysterious oilskin bag and realized what she was looking at, even after she had taken it to Jared and seen how instantly excited he had become over it, even after she had let the significance of the new find settle in—she could still think of nothing but the way Jared had kissed her when he had pulled her from the cave.

The police had caught Charlie "Coyote" Braddock and he confessed to planting explosives at the cave entrance in order to stop further excavating. And because the incident had generated heated debate on all sides—from those wanting the cave sealed to those wanting it opened as a tourist attraction—Erica and Jared had stepped up their race to find the most likely descendant of the skeleton. The oilskin bag Erica had found that morning seemed about to provide them with an unexpected clue.

The bag had contained a parchment, mildewed but still legible, that turned out to be the land grant to a property called Rancho Paloma, deeded to someone named Navarro. The landmarks drawn on the deed— *la cienegas* (the marshes), *la brea* (the tar), *El Camino Viejo* (the Old Road)—marked off a section of prime Los Angeles real estate that was clearly defined even today. El Camino Viejo had undergone many name changes since the Spaniards—Orange Street, Sixth Street, Los Angeles Avenue, and Nevada Avenue—until its present-day name was settled upon: Wilshire Boulevard.

So now Erica and Jared were at the office of the Los Angeles City Archives, where they had spent the morning going through public records dating as far back as 1827, sitting at tables piled with documents, reports, bound volumes, maps, photographs, computer disks and videotapes. Jared was running searches on titles and deeds and land grants while Erica was tracing family names.

She finally leaned back and stretched, taking a moment to watch Jared as he sat in deep concentration over old records. The kiss had been both urgent and tender, and when she had parted her lips, his tongue had touched hers. It had been over in an instant, but it had packed more punch than a lifetime of hand-holding and stolen glances. Jared had lit a fire in her that continued to burn even now, so that when he reached for his coffee, she thought it was the sexiest gesture she had ever seen. "Any luck?" she asked.

He rubbed the back of his neck and looked at her. Erica could swear she saw an arc of electricity zap from his eyes to hers. Those dark irises positively smoldered. "As near as I can figure, Rancho Paloma was carved up and sold to newcomer Americans in 1866," he said in a voice that betrayed a desire to speak of more intimate things than historical records. Or so Erica imagined. In truth, she had no idea what Jared was thinking. After that one impulsive kiss there hadn't been another.

"So is that when the deed was buried in the cave?" she said. "In 1866?"

Because of the explosion and cave-in, and subsequent clearing of the rubble, there was no way to accurately determine at which level the deed had been buried.

"Perhaps. Maybe someone was trying to stop the sale and thought that burying the deed would do the trick."

"But why in *our* cave? Why bury the deed to property in the cave of the First Mother?"

Jared absently massaged his jaw. "It's almost as if," he murmured, "by burying the deed in the cave, someone was symbolically giving the land back to the First Mother."

"Someone connected to her perhaps, a descendant?"

Their eyes met and the same thought occurred to them both at the same instant: "If that's so," Erica said in sudden excitement, "and if we can find the present-day descendents of these original Navarros, then chances are we might find the identity of our skeleton!"

Jared pushed his chair back and stood up, lifting his arms above his head. Erica feasted her eyes on the way his shirt pulled over sculpted muscles. "What have you found on the Navarros?" he asked. Jared was having a hard time concentrating on the task that had brought them here. His mind was filled with the incredible story Erica had told him after she had crawled out of the collapsed cave.

Jared had sat with her while she calmed down, and she had told him a remarkable tale about being abandoned when she was five years old and living in foster homes until she had been rescued by a woman lawyer she didn't know. And that was why she was fighting so hard to save the Emerald Hills Woman, she said, because no one else was going to. Now he understood her motivation. According to the legal system, sixteen-year-old Erica was supposedly already being taken care of by the state, and yet a serious misrepresentation of the facts of her case had been about to cause such a miscarriage of justice as to toss the girl into a penal system from which she might never emerge. What the attorney had done was see the *personal* aspect of the case. Erica had not been just a number on the court docket, but a person with rights. Just like the Emerald Hills Woman, who was likewise supposedly being taken care of by the state, yet who was about to be buried, to be forgotten forever.

He wished he could have met Lucy Tyler. After she was appointed guardian ad litem to Erica, she found a better foster placement for her and made regular visits. "She became my mentor," Erica had explained. "God knows what she saw worth salvaging in me, but I wanted to please her and do well for her. I think that deep down I had no sense of self-worth, so my motivation to make something of myself didn't come from a belief in myself but rather that I believed in her. I took her name after I graduated from high school. She died the week I received my Ph.D. Lymphoma. She had kept it a secret so I wouldn't be distracted from my studies."

"Not much," Erica said now in response to his question about the Navarros. She had been going through a large book titled, *California's Founding Families*. "All it says in here is a Navarro family lived on Rancho Paloma. But it gives no further information about them. There are thousands of Navarros currently residing in LA County. Even if we decided to check each one out, that would be assuming the Navarros of Rancho Paloma even stayed in LA."

He nodded. "Well, I'm hungry. There's a burrito stand downstairs. Do you want beef or bean?"

"Chicken," she said. "And any diet soft drink." She watched him go, marveling at this sudden and unexpected turn in her life. Of all the men who had tried to penetrate the barrier around her heart, Jared Black, her old enemy, was not the one she would ever have predicted to be the victor. What now? Was the next move hers? But how could she be sure he had meant to start something with that kiss? What if he regretted it and wished he could take it back? Suddenly the future, with its promise of mystery and surprise, both excited and frightened her.

She forced her mind back to reality: how to link the deed to the cave?

Erica contemplated the formidable mother lode of historical evidence available for their search: newspaper archives; birth, death, and marriage records; the license bureau; county tax assessor; police files. There were thousands of records, annals, chronicles, memorabilia, memoranda, rolls, registers, statistics, lists, ledgers, public papers, and court transcripts.

Where to begin?

Deciding to start with statistics—to see if she could find any Navarros that had died between 1865 and 1885—she sat at an available computer terminal and selected the database. The records that far back were sketchy, with question marks following many of the names. When Jared came back with lunch and sat next to her, unwrapping the aromatic burritos, she said, "Maybe we should just take out an ad in the paper. 'Anyone with information on the whereabouts of Mr. or Mrs. Navarro, circa 1866 . . . ' "

He shook his head and laughed.

Erica took the cap off her diet cola. "I feel like filing a missing persons report!"

They ate in silence for a while as they watched others come and go—teachers, historians, writers, people doing genealogical research on their families—until Erica realized she was staring at a red-haired young woman who was asking the clerk for help tracking down the ancestors of a family named McPherson, who had come to Los Angeles at the turn of the century. "They were my mother's people," Erica heard the young woman say.

And Erica felt her heart leap.

Quickly setting aside her burrito, she returned to the computer terminal, closed the statistics database, and opened up the LAPD database on closed and noncurrent files. Search parameters were listed by division, department, and date. She selected Missing Persons and stared at the screen for a long moment before she was aware of the idea that had begun to form in her mind: *Was my mother's disappearance ever reported?*

Although she had tried to search for her family years ago, the computer database that was available now hadn't existed then. Searching had required going through vast quantities of paper files and records, a time-consuming and ultimately futile task. But now, on a sudden hopeful impulse, instead of searching for Navarros Erica typed in "1965," the year her mother had arrived at the hippie commune. She added: "female," "Caucasian," "pregnant," and "under thirty years of age." Telling herself that it was a long shot, she nervously drummed her fingers as she waited for the results to appear. What were the chances anyway? It was only a guess that her mother had run away from home to become a hippie. She could have left with her parents' knowledge. Maybe they were even glad to be rid of her, so no missing persons report would have been filed.

When the results came back, she anxiously scanned the names of girls reported missing. A lot of teenage runaways that year, some pregnant. *Any one of these could have been my mother.*

She scrolled back and read the list more carefully, silently mouthing the names to see if any rang a bell.

Then: *Monica Dockstader. Seventeen years old. Brown hair, 5'7", 140lbs, four months pregnant. Last seen Greyhound Bus Station, Palm Springs.*

Dockstader. It resonated with something in the far reaches of her mind. And the date! June. Which meant Monica Dockstader's baby had been due in November. The month Erica was born.

Going to the main desk, Erica requested microfilms of newspapers from 1965, confining her search to the *Los Angeles Times* and the *Herald Examiner.* She carried them to a viewer and, with trembling fingers, loaded the first film.

It took less than five minutes.

"Oh my God!"

Jared looked up. "You've found something?"

"I think I've found . . ." She turned wide eyes to him. Her voice dropped a notch. "My mother . . ."

He came to stand behind her and frowned at the newspaper headline on the viewer: *"Heiress of Palm Springs Date Empire Vanishes. Search Under Way. Reward Offered."* The thirty-five-year-old article was brief, with statements from the girl's parents asking her to come home. "She is currently going by the name Moonbeam," Kathleen Dockstader, Monica's mother, had told the police.

"Moonbeam . . ." Erica whispered. The baldheaded man, thirty years ago, telling the social worker, "She went by Moonbeam."

"Looks like she wasn't kidnapped," Jared said. "She ran away. The only reason the case got even this much press is because the family was wealthy. It says here the Dockstaders were the oldest and largest exporters of dates in the United States. I wonder if they're still in business."

Erica reached out and touched the monitor. Were the two distraught middle-aged people in the news photo her grandparents?

Jared leaned closer. "Good God, Erica. Look at the photo at the bottom of the page. That girl, Monica Dockstader. She could be a younger version of you!"

✳

"Does any of this look familiar to you?" Jared asked as he guided his Porsche off Highway 111 and onto Dockstader Road.

Erica looked out at the rows of stately date palms that went on for what seemed like miles, and beyond, tawny desert backed by mountains capped with snow turning pink in the setting sun. "No. But I was born in a commune up north and as far as I know didn't leave until I was taken to the hospital in San Francisco. I was five years old then, and after that I was placed in foster homes. I don't think I've ever been here."

On the Internet they had found a website for Dockstader Farms, over a thousand acres of rich date palms located near Palm Springs in the Coachella Valley, boasting a restaurant, gift shop, and tours of the grounds and packing plant, with free samples to all visitors. The website had a section titled "About Our Family." Erica had expected it to be the story of the Dockstaders. Instead it was a description of the *corporate* family—from vice president on down to the date pickers.

Erica had telephoned from the archives office to be told that Mrs. Dockstader was not taking any appointments and would not be available until she returned from a six-month vacation. Erica had briefly considered telling the secretary who she was—surely Mrs. Dockstader would be available for her long-lost granddaughter—and then thought it might be better to simply drive out here. News like this should not come over a phone and through a secretary, and it couldn't wait since Mrs. Dockstader was leaving tomorrow.

They drove past a sign that said "Established 1890," past the visitor parking lot, and followed a small paved lane flanked by massive oaks and willows. When they came to a sign that said "Private Residence, No Public Access Beyond This Point," Jared kept driving. Erica closed her eyes and felt her heart gallop. She knew what they were going to find at the end of the lane: a huge Victorian gingerbread built at the turn of the last century, filled with antiques and family history, and at its heart, Kathleen

Dockstader, a kindly, grandmotherly seventy-two-year-old widow with arthritic hands and white hair. Erica could almost smell the woman's lavender scent as she said tearfully, "Yes, I am your grandmother," and took Erica into a loving embrace.

The lane came to an end at a curved driveway and the oaks and willows gave way to palatial green lawns, elegant fountains, and a house that looked as if it had been built in the future. Constructed half of blinding white stucco and half of glass, the Dockstader residence was a single-story, low-profile house with cool, clean lines, lacking clutter and decoration, part Santa Fe, Erica thought, and part botanical greenhouse. A Rolls Royce was parked out front, and a man in a butler's uniform was loading matched luggage and a set of golf clubs into the trunk.

When Jared parked the car, he looked at Erica. "Ready?"

"I'm nervous." She impulsively took his hand. "Thank you for coming with me."

"I wouldn't miss this for the world," he said, giving her hand a squeeze. "This woman has been searching for you for thirty-five years. She even offered an impressive reward to find you." His smile broadened. "I hope she has smelling salts handy."

She looked into Jared's eyes, which she realized weren't shadowy after all but an expressive gray that made her think of openness and honesty. "Something I have wondered all my life . . . did my mother ever go back to that commune and search for me? Maybe she didn't know about the man taking me and the woman who died of a drug overdose to a hospital in San Francisco. What if she has been searching for me all this time?"

"Maybe she came home, maybe she's here," he said, turning his eyes to the glass-and-stucco structure set like an architect's model among perfect trees and shrubs.

They were stopped at the front door by the butler. "Please, it's urgent," Erica said to the man. "Tell Mrs. Dockstader that we've come regarding her daughter."

They were shown into an entryway painted in soft desert tones with a limestone floor that shone like glass and a skylight exposed to the flawless desert sky. They were kept waiting for nearly thirty minutes, during which daylight faded and muted house lights came on.

The woman who finally appeared was neither kindly nor grandmoth-erly. "I am Kathleen Dockstader," she stated abruptly to Jared. "What is this about my daughter?"

Erica was rendered momentarily speechless. Deeply tanned and wear-ing pink Bermuda shorts and a white golf shirt, with blond hair caught up behind a visor that read *Dinah Shore Golf Classic*, Kathleen Dock-stader, fit and athletic, looked years younger than her actual age.

Erica found her voice. "My name is Erica Tyler, Mrs. Dockstader, and I have reason to believe I am your granddaughter."

The woman looked at Erica for the first time. Her face froze. She blinked. Then she said, "Why?" Her voice was cold.

Wishing they could go inside and sit down, wishing she would be offered frosty iced tea to help her lips and tongue form the proper words, Erica told Mrs. Dockstader her story, ending with finding the missing persons report and news article at the office of archives.

"Miss Tyler," Kathleen said impatiently, "I am getting ready to embark on a world golf tour. My plane leaves tonight. I do not have time for speculation. Show me proof." She held out a hand which, with weathered skin and ropy veins, was the only evidence of her real age. "Birth certifi-cate? Letters? Photographs?"

"I have nothing."

The woman pursed her lips. "Just a story. That I'm supposed to buy." She turned to go. "You are wasting my time."

"Mrs. Dockstader," Erica said hurriedly, desperation in her voice. "I have memories of living in the woods with a lot of people. I think it was a hippie commune. I remember a ride in a car from the woods into the city, and the man who was driving, who had long hair and a beard, took me and a woman to a hospital. He didn't stay long. He said he wasn't the woman's husband and I wasn't his kid and he didn't know her real name. I vaguely remember a nice lady, a social worker, asking me ques-tions. My name and my birthday, things like that. I told her I was Erica but that I had never had a last name. But I knew how old I was and my date of birth, so they made up a birth certificate for me. They investigated the commune. I overheard a man reporting that my mother, who called herself Moonbeam, had ridden off with a biker, leaving me with the hippies. That was when I was made a ward of the state. That's all I know. That's all I can tell you."

Kathleen's lips curled in a dry smile. "Do you think I don't know what you are after? I know your type, preying upon rich old widows."

"Pardon me, ma'am," Jared said, "but I'd hardly call you old."

She shot him a look. "Don't patronize me. I am old and rich and without heirs, which makes me a target for con artists and gold diggers. You aren't the first to claim to be my granddaughter. Anastasia Romanov didn't have as many impersonators! The story of my daughter's disappearance in 1965 is well-known, as well as the fact that she was pregnant. I put ads in papers all over the country. I offered rewards. You would be surprised how many 'granddaughters' came out of the woodwork. I must say, your story of being raised in a hippie commune is new, if a bit melodramatic. Now if you will excuse me."

"I don't want money. I am not here to lay claim to *anything*. All I want is to find out where I came from, who my family is. Who *I* am."

"Young woman, my hopes have been raised and dashed so many times that I've gone beyond the point of caring. Whatever your scam, it won't work here."

"But . . . don't I resemble your daughter? A moment ago, when you came in, the look on your face—"

"You are not the first to notice your resemblance to an heiress and try to cash in on it. And my daughter did not have distinctive features. She was merely pretty, as you are."

"Who was my father?"

Aristocratic eyebrows arched. "How should I know who your father was?"

"I mean, who got your daughter pregnant?"

Kathleen made an impatient sound. "I have to insist you leave now."

"Mrs. Dockstader, did my mother ever suffer from severe headaches, like migraines, that made her see things, hear voices? Do *you*, perhaps?"

Kathleen went to the wall and pressed a button on an intercom panel. "Security, will you come in here please? We have visitors who need to be escorted off the grounds." She walked out of the room.

"Mrs. Dockstader," Erica said, following her. "Believe me, everything I have told you is true—" She stopped.

Across a living room filled with white carpeting and white statuary, above a pale limestone fireplace, hung an enormous canvas painting of two suns, one blazing red, the other glowing yellow.

Jared caught Erica's arm, and said quietly, "We'd better leave or she'll have us arrested." And then he, too, stopped and stared at the canvas. "Good God," he said. "It's the painting from the cave!"

Erica looked around for Kathleen Dockstader, but the woman had disappeared, and in the next moment a large man wearing a blazer and a badge that said *Dockstader Farms Security* appeared in the doorway. Erica and Jared left wordlessly, jumping into the Porsche and speeding back down the lane.

As they joined the traffic on the foothill highway, Jared took his eyes off the road to glance at Erica. Staring straight ahead through the windshield, she presented a tight profile to him, and eyes sparkling with tears. He wanted to stop the car and take her into his arms and kiss her the way he had when he had pulled her from the cave. He wanted to turn the car around and go back to Mrs. Dockstader and outline to her precisely what a heartless bitch she was. He wanted to find dragons to slay.

"Are you okay?" he said instead.

She nodded wordlessly, her lips pressed together.

When they stopped at a red light, Jared looked to the right—where golf courses and exclusive resort hotels were bathed in expensive illumination as if to defy the stars that were beginning to appear—and then ahead where traffic streamed through blocks of restaurants, shops, and gas stations, brake lights flashing red. Then he looked to the left, where a road climbed steeply into foothills covered in scrub, boulders, and wildflowers. When the signal changed to green he turned left. Erica did not protest.

The stars were out and the moon starting to rise when they reached a summit thick with pine trees and forest silence. Erica hadn't spoken a word since leaving the Dockstader house, and she continued to sit mutely when Jared finally pulled the Porsche to a stop at the edge of a forest and killed the headlights. At once, the stars seemed brighter, the heavens closer. The air was chill with a bite in it.

Jared turned in his seat and looked at Erica, waiting.

"She's my grandmother," Erica said softly after a moment. "And she knows it." She turned to face him. She was shockingly pale. "Did you see the look on her face when she first saw me? It was a look of recognition. Why, after spending so much money and effort to find me did she turn me away?" Erica looked down at her hands. "In the missing persons report it said that Monica was four months pregnant, which means her baby was due in November 1965. *I* was born in November 1965. Why is my grandmother rejecting me?"

"You can't see into another's heart." Jared stretched his arm along the back of the seat so that his fingertips touched her hair. The forest darkness seemed to close in around the car, as if to give the occupants privacy. Or perhaps to listen, to hear what they had to say. "When Netsuya died," Jared said quietly, "I ran away to hide from the world. I was found by marine biologists. All my father could say to me when I was brought home was how I had embarrassed the family. He later apologized and tried to take back his words, but words once spoken are hard to take back. Things haven't been the same between us since."

He touched a curl at the nape of her neck. She trembled. The night grew darker, the stars brighter. Golden eyes blinked in the brush. A night bird called nearby—a lonely, mournful sound. "When I was growing up," Jared continued, "I dreamed of being an architect, but my father wanted me to be a lawyer, so I became a lawyer. I've always admired and re-spected him, but in that instant, when he said I had embarrassed the family, I saw a complete stranger, a man I didn't like. And I thought I could never forgive him. But now . . ." He sighed and looked ahead through the trees. "Hearing your story and seeing Mrs. Dockstader's re-action is making me think that parents and grandparents, sisters and brothers are really just people and they can't be perfect. Give her time, Erica. You know she's thinking about it."

She finally looked at him with amber eyes like those of the forest dwellers watching them. "But the painting. Jared, that has to be where I saw the vision that has been haunting my dreams ever since I was a child."

He frowned. "Vision? What are you talking about?"

She opened the car door and got out. Jared followed. From this high point they could see below, the Coachella Valley stretched to the horizon like a black sea glittering with starry reflection. They stood for a moment breathing in the cold mountain air, inhaling the scent of pines and loamy soil. Then Erica set foot upon a wilderness trail illuminated in the moonlight.

Jared fell into step beside her as she explained: "The painting in the cave—I have had a recurring dream about it ever since I was little. That was why I asked Sam to assign me to the project, when I saw it on the news. I allowed Sam to believe I was desperate for the assignment because of the Chadwick shipwreck fiasco, that I wanted to restore my reputation. But that wasn't the reason. It was because I have been dreaming of that painting all my life and I thought I could find answers in the cave. Instead, there is only more mystery."

They came upon a stream, gurgling, whispering, as if telling secrets. When Erica shivered, Jared removed his jacket and placed it around her shoulders. "You asked Mrs. Dockstader about headaches, why?"

"I've suffered from them ever since I can remember—not just normal headaches, but something like migraines. Powerful, strong. My teachers always thought I was faking them. They said I did it for attention or to get out of a test. One school nurse believed me and had me looked at by a doctor. But I was a welfare case, so I didn't get much more of a work-up than the doctor looking in my ears and telling me to say Ah. It was when I collapsed on the college campus that someone finally took me seriously. I've been through all kinds of tests and programs, seeing headache specialists, neurologists, even psychologists. No one knows what causes the headaches, but what really baffles them is the auditory and visual phenomena that sometimes accompany them."

The glade through which the stream ran stood in moonglow, with boulders and catkins and the trickling water looking silver and mercurial. It was as if all color had been washed from the world, leaving only the hues of ghosts. "What kind of phenomena?" Jared asked, noticing how the moonlight had turned Erica's tanned skin ivory.

"I see things. Sometimes I hear things."

"Why didn't you tell me about the dreams?"

"Because I thought you would laugh."

"I'm not laughing."

Their eyes met in moonlight. "I know."

"What are the visions like?"

She rubbed her arms. "The first time I had a spell, that I can recall, it started with a blinding headache. I don't know if I fell asleep or phased out, but I suddenly saw thousands of butterflies in the classroom. Beautiful, dazzling, flying all over. And when I came to I was in the nurse's office. My first words were, 'Where did the butterflies go?' And the nurse said, 'What butterflies?' That's why I was never adopted. It was because of the headaches. No one wants to adopt a sick child."

Erica ran her gaze over the nearby mountain peaks that blotted out the stars. Her eyes were searching, as if she expected to see someone standing there, high up. "I went through a phase of being always packed and ready to go for when my parents came for me. Whenever I was transferred to another foster home, I called the social worker to make sure they would give my mother the new address. Sometimes I would call social services and ask if my mother had called. But she never did." Erica's voice went hard. "She just didn't want me."

Jared touched her elbow. "You don't know that."

"Then what about the biker she ran off with?" Challenge in her tone.

"That was something you overheard from a man who was quoting hearsay. Maybe she meant to go away for only a weekend. Maybe she had planned to come back for you but something happened. Erica, you might never know what really happened to your mother."

She shook her head, bitterness in the gesture. Then she knelt by the stream and dipped her hand into the water. Jared surveyed their surroundings, trying to recall what he had read about mountain lions in this area, and then realized that even though they had come only a short distance from the car, it couldn't be seen through the trees, nor could the lights of Palm Springs. He watched Erica take a sip of the crisp alpine water, and when she stood and ran her hands down her skirt, he said, "There's more, isn't there? Something you aren't telling me?"

She shook her head, avoiding his eyes.

"Erica, I nearly went out of my mind when you were trapped in the cave. I didn't know if you were dead or alive. For the first time since Netsuya died, I realized I cared about someone else. I think it started when I saw you confronting Charlie Braddock with that tomahawk. There you stood in your high heels and cocktail dress, brandishing an ax at this towering giant. And then at Sam's secret meeting in Century City, the way you stood up to him and the others, how you fought for the rights of a woman who died two thousand years ago. You're such a fighter, Erica. And seeing you like that reminded me that I was once a fighter, too, before Netsuya died."

She turned away and walked a few steps until she saw in the moonlight petroglyphs carved on a boulder: human stick figures with bows and arrows hunting large animals. She traced them with her fingertips, and said, "These are so old." She turned tear-filled eyes to him. "Everything I deal with is old and dead. I want *life*, Jared."

He took her by the shoulders. "Then let me in. Tell me what you haven't told me."

She started to cry. "Jared, did my mother leave me because of my sickness?"

He stared at her. "Good God, is that what you think?"

"Because I was having the headaches, I was difficult to take care of! That's why I was never adopted! One family tried to keep me—the Gordons. They were very sweet and tried hard, but Mrs. Gordon just couldn't cope with my spells that could happen anywhere. So they gave me back to child welfare services."

"Erica, you can't blame yourself for your mother leaving you. You were just a baby. My God, is this why you never married, why you aren't in a relationship? Because of the headaches and fainting spells? In the weeks we have been working at Topanga I haven't seen it."

"I'm very careful," she said as the tears flowed down her cheeks. "I know the signs. When I feel a certain tension in my neck or hear a roaring sound, I know I am about to have one of my spells, so I quickly go to my tent and be by myself until it passes. I can't burden another human being with that responsibility of taking care of me. And I am terrified of having children because I think it might be hereditary."

"*I* would take care of you." He pulled her to him suddenly and kissed her hard. Erica's arms went around his neck. She clung to him for a long, breathless moment.

Then he drew back, and said, "Erica, I've just been going through the motions of life. My heart hasn't been in the fight for the Emerald Hills cave. *You're* the one who's been putting up the real fight. I admired you four years ago when we squared off on the Reddman case. And I admired you last year, too, during the whole Chadwick incident. It wasn't your fault that the shipwreck was a hoax. Chadwick managed to fool the world's top underwater archaeology experts. You were just one part of a whole team. Your job was to authenticate the Chinese pottery, and that you did admirably because the pottery was *not* fake. And the way you stood up for your side of it, and your public apology for your part in it, that, too, was very admirable. But I've done nothing since Netsuya died. I've hidden behind a mask and mouthed empty words. You make me remember what it's like to be alive and fight for causes again."

He took her face in his hands. "I never thought I would fall in love again and here you are, warrior-woman, good and strong and wise."

He kissed her again, more slowly and tenderly this time, until the kiss grew urgent, and passion and need overwhelmed them. Jared lowered Erica to the cool sweet grass and high overhead, the stars so old suddenly looked brand-new.

Chapter Sixteen

ANGELA
1866 C.E.

Ghosts haunted her.

Not just people-ghosts but the ghosts of memories and years past; the ghosts of trees and sunsets, of love and sadness, of words spoken in anger and in the dark. Even Angela herself was one of the ghosts who haunted her on this morning of her ninetieth birthday, following her, whispering about remembrances of times long past.

Throughout the day, as she had gone through this hacienda that had survived eight decades of floods, fire, and earthquakes, making it the oldest house in Los Angeles, Angela was remembering things for the first time in eighty-five years. The lost years, she had always thought of them, for she had no memory before her sixth birthday in this house. Her hair was white now, as white as the snow that capped the San Gabriel Mountains in winter, but her back was still straight and she walked without aid, and her mind was as sharp as glass. But when she had awakened at the dawn of this ninetieth birthday, it had been to find her mind filled with perplexing, long-forgotten memories.

Like a crowd of unexpected party guests, recollections of events from decades ago had swirled in kaleidoscopic color and noise as she lay watching the sunrise shed new light across her bedroom. Inexplicably, she had found herself thinking of baskets woven by Indian women and recalling that the patterns in the weave contained a story. And then she heard herself, eight years old, asking Doña Luisa: "Mami, why is the village named for angels?" And Luisa had answered: "Because it was built upon sacred ground. What other reason could there be?" Stories of Coyote the Trickster, and Grandfather Tortoise who causes earthquakes sprang into her head. And then Angela was remembering a warm afternoon long ago when the new plaza was being dedicated by Governor Neve and everyone had been given a little cross made of tin. She had stood there with her parents . . . or had it been just her mother? The colonists from Mexico numbered forty-four that day, eighty-five years ago. Such a small population . . . She frowned. But no, there were others there, standing away from the celebration, silent onlookers with flat expressions. The Indians. They had numbered in the thousands that day. How many were left? A few hundred.

But there was a blank space among the memories, as if in all this remembering she had forgotten something.

After she had bathed and dressed with the help of her personal maid, and then had drunk her morning chocolate and silently recited her first prayers of the day, she had gone straight to the kitchen, thinking that the thing she had forgotten involved the food for today's feast.

Because Angela's large family was now a cultural mix of Spanish, Mexican, and American, all tastes had to be considered. Along with tortillas, tamales, and frijoles there would also be Spanish-style seafood and American-style beef. The huge kitchen with its three enormous ovens, massive tables, and deep fireplace was already, at this early hour, alive with the bustle of Indian women cooking, gossiping, filling the air with exotic aromas and words. Angela paused to inspect the *puchero*, a stew made of knucklebone, meat, vegetables, and fruit, layered and set to simmer for hours. The mistake was in stirring. Puchero must never be stirred. She lifted the lid and found that the layered stew was cooking nicely.

When all seemed to be going well in the kitchen, Angela wondered if the thing she had forgotten involved the musicians and the dancers. Or had she perhaps forgotten to invite someone? Were there enough chairs, plates, garden lights? For even though the party was being held in honor of her birthday, Angela insisted upon overseeing all the arrangements herself.

She stopped at a window to look out across the rolling hills in the haze. Spring was over, the flood season had passed, now it was summer, the season of smoke. Soon would come the desert winds that annually cleansed the air by driving it out to sea, after which came the fire season, when mountainsides raged with brushfires. There was comfort in the progression of the seasons and the predictable cycle of nature. Benevolent California, she thought wistfully. And once in a while the ground shook to remind Angelenos that they were mortal.

She continued through the house, searching for something to fill the empty space among her clamorous memories. She stopped at the bedroom that had been Marina's, thirty-six years ago. On that very bed, the eighteen-year-old had wept and confessed her love for a Yankee. Angela had not heard from her daughter since, and not a day had gone by in the ensuing thirty-six years that Angela had not taken a moment to send her thoughts across the distant horizon and say a silent prayer to the Blessed Virgin to watch over Marina and keep her safe.

In the corridor, she came upon the set of four upholstered antique armchairs that had been brought to California long ago by Doña Luisa. The brocaded silk was worn and faded now, and the veneered arms and legs nicked from the assaults of grandchildren and great-grandchildren. The chairs were to have been a wedding present to Marina. But Marina had run away and the chairs had stayed.

Angela trailed her fingers along the antique wood and thought: We five came together from Mexico. But why can I not remember that journey from Mexico? Why do my memories begin on my sixth birthday?

Voices interrupted her thoughts. Two grandsons talking as they came along the colonnade. "The cattle haven't been doing well since the drought." And the words triggered another memory. Cattle. Angela five years old and watching strangers arrive with large, frightening beasts. There was never meant to be cattle on this land. They were brought from across the seas. That is why they are dying.

"And Captain Hancock has found oil seeping onto his property. It makes the land useless for crops and grazing. We are not far from the tar pits. We might have oil, too. We must convince Grandmother she should sell the rancho while the land is still good."

"Everyone is selling. The Picos and the Estradas have sold much of their land to Anglo newcomers, George Hearst, and Patrick Murphy. We would be wise to do the same."

The men were accompanied by women in wide, sweeping crinolines. Angela herself did not wear the heavy cumbersome frame beneath her gown, but simply a petticoat. And she had stopped wearing a corset fifteen years ago. Women's fashions, she thought, were becoming more and more torturous.

She greeted her grandsons and their wives with a smile and open arms. It was always so wonderful to have the family gathered together.

Navarro wasn't here, of course. He had died twenty years ago, exactly sixteen years after the night Angela stabbed him. Outside of Carlotta, no one knew about the attack. On that fateful night, when Angela had seen that Navarro still lived, she had summoned a doctor, who had stitched and bound the wound, and helped put her husband to bed. The doctor was paid for his secrecy and when Navarro regained consciousness he had ordered his wife and eldest daughter not to tell anyone the truth of his condition—a man stabbed by his own wife was too humiliating.

And of course, Marina wasn't here either.

Six months after her sister disappeared on the night of her wedding, Carlotta received a letter from Marina saying she was safe. Carlotta had written back to say that their father wasn't dead, that he had survived the knife wound and that she could never come home, he would kill her for having run off with an *Americano*. Carlotta never heard from her sister after that, and when Navarro died twenty years ago, the family had no idea where to write to Marina to tell her it was safe to come home. They also had no idea if she was even still alive.

"We've come to collect you for the photographer, Grandmother," the grandsons said, flanking her on either side, each to take a frail arm. "He is getting ready to take pictures. It's the light, he said. The light is perfect right now."

But there was something Angela had forgotten, if only she could remember what.

✳

In September of 1846, at the outset of the Mexican War, there was rebellion against the American forces occupying the Pueblo of Los Angeles. An American fur trapper named John Brown rode five hundred miles in six days to inform Commodore Stockton in Monterey of the resistance. U.S. troops were immediately dispatched and, shortly thereafter, the *New York Herald* sent a cub reporter named Harvey Ryder to cover the story.

That was twenty years ago. Ryder never returned to New York.

"Ironic when you think about it," he was saying now to the photographer who was setting up his equipment beneath the banyan trees near the Navarro hacienda. "The Spaniards came here three hundred years ago looking for gold and when they didn't find it they wrote California off. Gave it away to the Mexicans and then the Mexicans lost it to the United States. And then gold was found." He laughed. "I'll bet their king wishes he'd never given up this gold mine! These folks should be glad the Americans came along. Without us that gold would never have been found. It would still be in the ground and Los Angeles would still be a cow town of five hundred people." He pushed his bowler hat farther back on his head. "Well, it's still a cow town, only now it's a cow town of five *thousand* people."

The reporter fixed his eye on an Indian woman walking by with a basket of fruit on her head, her long braids swaying. "The *New York Herald* sent me to cover the war with Mexico," he said to the photographer who was either listening or not. "I was supposed to report on the war, but it was all over by the time I got here. Never went back to New York, though. Gold was discovered right after the treaty was signed and, like everyone else, I went north to make my fortune. Found a little gold. Not much.

Knocked around in Oregon for a while after that. Got married and divorced. Even have a couple of kids somewhere. Then I ran into an old friend in San Francisco, who told me the *Los Angeles Clarion* was looking for a reporter."

Servants were getting the garden ready for the party. Bowls of fruit had been set out, from which Ryder helped himself. "This place is growing," he said as he peeled an orange. "No doubt about it. Everybody's buying up the ranchos and naming towns after themselves. Met a dentist by the name of Burbank the other day, bought himself a Spanish land grant in the eastern part of the San Fernando Valley. And Downey, same one who was governor a couple years back, subdividing his rancho and selling lots. Some folks are even keeping the Indian names, they think it's romantic." He shook his head. "Like Pacoima and Azusa sound romantic?"

He separated a wedge of orange and popped it into his mouth, juice squirting down his chin. "Angelenos are an unpredictable breed. You think all they do is gamble and take siestas. But you should have seen them when war between the states broke out. This town was instantly divided over the issues of slavery and secession. I am talking all-fired, gun-shooting passionately divided. Half the menfolk rode off to fight for the Confederacy or the Union, the other half stayed home and tore the town up with drunken fistfights and gun battles. But the war issue was quickly overshadowed by the drought of '62, which devastated the cattle industry here. Close on its heels was the smallpox epidemic that carried off half the Indians. Seemed ironic to me, as the Indians were the ones who worked the herds. When the cattle died, seemed like there was no more need for the Indians." He smiled and looked at the photographer for approval. The man kept working.

"Got a serious bandit problem here though. Mostly ne'er-do-wells if you ask me. They claim they're taking revenge on the Yankees for stealing their land. Hell, it isn't stealing! A lot of those old Spanish land grants weren't valid. No U.S. judge is going to allow a crude map with someone's name on it to stand as legal title. The Mexicans didn't even do proper surveys. Just rode out to some trees, drew them on the map, then rode south to a rock, drew that, then rode over to a creek, drew that, and they called it legal. That's how they took it from the Indians. Now, the Americans did it properly, came in with surveyors and lawyers and obtained the land fair and square. But you can't make the *banditos* understand that."

He ate some more orange and inspected his fancy satin waistcoat for drops of juice. "Lotta lynchings hereabouts, too. Hotheaded group of Texans living out in El Monte, call themselves the El Monte Rangers, darned near started a civil war right there in town when a comrade name of Bean—brother of Judge Roy—was found dead in a field near the Mission. Those old boys rode through shooting at everything in sight and strung up just about anything that didn't move.

"Can't blame the people for turning vigilante, though. You have one sheriff and two deputies covering the whole county, and one marshal as the only lawman for the town. Folks are forced to take the law into their own hands. 'Course, Los Angeles isn't a town anymore. Got promoted. Five thousand people living in twenty-eight square miles are now officially a *city*—leastwise according to the California legislature. But I tell you my friend, I've seen Paris and I've seen London. And Los Angeles is no city."

He removed his hat and fanned himself with it. "But I predict someday it will be. The railroads are coming, and with them, hoards of new immigrants from the East hungry for land. You don't see many Indians anymore. Used to be there were thousands but over the past quarter of a century, despite a few uprisings, they died, the Missions were secularized, the Indians were let go, and they just vanished, mostly to death."

As he licked his fingers and then wiped them on his handkerchief, he looked around the grounds for the family. He had sent a couple of men to round everyone up for the portrait. He was supposed to interview the matriarch, Señora Angela Navarro, and ask her how it felt to be ninety years old.

"Something mysterious happened in this family back in 1830," he said as the photographer continued to set up his contraptions and plates and squint frequently at the sun. "The youngest daughter disappeared on her wedding night and Navarro, who owned this rancho, took to his bed with an inexplicable illness. Bedridden for weeks, I hear, and when he recovered he was a different man. Ceased to have any interest in the running of the rancho, so his wife was forced to take over.

"The story goes that at first few people had taken her seriously, since she was only a woman and Navarro *was* still on the scene. But one year the winter rains were coming and the señora warned everyone that there was going to be a terrible flood. She even had her workers digging drainage ditches on the downslope of the property. Other rancheros didn't listen to her, so when sure enough the plain flooded and crops were destroyed, Rancho Paloma was spared because of the runoff canals. After that, they started listening to her. When she cut back on cattle production and introduced citrus groves and vineyards on the property, the other rancheros said she was crazy. But look what's happening on the other ranches. The cattle are all dying and the owners are being forced to sell their land. Not Angela Navarro. Some say she's the richest woman in California.

"I remember seeing her for the first time, when I came out here in forty-six. I was coming up the Old Road when I saw her. Magnificent, she was. Oh, I'd seen horsewomen back in New York, but Angela Navarro rode like a man. No sidesaddle for her. And wearing a man's broad-brimmed black hat, like the Mexican cowboys wear. They say she had ridden her property every day inspecting the orange and lemon orchards, rows of grapevines, avocado groves, until she became a fixture of the landscape. Was forced to switch to a carriage when age finally caught up with her."

He pulled out his pocket watch and clicked it open. Supposedly all the old *Californio* families were coming to the party, plus wealthy Anglo newcomers. Treating her like royalty. As if she were a queen. He laughed at his private joke. Angela Navarro, Queen of the Angels!

"Besides running the rancho," he continued out loud although the photographer was clearly more interested in his chemicals, which was okay with Ryder since his soliloquy was by way of preparing the article he was going to write, "she also channeled her energies into good works and demonstrations of civic pride. Yes sir, Navarro's widow has been a real force in this town. It's because of her that wooden sidewalks got put in so that ladies could walk down the street without trailing their dresses in mud or dust. She helped fund the Catholic Sisters of Charity in 1856, which established an orphanage for children of all denominations. She also helped fund the first hospital, and twice a year on Christmas and

Easter she distributes food and clothing to widows and orphans. When the city's first board of education was established in 1853 by the city council, Angela Navarro was one of the original members, and when Public School Number One was built on the corner of Spring Street, it was Angela who insisted that the school be open to girls as well as boys. So just remember, mister, that you aren't going to be taking a picture of just any ordinary person."

"I'm ready," the photographer finally said.

✳

Angela's nine children had produced over thirty grandchildren, from whom had sprung great-grandchildren too numerous to count. Not all had survived, just as not all her own children were still alive. Carlotta had died long ago in Mexico, but Angelique and her American husband, Seth Hopkins, who had struck gold in the north and came down to start citrus orchards, were here, along with their children. Yet despite this large family whom Angela had come to regard privately as her "little tribe," she still acutely missed Marina.

Perhaps that was the missing piece in her mind. Marina.

The photographer seated Angela in a big ornately carved chair that resembled a throne, and surrounded her with sons and daughters, grandchildren, and great-grandchildren. She wore a somber black dress with white lace collar and cuffs, and a small white lace veil pinned to her white hair. There was much arranging and rearranging of the participants, as the photographer tried to get the whole family into one shot. But children squirmed and babies cried and men cursed the heat, so the taking of the pictures was quickly becoming an ordeal. Only Harvey Ryder seemed to be enjoying it as he sat back in the shade, eating an orange and keeping his eye on the plump rear end of one of the Indian women.

In the midst of all the commotion and complaining and changing seats and removing hats and putting hats on and telling the photographer what would be best, Angela suddenly stiffened. Ryder, his instincts honed over the years, immediately saw it and was on his feet. The strangest look had come into the old lady's eyes.

No one noticed at first that Angela had risen to her feet. But when she started to walk away from the gathering, and the photographer said, "Excuse me, ma'am, we need you in this," Angelique immediately went after her.

"Grandmamá? Are you all right?"

Angela came to a standstill at the edge of the garden where a low stone wall separated the house from the farm buildings. Her eyes, encased in folds of skin and surrounded by wrinkles, but still sharp and bright, were fixed on the lane that led from the Old Road.

The others came to join her as they all expressed their worry, insisting that Grandmother sit down, wondering if they should call a doctor, fussing and fretting while Angela stood stock-still and watched the lane.

Presently everyone fell silent, and on the wind they could faintly hear the sound of horses' hooves, the creaking of wagon wheels. Before they could even see who it was, Angela's lips lifted in a smile, and she whispered one word: "Marina."

And in the next moment, as the crowd stood spellbound, they saw the wagons and the people on them, and the piles of luggage, signs of travelers from a great distance. On the seat in the first wagon, a one-armed man with white-gold hair and a white beard, and next to him a handsome middle-aged woman wearing an out-of-date gown and bonnet. In the second wagon, a younger man with a woman at his side, two children between them. And in the third wagon, a teenage boy holding the reins.

"¡Dios mio!" declared one of Angela's sons, a man in his sixties who bore a resemblance to Navarro in looks only, not in temperament. "Mamá!" he cried. "It is Marina! She has come home!"

The company ran to greet the visitors, swarming upon the wagons like a village welcoming soldiers back from a war. Angelique stayed behind with Angela, at the garden wall, watching the scene through tear-filled eyes. Hooking her arm through her grandmother's, she felt the older woman tremble with excitement and saw tears sparkle on Angela's withered cheeks. "It is indeed Auntie Marina," Angelique said in amazement.

It was a jubilant procession that accompanied the wagons to the hacienda, with the adults cheering and children happily running about. Only a handful of them remembered Marina, but they had all heard stories about her. Her sudden appearance was like the appearance of a saintly apparition. Everyone, including the flustered photographer and the cynical reporter, sensed the magic of the day.

Finally, the wagons pulled up to the stone wall, and Marina stayed for a moment on the seat, looking down at her mother. Then, with the help of her brothers, she climbed down and went into her mother's arms as if they had said farewell only yesterday, instead of thirty-six years ago.

✳

The ghosts were back. Whispering, teasing, reminding her of things long ago. Angela saw through the open shutters the position of the moon: it was nearly the midnight hour.

She lay wide-awake in the four-poster bed where she had given birth to her children, and she thought what a full day it had been. The food, the music, and the dancing. All her friends who had come, the old Spanish *rancheros*, the Mexican craftsmen, the Anglo newcomers. Even dignitaries such as Cristóbal Aguilar, the mayor of Los Angeles, and a message of birthday congratulations via telegraph from the governor in Sacramento. And Marina coming home! A satisfying day for any woman. But even so, there was still the empty spot in her mind, the one she had woken with the previous dawn.

In this dark and silent hour when her thoughts were clear, she began to realize that it was not so much something she had forgotten as something she must do. But what?

Angela got out of bed and into her slippers. She smiled at all her birthday gifts. Her two most prized were the pink Aztec figurine from Angelique and watercolors Daniel had painted in China. When she had declared what a tragedy for him to lose an arm to a bandit's bullet, Daniel had said, "Praise the Lord it wasn't my painting arm!"

Drawing a shawl around her shoulders, she slipped the jade statuette into her pocket, thinking that she would be needing the luck of an ancient goddess with her tonight, then she took a candle and walked down the dark and silent colonnade, past closed doors where people slept, until she came to a room at the end.

This was her private study, with its massive iron chandelier, heavy furniture, bookshelves to the ceiling, and a fireplace so big a person could stand inside it. On the desk were stacks of letters waiting to be answered, people asking for money, for advice, for the opportunity to do business with her. As Angela's eyesight was no longer what it used to be and her trembling hands could no longer write legibly, she employed a secretary to help her. But she never missed a day without sitting at this desk and going through the books, the accounts, the receipts and bills.

This had once been Navarro's seat of power, where he had received important visitors and dispensed favors like a king, or meted out punishments like a despot, where he had reprimanded his children and upbraided his workers, and signed contracts and agreements involving great amounts of money, and traded in goods both legal and illegal. He had helped his friends and destroyed his enemies in this room. He had once even received the Governor of California here and had had the arrogance to remain seated when the man entered. Navarro had sat upon this magnificent thronelike chair and worked his balance of good and evil, and in all the years he ruled here he never once allowed Angela across the threshold.

She recalled now the night she had visited Navarro as he lay in bed recovering from the stab wound. Although he had lived, he had lost a lot of blood, and a subsequent infection had rendered him bedridden for weeks. In that time, Angela had taken over the temporary running of the rancho, as was the local custom which allowed for wives to act as *rancheras* during a husband's absence. She had gone to his bedside and looked down at him as he had lain helpless, and she had said: "This land is mine. I do not care what you do after this, but you will never run Rancho Paloma again. And if you ever touch me or one of my children again, I shall stab you until you are dead." When he had finally recovered and had gone into his study to resume his work, he had found her behind the desk, going over the ledgers. Their eyes had met in a brief, silent challenge. Then Navarro had turned and quietly left. He never entered the study again.

She now unlocked a drawer and took out an oilskin bag, tucking it under her arm. Then she left and padded silently along the colonnade until she reached the bedchamber where Marina and Daniel Goodside slumbered.

As she tapped lightly on the door, knowing that middle-aged women slept lightly and middle-aged men slept like the dead, Angela marveled again at her daughter's story. The first ten years she was married, Marina had stayed home in Boston to give birth to four children. Then Daniel was called to the ministry and they had joined a mission to China. They went, babies and all, and there they spread the word of God for twenty-five years. Marina had explained that when she thought it was safe to write home, that she decided Navarro was so old that he was no longer a threat, she had tried to get letters out, but it was difficult. Many Chinese did not trust foreigners. One letter that Marina saw personally aboard a ship went down with the ship in a storm.

And then, just a year ago, Daniel's term of service had come to an end and he was retired from the mission. They sailed first to Hawaii, where Marina began again to send a letter, but decided after a first effort that it was better to just come instead. She hadn't had much hope that her mother was still alive or that the Navarros were even still here. But . . . to arrive on her mother's birthday!

Angela took this as a sign. It was all meant to be. Just as Marina was now meant to accompany her on a final journey.

When Marina opened the door, Angela said, "Get dressed. You must come with me."

"Where?"

"We will need a carriage."

"But Mother, it is late."

"The night is warm."

"Can it not wait till morning?"

She said, "Daughter, the past is a very insistent voice inside me tonight." And she added, "We must take Angelique as well."

✳

Angelique, forty-two years old and plump from seven pregnancies, had taken the time to slip into a wide, cumbersome crinoline which left almost no room in the carriage for the other two women. But Marina, at fifty-four, was thin from years of hard work and sacrifice, and she wore a simple dress that was twenty-five years out-of-date, and Angela was small and frail. There was just enough room.

Her daughter and granddaughter protested as they were helped up into the carriage by Angela's loyal coachman. He had been driving her around the rancho for fifteen years, and he asked no questions now, roused from sleep in the middle of the night, to take his mistress on an urgent errand. And yet they did not refuse to go, for both Marina and Angelique knew that if they did not agree to go, Angela would make this journey on her own.

"Let us at least have Seth and Daniel accompany us."

But Angela shook her head. This was woman's quest. Let the men sleep.

When they reached the Old Road and the driver turned eastward, Marina said in alarm, "But Mother, it is dangerous to go into the town at night!"

"We will come to no harm."

"How can you know?"

When she didn't respond, Marina exchanged a fearful look with her niece. Then they both sought comfort in the sight of their driver, a large burly man wearing a long sheathed sword, with both a knife and a pistol tucked into his belt.

They rode through the countryside in silence and when they passed a familiar oak grove, Angelique explained to her aunt that the Quiñones rancho no longer existed. Pablo, who was to have married Marina thirty-six years ago, had recently sold the land to an American named Crenshaw.

When they neared the town they could smell the stench from the irrigation ditches into which plumbing from houses and shops all drained by means of wooden pipes. The streets were lit by lanterns hung outdoors by homeowners and shop owners, required by law. But the word was, gas lighting was coming to Los Angeles. The saloons were still brightly lit with honky-tonk music pouring out. Gunfire could be heard in the distance. Two men were fighting on the wooden sidewalk.

And they saw Indians sleeping in doorways, or staggering down the street, drunk on white man's liquor.

The carriage passed Public School Number One on the corner of Spring Street. On Temple and Main Streets, where the town used to have only adobe buildings, they saw how Yankees were taking over with new buildings made of wood and brick. Spanish patios and fountains were being replaced by architectural styles with fancy names such as Romanesque, Queen Anne, Colonial Revival, and using pillars, gables, and mansard roofs. Street names had been changed: what was once *Loma* was now Hill, *Accytuna* was Olive, *Esperanzas*, Hope, and *Flores* was now Flower. Changed because of the Yankees.

As they rode around the Plaza, which stank of a recent bullfight, Angelique told Marina that there was word of a new hotel that was going to be built here and that it was going to have a bath on every floor, gas lighting, and a French restaurant. At three stories high it was going to be the tallest building in Los Angeles.

But Marina wasn't interested. "Mother, why are we here?"

Angela didn't know, only that she must keep going.

They left the main town and continued on the northeast road, three women in a carriage driven by a silent driver. They passed Chavez Ravine, a canyon where the town had put its potter's field, a cemetery for strangers and the friendless poor, until finally they arrived at the Mission, its long narrow windows between tall buttresses making it look more like a fortress than a church. When Mexico had taken possession of Alta California, the new governor had abolished the Mission system and had either given or sold the land to his friends and relatives. San Gabriel had stood neglected for years, its Indians living in squalor, the walls and roof falling in, vineyards going to seed, until 1859, when the new American government restored the property to the Church. But it wasn't the same anymore. Shacks and shanties surrounded the once-beautiful church.

As they sat solemnly in the carriage, the driver waiting for his mistress to issue further orders, Angela entertained a dim memory of a garden that had once been here, and an Indian woman tending herbs, humming softly in the sunshine. But then fever and a coughing sickness had taken her, and she had stood weak and ill during the dedication ceremony at the new Plaza. After that, a donkey ride to the mountains by the sea—

Angela gasped. Suddenly she knew. Knowledge that had been buried in her heart for eighty-five years broke free of its prison and soared like a bird.

I was born in this place. Not in Mexico as my mother told me. Or rather, not as Luisa had told me. For Luisa was not my real mother.

And now she understood why her thoughts throughout the day had been filled with memories of her childhood. *Perhaps when we draw near to the end, we are also drawing near to the beginning.*

She also saw clearly what it was that had been haunting her all day—the feeling that there was something left undone, a final duty she had to fulfill. Now she knew what it was and why she had taken a midnight ride through Los Angeles.

She had come to say good-bye.

✳

As they neared the foothills they could smell the sea. They knew they were riding across Rancho San Vicente y Santa Monica, owned by the Sepúlveda family. They heard the bells on sheep grazing nearby.

When they arrived at the canyon, Angela saw the rocks with the petroglyphs but she had forgotten what they meant. She had a dim memory of being brought here has a child, someone telling her that she was going to learn stories. But Angela was never taught those stories. She didn't understand the significance of the cave, or its paintings, or why she felt that at one time this had been a very important place. She remembered riding here on her wedding night, and cutting off her braid.

Marina and Angelique accompanied her up to the cave. They unclamped a lantern from the carriage to light their way, and assisted the older woman, one on either side of her. Marina remembered this place. It was where Daniel had found her the night they started their life together.

They helped Angela inside. The cave was cold and dank, and smelled of centuries. The carriage lantern threw golden light upon walls covered in strange graffiti, and words carved into it: *La Primera Madre*. When they saw the painting of the two suns they gasped, it was so beautiful.

Bidding her daughter and granddaughter to sit, asking that they be silent, Angela eased herself down to the cold floor. The lantern stood in the center of the strange little circle, the faces of the three women cast in a surreal glow.

Angela sat for some minutes in the silence until she began to feel in her bones and in her blood what it was that had been missing. She closed her eyes. *Mama, are you here?* And she instantly felt a presence, warm, loving and protective. She realized that all her life there had been a hole inside her, a small area of emptiness so that she had never felt complete, had always felt she should be searching for something. She knew now what it was: her bloodline.

She suddenly understood why she had come here, why she had brought the oilskin bag with her, for it contained a parchment granting ownership of land to people who had no right to the land, whose ancestors dwelled far away. To the shock of her companions, Angela started digging into the floor of the cave, driving her ancient fingers into the hard earth. When Marina and Angelique tried to protest, she silenced them, and there was something in her voice, the set of her features, that made them obey.

They watched as the hole grew until she seemed satisfied. They did not know what was in the oilskin bag or why Angela placed it in the hole. They watched in fascination as she slowly scooped the earth back over it, covering also the jade Aztec figurine that had fallen from the pocket of her shawl. Angelique opened her mouth, but something silenced her. The Aztec goddess, that had seen her through some strange and beautiful times, was being consigned to the floor of this strange cave.

After she had finished burying the deed to Rancho Paloma, Angela felt a sense of peace steal over her. The land belonged to the First Mother and her descendants, not to the intruders, the invaders, but to the original people from whom it was stolen. As she patted down the soil, she thought: *I must tell the others. Marina, Angelique. They have Indian blood. Daniel, Seth . . . their children descended from this First Mother.*

She started talking, urgently now because she knew her time was short: "We are Indian, we are Topaa, we descend from the First Mother who is buried here. We are the keepers of this cave. It is up to us to continue to pass down the traditions and stories and religion of our people. We have to keep the memories alive."

They stared at her. "What is Grandmother saying, Auntie Marina?"

"I have no idea. She speaks gibberish."

"Is it a language she speaks? It's not at all like Spanish."

"You must remember this place," Angela said, not realizing she was speaking Topaa, the language she had spoken when she was a child and her mother had called her Marimi and told her she would someday be the clan medicine woman. "You must tell others about this cave."

Angela took Marina's hand, and said, "I named you Marina. I misunderstood the message in my dream. It was meant to be *Marimi*."

"Mother, we do not understand what you are saying. Let us take you out of this place. Let us take you home."

But Angela thought: I *am* home.

"Mother, please, you are frightening us." Angelique and Marina reached for her.

But Angela's thoughts were now upon the First Mother, who had trekked across the desert alone, outcast from the tribe, and pregnant. Yet she had endured. Angela looked at Marina, who had undergone rigors in China and endured much adversity yet had found the strength to work at her husband's side, and Angelique, who had suffered a great ordeal in a mining camp up north. And Angela herself, no matter what Navarro did to her, she kept her pride and self-respect and dignity. *We are the daughters of the First Mother. This is her legacy to us.*

Angela knew now why she had brought Marina and Angelique with her. Both would have, in another place and time, been clan medicine women for their tribe. But now they were married to Americans and had children named Charles and Lucy and Winifred. She closed her eyes and saw the silhouette of a raven against a blood-red sunset. He was flying to the land of the dead, where the ancestors had gone, and where they were waiting for her, Marimi, to join them.

Chapter Seventeen

She never used tricks. The ghosts that appeared were neither illusions nor the products of chicanery and hocus-pocus—or so Sister Sarah claimed. She always welcomed psychic debunkers to come to her Church of the Spirits in Topanga and run any analysis on her séances they wished. They would arrive with their cameras and recording equipment, heat sensors and motion detectors, the most sophisticated scientific devices of the day, hoping to catch her in a fraud. But they never did. Psychiatrists and men of the Church claimed the apparitions were the result of mass hysteria—people seeing what they *wanted* to see. But Sister Sarah maintained that her spirits were real and that she was the human conduit through which they passed from the realm of the Beyond to that of the living.

Erica was glued to the TV set in Jared's motor home. When she had found the documentary video on the 1920s' spiritualist, she had had no idea what a rich mine she was about to tap into: rare archival footage of Sister Sarah's sermons where audiences of six thousand were brought to their feet in ecstasy as they saw deceased loved ones materialize, with the charismatic Sister Sarah onstage in her flowing robes, arms outstretched, head back, eyes closed, quivering with spiritual energy.

She had been an astounding beauty. Film clips from the few movies she had made prior to being discovered showed a sultry, sloe-eyed siren who had been variously labeled vamp, goddess, seductress, femme fatale. Audiences loved her. Footage also included home movies made by Edgar Rice Burroughs on his Tarzana Rancho, where Sarah was a frequent visitor, along with Rudolph Valentino, Douglas Fairbanks, Mary Pickford. It was in those early days that her talent had been discovered, when she told fortunes to friends, counseled them on important decisions, and even helped the police locate a child that had gone missing in the Baldwin Hills. Word of mouth had spread, and she became more and more in demand for private séances. Sarah moved to larger venues, finding that she was just as able to summon numbers of ghosts as easily as one. People worshiped her. She reunited them with the dear departed. She was also the living promise of life after death.

While Sarah lifted her arms and eyes heavenward in the video, her audience breathless with spiritual anticipation, Erica consulted her watch. What was keeping Jared?

He had left hours ago for an urgent meeting with the Confederated Tribes of Southern California, hoping to dissuade them from putting a stop to DNA testing on the Emerald Hills skeleton. Their surprise move, resulting in a court order suspending all archaeological and forensic work in the cave, could ruin all possibilities for identifying the skeleton once and for all. Temporarily restrained from working in the cave, Erica had decided to take the time to pursue her search for the source of the painting in her dreams.

If Mrs. Dockstader was not her grandmother, and if Erica had never before set eyes on the painting over Mrs. Dockstader's fireplace, then her childhood dreams must have stemmed from another source. It seemed logical that since Sister Sarah bought this property and filled in the canyon, someone might have taken a photograph inside the cave and published it somewhere.

But Erica was having a hard time concentrating.

All she could think about was she and Jared making love beneath the stars. Was *this* what it was like to be in love? No wonder people wrote songs about it! She felt giddy and silly, happy and delirious. But scared, too, that it might all be just a dream, or that she might lose him before she even had him. Maybe that was all part of—

She suddenly stared at the screen. Restored film footage, taken in 1922, was showing Sister Sarah going inside the cave. Erica shifted to the edge of her seat.

The camera was on the south ridge and focused down on the cave entrance. Sarah, in her trademark white robe and hood, disappeared into the darkness while her entourage and reporters waited dramatically outside. When she emerged minutes later, her expression was transfixed. The voice-over said, "Did Sister Sarah experience a spiritual revelation in this cave as she later claimed, or was she acting? Shortly after she purchased the property, she had the canyon filled in, burying the cave so that we will never know what she saw in there."

The closing film clip of the documentary, shot in 1928, showed a distraught Sister Sarah in front of microphones and journalists saying farewell to her followers. The news had come abruptly and unexpectedly, when the Church of the Spirits was at its peak popularity. Sarah did not explain why she was dropping out of public work, only that it was "God's will." She then vanished from view and although efforts were made to find her—newspapers ran contests, reporters vied for the big story—Sister Sarah was never heard from again.

The documentary ended, and as Erica turned off the TV, she thought: It all comes down to the cave. It was the painting that brought me here in the first place, and others over the centuries were drawn to the cave—the people who left behind the spectacles, the reliquary, the crucifix, the braid, the spirit-stone, the Aztec fetish, the deed to the rancho. Sister Sarah. How are they all connected? How do they connect to the painting in Kathleen Dockstader's house? *How does it all connect to me?*

What she and Jared had found on the original owners of Rancho Paloma was that the Navarros had been a prominent founding family in Los Angeles. Apparently the matriarch, a woman named Angela, had been a major force in shaping the new town. One of the things she had accomplished was pushing for a city park where people could sit or walk, and where bullfights would not be held, as they were in the Plaza. The park was created in 1866 and originally called Central Park—its contemporary name was Pershing Square. Today, in the San Fernando Valley there was a school named Angela Navarro Elementary, in her honor. Erica and Jared had also found out that Angela Navarro had lived at Rancho Paloma and died in there in 1866, and that a legal hassle had ensued upon her death when the family couldn't produce the deed to the property.

Because it was buried in our cave. Whoever hid it there knew about the skeleton buried there, and who she was. And the people who visited the cave through the centuries knew who the woman was. DNA tests would at least point us in a direction.

"Hi."

She looked up at Jared's smile. Her heart executed a somersault. "Hi." Sister Sarah's séances weren't the only miracles that had taken place here. Jared had finally called his father. They had talked for an hour. It wasn't perfect, but it was a start. And Jared was going to design a house just for Erica. She said she liked the one the miniature Arbogasts lived in.

"I'm afraid I have some bad news. I can't get them to change their minds about blocking the DNA testing."

"We'll just have to keep trying."

He paused, smoky eyes filling up with the sight of her. Erica wondered if she and Jared would ever tire of the delicious thrill of suddenly being in each other's presence. "There's worse news, I'm afraid," he said. "The bones are going to be removed and buried in a local Native American cemetery."

"No! When?"

"As soon as possible. I'm sorry, Erica. You know, I never thought I would come around to your way of thinking, but I now believe that it's wrong to remove bones until a cultural affiliation can be identified. I've never been a religious or spiritual man, but we know that the woman buried in the cave was, and that the people who came and paid homage to her were spiritual people. We have to honor that, and we also have a duty to find who are the rightful caretakers of her final resting place."

He bent to kiss her.

Luke stuck his head through the door. "Uh, Erica? You have visitors. They said it's important."

She stepped outside and shielded her eyes against the sun. "Mrs. Dockstader!"

The older woman was dressed in white slacks and a pale pink blouse, with open-toed sandals and a small shoulder purse hanging from a long gold chain. Her eyes were hidden behind enormous sunglasses. "Tell me about the headaches," she said.

✳

Jared invited Kathleen Dockstader and her attorney to meet with Erica in his RV, which was more comfortable and more private than Erica's tent or the lab trailer.

"Dr. Tyler," the older woman began, "after you left I had my lawyer run a background check on you. As you seemed legitimate, an anthropologist working for the state with impressive credentials, I decided to check out your story. I hired a private detective to do a search on hippie communes, anyone who might have lived in one and could remember that far back. He tracked down someone running a tavern in Seattle, who had lived in a commune during the years my daughter would have. He said he remembered the Dockstader girl, a runaway heiress who didn't want to have anything to do with her mother's millions. They all admired her at the time. In retrospect, he thinks she was crazy. The detective asked him if he knew what happened to her. He said she left the commune with a musician on a Harley motorcycle."

Kathleen paused, clasping and unclasping her hands. It was just as Jared had speculated: after he and Erica left her house a week ago, Mrs. Dockstader hadn't been able to stop thinking about Erica. She had even canceled her world golf tour.

"And then there was this," she said as she signaled to the attorney, who retrieved a book from his briefcase, handing it to her. Erica was astonished to see that it was her high school yearbook from 1982, the year she graduated. Kathleen opened it to a page marked with what turned out to be a small black-and-white photograph that looked as if it had been clipped from an earlier yearbook. The girl in the picture had a bouffant hairdo that curled out at the bottom in a flip. "This was taken in 1965," Kathleen said. "When Monica was seventeen." She laid the picture next to the one of Erica. "You were both the same age in these photos. The resemblance is astonishing, isn't it?"

"We look like twins," Erica murmured.

Kathleen closed the book and handed it back to the lawyer. "But what finally convinced me that you were my granddaughter was when you asked about the headaches. My mother had blinding headaches. Not just migraines, but strange fainting spells during which she heard things and saw things. Visions. Apparently it is an inherited trait. She told me that a great-aunt suffered from the same thing. No one knew about it. It was sort of our family secret. Others pretending to be you, who had come hoping to claim a reward or inheritance, knew nothing about the headaches."

"Mrs. Dockstader—"

"Please call me Kathleen."

"Why did my mother run away?"

"Because we wanted her to stay at a home for unwed mothers and keep her pregnancy a secret. Afterward, we were going to place the child with one of Herman's sisters—Herman was my husband, Monica's father. The child would have been raised as a cousin. We believed that having a baby would ruin Monica's life.

"After she ran away, it devastated us. She was Herman's princess, the light of his life. When she left, something died in him. We placed ads in all the personal classified sections of major newspapers around the country telling her that we wanted her and the baby to come home. But . . . we never heard."

"Do you know who my father was?" Erica asked in a whisper.

"Monica would never tell us." Kathleen brought a monogrammed handkerchief out of her purse. "I have no idea who he was. She wasn't a bad girl. She was just spirited. You don't know how many times since the day she left us I've wished her father and I had spoken different words. She wanted to have the baby at home. She would have stayed with us." Kathleen turned shimmering, vulnerable eyes to Erica. "You would have been raised in our home."

"I don't know what to say."

Kathleen dabbed her eyes with the handkerchief. "Neither do I. This is going to take some getting used to."

They looked at each other, the younger woman scrutinizing the older woman's face for signs of similarity—they shared the same widow's peak hairline—the older woman looking at the face that would have been her daughter's one day.

"I wonder," said Kathleen, "if I might be permitted to see the cave."

"The cave?"

"If I may."

Jared escorted them both down the scaffolding, assisting the older woman down the steps while Erica produced a key for the padlock on the iron security gate. Inside, she turned on the fluorescent lights that bathed the cavern in a surreal glow, illuminating wooden timbers and struts, trenches carved into the floor, the wall covered with scarlet and gold suns and mysterious symbols, and finally the Lady, lying peacefully on her side beneath a protective transparent cover that looked like a glass sarcophagus.

Kathleen's sigh whispered like a breeze, her eyes were filled with wonder. "I know all about this cave," she said softly, as if not wishing to disturb the slumbering Lady, "the paintings on the wall, the words *Primera Madre*. It's all exactly how I imagined it to be."

Erica gave her a surprised look. "You've been here?"

"No no. This canyon was already filled in when I was a child. But I was told about it by someone who *had* been in here."

"Who?"

She smiled. "The woman who painted the canvas of the two suns that hangs in my living room. The woman who built a retreat here called the Church of the Spirits. Sister Sarah, my mother. Your great-grandmother. I was her love child. I was the reason she vanished."

*

"My mother always knew someone was buried in the cave," Kathleen said. She and Erica were sitting in the sun-filled living room of Mrs. Dockstader's Palm Springs house, going through albums full of pictures, news clippings, and mementos. "She sensed it, even though she had no proof. She even claimed that the spirit that dwelled in the cave had instructed her to build her Church of the Spirits on that spot."

"What happened to her? Why did she vanish?"

"She was in love with a married man, but his wife wouldn't give him a divorce. When my mother found out she was pregnant, she knew it would upset her followers, so she opted to vanish. She moved to a small town where there was no movie theater and where people were not likely to recognize her. I was born, and she raised me alone. I never saw my father. I don't know if they ever had contact after that. All I know is that it was very tragic. My mother died when I was twenty-two. She was buried in the cemetery in that small town, and to this day no one knows that the woman in that grave is the famous Sister Sarah."

"Is that why you wanted my mother to give up her baby?"

Kathleen smiled sadly. "I grew up witnessing my mother's sadness. She tried to hide it, but a child senses these things. I knew she was an outcast because she was an unmarried woman with a child. And I knew a stigma was attached to me as well. She passed herself off as a widow, so we lived a lie. We didn't want Monica to have to go through that."

Erica could barely take it all in. She felt like a starving person who had been brought to a feast. All the photos and stories, people who looked like her, were related to her, a vast family of aunts and uncles and cousins, and grandparents and great-grandparents going way back.

"This is," Kathleen said. "Daniel Goodside. He was a Boston Clipper ship captain. I found this picture in an old trunk. It was one of a pair of portraits taken in 1875. The one in the other frame was of a woman but it was too mildewed and beyond saving. On the back I could see the name written: Marina, wife of Daniel. I don't know anything about Marina, what her family name was. I assume she was also a Bostonian. He lost an arm, as you can see, maybe in the Civil War. He was something of an artist."

On the opposite page was a small watercolor done by Daniel Goodside in 1830—"*Medicine woman of the Topaa tribe living at Mission San Gabriel Arcangel.*"

"Topaa," Erica murmured. "I've never heard of that tribe."

Kathleen closed the book and rose. "Probably he meant Tongva. There was a lot of misunderstanding names and words back then. Come, let me take you on a tour of the property."

She linked her arm through Erica's. "My husband's father—who would be your great-grandfather—imported the first date palms from Arabia and started the farm back in 1890. I married into the Dockstader family in 1946, right after the war. I was eighteen. Your mother was born two years later, in 1948."

They were interrupted by a maid informing Erica that she had a phone call. It was Jared. "You'd better get back here. There's been a startling development."

＊

They heard robust laughter coming from Jared's RV. His visitor was a heavyset woman with ruddy cheeks and a strong handshake.

"Dr. Tyler, my name is Irene Young and I think I might have something of interest to you. I'm a phys-ed teacher in Bakersfield but my hobby is genealogy. I'm tracing my family tree and when I saw the news report about you finding the deed to a rancho that belonged to a family named Navarro I knew I had to come." She reached into her canvas tote bag and brought out a leather portfolio. "I've traced my family on my mother's side to a family named Navarro that lived on Rancho Paloma. Here is a picture of them." She held out an antique photo in a protective plastic cover. "You notice there's something written on the back. This picture was taken in 1866 on the occasion of this woman's birthday," and she pointed to a dignified elderly woman sitting in the center of what looked like a family grouping.

Irene went on to explain that she had contacted many of the descendents from the people in the photo, but that she wasn't able to identify one couple. She pointed to them.

Erica squinted at the one-armed man in the back. "My God! It's Daniel Goodside. My ancestor."

"What!" Jared said, looking at the picture.

"Goodside?" said Irene Young. "Is that his name? I assume he was married to the woman seated next to him."

"That would be Marina," Erica said, remembering what Kathleen had told her.

"She bears a strong resemblance to the woman in the center, who I assume is the family matriarch. Her name is Angela Navarro, which would make Goodside's wife a Navarro."

"My grandmother said she never knew Marina's last name, that she assumed she was a Bostonian. My God . . . Am *I* related to the Navarros?"

Irene pointed to a couple standing at the back. "These are my great-great-grandparents, Seth and Angelique Hopkins. Angelique was Marina Goodside's niece and the granddaughter of the matriarch, Angela."

Erica looked again at the picture. With a puzzled frown she reached for a magnifying glass and silently scrutinized the photo. "This woman is Indian."

"Unfortunately, I haven't been able to determine her tribe. I am assuming she would have been a Mission Indian—"

"Jared!" Erica said suddenly. "Kathleen has a watercolor that Daniel Goodside painted—of a Topaa woman!"

"Topaa! You think the people in this photo are of that tribe?"

"It all ties in, don't you see?" Erica was suddenly animated. "Daniel Goodside was interested in painting members of the Topaa tribe. He married a woman who was half or perhaps quarter Indian. A woman whose last name was Navarro. And then someone buried the deed to Rancho Paloma—Navarro land—in the cave at Topanga—Topanga!" she said suddenly. "No one knows what the word really means. There are several theories. But one thing agreed upon is that 'nga' means 'place of.' If a tribe named Topaa lived here, then it all falls into place!"

"Why have we never heard of them?" asked Irene.

"Maybe the Topaa were among the first to be rounded up and taken to the Mission. They would have been assimilated quickly. That would account for why we know nothing about their existence."

She turned to Jared. "With this new information we can stop the Confederated Tribes from taking the bones for reburial. Our skeleton might be the only evidence of a lost tribe. Now that we have a tribal name, we have a better chance of finding a likely descendent."

He smiled cryptically at her.

"What?"

"Erica, so far *you're* the most likely descendent."

*

Sam was unconvinced, as were the members of the Confederated Tribes, who had arrived with a coffin and a medicine man. Dr. Tyler's evidence was too thin, they said, if it could even be called evidence. It was time to lay the medicine woman to rest in Native American ground.

Erica refused to unlock the security gate to the cave. To Sam's frustration, he couldn't find his key and Jared had the only other one. They stood on the cliff above the cave, Erica barring their way, Sam threatening to take bolt cutters to the padlock. Erica looked at her watch. Where was Jared? He had called earlier and told her to stall the Confederated Tribe members until he got back. He had sounded excited although he wouldn't say why. But that had been hours ago.

"Who on earth is *that*?" Luke said suddenly, pointing.

They all turned to see Jared coming slowly through the camp, escorting two small, brown people, aged and bent, an elderly brother and sister living in East Los Angeles. Jared had found them through the Indian Studies Department at UCLA, where a massive database on California Indians was being compiled. Field anthropologists were going into the inner cities, searching for "hidden" or "forgotten" Native Americans.

He introduced them as the Delgados, Maria and Jose. "We know there were bound to be Indians who didn't become Missionized, who stayed in the villages and then later moved into the Pueblo to become assimilated into the Mexican population but marrying among only themselves. These two people claim that they grew up being told they were Topaa, but no one believed them because no one had heard of the Topaa."

The old woman spoke: "Many years ago we went to the museum and talked to the people there. They were scholars and very educated. They told us we were mistaken, that there was no Topaa tribe and that we were Gabrielino. When a writer came to our neighborhood to write a history of California Indians, and we told him we were Topaa, he wrote down 'Tongva' because he thought we were mistaken."

The brother and sister were born in 1915, both widowed now and living together. They had heard stories in their childhood and into their teens from a very old elder who lived to be a hundred. He had been born at the Mission and he had thought it was around 1830. Although the elder had never lived in a village, he had learned about village life from other elders at the Mission, and stories about the First Mother and how her spirit guide, the raven, had led her across the desert from the east. The elder had been the one who had told them to remember that they were not Gabrielino, which was the white man's name for their tribe. They were Topaa.

Mention of the First Mother startled Erica. "You heard this on the news or read it in the paper?"

The old woman laughed. "Papers! I don't read. And my brother, he don't either. We don't watch the news on the TV, always bad news, always guns and killing. My brother and me, we like game shows." Her grin was toothless.

Erica turned to Jared. "This is proof that they are really Topaa. There is no other way they could know that this was the cave of the First Mother if they hadn't heard it from elders."

"This man told us about the cave," the old woman said. "Can we go inside? Can we visit the First Mother?"

*

They were gathered in the cave, saying good-bye. Sam and Luke were the first to leave, wishing Erica and Jared good luck. They had a lot of work ahead of them. DNA analysis of the bones matched that of the elderly Indian pair, identifying the sleeping lady as a member of the Topaa tribe. Jose and Maria Delgado wanted a museum to be established to teach people about the Topaa. They wanted the First Mother to remain buried in the cave, with her grave protected from feet, but with the cave being kept open for people to visit. "It is what she would have wanted," the old man said. "People come here to talk to her and to read about her journey."

Kathleen Dockstader was the last to leave. She had canceled her six-month vacation to devote her time to searching once again for Monica.

"One thing mystifies me," she said to Erica. "The painting in my living room, the one of the two suns, painted by my mother. You say you've dreamed about it all your life."

"Since I was very little. Someone probably took a picture of it and used it as part of a Sister Sarah bio and I saw it somewhere, in a book or magazine, and I just forgot."

"That's what puzzles me because, you see, that painting was stolen when my mother disappeared and apparently was found later, and stored away in a police warehouse, waiting for the owner to report its theft. Five years ago, the painting was finally traced to me, I was contacted and that was when I acquired it. Before that, the painting had lain buried and neglected for seven decades. So you see, my dear, you can't possibly have seen it before two weeks ago."

"Well," Jared said when everyone had left and he and Erica were alone with the First Mother slumbering beneath her transparent sarcophagus, "this is irony for you. My job was to locate the most likely descendant, and she was here all along, right under my nose." He looked at the blazing suns on the wall. "Why do you suppose you dreamed about them when you had never seen the painting before?"

She didn't have the answer, although her speculation was that it could be some sort of race memory. "The suns are really circles, and the circle was sacred to the Topaa, as it is to many Native American tribes today. Perhaps I was merely dreaming of the sacred. Or perhaps it was a prophecy."

"A prophecy?"

She thought of the elderly Topaa couple. "That someday we would complete the circle."

Jared took her by the hand and, looking back at the skeleton, said, "Whoever she was, her journey is not done. It's up to us now to continue it." And as they left the cave and turned toward the setting sun, a raven swooped down from the sky and flew before them, as if to lead the way.